MIDNIGHT LIES

A WILDEFIRE NOVEL

ELLA GRACE

BALLANTINE BOOKS • NEW YORK

A Ballantine Books Mass Market Original

Copyright © 2013 by Christy Reece

Published in the United States by Ballantine Books, an imprint of The Random House Publishing Group, a division of Random House LLC, New York, a Penguin Random House Company.

BALLANTINE and the HOUSE colophon are registered trademarks of Random House, LLC.

ISBN 978-0-345-53839-0
eBook ISBN 978-0-345-53840-6

Cover art: Craig White
Cover design: Scott Biel

Printed in the United States of America

www.ballantinebooks.com

9 8 7 6 5 4 3 2 1

Ballantine mass market edition: October 2013

To all the Southern women in my life:
mother, sisters, aunts, and friends.
Your strength, courage, and
remarkable sense of humor exemplify
what it is to be a steel magnolia.

MIDNIGHT
LIES

CHAPTER ONE

Charlene Braddock slammed her laptop closed and hurled it across the bedroom. The hard thud as it crashed against the wall gave her no satisfaction or relief. Jealousy and bitterness sizzled and burned like acid inside her. After three years of trying and failing to regain her ex-husband's affections, she was no closer than the day he'd shoved the divorce papers in her face and demanded she sign them or else. Remembering that look in his eyes always made her shiver. He had been furious. Those steely blue eyes of his had blazed with a passion and intensity she had rarely seen. Instead of dissolving their marriage, she had wanted to tear off her clothes and let him work out all that anger and aggression on her body. When Quinn Braddock got worked up, her libido went into overdrive.

Of course, she'd done nothing of the sort, since she wouldn't have received the response she desired. Quinn's control was legendary. Fury might envelop him but it would never consume him. He kept his emotions on a tight leash. Even their final argument before he'd walked out the door for the last time hadn't produced any drama.

Sure, there had been full-blown anger, but he'd never let himself get out of control.

Not that Quinn was a cold fish. Oh no, there was definitely passion in him. She had felt and tasted its intensity. Early in their marriage, he had been insatiable. Back then their apartment had been small and there hadn't been a wall or flat surface where they hadn't screwed like minxes.

His career had ruined them. Long hours of work had left her alone with too much time on her hands. Quinn was a gifted doctor with an excellent reputation. Nice for him, but her life had become tedious. When she had complained about her boredom, Quinn's solution had been for her to find a job or do volunteer work. She had wanted to laugh in his face. She was the wife of a physician—she didn't have to do anything so mundane or common.

That was the day she'd gone out and had her first fling. Getting back at Quinn that way had given her immense satisfaction, so she had continued—discreetly, of course—enjoying the pleasures that illicit relationships could bring. Down-and-dirty sex with a variety of men brought delicious danger to a whole new level. Unfortunately satisfaction from each encounter only provided a temporary fix. Charlene had still wanted more. More of what, she didn't know. She had only known she wasn't getting it from Quinn. It became a vicious circle. The more he pulled away from her, the more she craved his attention, which increased her need to screw around even more.

It was all his fault. She had hoped one day he would understand that and come back to her.

Charlene glared over at the ruined laptop. The local online news report confirmed what she had long feared. Quinn had a new woman in his life. One who was, no doubt, giving him everything he wanted in the bedroom.

Memories of some of their happier times went through

her mind. Her eyes closed on a shiver of arousal. Vanilla sex with Quinn Braddock was better than the hard and rough stuff she got from all her other lovers combined.

Still, she loved the hard, often brutal sex play. Her newest lover gave "dangerous liaisons" a whole new meaning. He certainly had no issues with giving her all she could take. Sometimes he gave her much more than she could handle. Last time, it had gotten so rough, she'd been almost afraid she wouldn't survive. She had begged him to stop. Not that he had. He had told her his loss of control was because of his desire for her and not because he liked to inflict pain. She didn't care what his reasons were. As long as he provided the pleasure she needed, she would keep him. When that ended, so would their relationship.

But she wanted Quinn back, too. They could be good together again if he would just stop being such a tight-ass.

Charlene cursed the day he'd found her with that weasel Nate Lockhart. Not only had the bastard been a poor substitute for her husband, he'd been ridiculously unimaginative. Every time he did something to her, he'd ask if she liked it. Hell, he should have had enough balls not to care.

It had been a mistake to seduce Nate. Having her husband's friend screwing her brains out had been fun the first couple of times. Quinn wouldn't give her the attention she needed, so it had been another way to get back at him. She'd even gotten off on it when she had been having sex with Quinn, thinking how delicious it was to have him inside her where only hours before his friend had been pumping away.

She hadn't expected Quinn to walk in and find them screwing in Nate's office. It had been her little secret, exciting and dangerous.

Quinn's reaction might have been the most humiliating part of all. He had laughed. Even now, years later, she could hear that abrupt bark of laughter. He had seemed genuinely amused and almost relieved. Dammit to hell, how had it all gone so wrong?

This new woman Quinn was seeing . . . who was she? Of course, Quinn had dated several women since they had divorced. He wasn't a monk. But neither was he one to be caught on camera with a woman unless he wanted to be. Was this the woman who would finally take him away from her forever?

The photograph from the fundraiser had been frustratingly bad. The shot showed Quinn's profile as he looked down at his companion. But even the bad picture made it look as though Charlene's tall, gorgeous ex-husband was enamored of the woman. His half smile, with that sexy, quirky edge, had been only for the female beside him. The photo had just shown the back of the woman. Straight, thick hair fell halfway down her back. She was a blonde. Well, dammit, so was Charlene. And a real one at that. This bitch probably got her color from a bottle. And she was fat and wore frumpy clothes, too.

Charlene blew out a frustrated sigh. Okay, so she wasn't exactly fat, but she was nothing like Charlene, who spent hours each week with a personal trainer, honing her body to taut, slender perfection.

But at least Charlene was right about the woman's dress. It was definitely not designer made and was conservative by anyone's standards. With Quinn's talents, he was destined to move up in his career. He had a reputation to maintain. One would think he would be more careful in his selection of dates for high-profile events.

On impulse, Charlene grabbed her cellphone from the nightstand. She couldn't let it go . . . she had to try one more time. They'd had some good times, especially at the beginning. If she could just get him to stop being so uptight. His straight-shooter Eagle Scout demeanor had been charming at first but had worn thin after a while. Living with such perfection could be damn irritating.

He answered on the first ring, his groggy "Braddock" telling her she'd woken him. She refused to feel any guilt for interrupting what was probably much-needed sleep. This was important, dammit.

"It's me, Quinn. I need to see you."

An explosive sigh came through the phone, making her glad she'd woken him up. The asshole!

"What is it this time, Charlene?"

Her eyes roamed around the massive bedroom, searching for some new hook to get him to the house. The necklace draped casually on her dresser caught her attention. She hated the thing. Her taste in jewelry ran toward bold and spectacular. The pearl-and-diamond necklace was a Braddock family heirloom, much too understated and old-fashioned for her. Quinn had given it to her a couple of weeks before they married. She'd never worn it, but when he'd asked for it in their divorce settlement, she had gleefully declined. Just one more twist of the knife. He'd been more pissed about her refusal to return the necklace than he had been about finding her screwing Nate. Yes, he would jump at the chance to get it back.

"I've decided to return the Braddock necklace to you."

"Why? What's the catch?"

Dammit, he didn't even try to hide his suspicion.

"No catch. I hate the thing. But if you don't want it, I'll just—"

"Fine. I'll come by this evening and—"

"No, I'm busy this evening. You need to come right away or I'm selling it to a jewelry store."

The long pause that followed made her wonder if she'd

played her hand too forcibly. She had tried to entice him over to the house before and had been successful only a few times. But this was something he really wanted.

"I'll be there within the hour. Meet me at the door with it. I won't come in."

She smiled her satisfaction. *We'll just see about that.*

"Of course, darling. Whatever you say." She ended the call and raced to her closet. She had just the outfit for seducing a reluctant ex-husband back into her bed.

The cellphone in her hand rang. Charlene cursed, sure that Quinn was calling to cancel. She glanced down at the display. Recognizing the number, she sighed, part in relief, part in frustration. Phone to her ear, she opened her closet door as she said, "Darling, how are you?"

"Horny."

Her lovers were usually all about pleasing her. From the beginning, this man had been different. He never sugarcoated what he wanted. Sweet talk and flowers were not his way. And though occasionally he was too crass even for her, the things he did to her in bed made up for his inadequacies. Unfortunately this wasn't a good time for him to be horny and demanding.

"I'm sorry, darling, but I have an appointment in a few minutes. Can you come by tonight?"

"An appointment? With whom?"

Though she resented his nosiness, she hesitated in not telling him. His temper had a volatile edge. A couple of times she'd pissed him off and he'd gone way beyond the pain-filled pleasurable lovemaking she enjoyed and into something intensely scary. The last time that had happened, she'd had to hide the bruises for days.

"My ex-husband is dropping by to discuss our divorce settlement."

"I thought your divorce was settled a long time ago."

"It was, but I kept a piece of jewelry he wanted. I'm

redecorating my bedroom and came across it while I was putting things away for the workers to come in."

She winced. Dammit, now she'd probably have to do some kind of decorating just to keep him from asking about it later. If he ever learned she had invited Quinn over to get him into bed . . . She shivered at the thought.

"I'll be there tonight at six. Be ready for me."

A different kind of shiver swept through her. After their first time together, he had set ground rules and expectations. One of those was preparing herself for him. He had given her a list of do's and don'ts, including where to shave, what perfume and makeup to wear, what music to have playing when he walked in the door, and what food he required after their playtime had ended. And always, he wanted her naked.

"I'll be ready," she answered with her most sultry tone.

The line went dead and Charlene dropped the phone on the chair beside her. She only had a few minutes to get ready for Quinn. She pulled the lace-and-silk black negligee from its hanger and stripped out of her robe. Anticipation and nervousness made her normally graceful movements stilted. It had been years since she and Quinn had slept together. Would he notice that her breasts were larger and perkier? The plastic surgeon had done a marvelous job with them; Quinn had always been a breast man.

After slipping the skimpy gown over her head, she stood in front of the full-length mirror to assess her allure. Damn, she looked good. Though she had just passed her thirty-fifth birthday, she didn't look a day over twenty-five. Her tits and ass were sublime. There was no way in hell Quinn could resist her. So what if she'd slept around? It was past time for him to get over that.

The doorbell rang. She glanced sharply at her clock.

He was way too early. She hurriedly put on the necklace he was coming for and then took one last glance in the mirror. His timing didn't really matter. Even with the too-demure necklace, she looked fabulous.

Running lightly down the stairs, Charlene almost laughed with sheer happiness. Things would work out, she was sure of it. Quinn would be enamored of her again, take her to bed and do all sorts of delicious things to her. And tonight her lover could take care of any remaining sexual needs she might have. What had begun as a lousy day might well be her best ever. Her nipples tightened in anticipation of the coming events.

She opened the door. "Darling, it's so good—" Stopping abruptly, she stared. "What are you doing here? I told you I had an appointment."

Eyes gleaming wickedly, he moved forward, giving her no choice but to retreat to the middle of the foyer.

He closed the door behind him and sneered, "Is this the kind of outfit you wear to greet your ex-husband?"

Charlene held back a huff of exasperation. The last thing she needed was for him to be here when Quinn arrived. She should have lied when he had asked about her appointment.

"I was just about to change into something more appropriate."

"But he is coming over. Right?"

"Quinn? Yes, he'll be here in just a few minutes."

"Then there's not much time, is there?"

"Time for what?"

He came closer. "For this."

Charlene looked down at something gleaming in his hand. "What is . . . ?" She frowned, confused. "Is that my knife? Where did you . . . ? I've been looking all over the place for—"

The knife thrust toward her. So startled by the attack,

she barely felt the pain in her shoulder. Frozen, she stared up at him in horror. Then, as realization hit, she screamed.

In a gleaming arc, it came down again.

"No, stop, please . . . Stop!"

She stumbled backward and turned to run. Too late. Agony exploded in her shoulder and back. This time the pain was intense . . . urgent. Twisting around, Charlene screamed as she raised her hands to fight back, slapping ineffectually as the knife descended again and again. Slashing, ripping, destroying.

Blood was everywhere. He was ruining her beautiful gown. The pain was excruciating . . . unbearable. *Why, why, why?*

The floor appeared before her, slamming into her face. She lay, panting, too tired to cry, too stunned to speak.

A voice from above whispered silkily: "How about it, *darling?* Was it as good for you as it was for me?"

CHAPTER TWO

"Hey, sleepyhead. Wake up."

Samantha Wilde woke with a smile on her face. That sexy baritone growl did it to her every time. Rolling over onto her back, she blinked sleepily up at the harshly beautiful face of Quinn Braddock—surely the most perfect man on earth. Before she could kiss that perfection and entice him back to bed, her foggy brain registered that he was dressed.

"I thought you weren't going to the hospital until later today."

"That's still the plan. Charlene called and asked me to drop by for a few minutes."

She had never met Quinn's ex-wife, but had heard enough stories about the woman to make her glad she hadn't. Not that Quinn would talk about her. Everything she'd heard had come secondhand. The only thing Quinn had ever said was that he never should have married her. The look on his face when her name came up was enough to keep Samantha from asking more. Quinn was a warm and compassionate man, but a cold, hard look entered his eyes at the mention of his ex-wife.

Hiding her yawn behind her hand, Samantha gave a full-body stretch, wincing at her slightly stiff muscles. She had tackled a suspect yesterday when he'd tried to run. Though the perp had gotten the worst of it when he had tried to fight her, she still had some aches she needed to work out.

"Still sore?"

Nothing got by this man. She'd once told him that if he ever wanted to leave medicine, he'd make a great cop. "Just a little. A hot shower will help."

"I'll give you a massage tonight."

A shiver of anticipation swept through her. "All over?"

He lowered his mouth over hers and spoke against her lips. "Every soft, silky inch of you will know my touch."

Groaning her anticipation, Samantha wrapped her arms around his broad shoulders and pulled him closer. His mouth moved over hers for several long, satisfying seconds. She uttered a small sound of disappointment when he pulled away from her and stood.

"Gotta go."

Samantha propped herself up on her elbows. "Something wrong at Charlene's house?"

"No."

She wasn't put off by his abrupt answer. She just hated that his day was starting off on such a sour note. Considering the things she'd heard about Charlene, Quinn's relationship with his ex-wife was understandably strained. They'd been divorced for three years now, but Charlene had a tendency to call her former husband often. Samantha had no worries that Quinn would be tempted to go back to her. He might not have much to say about her, but if one read between the lines, his opinion of Charlene was just below that of his regard for slugs.

Hoping to erase the grimness from his face, she said, "I'll be working until at least nine tonight. Want to meet for a late dinner somewhere?"

As a new homicide detective, Samantha often had unpredictable hours. Fortunately Quinn's hospital schedule was just as grueling and time-consuming, so he understood about her crazy hours and limited time.

He leaned over and pressed a tender kiss to her forehead. "You'll be too tired to go out. Come over to my place and I'll make dinner."

Another reason she had fallen in love with Quinn Braddock. He loved to spoil and take care of her. Smiling her gratitude, she reached up and caressed his clean-shaven jaw. "I'll bring the wine."

He lowered his head again, moving his lips softly, confidently over hers. Samantha pressed upward, wanting a deeper taste. When he pulled away, her lips pouted her disappointment.

"Be careful. You're half a second away from having this sheet stripped away and me inside you."

A familiar delicious throb began. "Have time for a quickie?"

"You know we never can settle for a quickie." He glanced at her bedside clock. "Besides, even a quickie wouldn't work. Aren't you testifying again today?"

He was right on both counts. After their first night together, they had learned that their quickies could last for hours. She wasn't the most knowledgeable when it came to sex, but Quinn's expertise made up for her lack of experience. She couldn't imagine a man pleasing her more, inside or outside the bedroom.

Sighing her regret, she made a promise. "Let's plan for an extended quickie tonight."

"You're on."

Samantha watched in admiration as he went across her bedroom to pick up the car keys he'd left on the dresser. She loved the way he walked. For such a tall, broad-shouldered, muscular man, he moved with amazing agility and grace. She could only imagine that all of his patients, at least the female ones, fell instantly in love with him.

When he turned back, her expression must have revealed her thoughts, because he grinned and said, "Stop looking at my ass and get dressed. Telling the judge what delayed you probably won't win you any points."

So true. This was her second day of testimony, and if there was anything clear about the trial, it was that the judge disliked cops—and female ones in particular.

Before she could respond, he headed to the door, that austere, grim expression back in place. "See you tonight."

She grimaced in sympathy. When compared to meeting with a despised ex-spouse, facing an unfriendly judge didn't sound so bad. "I hope it's not too unpleasant."

"I just hope I can get out of there without strangling her," he muttered, and was out of the apartment almost before Samantha could register his astonishing statement. For Quinn to reveal his hatred was rare. Charlene must have really pissed him off this time.

Samantha dropped her head onto her pillow again. Her granddad would have approved of Quinn's restraint in not discussing other people. Though her hometown of Midnight, Alabama, had been rife with gossipers and busybodies, Daniel Wilde had looked upon gossiping as an evil deed. The fact that the Wilde family had often been the subject of those gossipers hadn't helped. And their hometown newspaper, *Midnight Tales,* had been the worst. Every salacious remark that had been whispered about the Wildes, they had printed as thinly veiled innuendos—skirting as close to libelous as possible without going over the edge.

But her grandfather would have approved of Quinn for other reasons, too. She had often worried that she would never find the right man. She had dated often but had never felt a real connection with anyone. Her sisters, Savannah and Sabrina, had called her a hopeless romantic, insisting that there was no perfect man out there. She had been almost to the point of believing that. Then she'd met Quinn.

Silly, but sometimes she worried that he was too perfect. That perhaps she was seeing only what she wanted to see. When she was a kid, how many times had she looked up at her daddy and thought him to be the most wonderful man alive? And what had he done? He had brutally murdered her beautiful mother and then had cowardly taken his own life. That had shaken Samantha's trust to the core and destroyed her innocence.

Then, years later, both of her sisters had thought they'd found their ideal matches, only to learn how wrong they'd been. With that history, why should she have faith in any man at all?

Now Savvy was back in Midnight for a short time to ready the Wilde mansion for sale. And she would most likely have to see the man who had shattered her heart. Life was just too damn unfair sometimes.

Even though Samantha and her sisters understandably had trust issues with men, they'd thankfully had one wonderful example. Daniel Wilde, their grandfather, had epitomized everything honorable and good. If Samantha could find a man half as fine as Daniel Wilde had been, she would call herself lucky. And unless she was seriously mistaken, that man was Quinn Braddock.

There was one major fly in her happily-ever-after ointment: Quinn wanted nothing permanent—he had made that clear from the start. Samantha, quite confident of her feminine powers, hadn't been worried when he had made that announcement on their first date. It was the first time any man had ever made that stipulation. Instead of being insulted, she had been amused, almost seeing his warning as a challenge. Weeks later, when she realized she was falling in love with him, she wasn't feeling quite so confident and was most definitely not amused.

After almost four months of dating, their relationship was intense, passionate, and more satisfying than anything she'd ever experienced. Even sex was exciting and thrilling. Before Quinn, her sex life had been about as bland as cold grits. She had decided that, for her at least, the idea of sex was much more enjoyable than the actual act. She was good at a lot of things . . . sex just didn't happen to be one of them.

Then, the first night she and Quinn made love, she had changed her mind. She had been terrified, worried that she would disappoint him. Quinn had been incredible. Patient and oh so very thorough in his intent to pleasure her. He had praised her, making her feel beautiful and sensual—sexually confident. Their lovemaking was everything she had wanted and so much more.

Still, even with the amazing connection they had, Quinn was never wavering in his stance on no commitment. He seemed to enjoy their relationship, laughed with her, talked with her, and made love to her until she was breathless and weak. But there had been no indication that he had changed his mind about anything permanent.

She wasn't giving up on her dreams, though. Beneath the façade of toughness she'd adopted to handle her job as a cop, Samantha was still the romantic her sisters had teased her about. The romance novels she had stashed away in bookcases and drawers throughout her apartment were testaments to her belief in a forever kind of love. And she was a small-town girl, with traditional values. That meant a wedding, babies, PTA meetings, Pee Wee football, and school plays. She wanted it all. Unfortunately the man she wanted to share all of that with had firmly denied wanting any of those things.

With an explosive sigh, Samantha sprang from the bed and headed for the shower. Her time was too limited to lie in bed and worry. Besides, staying busy had always been her answer to her troubled thoughts. As a teenager, she'd involved herself in every activity possible. It had made her numerous friends and paved the way for opportunities and honors many had envied. Little had those people known that all of that had been her way of trying to stay sane. Cheerleading, being the homecoming queen and class president, and taking dance and drama classes had all looked like fun and frivolous activities for a spoiled teenaged girl. That had been fine with her. Few saw beyond the shield she had erected to deal with the crushing pain of her parents' deaths.

She had eventually come to terms with her father's betrayal, but work was still her answer to her worries. Being a homicide detective definitely kept her mind from obsessing over things she couldn't change.

After her shower, she pulled her hair up in a tight, brow-raising bun, applied a minimum of makeup, then stepped into a somber black pantsuit and low-heeled black pumps. She hated that she was dressing for the judge, but couldn't deny it. Yesterday she'd worn what she had considered a conservative skirt and blouse. The judge had glared at her as if she were wearing a bikini. Hopefully an even primmer outfit would help.

The clock chimed eight times. Grabbing the purse she'd dropped on her dresser, she dashed toward the front door. A stomach rumble halfway there reminded her she hadn't eaten. Cursing softly, she detoured into the kitchen, poured a cup of coffee from the pot that Quinn had made, flipped the switch to OFF, and then looked around for something quick. The overripe banana on the counter or a cold Pop-Tart? Quickly deciding, she shook the foil-wrapped pastry from its box, dropped it into her purse, and headed out the door. Maybe she would call Quinn at lunch and see if he had time to spare. The delightful prospect of seeing him in the middle of the day gave her the boost of energy she needed.

Samantha ran down the stairs, enjoying the heady feeling of being young, healthy, and in love with an amazing man, gloriously oblivious to the horror her life was about to become.

Quinn parked his Audi across the street from Charlene's house. Instead of immediately getting out, he took a few seconds to center his thoughts and push aside his usual revulsion at seeing his ex-wife again. Hell of it was, he wasn't nearly as disgusted with her as he was with himself. He'd made some dumbass mistakes in his life, but marrying Charlene had to be the absolute worst.

An image of Sam came into his mind, instantly soothing him. How he'd fallen so hard, so fast, he would never know. He'd met her at the hospital. She'd been there to interview a shooting victim, and he'd been headed home after a grueling night in the ER. They had walked into the elevator together, along with a couple of other people. Someone had asked for a floor number to be pressed, and he and Sam had reached for the button at the same time. He'd practically smashed her finger and had turned to apologize. Whatever words he'd been about to say were instantly forgotten. Beautiful, brilliant sunshine had invaded his life in an instant.

After his divorce, he had vowed he would never become seriously involved with a woman again—or at least not until he was much older. Sam had changed his thinking. He wanted something long-term. Not marriage. He was done with marriage. After seeing his parents' ice-cold union and knowing what he came from, he should never have tried it in the first place. Those asinine decisions were in his past. But Sam . . . Sam was his future. She made him want more . . . something a hell of a lot deeper and permanent than the temporary sexual relationships he'd had since his divorce.

She had no clue that this coming Friday he had something special planned at his apartment. Her favorite restaurant was delivering an elegant meal. Amidst delicious food and wine, along with candlelight and soft music, he was going to ask her to move in with him.

Right now their hectic schedules prevented them from seeing each other every day. Living together would make it easier on both of them. Waking up beside her every morning was something he could definitely get used to. He hoped to hell he hadn't misread what he'd seen in her eyes. Finally he had found someone he could believe in and trust.

The screech of tires pulled Quinn from his thoughts. Out of the corner of his eye, he caught a glimpse of a dark, blurred streak as it zoomed by, like a vehicle leaving in a hurry. Someone most likely late for work.

Pulling in a deep breath, he got out of the car. This wasn't going to get any easier . . . might as well get it behind him. With quick, determined strides, Quinn headed across the street. Two minutes. That's all the time he would give Charlene. If not for the necklace, he wouldn't even consider coming back here.

He wasn't as stupid as she apparently thought. The necklace was to get him inside her house so she could once again try to seduce him back to her bed. That ploy hadn't worked the dozen or so times she had tried. Would never work. But he did want the damn necklace and was willing to stomach her presence for the two minutes it would take to reject her and get what belonged to him.

Sam's birthday was coming up in a couple of months, and despite the fact that the necklace was only ever given to a Braddock bride, he couldn't squelch the thought of having it reset and giving it to her.

Quinn was so focused on getting through the next few minutes with a minimum of drama that his eyes barely skimmed over the massive two-story, light brown brick house Charlene had gotten in the divorce settlement. Purchased eight months before their divorce, the house had never been home to Quinn. Before that, they'd had a perfectly nice condo in the city. Charlene had insisted that decorating her own home would fill her creative void.

A few weeks after they moved in, the unsatisfactory marriage he'd stubbornly been keeping together had unraveled further. Quinn had spent most of his nights on the sofa in his study. Then one day he'd gone to talk to a friend and had gotten his socks blown off. Seeing Nate and Charlene together had cleared up so many things. Instead of the fury other men might have experienced, Quinn had felt only immense relief. At last he could let go.

That day might have been the end of his marriage, but it was also the day he'd finally started living again.

Quinn rang the doorbell and waited. When there was no immediate answer, he pounded on the door and was surprised when it squeaked open. Charlene had probably left it open, thinking he'd just come inside. That wasn't going to happen.

Pushing the door open wider, he stayed on the other side and called out, "Charlene, I'm here."

The vile stench of blood attacked his senses and caught him off guard. The stink of violence was a scent he knew all too well. Unlike the hospital, where the smell was almost drowned out by antiseptic cleanliness, this was intense and brutal. The way it smelled in battle. He'd been an army combat medic. The foul odors of dismemberment and carnage were scents you never got used to or forgot.

He pushed the door open farther and saw the blood. Then he saw her. Lying on the floor, facedown, blood pooled everywhere. God, there was so much of it.

Training kicked in—Quinn didn't think, he acted. Rushing forward, he dropped to his knees, touched her neck to feel for a pulse. Was that a faint flicker? Holding her neck and head in place, he gently rolled her onto her back and saw immediately why there was so much blood. Her throat had been cut, nicked at the carotid artery.

Her eyes flickered open, their light blue depths glazed with pain. There was no recognition in them. Quinn had seen it too often not to know she was mere seconds from death.

"Charlene? Stay with me. You're going to be all right. Try to stay awake."

She opened her mouth to speak but there was only a gurgling sound.

Quinn's hand on her throat stopped some of the bleeding, but blood still seeped through his fingers. She raised her hand toward his face. Quinn grabbed for it but not before she slashed him with her nails across his face. He jerked back and her hand fell to the floor. One last gurgle emerged from her. Quinn watched as her eyes went still and unfocused in death.

Dammit, if only he'd come a few minutes earlier. The only thing to be done now was to call the police and alert them to a murder. Standing, he put his hand in his pocket for his cellphone. The door behind him slammed against the wall. Quinn whirled around.

A uniformed policeman stood at the door, his gun pointed at Quinn. "Take your hand from your pocket and put both of them in the air."

Following the officer's directions, Quinn raised his hands. "I was just about to call the police. She's dead."

"No shit. Looks like you made sure of that."

The sick feeling in his stomach sank lower in his gut. "I didn't do this. I tried to save her."

"Yeah, right. Just keep your hands up." The officer

glanced over his shoulder at his partner. "Cuff him and read him his rights."

Knowing that arguing would do no good, Quinn held his words. As his wrists were cuffed, he took one last look at the woman on the floor. She'd been a pathetic, miserable human being and he'd lost any affection for her long ago, but she hadn't deserved this sad and horrible end.

In the backseat of the patrol car, headed to the police station, one thought comforted him. At least he knew who he would call. Sam would figure out what to do about this mess. If there was anyone Quinn knew he could count on, it was Samantha Wilde.

CHAPTER THREE

Samantha sat rigidly in the back of the courtroom and did her best to push aside her fury at the imbecilic judge. Anger accomplished nothing. Having ground her teeth for the last hour, all she had to show for it was a massive headache hammering at her brain. She'd just completed her testimony and the judge had once again blatantly sided with the defendant. The defense attorney's dramatics should have been stopped long ago. At the very least, the man should have been reprimanded. Instead, despite the prosecution's numerous objections, the judge refused to stop the grandstanding.

The case wasn't cut-and-dried . . . she knew that. Despite the numerous television dramas depicting clear-cut cases that were solved in an hour, few were so unambiguous and easily resolved. This one was no exception. A young woman with a questionable lifestyle had been murdered. Samantha had no doubts that the woman's sometime boyfriend had done the deed. However, the judge had blocked so much of the prosecution's evidence, it was obvious the creep was going to be set free. How she would love to get up and tell the jury all she knew about the young man who sat behind the defendant's table with an innocent, injured look on his face.

How did her sister do this every day? Savvy was an assistant district attorney in Nashville and, from all accounts, thoroughly enjoyed her job. How could she work day in and day out trying to make sure justice was served and all too often watch the perps walk out the door, ready to commit the same crime or something even more heinous?

Being a cop was often frustrating but at least she could arrest the guilty party. The courtroom always seemed so arbitrary to her. Yes, there was justice, but it wasn't black and white. Not like it was out on the street.

The vibration of her phone caused a welcome distraction. The judge had been adamant about no phones in the courtroom. Since he already didn't like her, she wasn't about to call attention to herself. Easing out of her seat, Samantha quietly and happily left the courtroom and its ridiculous drama behind.

In the hallway, she dodged and weaved through small pockets of people as she put the phone to her ear. "Detective Wilde."

"Wilde, where are you?"

Her captain always sounded like he'd gotten up on the wrong side of the bed. She was used to his gruff manner. "At the courthouse. I—"

"You need to get back here ASAP."

"What's up?"

"We just picked up a murder suspect. Says he knows you."

"Who's that?"

"Dr. Quinn Braddock."

Before the captain finished saying Quinn's name, Samantha was running down the hallway to the double doors leading outside. The phone still at her ear, she ran out of the building and down the stairs. "Who's the victim?"

"His ex-wife, Charlene Braddock."

No. No way. "I'll be there in ten minutes."

Running with the speed of an Olympic sprinter, Samantha made it to her car in seconds. Her heart pounding with the dull thud of dread, she started the vehicle and took off with a screech.

This was a mistake, of course. There was no way Quinn would have committed murder. It was ridiculous to even consider him a suspect.

As she zoomed in and around traffic, her mind wouldn't shut out the voices of doubt. And the one voice that shouted the loudest reminded her of the comment Quinn had made as he'd walked out the door this morning. She could hear his voice as clear as if he sat beside her. *"I just hope I can get out of there without strangling her."*

Sick dread penetrated and began to wash away the denial. "Oh, Quinn . . . no."

Quinn sat alone in the interrogation room. Charlene's blood still covered his shirt. At least they'd allowed him to wash his hands, but the stench of death continued to fill his nostrils. He had been one of the lucky ones who'd never suffered from PTSD, but the smell of blood on his clothing was all too familiar and brought images to his mind he had worked like hell to forget.

Swallowing back the bile surging up his throat, he forced the horror of the past aside and concentrated on the here and now. They actually believed he killed Charlene. Sure, he knew the statistics. Knew that the largest percentage of murders were committed by family members or acquaintances of the victim. He wasn't naïve. What he was, was pissed.

From the off-the-cuff comments that had been made around him, the cops were ready to bag, tag, and haul him off to prison. Hell yeah, he knew he looked guilty. They'd caught him standing over Charlene's lifeless body, covered in her blood. And he had scratches on his face.

His DNA would most likely be under her fingernails. Hell, if they hadn't taken him in for questioning, he would've been disgusted with their ineptitude. But now he was becoming disgusted with their lack of investigation. They thought they had their killer; why look elsewhere?

He had wanted to contact Sam, but when it came time to make his one call, he'd done the sensible thing and called his attorney instead. His request that Detective Wilde be notified had been met with speculative interest. He knew she would come as soon as she heard. After having so many of the officers treat him as though he had already been found guilty, he looked forward to Sam's unerring trust. She would be the voice of reason in this insanity.

He had no illusions or expectations that she could convince anyone he wasn't guilty. The investigation would have to prove that. But she would make sure the investigation took place. Sam wouldn't leave him hanging out to dry as her co-workers apparently wanted to. He couldn't deny another reason he wanted to see her. She would soothe the raging rivers roaring inside him. Control was a vital part of his makeup, but he could feel it eroding as each slow minute ticked by.

The image of Charlene's body wouldn't leave his mind. Admittedly he had no affection toward the woman who had lied to him almost from the moment he had met her, but no one deserved the death she had endured. Had this been a random act of violence? Though blood had covered most of her body, he had noted that she wore a nightgown. Had she answered the door that way or had someone broken in and stabbed her? Had she planned to greet him in her nightgown and opened the door to her killer instead? Were there things missing from her home? If so, hopefully that would help the police see that he hadn't been involved. Charlene had nothing he wanted, and since he hadn't had any of her items on his person, if things were missing, then the killer or killers had them.

He amended the thought. There was one thing he did want—the Braddock necklace. He had given it to Charlene a couple of weeks before their wedding. Her lack of enthusiasm for the gift should have given him a clue. She had hated it. Even on the few occasions he'd asked her to wear the thing, she had scoffed and refused, yet she had declined to return it at their divorce. He hadn't been surprised . . . that was Charlene's way. Quinn had chalked it up to a lost cause.

A slight noise caught his attention. Sam came through the door like a small tornado on a mission. He had often marveled that someone so incredibly delicate-looking could work in such a tough profession. Samantha Wilde destroyed every stereotype he'd ever heard about homicide detectives.

Sitting at the table across from him, she asked softly, "What happened?"

The question didn't strike him as odd. It was a reasonable one. "The door was partially open when I got there. I found her lying on the floor. She was bleeding out. I tried to save her but it was too late."

"Did you see anyone leaving the house? Anyone suspicious?"

"No." A memory hit him. "I do remember hearing squealing tires, like a car leaving in a hurry."

"But you didn't see anyone?"

"No. Just a dark blur."

"A dark blur? Blue, black, brown? What color?"

"I don't know. I just caught it out of the corner of my eye."

"How do you know it was a car, not a truck or SUV?"

"I don't . . . not really. Guess I just assumed it was a car." He shrugged. "Sounded like a car."

She silently stared at him for several seconds. Finally she said, "How did you get the scratches on your face?"

"Charlene scratched me when I was trying to help her . . . I don't think she even knew who I was."

She went silent again, her brilliant green eyes piercing and direct, as if she were trying to drill through his brain. The truth slammed into him like a giant meteor crashing to earth. Sam wasn't looking at him as her lover, a man she totally trusted and believed in. She was eyeing him as a suspect. The lump of cement that had been churning in his stomach for the last hour solidified into a hard block and settled low in his gut.

"Samantha, I didn't kill her."

A pained and devastated expression flickered across her face before she replaced it with that of a professionally cool homicide detective interviewing a person of interest. "I didn't say you—"

"Not another word, Quinn."

He jerked his head up to see his friend and attorney, Bob Dixon.

Bob kept his steadying gaze on Quinn but his words were for Sam. "I'd like to confer with my client."

"I'm not working the case," Sam said.

"What's she doing in here if she's not on the case?" Bob asked Quinn.

"Samantha is my—" He caught himself. Was he risking her career by calling her his girlfriend? As hurt as he was by her attitude, causing her problems wasn't something he wanted.

"Your what?" Bob asked.

"My friend."

"Friend or not, she's a cop. What'd you tell her?"

"What I've told everyone since I got here. The truth. Charlene was near death when I arrived at her house. I tried to save her but couldn't."

Bob nodded and turned to Sam. "As I said, I need to confer with my client."

Nodding her agreement, she headed to the door. "Let us know when you're finished."

She didn't say another word to him, didn't even look at him before she left. Shit. Did she actually believe he was capable of murder?

Samantha made a beeline to the ladies' room—one of the few places in this building that she could hide. She rushed to the last stall and locked the door. Finally she allowed herself to breathe, taking slow, even breaths. Feeling no better, she closed the lid on the toilet, sat down abruptly, and put her face on her knees. It had been years since she had fainted, but she recognized the signs. She had been seconds from falling face-first onto the floor.

She told herself that Quinn's emotionless comments to her questions weren't suspect. He was a very controlled person—that was his nature. And the scratches on his face? It made perfect sense that an injured victim would lash out, not knowing that someone was trying to help. The comment he'd made about strangling Charlene . . . people joked about stuff like that all the time. It didn't mean they meant the words.

Insidious doubts once more drilled into her blind faith. Hadn't she wondered if this man who seemed perfect for her was too perfect? Hadn't she questioned if what he had shown of himself was just a façade, because it was what she had wanted to see? Just how well did she know Quinn?

She had thought her father to be flawless, too, only to learn that a monster had been lurking beneath the surface. She had loved her father, Beckett Wilde, with all her heart, believed him a hero in every sense of the word. He had proven how very wrong she could be.

Admittedly she had been ten years old when that happened. It was normal for a child to look at a parent as a larger-than-life, extraordinary person. She was an adult now. She knew people were all too human. Despite Quinn's seeming perfection, he was as human as anyone. Had his fierce control finally snapped?

Samantha raked her fingers through her hair, barely aware that it came loose from its knot and tumbled down over her shoulders. How could she even consider Quinn a killer? This was a man who'd held her in his arms when she had sobbed over a sappy, sad movie a few weeks ago. A man who made love to her with an intense passion intertwined with an aching gentleness. He had laughed at her lack of skills in the kitchen, joined her in singing an old rock and roll song she had been humming one day. He had told her about losing his first pet, Harry the hamster, and how he had buried it beneath his mother's prized zinnias because he wanted his friend's grave to be beautiful.

Quinn was a physician, saving lives daily. He would never take one. Yes, all right, he had served in the army, but that was war against the enemy. And he had been a combat medic, putting his life on the line to save others. He was everything heroic and brave. Just because he seemed too good to be true didn't mean he wasn't exactly as he appeared to be.

Everything they had shared over the past four months showed that he was exactly what she believed him to be. Quinn Braddock was not a killer.

But then why didn't he talk about his past? The hamster story had been one of the few things he had shared. She knew his parents lived in Virginia, but only because she had asked him. He'd admitted he and his parents had never been close and that he hadn't seen them in years.

After graduating from college, Quinn had joined the army, choosing to serve his country. When he'd left the service, he had pursued medicine. He had an excellent reputation as an ER doctor in one of the largest hospitals in Atlanta. All these things showed a man of honor, integrity, and caring. His decisions and career choices reinforced her faith in him.

But what if Charlene's death hadn't been cold-blooded murder? Quinn had made no secret of his hatred for his ex-wife. What if he had gone over there and lost his temper? Beneath the cool control were simmering passions she had yet to see unleashed. What if that control had snapped?

Why had he gone over there in the first place? He had never said—only that she had called and asked him to come. If Charlene had called, why hadn't she heard the phone ring? His cellphone had been on the nightstand, right next to hers. Why hadn't she heard it?

Samantha pushed her fingers through her hair again and stood. This merry-go-round of questions and suppositions was getting her nowhere. She needed to get the full facts. The only way to get to the truth was to investigate the evidence.

After washing her hands and patting her face down with a damp paper towel, she felt marginally refreshed. The instant she opened the door, she was wishing she had stayed inside the bathroom.

Larry Kennedy appeared in front of her; apparently he'd been waiting for her to come out. "Captain Mintz is looking for you."

Larry was a fellow detective and one of the few cops who'd made it clear that he didn't approve of her. His deep-set eyes gleamed with unhidden malice. It hadn't helped that she had turned him down for a date her first week on the job.

With a silent nod to let him know she'd heard him, she turned away. She and Kennedy had already had several small altercations. The last thing she needed to do was get into another verbal sparring match. Not when her world was falling apart around her.

"Guess you should be more careful who you date," Larry called out.

Samantha kept walking. She wouldn't give the jerk the satisfaction of acknowledging his comment. His opinion meant less than nothing.

She knocked on her captain's door, and when he called for her to enter, she took a steadying breath and opened the door.

"Wilde, have a seat."

Stone-gray hair, military posture, and a fairness she admired—this man's opinion meant a lot to her. He had taken a chance on her, gone to bat for her, and mentored her.

She dropped into the chair in front of his desk and took another deep breath. Her nerves were rattling inside her like sizzling kernels of popcorn. Hopefully, after her meeting here, she could gather more information and then find a quiet place to sort it all out.

"I understand you and Dr. Braddock are friends."

There was no reason to hold back with the captain. "We're more than friends. We've been dating for about four months now."

"I see."

"He's not the kind of man who would do this." She swallowed and added, "I believe in him."

Bushy black brows arched, showing his doubt. She silently cursed her less-than-convincing endorsement. She'd never been able to lie worth a damn. She did have doubts, dammit. She hated that she had them, but they were there whether she liked it or not.

"It doesn't matter whether you believe he's innocent or guilty. The evidence will prove the case."

"Who're the lead detectives?"

"Murphy and Kennedy."

She felt a little relief. Joe Murphy was one of their finest and would hopefully temper Kennedy's ass-hat tendencies. And despite the unfriendly relationship she had with the man, Larry Kennedy was known to be a competent detective.

"I'll help where I can."

"No, you'll stay out of it. Understand?"

She nodded. Yes, she would officially stay out of it, but that didn't mean she wouldn't investigate on her own. There was no way she could just sit back and do nothing.

"Of course." She put her hands on the arms of her chair as if to get up. "Was there anything else?"

His hard look told her he didn't believe her, but thankfully he let it go. "That's it."

Samantha walked as sedately as she could from her captain's office. First she would watch the interview she knew would be conducted soon. Then she would go to the crime scene. She had to see it for herself. She had to find proof that Quinn was innocent.

And if he isn't? her mind whispered. Then she would deal with the fallout.

CHAPTER FOUR

"Okay, tell me again why you went to see your ex-wife, whom you admittedly had a rancorous relationship with."

Quinn ground his teeth together. This was the tenth time they'd asked the same damn question. Bob sat beside him, ready to stop the questioning if he felt it necessary. Since Quinn had nothing to hide, he'd seen no problem with the interview. Problem was, they were getting nowhere. Since he was telling the truth, he wasn't going to change his story. And since they didn't believe him, they were going to continue to ask the same frigging questions to try to trip him up.

"As I said before, she called me this morning and asked me to come over. She told me she had changed her mind about a necklace she retained in the divorce settlement."

"And this necklace . . . where is it?"

"I have no idea. I assume it's either still in her house or the killer took it if he robbed the house."

"And how did you get in the house? Do you have a key?"

As patiently as possible, Quinn answered, "As I said, when I rang the doorbell and no one answered, I knocked. The door pushed partially open. I called out her name. When she didn't answer, I pushed the door open farther and that's when I smelled the blood."

Detective Kennedy smirked. "Must have some nose on you, Doc. Smelling blood from that far away."

"Once you've smelled the blood of violence, it's not something you forget."

"And how is it you know about that?"

"U.S. Army." He left it at that. If the detective didn't understand the violence of war, he wasn't about to explain it.

"If you pushed the door open and saw her there, why didn't you call the police immediately?"

"I'm a doctor. I save lives. I thought I could save hers." Quinn refused to feel regret for that. If he had to do it over again, he'd do the same damn thing. Saving lives would always be his priority.

"Your wife screwed around on you. Bet that pissed you off."

"She was my *ex*-wife. And yes, when I was married to her, it did piss me off. After we divorced, I didn't care who she slept with or how many."

"How many times would you say you've seen your ex-wife since your divorce?"

Quinn shrugged. "I don't know a number. She called me every few months and asked me to come over."

"For what?"

"For a multitude of reasons. Sprinkler system went out, she couldn't get the gas fireplace to work, she found a book in the study she thought was mine."

"Sounds like she wanted to get back together with you."

"She knew that wasn't possible."

"Did you have violent arguments with her when you went to see her?"

"I don't have violent arguments."

"You don't get pissed?"

Oh yeah, he got pissed. In fact, at this moment, he'd like nothing more than to smash the noses of these two pricks who were making it clear that they thought he was a murderer.

"I got over being angry with Charlene a long time ago."

"Something like that . . . that's a hard thing to get over. Seems like a man would hold a grudge against any woman who screwed around on him."

Kennedy's smirk was getting on Quinn's nerves a hell of a lot more than his questions. The man was trying to rile him. Little did he know that Quinn had trained himself long ago to hold his emotions in check. The look he gave the detective was unflinchingly direct. "I don't hold grudges. I've gotten on with my life."

Murphy began again, "And you went to see her this morning, for what?"

That was it. That same damn question marked the end of his patience. Quinn gave Bob a look and his attorney immediately intervened: "Okay, that's it, guys. You've asked these questions six ways to Sunday and Dr. Braddock's given you the same answers. He's been more than cooperative. Either charge him or we're walking."

They didn't have enough evidence to charge him, that much was obvious. For the first time in hours, Quinn felt the slightest loosening of tension in his muscles. He had to force himself to sit still as he waited for them to tell him he could leave.

Detective Murphy gave a brief nod. "Fine. We'll be in touch soon."

Quinn stood and, without another word, walked toward the door. Detective Murphy stopped him with another question. "By the way, what does the necklace your ex-wife was going to return to you look like?"

He sighed and turned back around. At least this was a new question. "It's an antique pearl-and-diamond necklace on a silver chain. The diamonds are shaped like stars; the pearls look like small moons. The largest stone is a diamond shaped like the sun."

"Sounds expensive."

"I've never had it appraised but it's been in my family for a long time."

"We'll be on the lookout for it."

Knowing nothing he said right now would help his case, Quinn turned back around and went out the door. His eyes scanned the large room. Stupid, but there had been a small part of him that hoped Sam would be waiting for him. They had plans to see each other tonight. That had been before his world had exploded. Hell, after the way she had looked at him earlier, why did he even want to see her?

"We'll get this sorted out, Quinn."

He turned to Bob, who'd been his friend long before he was his attorney. "I know. It's just frustrating that they don't want to look further than what's in front of them. While they're trying to pin it on me, the real murderer is getting away."

"Murphy and Kennedy have a good reputation. They'll investigate and find the killer."

He nodded, but damned if he believed his friend's words right now. "You need me any more today?"

"No, let's meet tomorrow morning at ten. Can you work that?"

He'd have to rearrange his schedule again, but what choice did he have? "I'll meet you at ten at your office."

Bob gestured toward the left side of the parking lot. "I'm over there."

"I'll take a cab. Need to think things through."

"Don't do one of your marathons when you get home, okay?"

His friend knew him well. Though his mouth felt like it would never lift in a smile again, he managed a small grimace. "Maybe just half a marathon."

Slapping him on the back, Bob turned to go to his car.

Quinn raised his hand to hail the cab coming his way,

his tired mind reeling with a myriad of thoughts. One issue clamored and clawed for predominance over all the others—Sam's doubt.

He didn't let his guard down often. Charlene had been an anomaly—one he deeply regretted. But Sam . . . ? Of all the people Quinn had thought he could believe in, Samantha Wilde had been number one on his list. And now he had to wonder if he had ever known her at all.

Samantha drove through the exquisitely landscaped subdivision toward Charlene Braddock's house. After watching Quinn's interrogation, she had gone home for a handful of ibuprofen and a change of clothes. And she had needed to decompress. Listening to Quinn's calm, even answers to Murphy's and Kennedy's questions hadn't made her feel any better. Nothing had tripped him up. She told herself that was because he had nothing to hide. But his unemotional demeanor was eerily scary.

As a cop, she had learned to pick apart words and read between the lines. Nothing he'd said made him look guilty. So why then did she still have her doubts? Why couldn't she have full faith that Quinn was innocent?

She turned onto Mallard Lane, where three police cars were parked in front of a stately brick home. Quinn once mentioned that he and Charlene had bought the house about a year before their divorce. This area of Atlanta was one of the most exclusive and expensive. And while Quinn's condo was nice, it was nothing like this.

She pulled to a stop about a half block away from the house, got out, and started walking. First she wanted to get the lay of the land. Who had been around when the murder took place? It had been early morning, so there should have been people leaving for their jobs, joggers, maybe some yard workers.

Summer in the South meant that people did their outside activities in the early morning or evening. Though the houses weren't close together, anyone on this street should have been able to see something. If not the actual murderer, at least perhaps a strange car in their neighborhood.

She knew Atlanta PD would be thorough. They would have already canvassed the area, looking for witnesses. Sometimes, though, it helped to go back and look for the less obvious. Samantha refused to consider that she was grasping at straws. This was all part of being a cop, even if this time there was an edge of desperation to her investigation.

"What are you doing here, Wilde?"

She turned around and faced Joe Murphy. "I had to come. I won't get in the way but I need to know what you guys know."

"Did you see Braddock this morning, before he came here?"

"Is that an official question?"

"Would the answer be different if it was?"

"No, of course not. Yes, I was with him this morning before he came here."

"Did he say why he was coming here?"

"He said Charlene called and asked him to come over."

"For what reason?"

"He didn't say."

"Were you in the same room with him when she called?"

Even though there was something about him that reminded her of her grandfather, she refused to blush as she said, "I was in the same room with him, but I was asleep."

"Did you hear the phone ring?"

"No, but I was in a deep sleep. I wouldn't have heard an earthquake."

She held her breath. Would he question her further? She had wondered why she hadn't heard Quinn's phone. But it was the truth. She had been exhausted last night. Quinn had managed to shower, dress, and make coffee all without disturbing her. Not hearing a phone that was on his side of the bed wasn't a surprise.

"How long have you known him?"

"About four months."

"What do you know about him?"

"That he's a good man. Was a medic in the army. Has an excellent reputation as an ER physician."

"You ever meet his ex-wife?"

"No."

"What'd he tell you about her?"

"Nothing."

She had answered too fast. And the damnable thing about it was, she had told the truth. Quinn had told her nothing about Charlene. It was that stupid remark this morning . . . she couldn't get it out of her head.

She quickly added, "The only things I know about her, I heard from some of his friends."

"Oh yeah, and what'd they say?"

"What you already know. That Charlene was unfaithful and wasn't a particularly nice person."

When he remained silent, she went on. "There are probably a half dozen men or more who could have done this. You need to talk to them."

Samantha slammed her mouth shut, cursing her runaway tongue. Even to her own ears, her tone had held a frantic edge.

His brushy brows, the only hair he had on his head, arched as his light brown eyes pierced her. "Do you think he's guilty?"

"Of course not."

"So why are you here?"

"If it was someone you cared about, would you be able to stay away?"

He considered her for several seconds and then shook his head. "No. But if the captain finds out you were here, your ass is grass."

"I'll stay out of everyone's way."

"If he finds out I didn't tell you to skedaddle, he'll chew my ass but good."

"He'll never hear it from me. Now, tell me what you know."

She released a silent, relieved sigh when he said, "We figure she knew the murderer. No evidence of forced entry."

Puzzled, she looked up at him. "But she might have answered the door to anyone. In a neighborhood like this, you don't expect a killer to come to your door."

"Maybe so, but I doubt she would have answered the door to just anyone in what she was wearing." Murphy shrugged. "We figure she knew him well."

"What was she wearing?"

"A sexy nightgown."

"How sexy?"

"She was practically naked."

Had Charlene been expecting someone other than Quinn? One of her lovers? Or had she worn the gown hoping to entice her ex-husband? If she had been expecting someone else, why would she have invited Quinn over?

"What else?"

"Preliminary report from the ME says she was stabbed thirteen times. Carotid artery was nicked, so she didn't bleed out immediately but it didn't take long. Blood spatter wasn't that bad, so the artery was probably one of his last jabs."

A crime of passion. She had seen it happen before. Her own mother had been stabbed repeatedly like that. And her mild-mannered, charming father had done the deed. She shoved that thought aside. It had no bearing on this case. None at all.

However, that kind of overkill did reinforce the thinking that Charlene had known her murderer. Anger like that was intimate . . . very personal.

"What about the murder weapon?"

"Kitchen knife. Found about a yard from her body. Killer must've thrown it down when he finished. Unfortunately he wiped it clean before he threw it down."

"Was the knife from the victim's kitchen?"

"Yeah, looks like it. There's one missing out of the case on the counter."

"Anything stolen from the house?"

"Not that we can tell. Doesn't look like anything has been disturbed." He paused and then added, "Well, except for one thing."

"What's that?"

"A laptop computer in the master bedroom. Looks like it was thrown against the wall."

She nodded absently. Their tech people would check it for emails and anything incriminating, including fingerprints.

"Oh, and that necklace Braddock wanted. It's not there, either."

Yes, the necklace. The one Quinn hadn't mentioned to her. Why hadn't he told her about it? All he'd said was that Charlene had called and asked him to come over.

"Anyone see anything?"

"Found just one person so far. Lives next door. Said she saw Braddock cross the street and go into the house. When she looked out again, our guys were already on the scene.

"Neighbors on the right side were still asleep, the one

diagonally across the street on the left was awake but didn't look out until she saw the police stop in front of the house. Neighbors in the gray brick house directly across the street would've had the best shot at seeing straight into her door. Unfortunately they're not there. According to the other neighbors, they left for vacation two days ago."

"How'd the on-scene officers get here so fast?"

"Had a couple of break-ins over the last few weeks. The Neighborhood Watch asked for some daily drive-throughs. Kid's a rookie cop." He looked down at his notes. "Name's Mike Kindred. Said he saw the front door open and stopped to investigate. Found Braddock standing over the victim's body."

Despite the ninety-degree temperature, chills swept up Samantha's spine. The image of Quinn covered in blood, standing over the body of his dead ex-wife, was something she was glad she hadn't seen for herself. Her imagination was more than enough to turn her stomach.

"Is Kindred still here?"

Murphy shook his head. "Left about an hour ago."

She jerked her head toward the house. "Okay if I go in and look around?"

He considered her for several seconds, then said, "Yeah, most everyone's gone."

"Thanks, Murph."

Giving her a quick, kind smile, he turned to walk away. Unable to stay out of it, she called out, "He didn't do it."

"I hope you're right."

She knew he wouldn't be moved by her words, but she couldn't resist making sure he knew she believed in Quinn. She ignored the whispers of doubt that continued to reverberate in her head.

CHAPTER FIVE

Quinn stood beneath the hot blast of the shower and scrubbed himself raw. A physician sickened by blood would be funny if it weren't so damn stupid. Blood in the hospital didn't bother him, because he knew what to do and what to expect. Even when there were complications, events were within his control.

On the battlefield, he'd had no control. Explosives and roadside bombs were impossible to predict. He had survived by focusing totally on his job. Without that fierce concentration, he wouldn't have come back alive.

That hard-earned control was slowly slipping away. He had no idea who had killed Charlene. And based on what had happened at the police station, he was apparently the only suspect.

A dark, sick feeling in the pit of his stomach wasn't something that came along often, but when it did, he took notice. This was the way he'd always felt right before some major shit went down.

Hell, what could happen next? He was already a suspect in the murder of his ex-wife. And his girlfriend wasn't sure he was innocent. Wasn't that enough?

Turning off the water, Quinn grabbed the towel from the rack and dried off quickly. It was going on nine o'clock. Would he hear from Sam?

All day long, he'd blocked out everything but the here

and now. The focus that had seen him through two tours in Iraq and one in Afghanistan and made him a successful physician had seen him through the day. But now, with Charlene's blood finally washed away and the horror of the day growing dimmer, the ache in his chest grew.

He had known he and Sam were keeping secrets from each other. They'd gone from instantaneous attraction to burning up the sheets. With their busy schedules, most of their spare time was spent in bed. They were good at sharing their bodies but not much else.

And to be fair, what he knew about Sam was probably a whole lot more than what she knew about him. He knew she had grown up in Alabama and was one of identical triplets. Her sister Savannah was an assistant district attorney in Nashville, and her sister Sabrina was a private investigator in Tallahassee. He knew her parents were dead and that her grandfather had raised the sisters. She loved sappy love stories, had a caring heart, and her smile could make his toes curl. And just the sound of her silky voice could turn him on.

He slid into a pair of jeans, slung the towel around his neck, and padded to the kitchen. It had just occurred to him that he hadn't eaten a damn thing all day. Maybe that was where his feeling of impending doom came from. As he threw together an omelet, he thought about the things he'd never told Sam. Would he ever have the chance now? Hell, maybe it was best she didn't know what kind of screwed-up background he'd come from.

Turning away from the stove, Quinn was unsurprised to find her standing at the entrance to the kitchen. Dressed in khakis and a sleeveless white shirt, she looked clean, pure, and so damn beautiful the ache in his chest grew. A small part of him that still believed in a future for them had been sure she would come.

He raised the plate he held in his hands. "The omelet is big enough for two."

Sam's smile wasn't as bright as usual, but at least she had one. "Thanks. My cold Pop-Tart from twelve hours ago has worn off."

He grabbed two forks from the silverware drawer, sliced the omelet, and slid half of it onto another plate. He turned and asked, "Orange juice or milk?"

A slender hand touched her stomach as she grimaced. "Better go for the milk."

She had a nervous stomach—something he had learned the first night they'd slept together. Whenever she was nervous or upset, her stomach went south.

He poured her a large glass of milk and an orange juice for himself. They sat at the bar together, silent. Normally they would be talking about their day, telling each other about an amusing or interesting event. There was none of that tonight.

Quinn quickly demolished his meal, the nourishment giving him a temporary sense of well-being. At least now he felt as if he could carry on a halfway decent conversation.

"How did the trial go this morning?"

She jumped as though startled. "What?"

He'd been so focused on eating, he hadn't noticed that Samantha had only taken a couple of bites of her omelet.

"You need to eat, sweetheart."

She flinched at the endearment and he felt the kick all the way down to his soul. Trying to ignore the hurt, he repeated, "Eat up and tell me how the trial went."

He watched her take another bite, noticing she chewed slowly as if she were having trouble swallowing.

"The trial . . . it was . . ." She shrugged. "It was the same as usual. The judge kept allowing the defense to take wild liberties."

"Think it'll go on much longer?"

"I don't know." She swung around to look at him. "Why didn't you tell me you were going to see Charlene to get a necklace back?"

This wasn't the time to tell her what he had wanted to do with the necklace. Now, as far as he was concerned, it could go in the trash. The damn thing would always have the taint of death attached to it.

"Didn't see the need to mention it to you. Wasn't that big of a deal."

Samantha bit the inside of her jaw, an old habit when she was upset. Quinn was holding something back, she could tell. He was good at keeping his thoughts to himself, but there'd been the slightest hesitation before he answered.

The crime scene had been like dozens she'd seen before. Nothing had stood out and told her the identity of the killer. From what she could tell, nothing in the house, other than the laptop, had been disturbed, and no items seemed to be missing. Whatever anyone wanted to say about Charlene, no one would dispute that her house, inside and out, was immaculate.

Charlene's cellphone had been found on her dresser in her bedroom. The log of calls, made and received, would be followed up on. If she had known her killer, were his name and number on the phone? Of course, Quinn's would be on there. Charlene had no landline phones, so she would have called him on her cellphone. But other names would be on there, too. One of them could be the murderer.

Nothing had struck her as unusual or strange when she was inside the house. It was when she walked out the door to leave that her world had blown up. A neighbor who'd talked to the police earlier decided she had remembered more and now wanted to chat in earnest. Samantha had learned more in that five-minute conversation with Marcie Ballou about Quinn and Charlene's disastrous marriage than she had in the months she had dated him. From Marcie's overexcited chattering, she had discerned that Quinn and Charlene's marriage was acrimonious the entire time they lived in the house together.

Why Marcie had opened up so completely was a mystery. Maybe it was because Samantha was a woman. Or perhaps Marcie wasn't a morning person, so when Murphy interviewed her, she hadn't been at her best. Maybe she'd been drinking, though there was no indication that the woman wasn't completely sober. For whatever reason, the instant she'd seen Samantha, she'd called her over and information had gushed forth like a geyser.

Samantha stared down at her plate, not seeing the congealing omelet in front of her as she remembered the disturbing conversation she'd had with Charlene's neighbor.

"Yoo-hoo! Hello, are you with the police?"

Samantha had been headed to her car across the street but stopped abruptly and turned. The woman, in her mid-sixties, was thin, with short, graying hair, and had a cigarette hanging from her mouth like it was a favored appendage. She was dressed in Capri pants and a summer top.

"Yes, I'm with the police. And you are . . . ?"

"I'm Marcie Ballou. I live next door to the Braddocks. Or rather, I live next door to Charlene. Well, I guess not anymore." She laughed, the sound an abrasive mixture of a little girl's giggle and the croak of a frog.

"Did you know Charlene well?"

"About as well as you can know anyone these days, I guess. She wasn't my best friend by any means, but we exchanged words on occasion."

"And did you see anyone this morning?"

"Well, like I told the police earlier, I was looking out my kitchen window around eight this morning and saw

Quinn . . ." She grinned and added, "Dr. Braddock, that is."

"Where did you see him?"

"He was parked across the street from Charlene's house. I knew it was him immediately. That car was all my husband talked about when Quinn—I mean Dr. Braddock—first bought it."

"What was he doing?"

"It was the strangest thing. When I looked out, he was just sitting in the car, staring out the window."

"At the house?"

"No. Just staring straight ahead."

"How long would you say he sat there?"

"Well, he was already there when I looked out, but I guess he sat there for maybe a couple of minutes more."

"Was he talking on the phone, perhaps?"

"No, I could see him pretty clearly. He was just sitting there. I almost went out and said something to him, but just when I was about to do that, he got out of the car and I knew immediately I didn't want to talk to him."

"Why's that?"

She shivered dramatically. "Because he looked furious. He marched across the street like he was on some sort of mission and his face looked like a thundercloud."

"Did you hear any arguing?"

"No, that's the thing. I heard nothing. Then, a few minutes later, I looked out again and saw a police car. Then, a little while after that, I looked out and there were more police cars, an ambulance, and a fire truck, too. It was like a television show."

"You said you talked to the police?"

"Yes, of course. That nice Detective Murphy. I just forgot to mention how angry Quinn looked."

"Anything else you forget to mention?"

"Only that I'm not surprised he killed her."

"Who?"

"Why, Quinn, of course."

"Why do you think he killed her?"

"That's pretty obvious, isn't it? He goes to her door looking mad as a hornet and a few minutes later she's dead?"

"Why aren't you surprised he killed her?"

"Because of their relationship. Even when they were married, it was terrible. I used to hear some of the most gosh-awful arguments."

"Was he physically abusive?"

"Oh no, I don't think so. Although there was that time at the pool."

"What happened?"

"I was in my bedroom and heard someone yelling. I looked out and Charlene was standing beside their pool, screaming at Quinn. Of course, all of the noise from their arguments always came from Charlene. When she got mad, she was as shrill as a seagull. Anyway, she was screaming about something."

"And what was Dr. Braddock doing?"

"He just stood there, looking at her. I couldn't see his face but I could just imagine how angry he must've been."

"Could you tell what she was angry about?"

"I couldn't hear the words. They stood there for a good five minutes. Her screaming, him just standing there."

"Then what happened?"

"Well, it was like something out of a movie. She slapped him across the face. He grabbed her, threw her over his shoulder, and went inside the house."

"Did you hear anything else?"

"No. It was quiet the rest of the night."

"Any other incidents like that?"

"No, other than every few days, I'd hear Charlene yelling about something."

"Anything else come to mind?"

"Well, all I can say is I'm surprised he didn't kill her before this. What with all the men."

"She was unfaithful?"

"Oh, I think 'unfaithful' is probably a mild word for what she was. And after he left, it got worse."

"Worse how?"

"There were even more men. Some were ones I'd seen before. Some came only once."

"Could you describe any of them?"

"I could try, but the thing is, they all kind of looked like Dr. Braddock. Tall and muscular, with dark hair. Guess you could say Charlene liked a certain type."

"Anything else?"

"No, not that I can think of. Quinn's an awfully nice man. When my husband fell off a ladder the summer they moved here, Dr. Braddock was so helpful. I always wondered why he married someone like Charlene."

Samantha wondered the same thing.

"Sam, where is your mind?"

She jerked her thoughts back to the man sitting beside her. After hearing Marcie's words, she was even more unsure of what had taken place today. How could a man go from the warm, caring person she knew Quinn to be to a cold-blooded murderer? It didn't seem possible. Quinn couldn't have stabbed Charlene the moment she opened the door. The knife had come from her kitchen. But what if he had gone into the house and then into the kitchen? Maybe they had argued . . . perhaps about that mysterious necklace. Maybe she had said something that had been the last straw. Had he taken a knife from the kitchen and followed her to the foyer, stabbing her repeatedly?

Her conversation with Marcie had been upsetting enough, but the real nightmare had begun when she'd gotten a call to come back to the station. When she had arrived, Murphy's sad eyes had been an indication that she wasn't going to like what he had to tell her. Kennedy's smirk had made her even more uneasy.

She had kept her focus on Murphy. "What's wrong?"

"What do you know about Dr. Braddock's family?"

Telling them she knew nothing about Quinn's family was the truth, but from Kennedy's increasing smirk, admitting that wasn't a good idea. Still, she wouldn't lie. "I know his parents live in Virginia and he doesn't see them often."

"What about his brother?" Kennedy asked. "He tell you anything about him?"

Revealing she didn't even know he had a brother would make it look worse than it already did. Her expression impassive, she said, "No, he doesn't talk about him."

"That's not surprising, since his brother was a psycho."

The queasy roil of her stomach became a tidal wave of nausea as Samantha said, "What are you talking about?"

Giving a glare to Kennedy, Murphy answered, "Looks like the brother raped and tried to murder a neighbor when he was just a kid. He went to juvie and ended up committing suicide when he was seventeen."

No wonder Quinn didn't talk about his brother. A rapist, almost murderer, who was now dead? Yeah, those weren't exactly the things you shared. Just like she had never told him about her father's crimes.

"Everyone has relatives who've done bad things. That doesn't mean he's a killer, too."

Kennedy laughed. "You really do have blinders on with this guy, don't you? There's plenty of research showing that killer tendencies run in the family."

She wanted to fly across the room and wipe the grin off of Kennedy's face. Instead she said calmly, "And there's plenty of research to refute that claim, too."

Head high, she had walked out of the room and then the building. When she'd finally gotten into her car, she had allowed herself to breathe. And she had argued with herself. Just because a family member was sick didn't mean the whole family was, too. She and her sisters were proof of that.

"Sam?"

She jerked, realizing she'd zoned out again. That went along with exhaustion and almost no nourishment. "Why have you never told me about your brother?"

Surprise and then pain flared in his eyes. "Dalton's been gone a long time."

"You had to know that this would come out in the investigation."

"Hell, Sam. I've barely had time to breathe since all this started. And what my sick brother did twenty years ago has no bearing on this." His eyes narrowed into slits. "Or is it that since my brother was a sick fuck, you think I am, too?"

"That's not what I said, Quinn. I got blindsided by the detectives today who told me about it. I wished you had told me."

"There wasn't anything to tell. He was sick and put away. Then he killed himself. End of story."

She drew in a silent breath and went another direction. "You said you saw a vehicle leave quickly before you got out of your car."

"No, I said I heard the squeal of tires, looked up, and saw a blur."

"If that was the killer coming from Charlene's house, how did you not see him? You were directly in front of her house. And you notice everything, Quinn."

"My mind was on other things."

Again he had hesitated before answering. Had he always paused before answering questions and she had just never noticed?

"Like what?"

"I was preparing myself to see Charlene. Seeing her was never a pleasant experience."

"Were you angry when you got out of the car?"

"No."

"Why didn't you tell me why you were going to go see her?"

"As I said . . . I didn't think it was that big of a deal. She got the necklace in the divorce. This morning she called and said she was going to give it back to me."

"Just like that, out of the blue? She gave no reason for her change of heart?"

"No, but you know it's not the first time she's tried to get me to come over. It worked today because I wanted the necklace."

"Do you have a photograph of it?"

"Why?"

"They searched the house thoroughly. It's not there."

"Do you want the photo so you can be on the lookout for it? Or do you want it to prove that it actually exists?"

Instead of answering, she stared at him hard for several seconds. His eyes met hers unflinchingly, challengingly.

"I met Marcie Ballou today."

"You went to Charlene's house?"

"Yes."

"I'm sure Marcie was more than happy to talk with you."

"She said you and Charlene argued a lot."

"Do you know many divorced couples who didn't fight before they split up?"

"No, but she said—"

"Samantha, do you think I killed Charlene?"

She hadn't wanted him to ask that question. How could she explain her suspicions when she didn't totally understand them herself? Her exhausted mind whirled with questions, doubts, and suppositions. She wanted to believe him . . . she really did.

Her hesitation gave him the answer. A blank look washed over his blue eyes, dulling their brilliance. He stood and said coolly, "Unless you're here in an official capacity, you'd better leave."

"Quinn . . . please. Don't."

"Don't what? You've slept beside me for months and you actually think I could do this thing? That I'm capable of murder?"

"It's not that I think you're guilty. It's just . . ." Hell, what could she say? She had doubts and they had only increased after talking with Marcie. And whether she wanted to admit it or not, learning about his brother had increased her misgivings.

A hand reached for her arm, and without thinking, she jerked back. She hadn't believed his face could get blanker than it already was.

"Get out."

Samantha went to her feet. Her knees wobbled as myriad feelings almost overwhelmed her. She didn't believe he was guilty but neither could she squelch the doubts. And still, even though she had them, she knew she was hurting him and it tore her to pieces.

"I'm so sorry, Quinn."

As she turned away from him, her thoughts whirled like a spinning top. Was it possible to love and distrust someone at the same time? How could she want to comfort him if she thought he was guilty of murder? How could she not trust a man who'd been so gentle and wonderful to her? How could . . .

"Dammit, Sam!"

Hard hands shoved her into a chair and then pushed her head toward her knees. "Take slow, even breaths."

Holy crap, she'd almost passed out again. She concentrated on breathing and the light-headed feeling dissipated. Now she was fully embarrassed. She peeked up at Quinn, noting the grim set of his mouth. He was angry. But if he was innocent, didn't he have every right to be furious? She was letting him down and breaking her own heart in the process.

His voice cracked like a whip. "Better?"

"Yes."

"When was your last period?"

The question seemed so out of left field, she could only stare at him.

"If you're pregnant, I want to know."

Weary and disheartened, Samantha raised her head and pushed her fingers through her hair. "I'm not pregnant."

"You didn't answer my question."

"Fine. I started my period this morning, around 10:02. Is that detailed enough for you?"

He gave her a grim nod. "Then you need to eat."

She stood slowly, grateful that her knees held and her head felt halfway normal. "I'll eat something when I get home."

"As much as I want you out of here, I'm not letting you leave like this." He whirled around and headed to the kitchen. "I'll make you a peanut butter sandwich."

She waited until he was in the kitchen before she grabbed her purse and headed to the door. He didn't want her here and she'd be damned if she'd fall apart in front of him again.

"Sam."

She should have known she wouldn't get out of here without him noticing. Still facing the door, she whispered softly, "I'm sorry, Quinn."

"Yeah, me too."

She opened the door and walked out. With every step

that took her away from him, her heart cracked. And at
the click of the lock behind her, it completely shattered.

Refusing to give in to the hurt, Quinn went about his
normal routine. He cleaned up the few dishes in the
kitchen, made coffee for the next day, and then changed
into running clothes. Late night runs were the norm for
him. It was a good way to let off the tension from the
day, and this one had brought that in spades.

Though he wouldn't let himself think about the betrayal he felt, he knew there was one thing he had to
take care of before he went through the door. He'd
never been much into denial and wasn't about to start
now. He was in trouble.

He grabbed his cellphone; Bob answered on the first
ring. "What's up, Quinn?"

"That defense attorney you told me about. I think I'm
going to need him."

"I'll have him contact you tomorrow."

"Thanks, man."

He ended the call before his friend could offer com-
miseration. He didn't need it. What he needed was a
good defense attorney who could figure out a way out
of this shit. And when it was over, he needed to figure
out how to live without a woman who had become the
most important person in his world. A woman who believed he was a murderer.

Quinn closed the door behind him. Bypassing the elevator, he headed for the stairway. When he had moved
into the city, after his divorce, he'd had a list of require-
ments he had given his real estate agent. One of those
was his need to live as high up as possible. Living on the
twenty-fifth floor gave him the opportunity to warm up
on his run. By the time he made it to the street, he was

ready for the hard runs he enjoyed. And at the end of his runs, the stairs gave him time to cool down.

The instant he was out on the street, Quinn took off like a bullet. This time of night, few people were around to distract him. This had always been his favorite time to run. Even in high school, when everyone in his house was asleep, he'd sneak off and run. Not that it had been necessary to sneak around. His parents hadn't given a damn. Their only concern was that he not bring any negative attention to them. Other than that, he could do what he damn well wanted.

It was on one of those midnight runs that he had saved his first life. That night had been an epiphany in many ways. Saving a woman's life had planted the seed in his mind of being a doctor. That seed hadn't taken root until years later but had waited patiently for him to acknowledge his destiny.

And that was also the night he'd discovered that his little brother was a psychopath.

CHAPTER SIX

Samantha stood in front of Captain Mintz's desk. The coffeepot in the break room was half empty, which meant he had consumed at least three cups of coffee. She had timed it just as she'd hoped. He would be in a mellower mood and hopefully more willing to grant her request.

She hadn't slept all night. Every time she closed her eyes, she saw Quinn's face. Dear heavens, she had hurt him so much. And the hell of it was, she still wasn't completely sure of his innocence. She wanted so badly to believe in him, but she couldn't. Not yet. Her only option was to prove his innocence or his guilt.

"What are you doing here so early, Wilde?"

"I need to take some time off."

Wise eyes studied hers. Didn't take a genius to figure out that yesterday's murder had everything to do with her need for time off. And she had long since decided that Captain Mintz was of genius status.

"How much time?"

"As much as I can."

"I'll give you four days."

She had hoped for two weeks but she'd take what she could get.

"Let's stop pretending for a moment that I don't know what you're taking time off for. If you get in the way of an ongoing investigation, you're out of here. You got that?"

"Yes, sir, I understand."

She was at the door when his voice stopped her. "For what it's worth, Wilde, I hope he's innocent."

"Thank you, sir." She closed the door behind her and whispered under her breath, "I hope so, too."

FIVE DAYS LATER . . .

"The good news is they have nothing more on you than they did before."

Quinn leaned against the bookcase in his attorney's massive office and shook his head. If that was the good news . . . "And I'm assuming the bad news is they still have no other suspects."

The lines in Homer Parker's aged face deepened as he grimaced. "Unfortunately, no. But with no further evidence, I doubt there's enough to bring it before the grand jury."

That was a relief but it didn't decrease the anger or frustration. Someone had killed Charlene in cold blood. No matter how he'd felt about her, she deserved justice. A secondary worry that he'd barely allowed himself to acknowledge hung over him like a dark cloud. The stigma of suspicion of murder hadn't exactly helped his career.

He was in emergency medicine, so most of his patients didn't give a damn about his personal life. All they wanted to know was whether he could save their lives or make them feel better. His patients weren't his concern; the hospital staff was. In the last week, he'd walked in on multiple conversations that had stopped abruptly. He had no doubt who had been the topic of those conversations. Doctors, nurses, and technicians he'd known for years were looking at him as if he had something to hide. They might not assume he was guilty like Samantha and the Atlanta PD did, but they sure as hell weren't treating him as if they believed in his innocence.

"I've hired a private investigator," Quinn said.

"That's your choice, of course, but I don't see the necessity."

That was because Parker's number one priority was keeping his client out of jail. Nothing else concerned him. But if the murderer was never caught, there would always be that doubt surrounding Quinn.

Leaning forward, he shook Parker's hand. "I appreciate your help."

"Call me again if you have the need."

Hoping like hell the need never existed again, Quinn walked out of the attorney's office and right into the path of Detectives Murphy and Kennedy. A sick dread filled him.

"Quinn Braddock, you're under arrest for the murder of Charlene Braddock."

Protesting his innocence would do no good. Figuring they'd cuff him, he put his hands behind his back. He was surprised when Detective Murphy said, "No cuffs."

"Dr. Braddock?"

Quinn glanced over his shoulder to see Parker standing behind him. The older man's wide-eyed, stunned expression would have been comical at another time. Looked like that help Quinn hoped he'd never need was going to be needed after all.

"I'll post bail as soon as it's set," Parker said.

Quinn gave a grim nod of acknowledgment. What was the point in speaking at all?

Samantha stood across the street from Charlene Braddock's house. They were arresting Quinn today. Murphy had called to let her know. She had thought about being there when it went down, but she knew Quinn wouldn't want to see her.

She had been on the case night and day for five days now. This morning she'd done something she had never done before—she had called in sick. Since her "vacation" was over, she was supposed to return to work. However, her investigation was far from over. The longer she investigated, the more convinced she became that Quinn was innocent. Problem was, she was the only one who believed it.

Actually, Murphy had his doubts, too, but this was a high-profile case and the DA had political ambitions. Whether Quinn's arrest resulted in a conviction or not, fingering a prime suspect would gain the DA and his office some mileage and extra publicity. And to hell with putting Quinn through hell.

At that thought, her conscience roared a heavy, disgusted sound. Her lack of faith in Quinn was indefensible. . . . She had never been more ashamed of herself. Using her past as an excuse for her suspicions would have no weight with him. She hadn't even considered trying to apologize or explain. Instead she had devoted herself 24/7 to either finding the real murderer or clearing Quinn. So far she had been successful at neither.

The laptop hadn't been as damaged as they had feared. The techs had easily accessed Charlene's emails and online accounts. The emails were unhelpful, mostly spam and receipts for online purchases. The largest amount of her activity involved shopping and a few posts on some social network sites. However, it was the last website Charlene had visited that had caused the most speculation. It was an online social news site for the Atlanta elite. The article covered a charity event that she and Quinn had attended last week. Samantha hadn't known that someone had captured a photo of them. Charlene had apparently seen it and had thrown the laptop across the room. The wall had a significant dent from her temper tantrum. Was that the reason she had called Quinn to come over?

The log of calls sent and received from Charlene's cellphone had been interesting. Over a dozen men's phone numbers were on her contact list, but she'd received only a few calls in the past thirty days. Murphy and Kennedy had interviewed the men on her contact list. All had admitted to a previous sexual relationship with Charlene but had sworn their relationship was over. And unfortunately every man had an airtight alibi.

The last call Charlene received had come from an untraceable burner phone. The identity of the caller remained a mystery.

Had that call been from Charlene's killer? The murder had been overkill, which usually indicated an intimate knowledge of the victim. So why an untraceable phone, unless the murder had been planned?

Charlene's neighbor Marcie Ballou had been both a curse and a blessing. She had blabbed to everyone within hearing distance about what she saw, what she thought, and what she suspected.

Yesterday Samantha had sat her down and taken her step by step through the morning of the murder. The process had taken the bulk of the day and had been a slow and tedious endeavor. What she learned confirmed her thoughts. Quinn hadn't had time to murder Charlene. He hadn't been in the house long enough to get inside, go to the kitchen, pull the knife from its slot, return to the foyer, and stab Charlene thirteen times before the first officer had arrived.

Samantha had gone through the scenario several times, clocking herself. Even when she sped through the house, the whole process took over two minutes.

Marcie had admitted that one of her morning shows

had gone off at 7:59 and that was the reason she had looked out the window. When a new show came on at 8:00 A.M., she had glanced out the window again and that was when she saw the first police car. And the police report bore the evidence of that time, also.

As soon as Samantha had confirmed that in her mind, she'd called Murphy. He had agreed that it was important evidence but said it wasn't going to prevent Quinn's arrest.

Samantha didn't care if she had to quit her job and devote herself full-time to proving Quinn's innocence. If that was what it took, she would do it.

Would he forgive her when this was over? She had grave doubts but she would make the attempt. If nothing else, he deserved to hear her apology in person.

"Hello there, can we help you?"

She whirled around, startled. A tanned, youthful-looking middle-aged couple stood several feet away from her. She had never seen them before. Since she had talked ad nauseam to every neighbor, she immediately knew they were Steve and Eileen Frazier, the couple who had gone on vacation two days before the murder.

"Sorry to be standing in your yard. I'm investigating Charlene Braddock's murder."

"Oh, we just heard about that," Mrs. Frazier said. "That's just awful."

Mr. Frazier immediately added, "But we don't know anything."

"Now, Steve, that's not right and you know it."

"No, I don't know it. You don't know if who we saw had anything to do with her murder."

Breath caught in her throat. Barely allowing herself to hope, Samantha said, "I was under the impression you two were on vacation when the murder took place."

Mrs. Frazier nodded. "We were supposed to be but Steve came down with food poisoning the night before we were scheduled to leave. So instead of taking off on Sunday like we'd planned, we ended up leaving Tuesday morning. Had to catch a direct flight to Puerto Rico to get on the cruise there."

"You saw someone at Charlene's house?"

"Well, we actually saw two someones."

Now that they were talking, Mr. Frazier seemed just as eager as his wife to share what they knew.

"What do you mean, two?"

"When Steve and I were in the car, doing our trip check, we saw a man walk up to Charlene's house and ring the doorbell."

"Trip check?"

"Yes, that's what we do just before we go on a trip to make sure we didn't forget anything. And wouldn't you know it, we did."

"So tell me what you saw."

"Well, we saw this man go up to the door and ring the doorbell. Charlene wasn't really a morning person, so we were a little curious about that."

"Of course, having a man show up at her door was nothing unusual," Mr. Frazier said.

Mrs. Frazier nodded. "Charlene did like her men."

Steering them back on topic, Samantha asked, "And did you recognize the man?"

Her heart sank when they both nodded.

"Was it her ex-husband, Quinn Braddock?"

"Not the first man but the second."

Samantha's patience was hanging by a thread. She was usually better at interrogation than this, but never had a question been so important to her.

"There was another man?"

"Yes, the first man was one we've seen a few times. Anyway, he went inside and that was that. We continued on with our trip check. Then when we realized we'd forgotten Steve's blood pressure medicine, I went back inside to get it. That's when I saw Quinn."

Her heart soared and her breathing increased. Was this the break she had been looking for?

"So another man was there only minutes before you saw Quinn Braddock, Charlene's ex-husband?"

"Yes, I saw Quinn walk across the road and I remember thinking that if that other man was still there, someone was going to be embarrassed. But he went inside and we left right after."

This was what she had been hoping for. Two eye witnesses who could testify that Charlene had a male visitor right before Quinn had arrived. This stranger was the man who had killed Charlene.

"Mr. and Mrs. Frazier, would it be possible for you to come down to the police station and talk to a sketch artist?"

"We have an awful lot to do today," Mr. Frazier said.

"Now, Steve, we've got to do our civic duty. Charlene wasn't the nicest neighbor in the world but she sure didn't deserve to be murdered."

Though Mr. Frazier grumbled again, Samantha knew that Mrs. Frazier's wishes would prevail.

Turning away, she pulled her phone from her pocket and tapped in the number for Murphy. At last she had proof positive that Quinn was innocent. With Mr. and Mrs. Frazier's statement, along with Marcie's testimony about the timing of Quinn's arrival, the charges would definitely be dropped.

And once it was over, she would go to Quinn and ask his forgiveness. She refused to contemplate that he wouldn't grant it.

Quinn was standing in the processing room, waiting to be fingerprinted, when Detective Murphy walked in and announced, "Charges have been dropped. You're free to go, Dr. Braddock."

Parker, who was standing close by, said, "How's that?"

"We have two witnesses who saw a man go into the victim's house only moments before Dr. Braddock arrived. Based upon that and other things we've uncovered, all charges are being dropped."

"What about the man that was seen? Has he been identified yet?" Quinn asked.

"No, but we've got a sketch artist working on it."

"I'd like to see it when it's done."

"You bet."

Before Quinn could say anything else, a young woman popped her head into the room. "Murph, the captain wants to see you."

He nodded, but instead of leaving, Detective Murphy continued to stand in front of Quinn as though he wanted to say something.

Quinn raised a questioning brow, wondering if the detective was going to give him a warning or an apology, or perhaps more information. He got nothing. Just a hard, searching look and then the man walked out the door without another word.

"Well, Dr. Braddock," Parker said, "looks like this time it's well and truly over."

Yeah, with the exception of finding the murderer. But that wasn't something his attorney was concerned about. Parker had done what he was hired to do. Now it was up to the police to go after the real killer. And while he appreciated that the charges had been dropped, he hoped to hell the real murderer could be caught. Until he was, that cloud of suspicion would continue to hover.

With an odd sense of déjà vu, Quinn once again shook Parker's hand and walked out the door. Halfway across the crowded room, he stopped. Stupid, but he wanted to see Sam's face when she learned that he wasn't guilty. Would she be surprised? Why the hell should he care? Still, he couldn't help himself.

He stopped at the large reception desk. "Is Detective Wilde in?"

Not bothering to look up from the report he was reading, an officer answered, "She's on vacation this week."

The news deflated any good feeling. So Samantha had gone out of town while he'd been fighting for his freedom. If that didn't show him where her mind and heart were, nothing would.

Quinn stalked out the door. To hell with her.

CHAPTER SEVEN

Standing before the full-length mirror in her bedroom, Samantha ignored the terror in her eyes as she forced her frozen lips upward into some semblance of a confident smile. A small, still voice inside her said that this was the wrong way to go. That Quinn needed her remorse and love, not a sexy siren. Perhaps if she were more confident of him, she might consider just showing up at his door like normal and asking his forgiveness. But as unsure as she was of Quinn's feelings, how could she not arrive dressed for battle?

She was going in with full armor. The body-hugging sleeveless black dress stopped several inches above her knees, its plunging neckline only a fraction above indecent, the next-to-nothing back showing more bare skin than some swimsuits. Black stilettos adorned her slender feet, making her already long legs look even longer and sleeker. Her hair, which she knew Quinn loved, flowed over her shoulders to the middle of her back in a smooth stream of golden silkiness.

For the first time in a long time, she was using her looks to influence someone. The person in the mirror wasn't Samantha anymore, and this outfit was certainly not something she felt comfortable wearing. This woman resembled the old Samantha Wilde. Looking beautiful every moment of every day was what she had once strived for with single-minded focus. She didn't miss those days of being more concerned about her looks than she was about her studies or the world around her. That kind of narcissistic self-containment had seen her through high school. In college, away from the stifling image she had created for herself, Samantha had come into her own.

She had entered the University of Georgia a naïve and self-centered young woman with no real clue of what she wanted to do with her life. For the first couple of months, she had maintained the same type of lifestyle and attitude she'd had in Midnight. With little effort, she had been instantly popular, gathering friends around her like always.

And then she'd met Simon Endicott. At first Samantha had thought of him as a stereotypical shy and awkward young man who was afraid to ask her out. It had never been in her nature to rebuff or look down on anyone, and though it took some time, she'd managed to draw Simon out of his shell. She was soon glad she had. Simon became a good friend. With his sweetness and his razor-sharp wit, he could always make her day brighter.

Then came the day that he didn't come to class and a dozen of her phone calls and texts went unanswered. Days later, Simon's lifeless body was found about twenty miles from campus in the Oconee River.

Samantha had been devastated. Memories of her parents' deaths were never far from her mind. With Simon's passing, her nightmares returned full force.

At first the police had ruled it an accidental drowning. Samantha's instincts told her something else. His relationship with his stepfather had been volatile. Simon hadn't talked about him much, but she'd seen the fear and disdain in his eyes when the man's name came up.

It had been beyond frustrating when she had gone to the police with her suspicions. Being treated like a beautiful, clueless ditz had never sat well with her. She might concentrate on her looks more than she should, but that didn't mean she didn't have intelligence and depth. Finally she found a female homicide detective who listened to her. And eventually, though it took much longer than it should have, Simon's stepfather was arrested and then convicted.

Simon's death changed Samantha. She grieved for her friend and missed him daily, but it also gave her a focus she had never possessed before. From then on, she had known she wanted to help bring murderers to justice. She had changed her major from fashion merchandising to criminal justice, toned down her looks to reveal her serious side, and never looked back.

Tonight she was putting all of that aside. If her looks and sex appeal could sway Quinn and get him to listen to her, then she would use them.

Quinn had never seen her like this. Whenever they'd gone out, to elegant parties or a nice restaurant, she had dressed femininely but conservatively. She loved beautiful clothes and still wanted to look attractive, but she no longer felt the need to use her looks to deflect attention from what was going on inside her. Tonight that was different. Remorse, self-contempt, and more than a little fear swirled like a violent whirlpool inside her. If Quinn didn't forgive her poor judgment and lack of faith in him, what would she do?

She turned away from the mirror and the vulnerability she saw in her eyes. She couldn't let that show when she saw Quinn. He would see remorse and love but she couldn't let him know how much she was hurting, too.

Hiding behind a beautiful façade had been her best defense when she was growing up, and while she knew Quinn wasn't going to forgive her just because she looked sexy, if she could just get him to soften at all, then hopefully he would listen to what she had to say.

Refusing to glance in the mirror again to see if she'd managed to veil the vulnerable look, Samantha grabbed her purse and car keys and walked out of her apartment. Optimism had seen her through some tough times; this would be no different.

Quinn would forgive her—she wouldn't take no for an answer.

Quinn was on his third scotch before he began to feel the slightest easing of his muscles. Running had always been his outlet for his troubles in the past. For the first time in his memory, physical exercise held no appeal. Getting drunk seemed to be just the thing to get over the hell he'd lived for the past week.

Sprawled in his oversized recliner, he downed half the contents of his glass in one long swallow. The alcohol dimmed the memory of the last time he'd been in this chair. Sam had been with him and they'd watched a sappy old movie. At the admittedly sad and depressing ending, he'd asked her if she enjoyed the movie. Instead of answering, she had buried her face against his chest and cried buckets. Quinn had held her, soothing her with words and caresses. After she had calmed, she had kissed him. Her lips had been lusciously soft and slightly salty from her tears. He remembered thinking it was the sweetest kiss he'd ever had.

The hurt he felt at her defection had diminished. Some of the relief was alcohol related but a small, still-sober part of him knew he'd retreated to the place he went when it all became too much. Compartmentalizing and locking away the pain was how he'd learned to deal. Didn't matter that this time it was more difficult than any other time. He would get there . . . eventually.

He hadn't seen Sam since she'd left his apartment that night. The night he'd learned that the woman he had intended to ask to move in with him thought he was a murderer. Of course, he had canceled the special dinner he'd had planned for Friday—she hadn't even known about it anyway. Instead, he'd taken a long run through the city. With every mile, his resolve had grown firmer. He was done with making mistakes. After his divorce, he'd sworn he would never let his guard down again. And then what the hell had he done? He'd fallen for a woman who thought he was capable of murder.

The ringing of the doorbell was an easily ignored irritant. The incessant pounding on his door just as easy to disregard. Whoever it was would go away eventually. He didn't want to see or talk to anyone for the foreseeable future. In a day or two, when he'd regained some perspective, he'd go back to caring about the living. For right now, he didn't give a damn about anyone.

The jiggle of the doorknob was barely a warning before the door was shoved open, and in seconds Samantha stood before him.

He glared up at her. "What the hell are you doing here?"

"I came to apologize."

A grin stretched his mouth but he figured it looked more like a snarl. "Oh yeah? Nice of you."

Her hands clutched her purse in front of her as if she were nervous. When her eyes flickered over the drink in his hand, he knew the reason for her unease. She didn't like people to drink too much. Said it showed a lack of character. Hell, since she'd thought he was a murderer, he wouldn't have figured she could think less of him.

He raised his glass. "Want a drink?"

"No. I want to tell you how sorry I am for not believing in you."

"Guess that means you heard the news."

"Yes, I heard. I found out by—"

He abruptly surged to his feet and released a humorless bark of laughter when she jumped away. "So you know I'm not a murderer but you're still afraid of me?"

"I'm not afraid of you, Quinn. You startled me . . . that's all."

He didn't hear her words. For the first time, he noticed what she was wearing. Or holy shit, what she wasn't wearing. She looked like a wet dream on Viagra. Silky blond hair reached down toward her delectable ass, the sexy, skintight dress showed every luscious curve of her beautiful body to its best advantage, and the fuck-me shoes had him hard in an instant. He wrapped his hand around a soft, slender wrist. "Show me how sorry you are."

"What?"

"Show me just how much you regret thinking I'm a murderer."

"Quinn, going to bed with you isn't the reason I came over here."

"Really? Is that why you're dressed like a porn star?"

Instead of acting insulted or angry, she froze, and a vulnerable, childlike expression flickered across her face. The look was so fleeting, he almost thought he imagined it. That didn't lessen his regret. Hell, he wasn't usually such a prick, even with people who'd stomped on him like he was dog shit.

"Sorry, Sam." He backed away and dropped down into the chair again. "You'd better leave. I'm not fit company."

"Let me make us something to eat and then we can talk."

She looked so hopeful and eager to please, Quinn couldn't have resisted if he'd tried. "Yeah . . . food sounds good. You fix something and I'll just sit here and relax."

Though her gaze dropped to the bottle sitting beside his chair, she didn't try to take it from him. A good thing, since he wasn't about to give it up. This was the best he'd felt in days.

"You want anything in particular?"

He shook his head. "Make whatever you like." And because he figured he was letting her off too easy, he added, "I don't give a damn."

Her legs decidedly shaky, Samantha turned away and headed to the kitchen. She guessed it could have gone worse. At least he hadn't thrown her out of the house. She needed to get some food in him, sober him up. He knew that being around people who drank too much made her nervous, she had just never told him why. She had planned to at some point, but there never seemed to be the right time. The confession "Oh, by the way, my drunken father murdered my mother and then committed suicide" wasn't something you just casually mentioned.

Since she figured he needed to get some food into his system as soon as possible, she didn't go for anything elaborate or time consuming. Grilled cheese and tomato soup had been a favorite of hers when she'd been under the weather as a kid. And though Quinn wasn't physically sick, she'd seen enough pain in his eyes to convince her he was sick at heart. To know that she was a big part of his pain hurt her in ways she had never felt before.

As she prepared the meal, she came to a decision. She needed to come clean about everything. Explaining she hadn't trusted him because of her father's horrible betrayal might seem like a lame excuse; nevertheless, it was the truth. She should have trusted Quinn. Her love hadn't been strong enough to stand up to the suspicion. But now, having come full circle, she would never doubt him again.

Samantha prepared a tray, figuring Quinn wouldn't be steady enough to come into the kitchen to eat. As she finished the preparations, she wondered if it would be possible for him to open up to her, too. They might have been as intimate as two people could be, but there were so many things they still didn't know about each other. She hadn't pressed for anything because of her own dark past. Had he done the same? Other than an unfaithful wife, who else had hurt Quinn?

Carrying the tray on which she'd placed a bowl of soup, two sandwiches, and a cold glass of milk, she headed to the living room. She stopped at the door and took in the scene. Quinn was passed out in the chair, snoring. Should she try to wake him? Since she avoided people who overdrank, she had little experience with drunken people. Though she'd seen her share of drunks as a cop, she didn't usually try to sober them up—she arrested them.

She placed the tray on the table beside the chair and shook his shoulders gently. "Quinn, can you wake up and eat something?"

Glazed, bloodshot eyes popped open as if he hadn't been asleep at all. With a sweet, almost goofy grin, he said, "Hey."

"Hey yourself. Can you eat something?"

He grabbed the hand on his shoulder and tugged, pulling her down into his arms. "Oh yeah, I definitely have an appetite for something."

The instant his mouth settled on hers, her mind went blank. Masculine, scotch-flavored lips moved powerfully, insistently, with a devouring need she didn't want to resist. It felt so good to be in his arms again, to feel the strength of his embrace, his body hard and warm against hers. Groaning with pleasure, Samantha let desire control her thoughts. Need overwhelmed all the events of the past week. In Quinn's arms, reality disappeared.

A large, strong hand glided up the outside of her thigh, moved between her legs, and pressed against her mound. She arched into his hot hand, moaning at the throbbing need only this man could quench.

"Oh, Quinn," she whispered, "I've missed you so much."

His answer was a dry, raspy laugh. Before she could consider why the sound bothered her, she heard a small ripping noise and then his fingers plunged deep inside her. Samantha gasped at the abrupt intrusion. Quinn soothed her, muttering incoherent words in her ear. Whether it was his fingers, his sexy voice, or both, she didn't know, but suddenly she found herself on the edge of an orgasm. Awash in a soft, delicious heat, she plummeted toward a dark, velvet abyss and then soared upward into ecstasy. Only with Quinn had she ever reached such glorious heights.

As shudders of the aftermath quaked through her, she said huskily, "Let's go to bed."

"Here's fine," he muttered.

"But I—"

Effortlessly lifting her, Quinn settled her over him so that she straddled his hips. She didn't know when or how he'd unzipped his pants, but before she knew it, he was pushing her down and driving deep inside her.

"Quinn?"

As if she hadn't spoken, his hands grasped her hips and his fingers dug deep into tender skin as he lifted her up, then pushed her down, repeating the motions over and over.

Her mind might be in shock at his unusual lack of finesse, but her body knew what to do. Arousal zoomed through her like a rocket. In the throes of another impending, explosive climax, Samantha gazed down at Quinn's face. The dispassionate, blank expression wasn't what she had expected. The coolness in the depths of his blue eyes made her wonder if this was more about punishment than pleasure. He was still angry. They should have talked before making love. But she had been so happy to be back in his arms, she had pushed aside her real purpose for coming here.

An instant later, rational thought disappeared. Like lightning, orgasm struck with swift, piercing intent. Her thoughts glazed with mindless bliss as her body rode another wave of exquisite pleasure. Quinn's thrusts became deeper, more forceful, and then he stiffened. Grabbing her shoulders, he pulled her down for a hard kiss as his release flooded inside her.

Samantha's forehead was leaning against his shoulder as breaths shuddered from her body. He'd never taken her so carelessly before, and while a sober, still-tender emotion told him he should feel guilty, he refused to acknowledge it. She had come here for one purpose and he'd given her what she wanted. They'd both gotten off. That was it and nothing more.

"Quinn?" she whispered.

He should tell her to go home. He'd said he wasn't fit company and he'd just proven that. But no, he wanted more. Hell, he deserved it, didn't he? After what he'd been through this week? After what she'd done to him? Didn't he deserve a few hours of peace inside her beautiful body?

He pushed her off him and stood. Then, lifting her in his arms, he carried her to his bedroom. With a sexy feminine groan of approval, she wrapped her arms around his shoulders and pressed kisses to his neck. She was telling him she wanted more, too.

Bracing her against the edge of the mattress, he stripped

the dress over her head and gazed down at her breasts. Samantha had a beautiful body and she used it to her best advantage. Cupping her breasts in his hands, he pressed them together and bathed them with his tongue. At her gasping "Yes," Quinn covered a gleaming nipple and sucked hard. Sam's fingers threaded through his hair as she pressed him deeper against her . . . her purring moans of pleasure sent him to the edge of explosion.

Everything she did said she wanted him as much as he wanted her. There was no point in making her time here a waste. Pulling away, he pushed her onto the bed, stripped quickly, and was nude in seconds. Crawling onto the bed, he was on top of her and in her again, where he planned to stay for as long as he damn well pleased. He ignored her beautiful, glowing face, the glittering emotion in her soft green eyes, the delicate hands skimming over his shoulders and back. This was sex for fulfillment and nothing more.

Covering her mouth with his own, he devoured her sweetness, taking everything she was so willingly offering. The small, soft whimpering sound she released as she wrapped her arms tighter around him barely penetrated the haze of lust. This was what she'd come for, wasn't it?

Warmth and light hit her face, waking her from the depths of a dreamless sleep. She rolled over and reached out for Quinn. What she found was a cold, empty space.

Hearing a noise, Samantha sat up and then swallowed a soft gasp. Quinn stood at the bedroom door, already dressed for the day. Her black dress was draped over his arm; ripped, minuscule panties hung from his fingers.

She smiled hesitantly at the feminine, fragile-looking things in his large, masculine hands. She whispered softly, "Good morning. I—" but broke off her words the instant she looked at his face. Never had he seemed so cold and emotionless.

"Quinn? What's wrong?"

He threw the dress and panties onto the bed. "Your shoes are on the floor. Get dressed."

"What?"

"I said—"

"I heard what you said. Why are you acting this way?"

"What way?"

"Like you hate me." She breathed a silent, shaky breath. "Look, I know you're still angry . . . we should have talked. I shouldn't—"

"Angry? Hell, Samantha, you've never seen me angry, and believe me, you don't want to."

"Last night you—"

"Last night was about one thing only and you know it."

A lead balloon of dread lodged in her stomach. She knew the answer even as she said, "And what was that one thing?"

His shrug was casual, uncaring. As if every single word from his mouth weren't ripping her heart to shreds. "We were both horny. You got what you came for. And baby, you came plenty."

A tidal wave of hurt and humiliation washed over her. How incredibly stupid and naïve she had been. Of course Quinn hadn't forgiven her. She'd never even had the chance to offer an explanation. He had taken what he wanted because she'd shown up looking like she was ready to give him anything he desired. And she had.

Quinn had used her and she had let him. She had no one to blame but herself. How could she be so incredibly stupid?

Unfortunately Samantha wasn't sophisticated or experienced enough to pretend anything less than complete devastation. "Quinn," she whispered, "you never gave me a chance to explain. To tell you how sorry I—"

He turned his back to her. "Let yourself out. I've got to go."

She sprang out of bed. Grabbing her dress, she held it in front of her as she hurried after him. Yes, he had hurt her, but she had hurt him, too. She had to make him understand. "Wait. Please. Let me explain."

He turned at the door, his expression one of such cold arrogance and disgust, she stumbled to a stop. Never would she have thought the man who had so tenderly and fiercely made love to her these last few months could look at her like he hated her.

"What is it you're going to explain, Samantha? That you believed I was a murderer but the moment you realized I wasn't, you came back to me?"

"It wasn't like that . . ." She closed her eyes. This wasn't how she had planned to tell him about her father, but he was giving her no choice. "I've never told you this but . . ." She swallowed hard and said, "When I was a little girl, my father got drunk and killed my mother. No one would have ever expected that of him. I guess I wondered if you could be like him and I just hadn't seen it."

Instead of offering sympathy, which she didn't want anyway, his mouth curved into a mocking smile. "Again, my dear, thanks so much for your faith in me." He opened the door and said over his shoulder, "Leave the key behind when you leave." The door closed, leaving her speechless and alone.

Fury like she'd never known before surged, washing over her body with an intensity that had her sweating from the heat. The anger was good and healthy. It would sustain her until she could get away from here. Then and only then would she allow the pain to consume her.

She dressed quickly, not even bothering to look in the mirror. Besides, who the hell cared what she looked like anyway? She opened the door and, releasing a shuddering sigh, took the key from her key ring and threw it on the hall table.

Without a backward glance, she walked out the door.

CHAPTER EIGHT

Quinn finished the last suture on a patient and stepped back out of the way, allowing a nurse to finish up. He was through for the day and a thousand miles past tired. Problem was, would he be able to sleep any better tonight than he had for the last few months? He already knew the answer was no. Not since before Charlene's murder had he slept for more than a few hours at a time. Insomnia and exhaustion were the new norm for him.

Disposing of his gloves in the receptacle beside the door, Quinn stepped out of the exam room and breathed a sigh heavy with disgust. He was tired of it all. The not knowing who killed Charlene, the knowledge that while suspicion was no longer on him, the stigma of doubt remained.

And his own paranoia was almost as frustrating. Every time a patient came into the ER and gave him an odd look, he immediately assumed they were wondering if he was a murderer. Every sly glance from the hospital staff made him want to turn around and snarl that he was innocent. Each whispered word he couldn't make out had him wondering if it had been about him. He was fucking sick of it all.

And Sam. Oh holy hell, Sam. That was the worst part. The way he had treated her continued to pound into his conscience even months later.

The incredible hurt on her face had been real. How many times had he picked up the phone to call her? How many nights had he lain awake, aching for her? He hadn't contacted her and wouldn't. Yes, he felt like shit for the way he treated her, but that didn't negate what she had done to him. Having her believe he was a killer was bad enough, but as soon as he was cleared, she had come to him expecting things to be forgotten and forgiven. That was way too reminiscent of his entire marriage to Charlene. Sometimes sorry just wasn't good enough.

She had come to his apartment to seduce him. The way she had dressed left no doubt. And she had gotten what she wanted—they both had. But he had been rough with her . . . rougher than he'd ever been with any woman. He felt like shit for that. Still, the forgiveness she apparently thought would be automatic wasn't there. He doubted it ever could be.

Her explanation for doubting him might well have been true, but that didn't lessen the hurt. Everything they'd had before Charlene's murder all felt like a lie.

Why the hell did it matter anyway? He doubted he would ever see her again. Atlanta was a big city. She might be a cop here, but as long as no one else committed a murder around him, they should never cross paths again.

He ignored the aching, hollow feeling in his gut. He would get over it . . . eventually. He had no choice.

As was his usual routine, Quinn updated the patient's family. After answering their concerned questions, he did what he had been longing to do all day. He grabbed his keys and jacket and marched out the door. Settling into the plush leather of the car seat, he contemplated a late night run in Centennial Park. Nothing was stopping him, other than sheer mental and physical exhaustion, that is. The ringing cellphone beside him interrupted his grim thoughts.

"Braddock."

"Dr. Braddock, this is Detective Murphy."

Despite the knowledge that he had basically been cleared of Charlene's murder, Quinn couldn't help but stiffen. He hadn't heard from the detective in months. Any communication between him and Detective Murphy went through his attorney or Paul Haney, the private investigator Quinn had hired. And even though the PI hadn't dug up any new suspects, he was at least a good buffer between Quinn and the police department.

"What can I do for you, Detective?"

"I'm just calling to let you know that we still haven't identified any new suspects."

"That's what I'm hearing from my investigator. Why did you—?" And then it hit him. "You're closing the case?"

"No, we'll never close the case until it's solved, but unfortunately we can't expend as much energy on it as we have been."

Which, to Quinn, meant the same thing. The man who had cold-bloodedly murdered Charlene was never going to be caught. And the suspicion surrounding him would remain.

"I appreciate you letting me know, Detective. I'm going to keep my investigator on it. If he learns anything new, I'll have him contact you."

"I'm sorry we couldn't find the killer, Dr. Braddock."

"I am, too."

"It cost us a damn good detective, too."

"Who's that?"

"Detective Wilde. She left the force. I thought you knew."

Quinn was glad he wasn't driving, because he would've lost all focus. Sam had left the Atlanta PD?

"When?"

"About four months ago."

Just a few weeks after their argument. Did it have anything to do with him? *Stupid question, asshole.* She had loved her job. Had he hurt her that badly?

"No, I didn't know. I'm sorry to hear that."

"Yeah, well. Shit happens and all that."

Yes, it certainly did.

"She went back to Alabama. Last I heard, she and her sisters were going to open a private security agency in her hometown."

Guilt sliced deep. Sam had left the city and he hadn't even known. It suddenly hit him that the usually close-mouthed Detective Murphy was being more than a little chatty.

"Is there a reason you're telling me all this?"

"If it hadn't been for Detective Wilde, you might still be a suspect. In fact, you might be on trial right now. Did you know that?"

A sick feeling wedged in his gut. "I thought some witnesses came forward and said they'd seen another man."

"They did, but she was the one who found them. Took vacation and worked night and day on clearing your name."

She hadn't told him any of that. Why hadn't she? Had he given her a chance? No, he'd been so hot for her, filled with dark desire and a deep hurt. The next morning, he'd been disgusted with his weakness and had treated her like a prostitute he'd hired for the night.

"Why are you telling me this?"

"Because I've never seen anyone more devastated than

she was when she left the force. I thought you should know that."

Quinn couldn't figure out whether the detective was playing matchmaker or trying to make him feel even worse. Didn't really matter. Sam had left her job and moved away because of him.

"Thanks, Murphy, for telling me that."

"If you see her, tell her we want her back."

Was he going to see her? Could he go to her home and apologize? Would she forgive him? Whether she forgave him or not, he had to see her.

Eager to put his plans in place, Quinn promised he would relay the message and ended the call. Adrenaline raced through his blood. For the first time in months, he felt alive. He wasn't out of the woods by any means, but the knowledge that Sam had done all of that for him gave him hope. If she had cared about him that much, did she still have feelings for him?

He had to find out. But more than anything, he had to apologize.

MIDNIGHT, ALABAMA
WILDE HOUSE
WILDEFIRE SECURITY AGENCY

"I really hope you can help me."

Samantha watched the woman across from her closely. She'd said her name was Lauren Kendall and that the Wildefire Agency had come highly recommended. Since Samantha and her sisters had only just opened the doors for business, that news came as quite a surprise.

Lauren was frightened. The nervous fidgeting in her chair, along with her difficulty in keeping eye contact, made that obvious. Still, something was off about her story.

On the pretense of reaching for her iced tea, Samantha glanced over at her sister Sabrina, who was tapping her pen on the notepad in front of her. Was Bri getting the same vibes?

"You say this man has been following you for about a month?" Bri asked.

"Yes."

"When did you first see him?"

Lauren looked down at her hands, which were twisting nervously in her lap. "I was at a restaurant with some of my friends. He stared at me a lot, but I didn't really pay attention to him. But then I saw him the next day at my gym, which I thought was kind of odd."

"Did he speak to you?" Samantha asked.

"No. Just gave me one of those looks."

"What kind of looks?"

"You know. The creepy kind, when a guy's eyes go up and down your body like he's imagining you naked."

"And when did you see him again?" Bri asked.

"About a week later. I was at the grocery store and saw him in the parking lot, staring at me."

"Has he approached you . . . said anything at all to you?"

Lauren's gaze moved to the window as she answered, "No, not yet." Her eyes returned briefly to focus on Samantha, who'd asked the question. "But I know he will soon. I'm just so afraid of what he'll do when that happens. I need protection."

"You've gone to the police?"

"No, I didn't really have anything to tell them. I figured they'd say that until he does something to me, they can't act."

She was right about that, but still there was something not right. Or was there? Samantha glanced over at Bri again, who, surprisingly, instead of looking at Lauren, was glaring at Samantha. What was that about?

"So will you take my case?" Lauren asked. "Protect me until this guy goes away?"

"Can you give us a few minutes?" Bri asked. "My sister and I need to discuss some things."

"Oh, of course." Lauren haltingly stood, twisting the shoulder strap of her purse with her hand. "Should I wait out in the hallway?"

Samantha hit a buzzer on her desk. Within seconds, Wildefire's new receptionist opened the door. Standing barely over five feet tall, with soft ash-blond hair and a generous figure, April Cantrell had the pleasant kind of personality that instantly put people at ease. After raising four boys, all of whom were now out on their own, she had been looking for an office job to fill her time. After one interview, Samantha and her sisters had agreed that the calm, efficient April would be a perfect fit for the agency.

"April, would you take Lauren to the sunroom and see that she has some refreshments?"

"Of course." She gave Lauren one of her sweet motherly smiles and said, "Follow me, dear."

Samantha and Bri were silent as they watched the tall, incredibly beautiful Lauren practically glide out of their office. In just that short walk, the woman oozed sex appeal as if it were as natural to her as breathing.

The instant the door closed, Samantha opened her mouth to speak, but before she could say a word, Bri burst out, "I hate what he's done to you."

"What are you talking about?"

"That bastard Braddock. Before you met him, you would have called Lauren out on her lies. Instead, you kept looking at me as if to make sure your instincts were right."

Samantha held back a sigh. Quinn's first name was never mentioned in the house. If he was brought up at all, he was always "that bastard Braddock."

She wished she could deny Bri's claim but she couldn't. Confidence in her judgment had taken some near-fatal blows. First she had suspected Quinn of murder, destroying their relationship. Then she had shown up at his apartment dressed for seduction, in the silly, vain hope that he'd be so enamored that forgiveness would come quickly. Instead he'd used her and she had let him. To compound matters, she'd thrown her parents' deaths at him as an excuse for her poor judgment. His treatment of her should have come as no surprise.

After her fiasco with Quinn, her world had been teetering on the edge. Then, only days later, she'd learned some news that had sent everything free-falling and careening into another dimension, exploding everything she thought she knew.

Her sister Savannah had found letters from their granddad casting serious doubts that their father, Beckett Wilde, had actually murdered their mother. After hearing that, Samantha had barely known which end was up. So much of her life and the decisions she had made had been based upon what had happened to her parents. Her distrust of Quinn had been directly related to that one horrific event. And it had all been a lie.

Not only was her confidence in her judgment destroyed, the parameters by which she'd lived had been demolished.

Since those dark, chaotic days, the real killers of her parents had been arrested and were now in prison. That painful part of her past had been put to rest, though the remnants would remain for years.

It had been with mixed regret and relief that Samantha left her job in Atlanta. She had lost total faith in herself. Savannah's suggestion of forming a security agency seemed like the perfect solution. Being back with her family again, in her hometown that was dearly familiar, where she was loved and appreciated, felt right.

At some point, she would put those dark memories of Quinn behind her, too. It was just taking more time than she'd hoped.

Unable to deny or defend herself against Bri's accusations, Samantha chose to ignore them. "So what do you think Lauren is hiding?"

"You're not even going to argue?"

Blowing out an exasperated breath, Samantha stood. "What do you want me to say, Bri? Everything you said is right with the exception of one thing. You keep blaming Quinn for what happened and it's not his fault. I'm the one who betrayed him by not trusting him."

Bri snorted. "You were doing your job, Sammie. If he couldn't understand that, then he's an idiot."

"He's not an idiot, he was hurt."

"Yeah, and he hurt you to get back at you."

There were no secrets between the sisters. They knew what happened. Samantha wanted to say his treatment was justified but couldn't bring herself to that point. The hurt he had dealt her might have been deserved, but that didn't lessen the pain.

"Look, we've been there and done this before. It's over and done with. Even though Charlene Braddock's killer was never caught, at least Quinn is no longer a suspect. That's the most important thing."

Bri snorted again. "Yeah, heaven forbid he thank you for saving your ass."

"He doesn't know I had anything to do with clearing him."

"Yeah . . . right."

"What's going on?"

They'd both been so involved in their argument, neither of them had heard Savvy come in.

"We're just discussing a new case."

"Sounded to me like you were arguing."

Samantha shrugged. "Not arguing. Just having a lively conversation."

"About Quinn," Savvy said.

Samantha rolled her eyes and glared at Bri. Both she and Bri had agreed that they would keep anything unpleasant away from their sister for the next several months. Savvy and her husband, Zach, were going to be parents. Considering what had happened with Savvy's first pregnancy, no one wanted to do anything to jeopardize this one.

With her slender arms crossed over her chest in a stubborn stance, Savvy narrowed her eyes and targeted both of them. "Okay, you two. I know you're only trying to protect me, but I'm fine. The doctor has said we're both doing great. So stop keeping things from me or it's really going to piss me off."

"Sammie and I both think Lauren is hiding something."

"Why's that?"

"Well, first of all," Samantha said, "she said we came highly recommended."

Savvy and Bri both laughed, bringing much-needed humor into the room.

"I'd love to know the person who highly recommended us to her. Apparently they've heard of us without any effort on our part," Bri said.

That was all too true. The agency was in its infancy. Samantha and Bri had just returned from a two-week training event in Birmingham. Savvy was going to wait on her training until after the baby was born. They'd had no cases, done no advertising. They barely existed, except on paper and in the phone book.

"Could Brody or Logan have made the recommendation?" Savvy asked.

Brody James and Logan Wright owned a security agency in Mobile. Both men had served in the army with Zach and had been a tremendous help to the Wilde sisters when they had decided to form their own security agency. The men had also offered to send business their way.

Samantha shook her head at Savvy's question. "Right after Lauren called and made the appointment with us, I called Brody and asked. He said neither he nor Logan had ever heard of her."

"So why do you think she came to us?" Savvy asked.

Bri shot Samantha a challenging look. Ignoring her sister's obvious goading, Samantha said, "I think her fear is real, but I also think she knows who her stalker is and figures we're such amateurs, we wouldn't see through her."

Bri nodded. "I agree. But why not tell us the truth? We'd still help her, whether she knows her stalker or not."

"Why don't we ask her?" Samantha said. If they were going to help Lauren, then she was going to have to come clean with them.

Savvy and Bri both nodded their agreement.

Samantha hit the intercom buzzer.

"Yes?" April answered.

"Would you ask Lauren to come back into the office?"

"Absolutely."

Seconds later Lauren entered and stood in the middle of the room. Still twisting the strap of her purse, she asked shakily, "So, will you take my case?"

"We have a few more questions," Samantha said. She nodded at the chair Lauren had sat in before. "Have a seat."

Amazing how someone could look afraid, relieved, and beautiful at the same time, but Lauren managed to do all three as she settled into the chair. She gave each of the sisters a bright, encouraging smile and said, "What else did you need to know?"

Seeing no reason not to go for the heart of the matter, Samantha said, "Why are you lying about not knowing your stalker?"

The confident smile disappeared, replaced by a surprising vulnerability. "I was afraid you wouldn't take the case if you knew the truth."

"I can guarantee we won't take it if you don't tell us the truth," Samantha said.

"He works for Armando Cruz." Lauren spoke with such quiet drama, it was apparent that she expected the name to be recognized.

Samantha glanced at Savvy, who was looking as clueless as she herself felt. She then looked over at Bri and was surprised to see dark fury in her sister's expression.

"You know who she's talking about, Bri?"

"Yeah, I do." Bri sprang from her chair and went to the window. Taking a brief look outside, she turned back to Lauren. "Did you make absolutely sure he didn't follow you here?"

Lauren nodded vigorously. "I took two buses, paid cash for a used car in Birmingham and used a fake name. No one followed me."

"You'd better hope to hell you're right, because if you've brought that scum to my town and endangered my family, Armando Cruz will be the least of your problems."

Feeling decidedly uneasy, Samantha said, "Maybe you should clue Savvy and me in on who this Armando Cruz is."

"He's a drug lord out of Mexico," Bri answered. "He relocated to Miami a few years ago. He's been tied to a half dozen or so murders, but the cops can't make anything stick."

"He's responsible for three times that many," Lauren said.

"How do you know this?"

"I've been his mistress for over two years."

Few things surprised Samantha or her sisters anymore. After learning the truth of their parents' murders, nothing seemed impossible or shocking.

Bri, who'd been keeping a watchful eye out the window, looked over her shoulder to Lauren. "This man that's stalking you . . . he's not really stalking you, is he?"

"No, he's trying to find me to bring me back to Armando."

"Why?" Savannah asked.

Lauren shrugged delicate shoulders. "Armando told me more than once that I'd have to die to leave him."

"How long have you been trying to get away from him?" Savvy asked.

"Almost from the moment I met him." Eyes haunted, her smiled strained, Lauren suddenly looked much older than the lovely young woman who had walked confidently into their office.

Sensing there was more to the matter than Cruz just wanting his mistress returned, Samantha said, "What's the other reason Cruz wants you back?"

"What do you mean?"

"She means, do you have information that could put him away?" Savvy asked.

"Not really. I may have picked up some things every now and then."

Not for a minute did Samantha believe her. But they would get to that later. "Why did you come to the Wildefire Agency?"

Before Lauren could answer, Bri did it for her. "You thought since we were new, we might be so grateful for the business, we wouldn't ask many questions."

"I—"

Savvy leaned forward. "You have to be totally honest with us if you want us to take your case."

Lauren's eyes went wide. "You're still considering taking me on?"

Samantha shot Bri a searching look. She had total faith in her sisters' abilities, but now that Savvy was pregnant, she wasn't sure taking this case was the right thing to do. Protecting her sister and her baby was priority number one.

A huff of exasperated breath came from Savvy. "I saw that look, Samantha Camille Wilde."

Samantha shrugged. "So? Is there anything wrong with wanting to make sure you and the baby stay safe?"

"No, and I appreciate it, but I'm not going to allow you, Bri, or my gorgeous, overprotective husband to treat me like I'm made of spun glass. I'm pregnant, not sick."

Turning back to Lauren, Savvy ignored the looks both Samantha and Bri were giving her and said, "What exactly did you think we would do, Lauren? Kill this man if he came close to you?"

"I hadn't really thought it through. I need protection." Her chin lifted slightly. "And think what you want of my reasons for choosing you, but I did hear that one of you is a former cop, so I figured you could protect me."

"Until what?" Samantha asked.

"I don't know what you mean."

"I mean, how long will you need protection? Do you think Cruz will eventually give up and just let you go?"

A deep furrow appeared in Lauren's brow as if this had never occurred to her. She confirmed Samantha's thoughts with "I guess I haven't thought that far ahead. I just wanted to make sure he doesn't catch me. I hadn't thought about what happens next."

"Do you have family, Lauren?" Savvy asked.

"No." She surged to her feet and began to pace. "Look, I know I should have been honest before, but I wasn't sure how you'd take to protecting me from someone like Armando." She whirled around. "I have money . . . lots of money."

Samantha met her sisters' eyes. They were wondering the same thing she was. "How much?"

"Close to two million dollars."

"And how did you get this money?"

The pacing increased, revealing more than any words Lauren could say.

"You stole it from him," Savvy said.

Jerking to a stop in the middle of the room, she snarled, "I earned that money. He would only give me enough to buy clothes or jewelry. I deserved it and a whole lot more."

"How did you steal it?"

"I didn't steal it, I took what's mine."

Resisting the urge to roll her eyes, Samantha said, "How did you take it?"

"I drugged his drink one night, took his banking passwords he kept in a notebook, and withdrew the money from some of his accounts. I did it over several months so he wouldn't notice it." She shrugged. "He had millions and millions in those accounts. I knew he wouldn't miss a few thousand here or there."

As if suddenly exhausted, Lauren returned to her seat, inelegantly slumping into her chair. "That's it . . . that's the full truth."

"So the real reason Cruz is after you has less to do with wanting you back in his bed and more to do with recovering the money you took?"

For an instant, Samantha thought she was going to take exception to that statement. Then, as if deciding that disagreeing wouldn't help her case, she shrugged and said haltingly, "Perhaps . . . maybe. I don't know."

"So is there a man following you or not?" Samantha asked.

"I don't know. Someone will be coming for me soon. I do know that."

Savvy stood and went to the door. "As you might imagine, Lauren, my sisters and I need to confer again. Are you staying anywhere right now?"

Lauren shook her head. "No. I came here as soon as I got into town."

"Then you need a place to stay for the night. We have plenty of room. I'll get April to show you to a guest room."

Tears filled Lauren's eyes and she once again looked like a fragile, terrified young woman. "Thank you."

While Savvy spoke with April about which room to take Lauren to, Bri looked over at Samantha. "I don't like this."

"Me either."

"But we're going to take it. Right?"

Samantha grinned. "Oh yeah. Definitely."

CHAPTER NINE

"I don't like this."

Samantha hid a smile as her brother-in-law voiced his disapproval of the Wildefire Agency's first case. Those had been her and Bri's exact words.

"What's not to like?" Savvy said. "Lauren's not even here at the house anymore. She's across town with Bri at your old house. No one's going to come looking for her here. We're all perfectly safe."

While Savvy and Zach argued, Samantha stood at the kitchen window. Even in early November, the grounds in the back were beautiful, a testament to the tireless work her mother and grandfather had put into them. They had wanted an oasis of beauty for the family to enjoy. Many barbeques and parties had taken place there, along with quiet moments of reflection.

As her mother had intended, the entire area was a place of serenity—with one stark exception, the darkened bare area where the guesthouse had once stood. Only a few months ago, her parents' murderer had burned it to the ground in an effort to kill Savvy and had almost succeeded. Zach had every right to be worried.

Construction to replace it hadn't started yet. Each time she looked out the window, there was the grim reminder of what had almost happened.

Samantha turned back to the couple sitting at the kitchen table. Despite her dismal thoughts, she couldn't help but smile at the scene. Though they were arguing, they sat next to each other, holding hands, with Savvy's head on Zach's shoulder. After what they'd been through to achieve their happy ending, the last thing she wanted was to cause them trouble. Zach was Midnight's chief of police. With only two deputies, he had his hands full already.

"What happens after you protect this woman from a hit man?" Zach asked. "You take care of one, another will replace him. If she has secrets this Cruz creep doesn't want known, he'll keep sending people after her until he succeeds."

"Not if we can bring him down," Samantha said.

The chair skidded on the tiled floor as Zach went to his feet. He stared at Samantha, then at his wife as if they'd both lost their minds, and said very quietly, "What?"

"Now, Zach," Savvy said. "We can't just let this man get away with what he's been doing. Not when we've got a way to stop him."

"Shit, Savannah. That's way past bodyguard services."

"What choice do we have?" Samantha asked. "Like you said, Cruz won't stop with one man. He'll keep sending people after her. Our only choice is to take out the big guy himself."

His eyes narrowed with suspicion, he asked, "Take him out how?"

Samantha snorted. "I'm not going to assassinate him, if that's what you're asking."

"Then what is your plan?"

"We gather all the intel Lauren has and take it to the DA's office in Miami. Bri said Florida officials have been after this guy for a while. Hopefully the information Lauren has will put him away. And that will either get Cruz out of her life for good, or, if she has to, she can go into witness protection."

"What exactly does Lauren know?"

"We don't know yet."

"Well, why the hell not? She's been in Midnight for three days."

Savvy cut her eyes over to Samantha, who sighed and said, "She's being evasive. First she said she didn't know anything. Then, when we pressed her, she said she's protecting us by not telling us."

Zach gave a disbelieving snort. "Sounds to me like she's playing games."

"We've asked Brody and Logan to help out," Savvy said. She shot Samantha a small smile. "We think she might be more inclined to open up with them."

"Why don't—"

The radio attached to Zach's belt squawked out the croaky voice of Midnight's police dispatcher, Hazel Adkins. "Chief, you there?"

Zach spoke into the mic. "Yeah, I'm here."

"There's a traffic accident over on the bypass, right in front of the motel. Three car pileup."

"Okay, I'm on my way."

Zach gave both Savvy and Samantha a hard look. "This discussion isn't over."

He walked out the door before Samantha could respond to his dictatorial tone. Zach's having final approval authority on their cases wasn't something she planned to let happen. She glanced over at her sister and swallowed her indignation. Zach's concern was understandable. They had almost lost Savvy; there had been three attempts on her life in as many days. That nightmarish time still lingered in everyone's mind.

"Don't worry, Sammie, he'll come around. He's just being super protective, with the baby and all. And I think he's trying to make up for all the years we were apart. Give him some time."

"I know. And he has every right to be concerned. Midnight doesn't need any more trouble."

"If we play our cards right, whoever Cruz sends after Lauren will never know she's here."

"You think Brody and Logan are going to be able to get anything from her?"

"My money's on Brody. Logan's too taciturn."

"Really?" Samantha grinned. "Want to place a little bet that Logan can get what we need before Brody does?"

"You're on."

"They should arrive soon. I told them to go on to the safe house." Samantha picked up her cellphone. "I'll check and see if they're there yet."

The doorbell chimed.

"You make the call, I'll get the door," Savvy said.

Samantha had just hit the speed-dial number for Bri when it suddenly occurred to her that they needed to be careful about answering the door. If Cruz's man had followed Lauren to Midnight, he would know she had come here.

She dashed from the kitchen and was in the middle of the foyer when she heard Savvy snap, "Well, she doesn't want to see you. You need to leave."

Surprised at the venom in her sister's normally sweet tone, she took another step and then jerked to an abrupt stop when she heard a familiar male voice growl, "Why don't you let her answer for herself?"

Quinn? He was here? In Midnight?

He almost made a huge mistake. When Samantha's sister opened the door, Quinn had almost grabbed and kissed her. Other than her hair being wavy and a darker gold, she looked just like Sam. Good thing he hadn't tried. The old saying "If looks could kill" fit her expression perfectly. If it was up to this woman, he'd be road-kill right about now.

Her eyes, so much like Sam's, glared up at him icily. "Samantha's not here."

She tried to close the door; Quinn stuck his foot out to stop it. "I saw her car in the drive."

Stubborn mutiny entrenched on her face, she said, "She's in another car. Leave. Now."

"Then I'll just wait till she comes home."

"No. She's not—"

"Savvy, that's okay. I've got this."

"Sammie, no, you don't have to talk to him."

Quinn's heart set up a thudding so loud, he could barely hear the sisters speaking. It felt like forever since he had heard that husky, ultra-feminine tone. He waited, holding his breath, until she appeared at the door.

"What do you want, Quinn?"

As receptions went, it was ten degrees below sub-zero. He had expected nothing less and deserved even worse.

"I'd like to talk to you."

"Everything you had to say you articulated perfectly the last time I saw you. Nothing more needs to be said."

In seconds Quinn took in her appearance. She looked like Sam, but a different one than he was used to. This was a much more casual Sam. Her hair was pulled back into a high ponytail, she wore minimal makeup, and her long legs were encased in faded jeans. An overlarge white shirt hung on her slender frame, hiding her curves. Quinn's gaze went back to her face, and the differences he saw there made his heart sink to his feet. The biggest difference was its thinness. And her shirt wasn't over-large because of its size. Hell, how much weight had she lost and was he the cause?

"Please, Sam," he said softly. "Just for a few minutes."

A war of emotions crossed her face. Quinn felt enormous relief when instead of saying no again, she nodded and said, "Fine. Let's go out to the porch."

The woman holding the door, Savannah apparently, said, "Sammie, you don't have to do this."

"I know that, Savvy. I'll be fine."

She gave her sister a strained smile, but when she turned her gaze back to him, the smile was gone. "Let's go."

Quinn backed away and stood on the porch. Feeling about as unsure and insecure as he'd ever felt in his life, he waited for her to join him.

She closed the door behind her and turned to him. "Say what you came to say."

"Have you been sick?"

She jerked as if he'd hit her. Dammit, an apology should have been the first thing out of his mouth, not a comment on her appearance. Concern for her health overrode his need for forgiveness.

Her answer was a curt "No" as the ice in her eyes froze harder.

Quinn tried again. "I'm sorry, Sam. For everything."

She considered him for several seconds. Quinn withstood the scrutiny, barely. What he wanted more than anything was to gather her in his arms and show her how very sorry he was and how much he had missed her.

"Apology accepted. Goodbye." She turned away from him as if she were going back into the house.

"Dammit all." Quinn grabbed her arm to pull her around and almost gasped at the bone-thinness of her forearm. "Shit, Samantha. How much weight have you lost? Are you not eating? What's wrong with you?"

"Quinn, you're not my doctor nor are you anyone who has a right to ask that question. You did what you came here to do. You've apologized. Now you can leave."

"It wasn't all one-sided, you know. You thought I was guilty of murder."

"For which I've apologized. We both screwed up. We're both sorry. End of story."

"No, it's not the end of the story by a long stretch. I know I messed up and I want to make it right."

She blew out a sigh, and for the first time since he arrived, there was the slightest thawing in her expression. "We were both guilty, Quinn. I'm sorry for not believing in you; you're sorry for . . ." She swallowed hard and then continued, "The things you said. Let's just leave it at that."

"I don't want us to be over, Sam."

"Haven't you learned by now that people rarely get what they want?" Her smile was sad but resigned. "We've been over a long time, Quinn. Maybe even before we started."

Turning her back on him, she walked to the front door and opened it. Before she disappeared inside, she said softly, "Some things just aren't meant to be. Have a good life."

She closed the door and was gone.

Quinn stood on the porch, staring at the door. *Aren't meant to be? Like hell.*

Striding from the porch, Quinn jumped into his car and drove away. He might not know exactly what he was going to do, but one thing he knew for sure—he and Samantha Wilde were not over. No way in hell was this the end.

CHAPTER TEN

Samantha sat alone on the sofa in the family room. Savvy had tried to get her to talk, but she had no words for what she was feeling. Besides, if she talked, she'd turn into a sobbing mess. She hadn't cried since before all of this began. Deep-freezing her emotions had shut down the waterworks. But now, as if a massive heater had been turned on full blast, a major thaw was taking place.

Saying goodbye to Quinn this time had been even harder than the last. It was obvious he felt bad about what happened. She felt bad about it, too, but it didn't change anything. She couldn't go through that pain again. Not ever.

"Are you okay?"

She turned to see Bri standing at the doorway, her green eyes filled with compassion and understanding.

"Who's with Lauren?" Samantha winced at the raw sound to her voice.

"Brody and Logan."

A smile stretched her lips, which felt odd, since smiling was the last thing she felt like doing. "Fifty bucks if one of them isn't in love with her by the end of the week."

Bri laughed softly and settled onto the sofa beside her. "You're on, but I think they're smarter than that."

"Love can wreak havoc with the smartest people."

"I know," Bri said.

The sadness in her sister's voice made Samantha feel even worse. Hell, what did she have to complain about? Bri was the one whose heart had been crushed twice—by the same man. Compared to that, Samantha knew her heartache was minuscule.

A small, soft hand touched her hair in a gentle caress. In an instant, Samantha gave up all pretense of being strong. Moving to the middle of the sofa, she put her head in Bri's lap and allowed the heartbreak to overtake her.

Only vaguely aware of her surroundings, she barely felt it when Savvy sat on the other side of her and began rubbing her arm and shoulder. Gentle words of comfort came from both sisters as Samantha at last gave in to her grief.

She had bottled everything up, worn herself out with work and anything else she could occupy her mind with. Human needs like eating and sleeping had become unimportant and sometimes impossible. Both Savvy and Bri had encouraged her to cry, but she hadn't been able to let go. Seeing Quinn had allowed that to happen. At least he had given her that.

Minutes later, shuddering out breaths, she raised her head and sat up. Tear-filled eyes blurred the images of her sisters, but she saw that both of them had tears in their eyes, too. Sniffing mightily, she said, "Who knew I had all those waterworks in me?"

Savvy took her hand and squeezed it gently. "I think those tears have been a long time coming."

"And now maybe you can let him go for good," Bri said.

"Did crying work for you?" Samantha asked.

"No. I was too mad to cry."

While Samantha knew that wasn't true, she wasn't

going to push it. The Wilde sisters had a lot in common, but they each handled grief in their own unique way. Savvy's had always been more open and out there. Samantha's had been bottled up for years. And Bri rebelled against every heartache as if each one were a demon she had to slay.

"Why do you think he came?" Savvy asked.

"To apologize. He said he was sorry."

"Sorry for what?" Bri snarled. "Treating you like a whore or costing you your job?"

"He didn't cost me my job. I chose to quit."

"But he's—"

"That's enough, Bri. Sammie doesn't need lectures."

Smiling at Savvy's warning and the corresponding huff of exasperation from Bri, she put an arm around each sister and pulled them close for a quick hug. "What would I do without you guys?"

"You'll never have to find out," Savvy said as she stood. "Now, who's hungry?"

A surprising answering growl came from her stomach, the first one in months. Perhaps this was what she had needed after all—an apology from Quinn and a cathartic cry. Life could apparently now return to normal. She got to her feet. "Let's load up and head to Captain Jimmy's. I'm in the mood for their seafood extravaganza."

Her delight apparent, Savvy practically ran out of the room. "Let me call Zach to see if he can meet us there."

Samantha turned back to Bri and said, "Did you learn anything from Lauren today?"

She snorted. "Almost nothing. I swear the woman can talk a blue streak and say absolutely nothing."

"Do you think she's lying and doesn't really know anything?"

"Beats me. I'm hoping Brody and Logan can spur some

kind of openness. I think you're right about her being more comfortable talking to a man."

"And it doesn't hurt that they both look like male models, either."

Bri looked genuinely shocked. "You think?"

"You don't?"

"I guess I haven't noticed. Maybe I should take another look."

Samantha considered her sister for several seconds. Bri had always been able to put on a brave face, but her sisters could read her better than anyone. The teasing glint in Bri's eyes hid a deep hurt only a few people knew about.

"You know, just because a man is good-looking doesn't mean he's scum. Not all men are like your ex-fiancé."

"I know that. Have you forgotten that my best friend is the most gorgeous man on the planet?" She headed to the door, a clear indicator the conversation was over.

Bri's best friend, Ian Mackenzie, had been her partner in their private investigation firm. When the Wildefire Agency was created, Bri had left him and the business behind. And while she swore there was nothing more than friendship between them, neither Samantha nor Savvy was convinced. Bri had definite feelings for the man, whether she wanted to acknowledge them or not.

The ringing doorbell stopped any further conversation they might have had. Samantha held her breath as Bri headed for the door. Had Quinn returned? She told herself she didn't want to see him, but if that was true, why was her heart racing in anticipation?

"I swan, Sabrina Sage, every time I see you, you've gotten prettier. Are you letting your hair grow out? I remember when it was longer than Samantha's. Hasn't it gotten cold out? This winter might just give us our first snowfall in nigh on fifty years."

Samantha exhaled with a sigh, which she told herself

was from relief, not disappointment. Gibby Wilcox, their aunt, was like a little whirlwind, sweeping through the door and sucking up all available air.

"We're just about to go to dinner at Captain Jimmy's. You want to go with us?"

Bri had asked the question, but Gibby's eyes zeroed in on Samantha, who stood a few feet away. "And are you planning on coming, too, young lady?"

"Yes, ma'am."

"To eat?"

Surprised she still had laughter left inside her, Samantha chuckled. "Yes, ma'am, to eat."

Beaming, Gibby answered, "Well, alrighty then, I'm sure not about to pass up a chance to clog my arteries a little. They need a good challenge."

Her sadness pushed aside for the time being, Samantha wrapped an arm around her aunt's shoulders and walked with her to the door. "Then let's go. I'm starving."

And she was pleased to realize that while "starving" wasn't accurate, she was at least hungry. Quinn was out of her life forever. Maybe now the sadness and heartache could be put behind her for good.

Quinn drove through downtown Midnight. Sam had told him a little about her hometown, but seeing it up close and personal made him more aware of who Samantha Wilde really was—a small-town girl with somewhat old-fashioned values. Other than her beauty, that was one of the things that had attracted him to her. He'd never seen such a unique blend of confidence and shyness. The first time she had smiled at him, he had been mesmerized, but it had been her first blush that had captivated and ensnared him.

He turned onto Magnolia Avenue and smiled at the

sight before him: a large fountain in the middle of the town square in the shape of a mimosa tree. He could only imagine that a much younger Sam had stood at the fountain and made wishes for her future. A grim thought wiped the smile off his face. One thing he was sure she hadn't wished for was an asshole like him in her life.

He turned a corner and spotted a restaurant with a sign in the window proudly claiming they served the best fried green tomatoes in Alabama. Quinn parked in front of Faye's Diner and got out of his car. Five seconds inside the restaurant, he became the center of attention. All conversations stopped and there wasn't one person in the crowded restaurant who seemed embarrassed to be staring.

Torn between backing out and shouting a big hello to the room at large, Quinn instead nodded to no one in particular, pulled out a stool at the counter, and sat. A tall, broad-shouldered woman with a fierce scowl and a slight mustache growled at him from behind the counter, "Whatcha want?"

He glanced up at the daily specials displayed on the wall. "Cheese grits and shrimp any good here?"

"If I make it, it's good."

"I'll have that with a glass of unsweet tea."

The woman glared at him as if he'd asked for an illegal substance.

"Something wrong?"

She shrugged, turned around, and shouted, "Give me a special and a fancy tea."

"Unsweet tea is fancy?"

Instead of answering, she gave him another glare and walked away.

A small, wizened-looking elderly woman hopped up on the stool next to him with the energy of a teenager. She grinned, showing an impressive mouthful of gleam-

ing dentures. "Don't pay Faye no mind. She got up on
the wrong side of the bed fifty-five years ago and she
ain't got over it."

Quinn backed away from the overwhelming scent of
garlic emanating from the woman and asked, "That
right?"

"You just passing through?"

"Yes . . . maybe."

"You don't know?"

No, for the first time in years, he had no clue what he
was going to do. He'd taken time off—two weeks. Considering the relief on the face of the ER department
head, he probably could have taken off a month without
any complaint. But that was another worry for another
day.

What he had hoped to do was ask for Sam's forgiveness and whisk her away to the beach to begin making it
up to her for being such a jerk. Overconfident jerk that
he was, he hadn't counted on her response. But damned
if he would give up.

"If I do decide to hang around a few days, know a
place I can stay?"

"There's a no-tell motel over on the bypass, but
you don't look that type. Molly Hanks has a bed-and-
breakfast on Cherry Lane. She usually closes down in
November until after the holidays, but I'll bet she'll
make an exception for you."

"I would hate to put her—"

The elderly woman waved away his objection and to
his surprise pulled out an iPhone and proceeded to
punch in a number. He listened as she arranged for
Molly Hanks to open her bed-and-breakfast just for
Quinn.

She ended the call, deposited the phone back into her
purse, and beamed up at him. "All taken care of."

Impressed with her efficiency, Quinn held out his hand. "Thank you, Ms. . . . ?"

She put a wrinkled, fragile hand in his and gave him a firm shake. "Inez Peebles. And you are . . . ?"

"Quinn Braddock."

"Samantha Wilde's beau?"

Surprised, he asked, "You've heard of me?"

Her laugh was the sound Quinn would imagine a hen gives as it lays an oversized egg. "Sugar, I'm the oldest person in Midnight. I've heard of everybody."

Quinn wanted to ask her what she had heard about him, but figured he wouldn't like the answer. With Inez, he soon learned it didn't matter whether he asked or not. He was going to get an answer.

"Don't know what you did to that girl, but you need to fix it and fast."

Apparently the entire town knew what an ass he'd been. Sam had once mentioned that there were few secrets in her hometown. Inez's bright, inquisitive eyes looked expectantly at him, waiting for his reply.

Usually the last person to share personal information, Quinn shocked himself by saying, "I'm going to do my very best."

"Good for you."

A large bowl of shrimp and cheesy grits was set in front of him, along with a pitcher-sized glass of iced tea.

"I'll leave you to your meal, young man. You enjoy your stay in Midnight."

"Thank you, Ms. Peebles. You've been extremely helpful."

As if he'd just given her the highest compliment, she gave him another bright, denture-filled smile as a pinkish blush tinged her cheeks. Without another word, she slid from the stool and walked away.

Feeling decidedly more optimistic than when he'd walked into the diner, Quinn dug into his meal. After one bite, Quinn decided that it didn't matter if Faye was as friendly as a pissed-off rhino. Anyone who could cook like this didn't need a pleasant personality.

He quickly demolished the meal. Feeling fortified and better than he had expected, considering his massive screwup with Sam, Quinn took his bill to the cash register. Faye was there waiting on him. Handing her a twenty, he said, "Keep the change. That meal was amazing."

Not cracking a smile, she took the money and deposited it into the cash register. If he thought complimenting her or giving her a hefty tip was going to soften her up, he was wrong.

Shrugging, Quinn turned and once again faced a roomful of curious people. He'd been aware of the stares as he ate his meal but had managed not to turn around and say anything. Now they couldn't be ignored. Hell, this town must not get many visitors if one stranger could cause such a stir.

Once again nodding at the room in general, he turned and walked out of the restaurant. The instant the door closed behind him, he heard a sudden raucous noise like a gaggle of wild geese descending at once. Apparently everyone now felt comfortable chattering about him behind his back. Weird, but he had a feeling he was going to like Sam's little town.

CHAPTER ELEVEN

Curled up on the window seat in her bedroom, Samantha tucked her favorite throw closer around herself and gazed out into the darkness. She'd had this crocheted throw since she was eight years old—a Christmas gift from Aunt Gibby. Its familiar soft warmth gave her comfort.

Dinner with her family had been just what she had needed. Zach had been able to join them, and with Aunt Gibby providing commentary on every subject, the entire meal had been entertaining and a great tension reliever.

The one subject everyone studiously avoided was Quinn and his unexpected appearance in Midnight. Surprises had never been her favorite thing. Whenever they happened, it always reminded her of the surprise visit her grandfather had made when she and her sisters were at summer camp eighteen years ago. He had come to tell them that their parents were dead. From that day on, "surprise" was an evil word for her. "Predictable" might sound less fun but at least it didn't usually carve a hole in your heart.

Had she made a mistake, turning him away? He had come to apologize. Something they both had needed him to do. But now it was over and she could let go. The sobfest she'd had earlier had been a good catharsis. A final step toward putting everything behind her. But starting anew with him? No, she couldn't. She and Quinn hadn't had a real relationship. All they'd had was a brief, intense affair. Their time together had been wonderful and deliciously satisfying physically, but it hadn't had staying power. If it had, their troubles would have been discussed and worked out.

She was no innocent party in what tore them apart. She knew that. If she had trusted Quinn, she would have known he wasn't capable of murder. It was painfully obvious her faith in him had been seriously lacking. Her fault, not Quinn's.

All of her life, she had relied on shallow romantic relationships because they had been so easy to control. Walking away from them had been effortless. While she had dated more guys than she could remember, only a couple of them had bothered to look beneath the façade of her looks to get to know the real Samantha. Those were the two she'd let down her guard enough to be intimate with. Both relationships had been ridiculously unsatisfying, each barely lasting a month. She had almost come to the conclusion that what lay beneath the surface of Samantha Wilde wasn't substantial enough to attract the kind of man she could fall for. And then she'd met Quinn.

"Want to talk?"

Samantha twisted her head around to face both Bri and Savvy, who were standing in the doorway. This was wonderfully familiar, too. From birth, when one of the sisters hurt, they all felt the pain.

Smiling, she motioned them in. Bri plopped down on the rug in front of Samantha. Savvy chose the rocking chair close by.

"I don't really know what to talk about. It's over and done with."

"Is it?" Bri asked.

"It has to be."

"But why, Sammie?" Savvy said. "You obviously still have feelings for him. And just from the brief glimpse I saw of Quinn, he cares for you, too."

How could she explain her feelings to her two staunchest defenders? They loved her no matter what. They didn't see that perhaps there wasn't much beneath the surface to love and admire.

"I don't think I'm capable of the soul-deep kind of love, Savvy. Not like you and Zach have."

The rocking chair creaked to an abrupt stop. Eyes wide with both confusion and surprise, Savvy said, "What are you talking about?"

"Despite all the things you and Zach went through years ago, as soon as you saw each other again, those intense feelings you'd been suppressing resurfaced. For ten years, even though you wouldn't admit it to yourself, you loved him. I just don't think I have that kind of depth."

Of all the reactions she had expected from her shameful confession, laughter wasn't one of them. Yet both sisters burst out laughing as if she'd just told a hilarious joke.

"I'm not kidding, you guys."

"I'm sorry, Sammie," Savvy said. "It's just that that's the most ridiculous statement I've ever heard you make. You have more heart and deep emotions than just about anyone I know."

Bri nodded but was more blunt in her evaluation. "That's pure bullshit, Sammie. Of the three of us, you're the one with the most tender and romantic heart."

"But that's just it. I think I idealized love and romance too much. And then, when it came time to step up and be in a mature relationship, I didn't have it in me to handle it. At the very first bump in the road, I ran like a terrified rabbit."

"Hell, Sammie," Bri said. "Having the man you're sleeping with become a murder suspect is not a bump in the road. It's a big-assed hill."

"But I—"

"No, wait, I think I agree with Sammie on this one, Bri."

Samantha wanted to cry all over again. She had wanted both her sisters to tell her she was being ridiculous. Now Savvy was agreeing with Samantha's assessment that she lacked depth.

Bri huffed out a breath of exasperation. "What the hell are you talking about, Savvy? We're supposed to be helping Sammie feel better, not tearing her down further."

"Hear me out, both of you. I'm not agreeing with you, Sammie, about your lack of depth. What I'm saying is, I agree that the first time you were given a chance at a real relationship, you blew it."

Bri snorted. "You're not exactly helping."

"Let me finish. You ran because you cared so much, Sammie, not because you don't have the depth necessary to love. You loved him so much it scared the hell out of you."

"Well, what kind of woman does that make me? Unable to stand by my man?"

"And what did you do after that initial reaction? You busted your ass to investigate and you're the one who cleared him. That's love, Sammie. The deep, heartfelt emotion that has staying power. You didn't run away and hide your head in the sand or under a pillow. You fought for your man in the most important way possible. You proved he was innocent."

"She's right," Bri said. "If you were lacking in emotional depth, you would have stayed out of it. Instead, you righted a wrong and prevented a major catastrophe for the man you love."

If it were up to her sisters, she would be nominated for sainthood. Samantha judged herself much more harshly. Had her motivations to clear Quinn been selfless, or had she done it out of desperation and fear that she had been wrong about him? Had she done it for herself instead of for the man she thought she loved?

"Stop it."

Samantha raised her gaze to her sisters again. Savvy was the one who spoke but Bri was nodding in agreement. "Stop what?"

"Stop questioning yourself in everything. You made a mistake; learn from it and move on."

"I believed the man I was in love with was a murderer. How can I trust my judgment? Learning the truth about Mama's and Daddy's murders reinforced my doubts. Hell, how do I know if I'm right about anything?"

"No one ever knows if they're right," Bri said. "Most of the time, I sure as hell don't. But you make a judgment with the facts you have and move forward. Nobody's perfect."

To her, Quinn had been perfect. There was a large part of her that didn't blame him for his harsh treatment. She had let him down in one of his darkest moments and had proved to him that she wasn't a woman he could count on. Maybe that was what hurt most of all.

But her sisters were right. She had to move on. She had screwed up royally and the best she could do was learn from her mistakes. That also included not becoming involved with Quinn again. Some might accuse her of being a coward, and she wouldn't necessarily deny the claim. The real thing hurt too much to put herself at risk again. From now on, she would limit herself to surface romances, and her motto would be "What doesn't touch you can't kill you"—a lame-assed mangling of Friedrich Nietzsche's famous saying.

Sure, Nietzsche would roll over in his grave, but she

was Samantha Wilde, a woman who had only recently learned that she was a coward.

"You're right, I do need to move on. No more morose Sammie." She took in both Bri's and Savvy's gazes. "Thanks for the pep talk. I needed it."

Bri shot her a grin. "And you're a terrible liar but it will be nice to see the old Sammie again."

"We've missed her," Savvy added.

Releasing a short, determined sigh, Samantha stiffened her spine and said, "Now let's talk about Lauren. How are we going to get her to talk?"

"Brody called with an update," Savvy said. "He said they're making headway but it's going to take some time to gain her trust."

"Time we may not have if Cruz finds out where she's hiding," Samantha said.

"That's why I'm headed back to Florida for a few days," Bri answered. "I've got contacts in Miami with their ear to the ground. If I can find out what Cruz's plans are, we'll be better positioned for our next move."

"Will you see Ian while you're there?"

The glare of warning that crossed Bri's face told Samantha to back off. Samantha fought a smile, happy to see that her sister finally seemed to be coming out of her deep freeze. Tyler Finley, Bri's former fiancé, had done a number on her. If the man weren't already dead, she and Savvy would have gladly done the honors.

Ian Mackenzie had been good for her. At one time, she and Savvy had wondered if they would ever again see the vibrant, incorrigible Bri they both adored. And though there were still occasional signs of disillusionment and bitterness, for the most part, Sabrina Sage Wilde had returned to the warm, wonderful, sometimes zany person she had once been.

"Ian's got his hands full since I left. I doubt that I'll see him."

Samantha met Savvy's eyes. Neither of them believed her. There was definitely something going on between Bri and her so-called best friend. When they were in the same room together, they could barely take their eyes off each other.

"Whether you see him or not, why don't you invite him for Thanksgiving?"

A rigid shrug of her shoulders was Bri's only answer. Samantha knew to back off. Still, she'd put the idea in Bri's head. Hopefully it would take root.

Savvy yawned and stood, patting her almost invisible baby bump. "I think Little Bit is ready for bed." Blowing a kiss to both sisters and saying, "Sleep tight," she left the room.

Samantha smiled over at Bri. "She looks good."

"And we're going to keep her that way. What do you think about trying to get her and Aunt Gibby to leave town?"

"I'd say you'd have a giant mountain named Zach Tanner to climb. There's no way he's going to let Savvy go away."

Bri got to her feet and began to pace. "You're right. And Zach can't leave because of his job." She stopped abruptly. "Then we need to get Lauren out of Midnight. Maybe take her to Mobile or even Biloxi."

"What's got you so worried all of a sudden?"

"Ian called just before I came in here. He's done a little more digging on Cruz."

"And?"

"It's even worse than we thought. Cruz is an animal. Even though he can't be tied to any of the murders he's suspected of, Ian checked them out. They're about as gruesome as they come. The man has no conscience. The last thing I want to do is put Savvy in danger."

"Then we'll just have to make sure we don't. Lauren is safe with Brody and Logan, but I agree, it'll be best if they take her to another town. If she has to stay here for any length of time, Midnight's gossipers are going to find out about her, no matter how diligent we are in hiding her."

Bri nodded. "You're right about that. And if anyone comes around asking questions, no one would hesitate to talk."

"I'll call Brody and Logan and talk to them about moving her to a new location. You go to Florida and see what you can find out. In the meantime, I'll stay here and keep a close eye on who comes into Midnight. If Cruz's goons manage to trace Lauren here, they'll have to ask questions and look around to locate her."

Laughing, Bri turned to leave. "Finally something the gossips are good for." Stopping at the door, she looked back over her shoulder, the laughter gone. "Sammie, you're one of the most beautiful people I've ever known, inside and out. Don't let this thing with Quinn take that knowledge away from you."

Swallowing around the sudden lump in her throat, Samantha asked, "How did I get so lucky to have such wonderful sisters?"

"You must've had awfully good parents."

How wonderful it felt to be able to say, "I certainly did."

"Night, Sammie."

"Night, Bri."

The door closed and once again Samantha looked out into the night. She had so much to be grateful for. That's what she needed to concentrate on. She had a great life, full of love and purpose. The thing with Quinn hadn't been real.

Leaning her forehead against the windowpane, she repeated softly, "It wasn't real." She ignored the little voice inside her that responded with *Then why the hell does it still hurt so much?*

CHAPTER TWELVE

"Samantha, it's good to finally see you out and about."

Smiling and thanking the umpteenth person who'd said the same words, Samantha once again refrained from explaining why she was just now "out and about." When she had returned home, she had been in no shape to gallivant around town, and surprisingly, Midnight's residents had accommodated her need for privacy. A good thing, since none of them would have recognized the morose, introverted Samantha Wilde. They only knew her as the perky and always-smiling former cheerleader. She hadn't been that person in a long time.

She didn't fool herself that the gossips hadn't been at work, though. Having often been their favorite topic of conversation, she was quite sure there had been plenty of speculation about her circumstances. Talk didn't really bother her. Most of the people in Midnight weren't malicious or spiteful—they were just nosy.

But her world had shifted once more. She and Quinn had apologized to each other and she could now move on. She was wiser and perhaps more wary than she had been before, but that was a good thing. Growth came from mistakes. That would be her takeaway from her massive screwup. Samantha Wilde had officially grown up.

She was beginning to feel like her old self again, albeit

a more mature version. The acceptance from her hometown was a stroke to her badly damaged ego. She had been the golden girl here, popular and pretty. Few had known what lay behind her smiling demeanor.

How odd that she had been considered the one least impacted by her parents' deaths. And though she had carefully built that façade to cover the pain, little had she known that it would come back and bite her on the ass. With a broad judgmental stroke, she had painted the murder-suicide of her parents with the same brush as the murder of Charlene Braddock. That had been massively wrong. The two hadn't compared at all. And to now know she had misjudged her father, too? Was it any wonder confidence in her judgment was at its lowest depth?

Nodding and waving at an elderly couple she had known since her birth, Samantha ducked into Deacon's Real Estate office. Even though it had been a boost to her spirits to visit the town again, she hadn't forgotten her real purpose. Midnight's residents often knew who was doing what before it actually happened. Mary-Jo Deacon, the town's only real estate agent, had a bird's-eye view when it came to newcomers. If anyone was looking for housing, temporary or otherwise, Mary-Jo was the first to know.

The instant the door closed, the older woman was running around her desk with her arms open wide for a hug. Her eyes behind her wire-rimmed glasses sparkled. "Samantha Wilde, how nice to see you again."

After returning the hug, Samantha took a seat opposite Mary-Jo, and they chitchatted about the cooling weather, Mary-Jo's grandchildren, and the time Mary-Jo's daughter dropped Samantha during the middle of a cheerleading pyramid to wave at a boy.

"I swan, I never thought Donna would end up marrying him. I'm glad she did, though. Bud turned out all right."

"All right" was a compliment in the South. And considering that Donna and Bud had eloped in defiance of their parents, that was high praise indeed.

Shifting the discussion toward her primary goal, Samantha said, "So how's business?"

Mary-Jo shook her head. "Almost at a standstill. Nobody's buying or selling. I've had to let go all my office help, and I only work about two days a week now."

"I'm so sorry, Mary-Jo. No new prospects?"

"Well, funny you should ask. I had a handsome young man come by day before yesterday looking for a house to rent."

Telling herself not to sound too interested, she said, "Is that right? So he and his family are moving to Midnight?"

"I don't think he has a family. He told me he just went through a painful breakup with his girlfriend and wanted a quiet place to heal."

Okay, even the romantic in her cringed at the lameness of that statement. Not because men didn't need that kind of time, just like women. But how many men would share that kind of information with a total stranger?

"Well, hopefully he'll like it so much he'll want to buy a house. Does he already have a job here?"

"I'm not sure. We're going to look at a few places tomorrow, but he's already told me that money isn't a factor."

At that, her inner voice began squawking up a storm. *A stranger comes to town with the vague excuse of a bad breakup, and money is no object? What better way for one of Cruz's men to roam around town searching for Lauren without looking suspicious?*

Now she was extra glad that Lauren was gone from Midnight. She had talked to Logan and Brody late last night, and they had both agreed that taking Lauren to another town would be wise. She hadn't heard from them yet, but knew their plan had been to leave around three this morning. A friend of a friend of Logan's owned a time-share in Magnolia Springs. They would keep Lauren there until further notice.

She would have liked to ask more, but if she delved any deeper about Mary-Jo's prospective client, there would be questions Samantha didn't want to answer.

Her smile bright, she got to her feet. There were several places to go and other people to talk to about a newcomer in Midnight.

"It was good to see you, Mary-Jo. Be sure to tell Donna I said hey."

"She and her family are coming for Thanksgiving. I'll tell her to give you a call."

"Wonderful. I'd love to see her again."

"Just wait till you get a look at her young'uns. I swear they get cuter every time I see them."

Figuring if she didn't get out of there, the proud grandma would soon be pulling out pictures, Samantha backed out the door with one last wave. Turning, she slammed face-first into a large, unmovable object. Embarrassed that she hadn't been watching where she was going, she looked up to apologize. Instead of the apology she'd planned, she snapped, "What the hell are you doing here?"

The words were appropriate but she inwardly winced at how breathless and weak her voice sounded.

Quinn let his gaze roam over the beautiful woman before him. She looked fresh and lovely and it took every bit of his self-control not to drop a kiss on that full, pouty mouth, pursed in disapproval. The fact that she would probably slug him if he tried was another deterrent.

"How are you?"

"I asked you a question. I told you to leave."

Quinn raised his brow. "I wasn't aware you were in charge of the whole town."

"There's no reason for you to stay."

"On the contrary. Midnight seems like the perfect place to spend my vacation."

"Vacation?"

He watched the color leave her face and battled his conscience. The last thing he wanted to do was cause her more pain. But he wasn't a quitter and he refused to believe this was the end of their relationship. They'd both made mistakes. He just needed to figure out a way back into her life. Hell, if he had to move to Midnight, then that's what he'd damn well do.

"It's been years since I've taken time off. There's a lot to be said for this charming little town."

"You didn't even know Midnight was on the map before you met me."

"And I have you to thank for that. Want to have lunch with me? It's chicken and dumpling day at Faye's."

She backed away, shaking her head. "You need to leave, Quinn. There's nothing for you here."

He struggled with staying still when all he wanted to do was reach out and pull her to him. He had let this go on far too long and he cursed himself for it. While he'd been in Atlanta, pissed at the world in general, Sam had been here, suffering. She had lost at least fifteen pounds, weight she hadn't needed to lose. Shadows beneath her eyes indicated she wasn't sleeping well, either. This was his fault. He shouldn't have treated her so badly in the first place, but neither should he have kept away from her for so long.

"I'm not going anywhere, Sam. Not till we've had a chance to talk . . . really talk."

"We have nothing more to say to each other."

"Yes we do. And until you agree to spend some time with me, sorting those things out, I'm going to be here."

Anguish briefly crossed her face, then her expression returned to the icy blankness she'd shown him yesterday. "That's not going to happen." She turned and walked away.

Quinn didn't try to stop her. He'd said enough today. All he could do was hope that she realized he was serious and that she would change her mind about talking to him. If they could just spend some alone time together, he knew he could convince her to give them another chance. He refused to believe anything different.

As he opened the door of the real estate agent's office, the first words out of his mouth shocked the hell out of him. "Mrs. Deacon, my name is Quinn Braddock and I want to buy a house here in Midnight."

Samantha sat on the park bench in front of the mimosa-tree-shaped fountain. For as long as she could remember, she had been coming here and making wishes. If the fountain ever gave up its secrets, her entire life story could be told here. As a kid, her wishes had to do with things like a puppy for Christmas or an elaborate dollhouse for her birthday. After her parents' deaths, she had wasted a whole year of wishes, begging for them to come back and for things to return to the way they had been. Between the fountain wishes and her prayers to the Almighty, her entire year had been all about asking for the impossible. After that, her wishes became more focused. She wished different things for her family members; Savvy and Bri had desperately needed those wishes to come true. And her grandfather had needed all the help he could get.

After she left for college, she had left childish things like pennies for wishes behind. But still, on visits home, she had returned to the fountain and made wishes—she'd told herself for old times' sake.

Today, she didn't care that it was silly superstition. That a penny thrown into the fountain had no bearing on a fervent, whispered wish. That no matter how much she wished something would come true, throwing a penny into the water would never make it happen. Long ago she had learned that when you wanted something to happen, you had to make it so. Wishes were for children.

Pushing aside all of that mature, logical mumbo jumbo, she withdrew a penny from her purse, closed her eyes, and wished . . . for what? She wasn't strong enough to wish Quinn away for good, but she was too cowardly to put her heart at risk again.

"That's either a powerful wish or a really bad headache."

Her eyes popped open. A good-looking man stood only a few feet away. With short brownish-blond hair, twinkling hazel eyes, and a charming smile, he was boyishly handsome. He was also a stranger.

"So which is it, a wish or a headache?"

"Actually it's both." Surreptitiously dropping the penny into the water, she stood and held out her hand. "I'm Samantha Wilde. And you are . . . ?"

"Quite enamored of your little town." Grinning, he shook her hand. "I'm Blaine Marshall."

"You said you're enamored of the town. Are you new here?"

"Actually, yes. Just got here a few days ago."

This must be the man Mary-Jo Deacon had mentioned. How coincidental that the one man she was determined to meet today had found her instead. Coincidences didn't usually pass the smell test for her. Charmingly boyish or not, he definitely put her radar on high alert.

"And what brings you to Midnight?"

"Would you believe I'm trying to find myself?"

"And you think Midnight is that place?"

The boyish grin reappeared. "Maybe not but things are definitely looking up."

Flirty banter had always come easily for her, or it had until she met Quinn. With him, she'd been tongue-tied, shy, and awkward. Even if this man was a hired assassin, she was glad to see she hadn't completely lost her touch.

Giving him the playful look she had perfected years ago, she said, "It's nice to meet you, Blaine. I hope Midnight meets your expectations." She turned to walk away and then stopped. Glancing over her shoulder, she smiled. "It just occurred to me that I'm famished. Would you like to join me for lunch?"

His eyes widened with delight. "I was just headed to Faye's Diner for a quick bite. That sound okay to you?"

Samantha hesitated. Would Quinn be there? He had mentioned Faye's. She couldn't handle seeing him again, especially when she was on a job. If Blaine was one of Cruz's men, she would need all of her focus on him.

"Actually, there's a new place around the corner, Cornbread Kitchen. I've been wanting to try it. Want to go there?"

"Sounds good."

They walked down the street and unfortunately had to pass by Faye's, where Quinn sat in a booth by the window. The dark look he gave her sent electricity zipping up her spine. It said they weren't over, that he would see her again. And damn the little voice inside her that shouted a gleeful *Yes!*

CHAPTER THIRTEEN

Two hours later, Samantha let herself into the Wilde house. Lunch had been pleasant but not especially informative. Blaine had a knack for talking about himself without telling her anything substantial. Others might not have noticed but she recognized the type. She had done the same thing herself for much of her life.

He had asked her out for tonight and she had turned him down. A risky tactic considering she wanted to determine if he was Cruz's man. However, she also knew a thing or two about pursuing a man. Turning him down while leading him on should make him even more interested.

That particular tactic hadn't worked with Quinn. When she had met him, she had tried to play her usual flirtatious games. After that first date, all pretense stopped. She had wanted him unlike anyone she had ever met. And to Quinn's credit, he hadn't taken advantage . . . he had seemed to feel the same way. Even when he had been bluntly honest about not wanting anything permanent, he had never tried to hide how much he wanted to spend time with her.

She dropped her keys and purse on the foyer table and took a second to breathe in the scent from the giant vase of lilies. For as long as she could remember, lilies had graced this table. Her granddad had started the tradition when he had first brought his bride, Camille, into the house. Lilies had been her grandmother's favorite flower, and even after her death, the flowers continued to fill vases throughout the house. It was a tradition neither she nor her sisters had been able to give up.

"Hey, find out anything interesting?"

Samantha turned to Savvy, who stood at the bottom of the stairway. "More than I thought I would but less than I needed."

"Hmm. Sounds very mysterious. Let's go to the kitchen and nibble on the chocolate cake Bri made before she left."

Her stomach rumbled in approval. The lunch at Corn-bread Kitchen had been enjoyable but skimpy. If they were going to compete with Faye's Diner, they were definitely going to have to step up their game. Faye had a tendency to overfeed her customers. "Sounds good to me."

Samantha waited until they were both seated, with slices of chocolate cake and large glasses of milk in front of them, before she sprang the news. "Quinn is still in town."

Her eyes wide, Savvy sat back in her chair. "Really? How do you know? Did you see him? Did you talk to him? What did he say? How long is he going to be here?"

Despite the subject matter, Samantha grinned at all the questions. "Yes, I did see him and did talk to him. He's taking some vacation time and decided that Midnight is the perfect place to spend it. He invited me to lunch."

"Did you go?"

"No, of course not. I told him yesterday that we were over. I haven't changed my mind."

Her eyes narrowed in doubt, Savvy took a giant bite of chocolate cake. Samantha had a feeling she did that to keep from expressing her opinion. She didn't blame her sister for her doubts. She had them, too. But what she also had was a strong sense of self-preservation.

Moving on to a safer topic, she said, "I walked through downtown, visiting to find out if there were any new-comers to the area."

"What did you find out?"

"Nothing till I got to Mary-Jo Deacon's office. She told me about a guy who contacted her to rent a house. He's new in the area, supposedly getting over a bad breakup or something."

"Was that Quinn?"

"Of course not. First, Quinn's only here for a few days, and secondly, he's not going to tell a complete stranger that he's recovering from a breakup. Hell, he barely told me about himself."

"That's why I think you need to give him another chance." She raised her hand when Samantha would have challenged the statement. "I'm not saying another chance at a relationship. I mean a chance to talk."

Samantha didn't bother to argue. It would do no good. "Anyway, to get back to the subject, after I talked to her, I was sitting at the fountain and was approached by that same man."

"Is that right?" Savvy's eyes gleamed with interest. "What did he say?"

"He told me he's trying to find himself in Midnight. We had lunch at that new place, Cornbread Kitchen."

"Wow, I'd forgotten how fast you can work."

"It wasn't like that." Her sister's remark wasn't meant to be hurtful, but it stung all the same. She had worked so hard to overcome the "flirts with anything with a penis" reputation some girls had given her in high school.

Savannah's eyes went wide with remorse. "Oh, Sam-mie, my gosh, I didn't mean anything by that other than I admire you. You have to know that."

Feeling like crap for snapping at her sister, she said, "I

know, Savvy. I'm sorry. I think I'm still rattled over see-ing Quinn."

"Okay, we'll get back to that in just a minute. What's this guy's name and what's your take on him? Did you get anything useful?"

"His name is Blaine Marshall. I Googled him on my phone, but there's not much there."

"You think he's one of Cruz's men?"

"I don't know. I'm going out with him on Friday."

"You think that's safe? If he's been sent here to find Lauren, he could use you as bait."

"I'll be prepared, don't worry." She took a giant bite of the scrumptious cake and closed her eyes in delight. How she wished she had just half of Bri's kitchen talent.

"Bri said she would call as soon as she got to Miami."

"Think she'll stop in Tallahassee for a quickie?"

Savvy snorted. "Like we'll ever know. She won't even admit there's anything remotely romantic between them."

"I'm not even sure she admits it to herself."

"Poor Ian."

"He can hold his own."

"I just hope he can hold it until Bri's ready for him."

The first time she and Savvy met Bri's business part-ner, they immediately decided he was the ideal man for their sister. And the sparks between the two were more than obvious. Bri, however, continued to deny them. Thankfully Ian was laid-back and easygoing, seeming to realize that Bri needed the space.

"Tyler Finley continues to be on my top five list of people I wish were still alive so I could slap the crap out of them."

Raising her glass of milk, Savvy said, "Hear, hear."

Scraping the last of the chocolate off her plate, Sa-mantha savored her last bite and stood. She took the empty plates and glasses to the sink, enjoying the con-tentment of her chocolate fix.

"So let's talk about Quinn."

She swallowed a sigh. The chocolate contentment immediately vanished. Turning, she shook her head at her sister. "There's nothing to talk about."

"You still love him, Sammie. You know that . . . right?"

Of course she knew that. One didn't get over a man like Quinn quickly. She was saved from having to answer when the doorbell rang.

Samantha peeked out the window and recognized the black SUV parked in the front of the house. "Brody's here."

"I'll let him in," Savvy said. Before she walked out of the room, she threw over her shoulder, "This discussion isn't over, Sammie."

Ignoring her, Samantha cut a large slice of cake and turned as Brody James walked into the kitchen.

The instant he saw what she was holding, his eyes lit up. "That for me?"

Laughing, she handed him the cake and said, "Milk or coffee?"

"Milk, please." Ever the gentleman, Brody waited until Savvy sat down at the table and then seated himself across from her. Winking, he asked, "How's Little Bit doing?"

"Wonderful," Savvy answered.

After taking a giant bite of cake, Brody swallowed and said, "Know what you're going to have?"

"No, we're not going to find out. As long as it's healthy . . . that's all we care about."

"I've never seen Zach so happy. You'd think he's done something nobody else ever had."

Savvy laughed, nodding. "He's taken a picture of me every day since we found out. It took some talking to convince him that my belly would not make a good Christmas card. By the time this baby's born, he or she will be the most photographed child in the world."

Settling beside Brody, Samantha said, "Speaking of doing something no one else has, have you gotten any information out of Lauren yet?"

"That woman . . ." Brody shook his head.

"What's wrong now?" Savvy asked.

"She's trouble wrapped in a pretty package."

"Do you think she's just not telling us what she knows, or she doesn't know anything and she's playing us for some reason?" Samantha asked.

"Oh, she knows plenty."

"But?" Savvy said.

"She's got nothing to back up what she knows. But if Cruz knows about her gift, she's in even more danger than we thought."

Savvy and Samantha looked at each other, then asked in unison, "What gift?"

"She's got some kind of photographic memory. Everything she's seen, she remembers. Cruz apparently took her to business meetings all over the world. She's got names and dates of every interaction since they began their relationship. She swears he doesn't know about her memory."

"Even if she's right, Cruz will still come after her, if for nothing else than his ego," Samantha said.

"I agree," Brody said. "We're going to record everything she remembers. It might not be proof enough to put him away, but it could damn well reinforce a case when it comes to trial."

"You guys make the move okay?" Samantha asked.

"Yeah. No problems." Brody shrugged. "If anyone was following, I would've seen. She's tucked out of sight." He grinned and added, "As Aunt Gibby would say, she's snug as a bug in a rug."

Both Samantha and Savannah grinned. Brody had become a favorite of Aunt Gibby's, and the feeling was mutual.

"So our plan is still the same," Samantha said. "Bri's digging for what she can in Florida. I'll keep an eye out in town for newcomers. Can both you and Logan spare the time to stay with Lauren?"

"One of us might have to go back to Mobile every few days, but she'll be safe whoever's with her."

"And I'm going to do some research on your new friend, Sammie," Savvy said.

"Sammie's got a new friend?"

Samantha nodded. "I met a man this morning, new to Midnight. He started talking to me out of the blue. I thought it was suspicious."

A tremble at Brody's mouth told her he was fighting a smile. "Men don't normally talk to you?"

Actually, they often went out of their way to do just that. Which meant Blaine might well be just a nice guy who was attracted to her. She wouldn't know until she delved deeper.

Samantha shrugged. "Just seemed a little too coincidental. Here I am looking for newcomers to Midnight and he suddenly appears before me."

"Yeah, I bet it had nothing to do with you being a beautiful woman."

She could feel herself blushing. Brody had flirted with her on occasion. With his gorgeous smile, velvet brown eyes, and hair the color of rich dark chocolate, along with a solid, muscular physique, he would catch the eye of most women. But not her. Though she could appreciate his looks, she had met him just after that terrible event with Quinn. He and his business partner, Logan Wright, had been called in to help investigate her parents' murders. Those things had influenced and colored everything. Nothing about those days made for pleasant memories. She told herself it had nothing to do with the fact that after her first meeting with Quinn, she hadn't been attracted to anyone else.

"It'll help to know as much as possible when I do the background check on Blaine Marshall," Savvy said. "What exactly did he tell you about himself?"

"Just that he's from northern Indiana. Is a CPA but left his job at a small accounting firm a few months ago. Says he's been traveling around, looking for a place to light. Thinks Midnight might be the perfect spot for him."

"Is he planning on working here as a CPA?"

"He didn't say. Said he was still trying to find himself."

"Did he mention family, ex-wife, children? Anything like that?" Brody asked.

"Ex-girlfriend, but he didn't tell me her name. Said all his family was gone."

Savvy stood. "That's enough to get started with."

"I'll try to get more information from him tomorrow night."

Brody's eyes cut over to Samantha. "What's tomorrow night?"

"I'm going out with him."

Brody was silent for several seconds. Was he going to object? This was her job, and while he was her friend, she wasn't going to let him deter her.

"Think it'd be a good idea to wear a wire?"

Actually, that was a good idea. Not only would it record their conversation, picking up nuances she might miss, it would be good protection. If Blaine was Cruz's hired man, then he could very well try to use her to get to Lauren.

"Yes, but I don't have that kind of equipment."

Brody stood, carried his empty plate and glass to the sink, and turned back to her. "I've got what you need at our office in Mobile. I'll get it and come back here tomorrow afternoon and show you how to use it."

Wishing she had Bri's gift for saying something outlandish to break the sudden tension, Samantha smiled her thanks at his offer. At his answering grin, she mentally shook her head. This was a good man, a war hero with the medals and scars to prove it. He was Zach's best friend and gorgeous to boot. Why couldn't she be interested in him? Brody had the kind of gentlemanly gentleness that any woman should find irresistible.

As if realizing she had nothing else to say, Brody gave a "See you tomorrow" to no one in particular and walked out of the kitchen.

The instant she heard the front door close, she turned to Savvy. "Why can't I be interested in him? He's such a good guy."

She should have known not to ask the question. Her sisters never lied to her and sometimes told her the painful truth. This time was no different. Looking both compassionate and slightly amused, Savvy said, "Because you're hopelessly and irrevocably in love with another man. That's why."

Since denying it would do no good, Samantha chose to ignore the statement. Heading to their new office, which had once been their grandfather's study, she said, "Let's go see what we can find out about Blaine Marshall."

"So did anything strike your fancy?" Mary-Jo's voice held a less-than-hopeful tone.

They were stopped in front of the real estate agent's office. The exhausted woman had shown him eight houses, all well within his price range but none that felt right. He refused to ask himself why he was spending so much time looking for a house he didn't know if he would ever live in. If Sam never forgave him, he would own a home that he might never be able to get off his hands. Even though he'd had some breaks in life, no one

would ever accuse him of being an optimist. So why the
hell was he pursuing this? Quinn gave a mental shrug.
He didn't have an answer. He only knew he was on a set
course and it led straight to Sam.

Midnight was a small town and the chance of finding the perfect home was slim. Not that he knew what
he wanted, but with every house Mary-Jo had shown
him, Quinn had found himself asking the same question: Would Sam like this house? So far, the answer had
been no.

"And there's nothing else?"

Her eyes narrowed, Mary-Jo considered him for several seconds. "Well, there is one more but I doubt it's
what you want."

"Why's that?"

"It's an old farmhouse on a small man-made lake.
Has twenty acres to it. Several developers have tried
buying it from the owner, but he refuses to parcel it out
or sell to someone who will divide it into lots. The land's
been in his family for over a hundred years. The house
is old but solidly built. Definitely needs some renovations, though. It's been on the market forever."

A memory clicked and Quinn's heart set up a hard
thud. "Can we take a look at it?"

"Sure." Starting her car again, she pulled back out
onto the road. "For a man who doesn't even work close
by or have family here, you sure seem determined to
have a house here in Midnight."

Yes, he was definitely acting out of character. Even
though he didn't plan to move to Midnight, he felt the
need to have a house here so that when he came back to
visit, he'd have a place to stay. This thing with Sam was
not over, no matter what she said. Before all of this happened, they'd been headed in the right direction. Charlene's murder had caused them to take a major detour,

but that didn't mean they couldn't get back to where they once were.

Since Mary-Jo didn't seem to know who he was or why he wanted a house here, he didn't bother to enlighten her. Not talking about himself had become a self-defense mechanism long before he met Sam. That had to change, because it had been the root of their problems. He had worked so hard on forgetting what he came from that maintaining a relationship based only in the present had felt natural. And because he hadn't wanted to talk about his past, he hadn't delved too deeply into hers. Unfortunately it had backfired. The first real challenge they'd encountered had all but destroyed them.

As they drove out of town, his mind returned to earlier today. Sam had been walking down the sidewalk talking animatedly with a man. Who was he? An old boyfriend? They hadn't looked affectionate with each other, but Sam had definitely been pouring on the charm. Was she already dating someone else?

"Are there any questions you have about Midnight?"

Pulled from his black thoughts, he answered Mary-Jo's question. "How old is the town?"

"It was founded in the early nineteenth century by five families out of Mobile. They decided to branch out and start their own town. Some of their descendants still live here."

"What's the population?"

"About fifteen hundred, give or take a few. We don't get a lot of new people coming to Midnight, and fewer who return after leaving. Well, except for the Wilde sisters. They came back just a few months ago."

"The Wilde sisters?"

Apparently recognizing she had his interest, she went on. "Oh, there's an interesting story there. In fact, more than anyone would've ever guessed."

"Why do you say that?"

She glanced over at him, her eyes behind her bifocals gleaming with excitement. "Well, of course, I'm not one to gossip."

Spoken as one who does exactly that. However, Quinn was more than happy to listen.

"Eighteen years ago this past summer, their parents died in what looked to be a murder-suicide. We moved to Midnight about a year after it happened, but people were still talking about it."

Emotion clogged Quinn's throat, making it hard to swallow. Sam had told him about her parents' deaths. And instead of talking with her, offering his sympathy and understanding, he had thrown her explanation back in her face and walked out the door. Hell, no wonder she didn't want to see him again.

"You said 'what *looked* to be a murder-suicide.' There were doubts?"

"Oh yes, in fact, the truth was just discovered a few months back. Turns out both the mother and father were murdered. The killers made it look like a murder-suicide to cover it up."

Shit. What that must have done to her. For eighteen years, she had believed her father was guilty of murdering her mother. To find out it was all a lie and cover-up must have brought great relief, but devastation, too. He should have been here for her, helping her through that time. Instead he'd behaved like an ass and hung on to his hurt pride. Hell, he hadn't thought he could feel worse.

"So what do you think?"

Quinn had been so immersed in his thoughts he hadn't noticed that they were now parked in a small clearing. Before him lay a small, sparkling lake. Opening the car door, he got out and took in the scenery. Even in winter, when nothing was growing or blooming, the lake and surrounding trees made an attractive and serene picture. He could only imagine how it would look in the spring.

He turned to the old farmhouse behind him. Two stories, with a giant wraparound porch and small individual balconies on the second floor—Sam had called them sleeping porches—and a tin roof. Even with the weathered exterior, shutters hanging askew from a couple of windows, and an obvious woodpecker's hole in the chimney, the charm was undeniable.

This had to be the place Sam had mentioned, he was sure of it. He remembered the conversation well. They'd been sitting in a noisy restaurant in Atlanta, eating dinner. Sam had been looking out the window, a wistful expression on her face. Quinn had asked her what she was thinking. Instead of answering, she had surprised him with the question *"If you could live anywhere in the world, where would it be?"*

Always too practical to be a dreamer, Quinn had said something like Tahiti or Hawaii . . . he barely even remembered his response. When he'd asked Sam the same question, she had surprised him with her thorough, detailed answer. He remembered every single word. Could almost hear her soft, dreamy voice, as if she had been in another world.

"There's a place right outside my hometown. An old farmhouse on a small lake surrounded by all sorts of flowering trees and shrubs. A friend of my granddad's used to own it, but he went into a retirement home. I don't even know if he ever sold it, but I remember visiting there when I was a kid. The house is beautiful, with a gigantic wraparound porch, hardwood floors, and sleeping porches for all the second-floor bedrooms. Once when we were visiting, we stayed long after dark. Savvy, Bri, and I sat on one of the sleeping porches and listened to the frogs from the pond and the fish jumping. It was so peaceful, almost magical.

"I used to imagine how beautiful it would be deco-rated for Christmas. The entire house covered in lights, reflecting on the lake. I loved the thought of sitting on one of the porches, curled up in a blanket, sipping hot cocoa."

She had abruptly stopped talking and given him a small, self-conscious smile. They'd gone on to talk about something else, but her words had stuck with him.

His mind already made up, he said, "What's the ask-ing price?"

Mary-Jo looked both stunned and excited . . . she was also apparently speechless. When she didn't answer, he said again, "Mrs. Deacon, what's the asking price?"

Recovering quickly, she named a price. Quinn was pleasantly surprised. The amount seemed more than rea-sonable. Of course, he hadn't yet seen the inside of the house. It could be full of vermin and need a complete gutting. Not that it mattered . . . his course was set.

"How much acreage did you say?"

"Right at twenty."

"How long's it been for sale?"

She grimaced. "Over five years without a nibble."

That was understandable. These days it was hard enough for some people to buy any house, much less one with a lake and acreage. He could do it, though. He'd have to sell some stock, but it could be done.

"Let me walk around the lake, then I'd like to see the house. If I see nothing to change my mind, I'll make an offer."

Leaving her with a stupefied expression on her face, Quinn started walking. The farther he went, the more sure he was of his decision. Sam loved this place. How could he not buy it?

CHAPTER FOURTEEN

Muffled conversations, squealing children, and the occasional plate being dropped rivaled the soft background music of the restaurant. Michelle's Place was one of the newer restaurants in Midnight. Offering a varied menu, it drew diners who were a mix of couples on dates and families with children. Samantha much preferred this atmosphere to that of a stuffy, overpriced restaurant in a big city.

She wasn't too sure Blaine felt the same way. She'd seen him wince more than once when the noise level increased.

Offering him a small, flirtatious smile, Samantha said, "So have you found yourself yet?"

He answered with a charming, self-deprecating grin. "That was probably the worst pickup line ever, wasn't it?"

Surprised laughter escaped her before she could catch it. "That was a pickup line?"

"I thought you would be impressed with my sensitive side."

"So you're not here to find yourself?"

"Not really. After my girlfriend and I broke up, I knew I needed a change. I quit my job and was mulling over where I wanted to move. I was going to Florida for a few days of sun. On the way, I happened to see a sign for Midnight. The name captured my attention, so instead of going to Florida, I came here."

"Are you usually that impulsive?"

"I can be."

Samantha leaned back in her chair and studied the man across from her. This was their second dinner date. And so far, despite numerous questions, she still didn't have a good grasp on who Blaine Marshall really was.

On the surface, he was an interesting, intelligent man who could converse on a multitude of subjects. Even though she was going out with him solely to determine if he was Cruz's man, both times she had enjoyed herself. There was no attraction there but he was a pleasant, entertaining dinner companion. That is, if he wasn't a hired killer.

He had asked several questions about her and her family. Samantha had been just as vague in her answers as he had been. Not that it really mattered what she told him. Blaine could ask just about anyone in this town and find out more than he could ever want to know about the Wilde family.

Their initial research showed Blaine was who he said he was. A mild-mannered former accountant from Indiana. He seemed uncomplicated, without mystery. She had dated her share of Blaines. Most of them had been nice guys. But still, she wasn't completely convinced of his innocence.

"You said you were headed to Florida. Have you spent much time there?"

Something odd flickered in his eyes. He shrugged, a little too nonchalantly. "Some." And then surprising her, his eyes narrowed and in a much harsher tone than normal he asked, "Why?"

Her heartbeat kicked up. Hmm. Definitely a Florida connection. Her expression one of surprised innocence, she said, "No reason. Just asking . . . getting to know you better."

As if realizing he'd revealed something he hadn't intended, he gave another one of his charmingly boyish grins. "Sorry. I like the beaches but not all my memories of Florida are good. That's where my girlfriend grew up."

"I see. So is that the real reason you were headed to Florida?"

Another grin. "You guessed it. She's visiting her family and I thought I'd give it one last shot. I'm just damn glad I saw the sign for Midnight or we never would have met."

"You've changed your mind about her?"

"Yeah. It never would have lasted."

"So what's your girlfriend's name?"

"I don't really want to talk about her. That's over and done with."

Samantha knew to back off. Shrugging, she said, "No problem. So have you had a chance to check out the beaches around here? Alabama has some of the most beautiful beaches in the world."

"Not yet. It's still a little cool for me."

Before she could comment that Indiana weather was a heck of a lot cooler than it was here, he raised the bottle of wine beside him and said, "Ready for more?"

She shook her head. "No thanks."

As he topped his glass off, he said casually, "I heard that you and your sisters have a security agency."

Though she maintained her bland expression, her heartbeat picked up again. They'd skirted around the issue of jobs and careers. This question sounded innocuous enough but she was on alert.

"That's right," Samantha said. "We're still fairly new at it."

She and Savvy had talked about this scenario. They

had agreed that Samantha would be a wide-eyed, clue-less girl who was just playing at this security thing. If Blaine was Cruz's man and believed she was incompe-tent, he would be more likely to let his guard down. Of course, he would also discover at some point that she had been a cop. She was prepared for that, too.

"How did you get started in something like that?"

She shrugged. "Just seemed like an interesting thing to do. I saw this television documentary about all sorts of exciting stuff people got involved with. We're just going to try it for a few months to see how we like it. If it doesn't work out, no big deal."

"But I heard you were once a cop."

She scrunched her nose up and fluttered her hand in a dismissive gesture. "Yeah . . . well, that didn't work out, either."

Seeming satisfied with her vague answer, he said, "So what kind of cases does the Wildefire Agency handle?"

"Oh, you know . . . security issues and things like that." She shrugged. "We're just learning this stuff."

She hated to sound this clueless, but if she went into detail, he'd definitely know she had a few more brain cells than he expected.

"You haven't had any cases yet?"

Oh, he was definitely digging. She was wearing the wire Brody had loaned her and knew he and Savvy were listening to every word and nuance of the conversation.

"Not yet but we're hoping something will come our way soon." She grinned and added, "Midnight isn't ex-actly a hub of excitement, and since we've not done any advertising yet, I doubt anyone outside of town has even heard of us."

"Samantha, how are you?"

She'd been so focused on playing her role, Mary-Jo Deacon was at her table before she knew it. Smiling her greeting, Samantha was about to pretend she didn't know that Mary-Jo and Blaine already knew each other and was going to introduce them. Instead Blaine started talking to the woman as if they were the best of friends. The man really could put on the charm when he wanted.

Samantha was content to watch them converse, her eyes on Blaine. He really was a nice-looking, pleasant man. The bland, even-keeled kind of guy she had always felt comfortable dating. Quinn had been completely different from any man she'd ever met. It was no wonder she'd found him so fascinating.

A week had passed since she'd run into him. Midnight was a small enough town for her to know that he had left. She told herself she wasn't disappointed that he had given up so easily. She hadn't wanted him to stick around and try to see her again . . . she hadn't.

There was a lull in the conversation and Samantha looked up from her inattention to see that both Blaine and Mary-Jo were looking at her. Apparently one of them had said something and she was expected to respond.

With a silent furious curse at her carelessness, Samantha gave them her most winning smile. "I'm sorry, I was just noticing how lovely your blouse is, Mary-Jo. What were you saying?"

Mary-Jo laughed. "Thank you, Samantha. You always say the nicest things. I was just saying that I finally sold the Hartley place. I remember you once told me how much you loved that house."

Samantha's heart sank a little. Silly, but she had hoped to buy the place one day. Her inheritance was more than enough to purchase and renovate the house. Being too pragmatic, she had talked herself out of it numerous times. Since she lived in Atlanta, it had made no sense to buy a house hundreds of miles away. Still, there was a

strong tug to her heart at the loss. If she had been thinking clearly the last few months, she might have made the
purchase. She loved living with her sisters again, but
Savvy and Zach would soon be parents, and though the
mansion was large enough to accommodate several families, she knew there were times they'd appreciate having
the place to themselves. If the guesthouse hadn't been
destroyed, she and Bri would probably have moved into
it. A newly wedded couple needed privacy.

Hiding her disappointment behind a bright smile, she
said, "Congratulations on the big sale. Who are the
lucky owners?"

"The buyer asked to remain private for the time being."

Now, that was interesting. "The Hartley family didn't
change their stipulation, did they?"

"No, and the new owner agreed to it. It will remain a
single-family residence."

Dismissing it as an oddity but nothing more, Samantha nodded and smiled through the rest of the conversation.

When Mary-Jo finally returned to her own table,
Blaine gave Samantha a wide grin. "She's a talker."

Samantha laughed. "That she is."

"So this place she sold . . . you had your heart set on
it?"

"Not really. It was just one of those silly dreams I had
as a kid. Did you have fantasies like that? Things you
wanted but when you grew older or gained more experience, you realized they would never happen or weren't
rational?"

An odd, fleeting expression crossed Blaine's face, and
once again Samantha felt as if she saw behind the pleasant mask to a man with a multitude of secrets. An instant later, the amiable smile was firmly in place. But
now her suspicions had greatly increased. Could the

seemingly mild-mannered, uncomplicated Blaine Marshall be Armando Cruz's man after all?

MAGNOLIA SPRINGS, ALABAMA

"Then on June 6, Armando took me to Isis, a nightclub in downtown Miami. We'd never been there before. I didn't want to go. I had a bad headache, but as usual, he didn't care. We sat in the back, hidden from view, like we usually did. His regular goons, Dallas Bartow and Ray Slatterly, were with him. Armando was in a lousy mood, worse than usual. Ray got a call on his cellphone. The music was so loud it was impossible to hear the conversation, but the look on his face made it clear it was bad news. He muttered something to Armando. I picked up the words 'lost shipment' and 'went sour.' Whatever had happened, it infuriated Armando. He ordered everyone at the table to get up."

For at least two hours, Samantha had sat in the living room of the safe house, out of view of the camera, and listened in both horror and awe as Lauren detailed her two-year nightmare with Armando Cruz. The young woman had already admitted to being a naïve, starstruck girl who had been impressed with the man's wealth and influence. She said she soon regretted her association with him but unfortunately it was too late. What followed were two years of abuse, both physical and mental.

"Armando grabbed my arm and pulled me with him. We went into a room in the back of the club. Armando threw me into a chair and turned around to Ray."

Lauren's detailed account of the violent argument and then the gruesome murder of Ray Slatterly would turn any sane person's stomach. Slatterly had apparently botched a job he'd been in charge of, and based upon Lauren's eyewitness report, Cruz had spared the man nothing.

"When it was over, Armando was covered in blood. Then he . . ." Shuddering, Lauren closed her eyes and swallowed thickly. "That's all I can tell you about that one."

"You need a break?"

The deep voice came from the man behind the camera. Logan Wright had barely let Lauren out of his sight since he'd met her. Though the man was as close-mouthed and reserved as they came, the tic in his jaw and the blazing fury in his eyes each time Lauren described her life with Cruz told the tale. Logan was enamored of the beautiful, damaged woman.

Lauren shook her head. "Just some water, maybe."

Savvy, who was sitting a few feet from Samantha, sprang to her feet and filled a glass from the pitcher on the table and handed it to Lauren.

The woman nodded her thanks and sipped her water. Then, with a determined breath, she said, "Okay, I'm ready," and began another account of one of Cruz's many illegal activities.

The cellphone in Samantha's pocket vibrated and she pulled it discreetly out, not wanting to disturb the taping. A surge of panic jolted through her as Ian Mackenzie's name flashed on the screen. It had to be about Bri.

Getting up as slowly and calmly as possible, Samantha made a sweeping smile of apology to no one in particular as she exited the room. The last thing she wanted to do was alarm Savvy.

She waited till she was in the bathroom with the door closed before she answered. "Ian? What's wrong?"

"Have you talked to Brina?" The urgency in his voice told her she was right to be alarmed.

"No, what's happened?"

"I'll tell you what's happened. Your stubborn, foolish sister is in over her head."

"Dammit, Ian. What?"

"She's gone inside Cruz's domain."

"What do you mean?"

"I mean she's gone undercover."

Trying to control the fear zooming through her, Samantha said, "Tell me exactly what you know."

"We had an argument. I won't go into detail but she left me a note saying she had an informant she was meeting. The next thing I know, I get a text with the damn evasive message of 'I'm in. Don't try to contact me.' "

Shit, shit, shit. Bri hadn't pulled one of her crazy stunts in a long time. That could only mean one thing. The argument with Ian had scared her. Nothing could be done about that now. She just needed to figure out how she was going to make sure Bri didn't get herself killed. After listening to Lauren's horrific accounts, Samantha knew that was a definite possibility. Cruz didn't react well to people who betrayed him.

"This man is not someone to cross, Ian. Bri could be in a lot of danger."

"Believe me, I've heard enough about the man to know that. He's the most dangerous kind of maniac. He's got the power to do what he damn well wants and more than enough money to pay off as many people as he needs to look the other way."

"I'll call her and try to get her out of there."

"Good luck." He paused and then added, "Tell her I'm sorry, will you, Samantha? I shouldn't have pushed her."

"I will, Ian." She closed the phone and blew out a ragged breath. It was as she'd feared. Ian had probably tried to get her to commit and Bri had run like a terrified deer.

Samantha was about to hit her speed dial to make the

call when Savvy knocked on the door. "Sammie, are you in there?"

Pocketing the phone, Samantha hurriedly turned on the faucet for water noise and called out, "Yes, I'll be out in a minute."

"Hmm, could you make it faster than a minute?"

Despite her worry, Samantha laughed. Savvy's increased need to use the bathroom was so normal and safe. Sanity in the midst of madness.

Opening the door, she said, "Sorry, I got a call from an old friend. Didn't want to disturb anyone."

Savvy grinned as she hurriedly unzipped her pants. "No problem. Little Bit's just pressing on my bladder more than usual today."

Leaving the bathroom, Samantha headed outside to her car. She would keep Bri's reckless behavior from Savvy as long as possible. Her sister didn't need any additional worries. And as soon as she confirmed that Bri was okay, she was going to make sure her sister knew how wrong she was for putting them through the stress. She wasn't above using Savvy as a weapon of guilt. Keeping her sister safe was more important than her feelings.

The instant she slid behind the wheel of her car, Samantha pressed speed dial for Bri, who picked up on the first ring. "Hey, I was going to call you in a few minutes. You'll never guess what happened."

Bri sounded thrilled and so very proud of herself. So much so that Samantha could feel her anger deflate. That didn't lessen the worry, though. "You're in Cruz's camp?"

"How did you—" Bri blew out an angry breath. "Ian . . . I told him to stay out of it."

"He's worried about you. And so am I. How could you do this without talking to me first?"

"I didn't plan it, Sammie. My main contact here in

Miami told me that the police have a man working on the inside. So I went to the cops and made them an offer. I'm going in as the undercover cop's girlfriend."

"And what did you promise them?"

"I told them we had evidence that couldn't convict Cruz on its own but we could use it to back up anything they had. I told them as soon as they arrest him and make their case, I'd give them enough to bury the bastard."

"Bri, you're going to get yourself killed. The man is a monster. I've been listening to Lauren's tapings. He has no conscience or morals."

"Which is exactly why he needs to be stopped."

She played her best card. "Have you thought about what this is going to do to Savvy? She's going to be worried sick about you."

"And that's why you can't tell her."

"How am I going to keep it from her?"

"Tell her I'm digging for info. Just don't tell her I'm going undercover."

"And how do you think she'll feel if something happens to you?"

"It won't, Sammie. I'll be fine."

"What did you and Ian argue about?"

"Nothing." Even though she was almost a thousand miles away, Samantha knew her sister well enough to recognize the defensiveness in her tone.

"Bri, you can't keep putting yourself in danger every time you get scared."

"I'm not. I'm doing my job."

Talking her out of this was hopeless. Samantha had known that even before she'd made the call. She had just hoped that invoking Bri's worry about Savvy would have made a dent.

"So what's your plan?"

"I'm meeting with the undercover cop today. He's

going to give me the lowdown on what he knows so far."

"He's not going to resent you coming in?"

"I don't think so. He'd told his handler he would need a female undercover soon. Apparently he's made some good inroads with Cruz and is being invited to some social events. Cruz never goes anywhere without a woman and apparently wants the men around him to have female companions, too."

"Be careful. Okay?"

"I will. I'll call you as soon as I can and give you a briefing."

"Sounds good. I love you."

"Love you, too, Sammie. Don't worry. I'll be fine."

Her stomach churning with worry, Samantha ended the call and got out of the car. She would listen to more of Lauren's accounts and then she was going for a long, body-aching run. The need to get away from everything for a little while was almost overwhelming. Running was her favorite way to relieve stress. Another thing she'd had in common with Quinn. Cursing herself for bringing him into her already dire thoughts, Samantha entered the safe house, determined to get through the rest of the day without thinking about Quinn at all.

CHAPTER FIFTEEN

Quinn stood in front of his new home. For the first time in his memory, he actually felt as though he had one. His condo was nice but had never really felt like home. The house he'd briefly shared with Charlene had never been a comfortable fit for him, either. And she had been a neat freak. Leaving a pair of socks on the bathroom floor had usually brought out her screeching tendencies.

The house he'd grown up in had been just as uncomfortable. His parents had been so absorbed with impressing those around them, they hadn't had time to actually enjoy what they had. He'd learned long ago that a large house and many possessions did not make a home.

He had a lot of work ahead of him. No one had lived here in over five years. Fortunately, even though it was almost a century old, the house was well built. However, it needed painting, both inside and out, a new roof, updated plumbing, and a central air-conditioning unit. And since he could only get down here every few weeks, he wouldn't be able to supervise the renovations. He had someone in mind for that, but had no clue if she would be interested.

"What the hell are you doing here?"

Cursing softly, Quinn turned to face a perspiring and furious Sam. He hadn't meant for her to find out this way.

"I bought this place."

Her eyes narrowing, she stalked toward him. Quinn swallowed hard. Damn, she looked good. Locking his jaw, he ground his teeth together as he tried to control his body's reaction. Dressed in spandex shorts and a white University of Georgia T-shirt, her beautiful body glowed. The glistening moisture on her skin made him want to lay her down and lick her from head to foot. The memory of those long, elegant legs wrapped around him while she undulated beneath him shot fireworks through his blood.

Hungrily and warily, he watched her come closer. When she stopped inches from his face, Quinn inhaled her scent, a mixture of delicate perspiration and the subtle, lingering fragrance of Sam's favorite perfume. Ah hell, there went his control. The hard-on he'd been determined to prevent sprang to full-fledged life. Since there wasn't a damn thing he could do about that, he concentrated instead on keeping his hands to himself. From the way she was looking at him, she'd slug him if he tried anything.

"Dammit, Quinn, haven't you hurt me enough?"

Astonishment at her words pulled him out of his lustful thoughts. "What the hell are you talking about?"

"You knew I wanted this house. You don't even live in Midnight. Why else would you buy the place if it wasn't to hurt me?"

Quinn didn't know if he'd ever been this speechless. She thought he had bought this house to hurt her? When all he could think about was being close to her?

"Why would you think something like that?"

"I don't know. You tell me."

Now wasn't the time to tell her he'd bought the house so he'd have a place to stay when he came to see her. That he had hoped she might consider moving into it and overseeing the repairs.

But she needed an explanation and the only one he had that wouldn't make her go ballistic was "I bought it for us."

Alarm flared briefly, making the leaf green of her eyes blaze a brilliant emerald. "There is no 'us.'"

Closing the distance between them, he said quietly, "Are you sure, Sam?"

The alarm deepened and he knew she wanted to back away from him. He was damn proud of her that she didn't. Instead she raised her chin and glared. When he stepped even closer, her body went stiff as if poised for flight.

"What are you scared of, sweetheart?"

"I'm not scared."

He might have believed her if her voice hadn't been trembling. Lifting her chin with his finger, he gently traced the edge of her jaw. "Sam . . ." Lowering his head, he whispered a soft kiss across her lips. "Please . . . baby . . . I'm sorry I hurt you."

She moaned beneath his mouth and opened hers for a deeper connection. Though everything within him urged him to give her the soul-deep kiss he wanted, Quinn kept it as gentle and unthreatening as possible. He'd hurt her before, damned if he would do it again.

Pulling away slightly, he looked down, hoping to see acceptance and forgiveness. It wasn't there.

Samantha backed away, shaking her head. She couldn't believe she'd almost given in. Even now, just from that one kiss, she could feel her body softening, preparing itself for more. Her libido might be a traitor, but her mind and heart made the decisions for her. They told her to get the hell away from him.

"Go home, Quinn. There's nothing for you here."

"You're here, Sam," Quinn said quietly.

Unable to respond without falling apart, Samantha

turned around and took off running. She could feel Quinn's eyes on her until she disappeared from sight.

With every step, the anger and hurt grew. How could he do that? He had bought the house that she had always dreamed of owning.

She hadn't planned to run such a long distance tonight, but visiting the Hartley place before the new owners took possession had seemed like a good idea. One last goodbye before it belonged to someone else permanently. Never had she considered that it would belong to Quinn.

He had said he bought it for them. There was no them. And he had accused her of being afraid. She had denied it, but in her heart, she knew that to be the case. She couldn't take the risk. Not again.

Even though it was past dusk, Samantha had no problem following the road that led her home. She'd run this way hundreds of times before. And if it became too dark, she had a small flashlight she could use. But for now, she kept her pace steady as she headed farther away from the man who had crushed her heart once again.

The sound of a vehicle coming up behind her brought her out of her dismal thoughts. Automatically, she moved over to the shoulder. For an instant she wondered if it was Quinn, but when the speed didn't decrease, she relaxed and continued running. Even though it was now dark as pitch, both her clothes and her shoes were made of reflective material and she was completely off the road. She was perfectly safe.

Her mind returning to Quinn's outrageous behavior, Samantha didn't realize she was in danger until it was almost too late. An engine raced as the vehicle behind her sped up. Before she could wonder about that, she heard the sound of spinning gravel. The car had gone off the road, onto the shoulder. Without turning, she knew it was closing in, aiming right at her. Instinct born of survival had her leaping sideways into the bushes a half second before the car would have slammed into her body.

She landed on her side and then rolled, cursing as soft, exposed skin met a giant briar patch. In an instant, fury gave her a surge of adrenaline. Bouncing to her feet, she watched as the vehicle continued down the road at a high speed. Holy hell, had someone just tried to kill her?

"You're sure you're okay?"

"Are you sure you can't describe the car?"

With her mind still spinning from her tumble and her body aching from the multitude of bruises and scratches, Samantha nodded at Savvy's question and then shook her head for Zach's. Those were the best answers she could give right now.

She had called Zach on her cellphone and told him what happened. He'd told her to stay hidden in the bushes until he got to her. She knew what he was thinking. Whoever it had been might come back. To check and make sure she was okay or to finish the job? She didn't want to find out. Ordinarily she felt quite comfortable in a one-on-one confrontation. She knew how to defend herself. But she wasn't armed and she was bruised. It wouldn't have been a fair fight and she would have been on the losing end.

In the end, no one had returned to either check on her or finish the job.

When Zach arrived, he had insisted on taking her to the medical clinic. Samantha hadn't argued. She knew nothing was broken but she wanted to get cleaned up before her sister saw her.

Keeping the incident from Savvy would have been impossible. Samantha had scratches and bruises on her face and most of her body. It would take days for them to go away. While the on-call doctor had cleaned her up with antiseptic and given her a couple of stitches on her side where a sharp rock had dug deep, Zach had gone to tell Savvy.

The instant her sister had walked into the clinic and let out a cry when she saw her, Samantha had wanted to kill the bastard who'd almost run her down. If this incident caused harm to Savvy or her baby, someone was going to pay.

His expression grim, Zach paced back and forth in the small examination room. Savvy sat beside her, softly touching her hand and looking both worried and furious.

"And you're sure the driver came after you?" Zach said. "He didn't just not see you?"

Samantha shook her head. "I heard him speed up as he approached. I got as far onto the shoulder as I could. He would have had to deliberately go off the road."

"But who would do something like that, Sammie? Everyone in this town loves you."

"Not everyone, sis, but I don't know anyone who hates me enough to kill me."

"Maybe they didn't know it was you," Zach said. "Maybe it was some idiot who happened to see an opportunity to scare the hell out of a runner."

"Could be. But if there's someone like that in Midnight, then he or she is one sick bastard."

"Well, we all know this town has got more than its share of sick bastards," Savvy said.

Zach pulled up a plastic chair and sat across from her. "I know you're tired and hurting, but your memory will never be as fresh as it is right now. I want you to take me through what happened, step by step. Okay?"

Samantha nodded. She'd been on the other side of interrogations many times. Zach was right. Now, while it was still fresh, uncolored by conjecture and not dimmed by time, she needed to recall every impression.

Closing her eyes, she cleared her mind of everything and went back to the first time she'd heard the vehicle.

"I'm on Sweetwater, approaching the four-way stop at Bayside. It's gone from dusk to ink dark in seconds. I hear a vehicle coming up behind me. Even though I'm already on the shoulder, I move farther away from the road. I'm not worried. Both my clothes and shoes have reflectors on them. I've run this road hundreds of times. My mind veers away from that and I pay little attention until I hear the vehicle speed up."

"How far away were you from it when the speed increased?"

"Maybe thirty yards or so."

"How could you tell it was speeding up?"

"Because I heard the engine shift gears." She opened her eyes. "It had a small engine. It was a small car or truck, maybe a four- or six-cylinder. The driver gunned the engine."

Zach nodded. "That's good. Close your eyes again."

Eyes closed again, she said, "I'm wondering about the increased speed. That's when I realize he's right behind me. I move even farther onto the shoulder, a little worried that he hasn't seen me. I hear a crunching, crackling sound and know the tires are hitting the gravel on the shoulder. He's gone off the road. The lights are bright and I know he's right on me, aiming toward me. I throw myself sideways, land on my side, then roll into a briar patch. Damn, it hurts. I'm back up in an instant. He's already several yards down the highway."

"What kind of lights did the vehicle have?"

"The front lights were harsh . . . I'm sure they were on bright, so no way he didn't see me. The—" She stopped abruptly.

"What's wrong?" Zach asked.

Her eyes opened wide as she just realized something. "I can't believe I didn't notice. I couldn't really see him because he turned his lights off after that. I only knew he was moving away from me because I heard him."

"He was trying to keep you from being able to identify him," Savvy said.

"I guess so." Rubbing her right temple where a headache was setting up camp, Samantha asked, "Why would anyone deliberately try to run me down?"

"I heard Quinn Braddock is back in town."

Samantha's head jerked up at Zach's statement. "Yes, he is. I saw him. He bought the old Hartley place."

Savvy gasped in surprise but Samantha kept her gaze fixed on Zach. She didn't like the tone of his question or the look on his face.

"He didn't do this, Zach."

"Are you sure? He was almost arrested for the murder of his ex-wife. And they never found her killer. You rebuffed him when he came to see you. Did you argue again?"

Yes, they had argued, but that had nothing to do with her almost getting run over.

"It wasn't him," Samantha said again. Knowing Zach would want more than her assurance, she added, "Quinn has an Audi, a large one. Eight cylinders. It would have had no problem picking up speed in an instant. This was either a small car or truck, I'm sure of it."

"Half the residents of Midnight have either a small car or truck."

Samantha nodded. "I know."

"Do you think this could have anything to do with Cruz?" Savvy asked.

"I doubt it. What's the benefit of maiming or killing me? It wouldn't help them find Lauren."

"Maybe the guy saw it as a way to get your attention . . . threaten or scare you." Going all motherly, as she tended to do with those she loved, Savvy stood and held out her hand. "Let's get you home and into a hot bath. That'll ease the aches."

Refusing to allow her sister to help her up, Samantha slowly got to her feet. She winced . . . her entire body was already stiff. She was going to be sore tomorrow.

"I'll take you both home and then I'll go hunting. Unless you have some old enemies you don't know about, this person is new to the area. I know most of the vehicles in this town. If I see one I don't know . . ." He shrugged.

She knew what the shrug meant. It was way past a long shot that the vehicle would be found and the driver identified.

As she thanked the doctor and made her way out of the clinic, Samantha's tired mind whirled with a multitude of questions. Who would want to hurt her and why? Did this have something to do with Cruz? Or was it someone from her past who held a grudge? Contrary to what her sister believed, there had been more than a few people in school who hadn't liked her. Holding on to a grudge for that long seemed unlikely, but who else could it have been? Some kids on a joyride, scaring the crap out of a runner just for kicks? If so, she'd like the opportunity to have a chat with them and their parents.

As much as she was hurting, she did feel good about one thing. Even though a future with Quinn wasn't possible and he'd hurt her with his purchase of the house she'd always wanted, at least she could assure Zach that without a doubt this had nothing to do with Quinn Braddock.

CHAPTER SIXTEEN

Quinn's first night in his new home had been about as miserable as he'd ever had. He'd spent two nights stuck in a dank, dark cave in Iraq under heavy fire and it hadn't been as bad as last night.

He'd fucked up. Again. Instead of rashly buying this place, he should've talked to Sam about it. Maybe that was the reason he wasn't prone to impulsive behavior. Dumbass moves resulted in major regret. Now he had to fix it.

Dressed before dawn, Quinn stood on the small pier of the lake and watched the sunrise turn the water into a sparkling ripple of golden light. The color reminded him of Sam's hair and how it could glow like sunshine. Had she ever experienced daybreak here?

He turned away from the spectacular sight and headed to his car. Last night guilt had consumed him. The hurt in Sam's eyes, which he had once again caused, had pained him a hell of a lot more than when she had thought him a murderer. Today that guilt had coalesced into a half-assed plan. He would apologize again. Then what?

They needed to air their differences, get beyond this. Because if she thought they were over, she was wrong. They hadn't even started yet. He'd never been a quitter. And one thing he knew for sure, quitting with Sam was out of the question.

Quinn pulled up in front of Samantha's home. She should be up by now, though the thought of a warm, sleepy Sam was a definite turn-on. How many times had he woken her with slow, teasing kisses until she was groaning for more?

His hands clenched the steering wheel as he forced his body to ignore the image he'd just created. Showing up with a hungry look in his eyes didn't exactly scream long-term relationship. She'd probably kick his ass or use her gun on him.

He focused on the stately home before him. When he'd been here before, he'd been so intent on seeing her, he hadn't really paid that much attention to the mansion. And that's exactly what it was—a mansion. He wasn't an expert in history or architecture, but he'd guess it to be at least a century and a half old. The tree-lined drive and surrounding grounds were just as impressive.

Sam came from a wealthy family . . . something else he hadn't known.

In northern Virginia, where he'd been raised, calling ahead of time was considered polite and necessary. Dropping in on someone was crude and common. Since his parents had deemed him crude from the moment he put on his first football uniform, that suited him just fine.

His jaw set, his intent clear, Quinn pushed opened the car door and got out. The minute he set foot on the porch, Samantha or one of her sisters would probably tell him to leave. This time he would not be pushed away. He and Sam were going to have this discussion whether she wanted it or not.

He was on the third step when the door opened and Sam stood there. He continued moving forward even as he braced himself for her immediate rejection.

"I'm glad you're here."

His heart kicked up an optimistic beat. "You are?"

"Yes, I've been thinking and you're right, we do need to talk." She opened the door wider. "Come on in."

Almost in disbelief, Quinn took the rest of the steps two at a time. This had been way too easy. The moment he saw her face, everything he wanted to say flew out of his mind. "What the hell happened?"

She touched the vivid bruise and scarlet red scratches on her right cheek. "I took a bit of a tumble last night."

"How? What happened?"

A slender, elegant hand lifted as if it was no matter. But it did matter . . . it mattered a hell of a lot. Quinn fisted his hands at his side to keep from reaching for her. The thought of her being hurt, in any way, twisted his gut.

"Come on in. Savvy made some hot apple cider yesterday. Would you like some?"

Quinn stepped through the door. He was only vaguely aware of the massive foyer and elegant surroundings. His total focus was on the marks on her face. And from the stiff way she was holding her right arm, he had a feeling the scratches and bruises on her face were just a small part of her injuries.

"What I want is for you to tell me what happened."

She grimaced. "I fell. No biggie."

He recognized evasiveness when he saw it. Deciding to let it go for the time being, he asked, "Where are you hurt?"

"Just some bruises and scratches. Really . . . it's nothing." She turned and said, "Let's go into the parlor."

Quinn followed her past several rooms. Though he was mostly focused on the stiffness of her gait, he glanced at the rooms they passed and admired the warmth of their décor. Someone had taken pains to make each room warm and inviting. The instant they entered the parlor, he knew why she had brought him to this particular room. It was cool, elegant, and downright unwelcoming. This was his mother's kind of room. Little warmth but plenty of pretension. He would imagine this was where visitors who weren't really welcome were brought. Pain stabbed at his chest that Sam had lumped him into that group.

"Have a seat. You sure you wouldn't care for some refreshments? Perhaps some coffee or hot tea?"

And she was acting like the cool, polite hostess. The loose khaki pants and long-sleeved white T-shirt, along with her ponytail, were casual and totally incongruent with her chilly attitude.

He shook his head at her offer. What he wanted was to break the ice she seemed determined to surround herself with. The Sam he knew wasn't this cold, emotionless woman in front of him. She was sweet, at times innocent and shy. And so damn sexy. She was putting on a performance and he wanted it to stop.

Because of that, he was deliberately blunt. "Are you ready to stop acting like a child and talk to me?"

Fire flared in her eyes. She opened her mouth to say something, most likely a healthy, equally rude retort. As quickly as the fire had appeared, it evaporated. She nodded and said, "You're right. I've been avoiding talking to you." She waved her hand at an uncomfortable-looking, flower-patterned chair. "Please, have a seat."

Her icy politeness only fueled his determination to crack that frozen exterior. He sat down just to have that out of the way. As soon as he was seated, she took a chair across from him and said, "I apologize for my outburst yesterday. I know you didn't maliciously buy the Hartley place to hurt me."

"I'm glad you're smart enough to figure that out."

The only reaction was a slight tensing at her mouth. Then she continued with what he was sure she felt was the sophisticated way to end a relationship. "However, you having a home in Midnight makes no sense. There's nothing for you here."

"Oh, I don't know about that. I've met some very nice people here and the weather is quite pleasant. I anticipate that I'll be spending all of my holidays and vacations here."

Heat hit her eyes once again and elation surged through him. Sam's coolness was slowly but surely melting.

"Quinn . . . seriously, that makes no sense. Tell you what, I'll buy the place from you. That way you won't be out anything."

"I have a better idea. Why don't you live there? You can oversee the repairs for me."

Like a rocket, she zoomed to her feet, the icy demeanor gone in a flash. "You jerk. I'm not your damn employee."

Figuring she was getting close to detonation, Quinn swallowed his triumphant laugh. This was the Sam he wanted to see. "You misunderstood. You wouldn't be my employee, as I hadn't planned to pay you." He shrugged. "After all, you'd be living there for free."

Her entire body trembling with temper, she snapped, "No, I will not live there and oversee your repairs. You've used me enough."

"What the hell are you talking about?"

"Sex, Quinn, that's what I'm talking about."

Stunned, he could only stare at her for a few seconds. Finally able to put together a coherent sentence, he didn't bother to temper his words. "What the fucking hell are you talking about?"

"That last night with you. That's what I'm talking about. You screwed me."

Now as furious as she was, he shot to his feet and stalked over to her. "We had sex and if I'm not mistaken, you were satisfied more than once that night."

"Yes, congratulations. Your penis did its job. You, however, were an ass."

Myriad emotions hit him at once—anger at her accusation, frustration at the situation, and fury at himself because he knew there was truth in her words. Calling on the control he'd honed over the years, Quinn nodded. "You're right, I was. And I'm sorry."

She gasped slightly, apparently not expecting the admission. Looking temporarily disarmed, she opened her mouth as if to speak and then stopped. Her head shaking in denial, she backed away. "I can't do this, Quinn," she whispered. "Not again. We want different things."

"Tell me what you want, Sam. Please. Don't just assume I won't give it to you. Let's talk it out."

Samantha held herself still and stiff as emotions snarled and clawed like vicious angry beasts, threatening to erupt. She wanted to throw herself into Quinn's arms. She wanted to demand that he get out of her house and her life. She wanted to shout that she loved him. She wanted him to tell her he loved her. She wanted . . .

No, she couldn't do this. Telling him she wanted something permanent would be pointless. That was the one thing he'd made clear he didn't want. And going back with him in hopes he would change his mind? She couldn't put herself at risk. What if he decided a few months from now that it was over? Better to take the pain now than face devastation later.

"What I want, Quinn, is for you to leave. I'm sorry for what happened. We were both at fault. Let's just leave it there."

"Like hell." He pulled her into his arms, covered

her mouth with his, and spoke softly against her lips. "Sam . . . don't, baby. I don't want to lose you."

She had always considered herself strong willed, but the instant Quinn whispered those words, she went weak. Groaning her surrender, she plastered herself against his body and let him take control. His mouth, gentle, insistent, authoritative, and delicious, moved over hers as if he couldn't get enough. All worries washed away as she gave herself up to the wondrous feeling of being in Quinn's arms again. Why had she waited so long? This was what she wanted . . . what she would always want.

"Sammie . . . I'm sorry to interrupt."

Samantha didn't know who moved first. Suddenly she was out of Quinn's arms and looking at her sister, who stood at the door, looking paler than Samantha had seen her in years.

"Savvy, what's wrong?"

Stark panic and fear in her eyes, Savvy whispered, "I'm bleeding."

Before Samantha could react, Quinn was there. He gently scooped Savvy into his arms, put her on the couch, and propped her feet on a pillow. Samantha went to her knees beside the couch and held her sister's hand.

Quinn's voice was gentle but authoritative. "How far along are you, Savannah?"

"A little over three months."

"Have you had bleeding before?"

"Not this time."

"This time?"

Samantha lifted her eyes briefly and explained, "Ten years ago. She had trouble with her first pregnancy."

Quinn turned his gaze back to Savvy. "Can your ob-gyn meet us at the clinic?"

Savvy shook her head. "He's out of town. He's referred all his patients to the doctor at the clinic."

Nudging Samantha slightly, he lifted Savvy in his arms again. "Okay, that's where I'm taking you." With her sister in his arms, he shot a glance at Samantha. "Call her husband and have him meet us there."

Samantha nodded and dashed toward the kitchen, where she'd left her cellphone. Savvy couldn't lose this baby, she just couldn't. Not again.

CHAPTER SEVENTEEN

Quinn paced back and forth across the clinic's small, utilitarian waiting room. He had placed Savannah on a waiting gurney and given her care over to someone else. Being on the outside, waiting for word, was an unusual experience for him. One he didn't like. But this wasn't his hospital or clinic.

Savannah was inside the exam room and Sam was with her. He'd never seen Sam so scared. He didn't know the story behind the loss of Savannah's baby ten years ago, but apparently they were afraid the same thing would happen again. Women were much tougher than they looked, and he knew from experience the Wilde women could handle a lot. He just hoped to hell that this time they didn't have to. Having Savannah lose this baby would hurt Sam, and if there was one thing he wanted to make sure of, he didn't want Sam hurt. Ever again.

Quinn closed his eyes. The kiss . . . before Savannah had come to the door. It had felt so damn good, almost as if things were back on the right path. Now he didn't know. What he was sure of was that he wouldn't let her go again. Not without a fight.

A tall broad-shouldered man in khakis and a light blue shirt burst through the front door. The stark expression of fear on his face told Quinn his identity immediately. This was Zach Tanner, Savannah's husband.

Offering a silent nod of acknowledgment—introductions could come later—Quinn said, "She's in exam room one."

With a curt nod of thanks, Zach continued his run, going through the door and out of sight. The fear and urgency were understandable. If it had been Sam on that exam table, Quinn knew he would feel the same way.

Soft footsteps and then a slight hitching sigh caught his attention. Quinn stood, realizing Sam had come out of the room. "How is she?"

Tears flooded her eyes and Quinn immediately thought the worst. "The doctor said it was just a normal discharge . . . mild spotting. That many women have the same problem and go on to have healthy babies."

"He's right. I've seen it happen dozens of times." He frowned when he saw no relief in her expression. "What's wrong?"

"That's exactly what she was told the first time. She can't lose this baby, Quinn. It almost destroyed her before."

Unable to just stand there and not hold Sam, he went to her. Approaching her slowly, in case he'd misread their earlier kiss, he held out his hand to touch her shoulder. With a small sob, she flew toward him; Quinn opened his arms and enclosed her in a strong, steadying embrace. Her face was buried against his chest, her golden-blond hair gleamed like silken sunlight, and her soft, slender body pressed against his. Quinn knew there was no place on earth he'd rather be right now than here with Sam, giving her whatever comfort she needed.

Samantha savored the strength of Quinn's arms. He held her as if he didn't want to let her go, offering her everything she wanted and needed right now. What would she have done without him today? He had been a rock. Though she wasn't prone to panic, the fear on Savvy's face and the knowledge of what could happen once again had almost frozen her in terror. Quinn had been the calm, solid solution. He had taken charge.

Pulling slightly away, she smiled up at him, wanting him to know whatever happened between them, she would always be grateful for his strength. "Thank you, Quinn."

His smile self-deprecating, he shrugged. "I was glad to help, small though it was."

She shook her head. "It wasn't small. You were calm and rational. Savvy needed that and so did I."

Blue eyes roamed over her face as if drinking her in. She saw so much of the man right now, perhaps more than she ever had before. Quinn was usually so very controlled that he was almost impossible to read. But right now, his expression showed caring, affection, and perhaps something even stronger.

"I know this isn't the right time or place, but I have to say it again, Samantha. Give us another chance."

"I—"

His fingers touched her mouth to keep her from speaking. "Don't give me an answer right now. Let's do this. I've got three days left before I have to go back to Atlanta. I know your sister needs you and you'll have to be there for her, but let's spend time together."

Panic flared within her. If he tried to seduce her, she would cave, she knew that. That kiss today proved she had absolutely no willpower when it came to Quinn Braddock.

As if reading her thoughts, he said, "No physical expectations, I promise. Let's just get to know each other better."

How could she say no to that? How many times had she wanted him to just talk to her, tell her about his background, his past. Even if nothing came of this, she couldn't resist the temptation of learning more about this man.

"Okay." Biting her lip, she said something she sincerely

hoped she didn't regret. "Since I need to be at the house to watch over Savvy, why don't you stay with us? There's more than enough room."

The bright smile he gave her made her catch her breath. Quinn was often humorous and would occasionally laugh, but rarely did he smile. If she hadn't already been totally enamored of him, that smile would have sent her over the edge.

"I'd like that."

Before she could respond, a sound behind her had her pulling out of Quinn's arms and turning.

Zach stood at the entrance to the waiting room. "She's going to stay here a little while longer and then I'm going to take her home. Dr. Watson said he believes she's going to be fine but he wants her on complete bed rest until her OB comes back next week."

Samantha nodded. "That sounds like good advice. I'll wait on her hand and foot, Zach. Whatever Savvy needs, I'll be there for her."

"Thanks, Sammie. I've got a deputy out sick with a stomach bug, so I'm shorthanded. Maybe you should call Bri and see if she can come help out, too."

Yes, she had to call Bri and let her know what happened. Knowing her sister, she'd be on a plane to Mobile within the hour. As much as she would like to have Bri home and out of harm's way, she would tell her the truth. That getting the information to put Cruz away was important. Even though she didn't want her sister in danger, she trusted Bri. Samantha could take care of Savvy, but only Bri had access to Cruz to gather the needed information.

Glancing up at Quinn, she said, "I have to go home and get Savvy's room ready."

"I'll take you home and then go grab my things."

Looking mildly amused at what he must have surmised from Quinn's statement, Zach nodded. "I'll bring Savannah home as soon as she's released."

Quinn and Samantha went through the door together. Her mind on the many things she had to do to make sure Savvy had what she needed, she was getting into his car before she realized that they'd been holding hands since they'd left the clinic. Having her hand in his had felt as natural and easy as if they had been together forever.

Another wave of fear washed over her but she pushed hard against it. Fear had controlled too much of her life lately. She was being given the chance to get to know Quinn, something she hadn't thought she would ever have. No matter what happened after he left, she wanted to have this time with him. And if this turned out to be a mistake? Then she would just have to deal with the fallout.

"I feel like such a fraud."

"Why?"

"Because I feel fine."

Despite Savvy's brave words, Samantha knew the truth. Her sister might feel fine physically but the shadows in her eyes said something else. She was terrified. And though Zach had been the rock Savvy needed him to be, Samantha saw a man equally frightened. Couldn't they catch a break? After all they'd been through, Savvy and Zach deserved total happiness.

Tucking her blanket a little snugger over her sister's feet, she winked. "Well then, milk it for all it's worth. Once Little Bit arrives, you'll be wishing for these extra days of rest."

"Do you really think so?"

The question broke her heart. Savvy was so strong, one of the bravest people she knew. To have her ask that question showed how much reassurance she needed. Samantha was determined to give her all she could take.

"Absolutely." Leaning down so her sister could see the sincerity of her words, she said, "You will have this baby, Savvy, and it's going to be healthy and beautiful."

Smiling through her worried tears, Savvy added, "And totally spoiled."

"Beyond redemption. This kid will want for nothing. I can promise you that."

"Thanks, Sammie. You always make me feel better." Moving slightly to get more comfortable, she asked the question Samantha had been dreading, "Did you get in touch with Bri?"

"Yes, she wanted to come right away but I convinced her to stay."

"I'm glad. I'd hate to put the Wildefire Agency's work on hold. Keeping Lauren safe and getting that creep put away for life is our priority."

"True, but taking care of our sister comes before anything else." Before she could object, Samantha added, "I told her I could handle everything here. After all, the only thing I'm doing right now is keeping an eye on Blaine Marshall and looking for any more newcomers in Midnight. That doesn't take much time, especially when I can get the information with a meal at Faye's once a day."

"Speaking of newcomers, let's talk about Quinn."

"What about him?"

Savvy snorted inelegantly. "Don't give me that, Samantha Camille. I may have been upset earlier but I know what I interrupted. You guys were wrapped around each other like you couldn't get close enough."

Heat swept through her, and though she told herself it was a blush of embarrassment, she knew that wasn't true. Just the memory of Quinn's mouth on hers, his hard body pressed into her, his arousal seeking to fit itself into her softness, caused her entire body to flush with need.

A soft laugh brought her out of her lusty thoughts.

Knowing her face was probably beet red, she tried for a wide-eyed innocent "What?"

"Let's just say if Quinn were here right now and I wasn't, he'd be a very satisfied man."

Samantha shook her head, unsure once more. "Oh, Savvy, I don't know what I'm going to do."

"Remember what you used to tell me? Don't overanalyze. Just let it happen."

"I invited him to stay until he has to go back to Atlanta."

"That's wonderful!"

"He said he wanted us to get to know each other. Nothing physical . . . just talking."

"That sounds perfect, Sammie. Isn't that one of the problems you told me you guys had? That you never talked enough?"

"Yes . . . but . . ."

"But what?"

Samantha plucked at the blanket covering her sister, unable to look in her eyes as she confessed, "What if I fall in love with him even more?"

"Is that possible?"

"I don't know. Even when I only knew a few things about him, he could consume my thoughts like nothing else. If I discover he's even more wonderful than I think he is, I honestly don't think I can let him go."

"Maybe you don't have to."

Samantha stayed silent. How could she explain her fears without sounding like a wimp? Here Savvy was, her child in jeopardy, possibly her health, and she was trying to make Samantha feel better. Admitting what a coward she was in the face of her sister's strength was too embarrassing.

Standing, she unnecessarily tucked her sister's blanket even tighter. "Maybe . . . we'll see. Now, is there anything special you'd like for dinner?"

Her eyes blinking sleepily, Savvy shook her head. "Surprise me."

Considering her limited talents in the kitchen, Samantha figured any surprise she gave Savvy wouldn't be a good one.

Going to the door, she opened it and looked back at her sister. "Everything's going to be okay. Believe that. Okay?"

Her green eyes wise beyond her twenty-nine years, Savvy nodded. "I never thought I'd ever have Zach back, so I know miracles happen."

"And this will be another one. I promise."

"You're right, Sammie. Everything is going to be fine. I just have to believe."

Closing the door, Samantha leaned against it and fervently asked for that miracle. No one deserved it more.

"How is she?" Zach strode down the hallway toward her, worry etched on his face.

"She's falling asleep. Says she feels fine."

Zach pushed his fingers through his hair, something she figured he had done a lot in the last few hours. "I've asked Brody to come back and help out at the station until my deputy gets back on his feet. I need to be with Savannah."

"I know you do, Zach, but hovering over her might make her more nervous."

"You're right. I'll do my best not to." He shrugged. "I just feel so damn helpless."

So did she.

She moved away from the door, toward the stairway. "Why don't you go sit with her? I'm going to see what I can find to fix for dinner."

"Don't worry about that. I called your aunt Gibby.

She's already got Faye fixing up a load of food for us. All we have to do is throw it in the microwave."

Samantha blew out a relieved sigh. Not just because she wouldn't have to cook, but also because when Zach had mentioned Gibby, she'd feared that meant her aunt would be cooking a meal for them. She adored her aunt, but one thing Gibby could not do was cook. Somehow, though, she had never caught on that people hated her cooking.

"I can go pick it up at Faye's."

The doorbell rang and Samantha tensed. That was probably Quinn. Now that the time had come, she was both eager and fearful of having him stay here.

"You want me to get the door?" Zach asked.

She shook herself from her stupor. The last thing they needed in this house was more drama. Whatever happened between her and Quinn, she didn't intend to involve anyone else.

"I'll get it. It's probably Quinn. He's staying here for a couple of days."

Behind the worry, she saw a glint of humor in his eyes. "Then I'll let you answer the door."

"We'll go get dinner and be back in a few minutes."

Zach nodded and opened the door to Savvy's room.

As Samantha headed downstairs, she lectured herself. Just because he would be here for a few days didn't mean anything. They were going to talk, nothing more.

Vanity made her stop in the half bath just off the hallway. When she saw the pale woman with the wild hair and worry-filled eyes, she grimaced at her and walked away. It would take more time than she had to repair her appearance. Besides, Quinn had seen her many times without makeup.

A smile fixed on her face, she opened the door and then pulled back slightly. She hadn't expected Blaine Marshall to be on the other side of it.

CHAPTER EIGHTEEN

His smile holding a touch of uncertainty and almost shyness, he held out a colorful bouquet of fall flowers. "Sorry to just drop in on you like this. I heard about your accident and then when you didn't answer my calls, I got worried."

"How did you know about my accident?"

"I had breakfast at Faye's this morning. Merriam, the clinic's receptionist, mentioned you were at the clinic last night, and then one of the deputies—I can't remember his name—said someone tried to run you over."

Nothing was private in this town. "I'm fine. Just a few scrapes and bruises. And I wouldn't say someone tried to run me over. That's a bit of an exaggeration. I was jogging at night and the driver didn't see me."

"That's a relief, then. So everything's okay? When you didn't answer your phone, I got worried."

He wanted her to invite him in and wasn't being all that subtle about it, either. His gaze darted around, as if he were trying to see inside the house. She didn't want him here. With Savvy's problems and Quinn on the way over, the last thing she wanted was to have a visitor.

Still, their curious discussion the other night about Florida had raised red flags that required further investigation. Both Savvy and Brody, who had heard the conversation, had agreed there had been something suspicious in his voice. So until she knew, one way or the other, about Blaine's possible connection to Cruz, she needed to maintain some semblance of interest.

She smiled her appreciation at his concern. "Everything's fine. I left my cellphone in my car. Didn't even know you had called." At least that much was true.

"I guess, after your accident, you wouldn't feel like going to dinner and a movie tonight?"

He looked so hopeful and lonely, Samantha felt guilty. Even though she didn't trust the guy, she almost felt sorry for him. She grimaced an apology. "I'm still a little sore from my fall last night. Maybe I could take a rain check."

"I understand. I—" He broke off at the sound of a car coming down the drive toward the house.

Samantha held back a sigh. Now she would have to explain each man to the other.

Blaine watched as Quinn's black Audi pulled up and parked beside his older model Toyota. "Looks like you have company."

"He's a . . . friend . . . staying here for a few days."

Turning back to her, he nodded. "I heard rumors. Guess they were true."

"What kind of rumors?"

"That you'd recently broken up with someone. Looks like that didn't stick."

The Wilde family was no stranger to being the subject of Midnight's gossipers. In earlier days, Samantha had purposely fed those voracious rumormongers. Focused on her, they had left Savvy and Bri alone. Of the three of them, she had felt better equipped to handle the maliciousness that had followed their parents' deaths. But that was years ago and she was long past willing to feed those particular vultures.

"Midnight is full of lies and half-truths. Beware of what you hear."

Her words were sharper than intended and she immediately regretted them. Alienating this man was certainly not the right way to go about gaining his trust.

Oddly he didn't seem put off by her blunt statement. "Someone as beautiful as you being unattached was too good to be true anyway."

With Quinn stepping up on the porch, it wasn't a good time to try to explain anything. She sniffed the flowers appreciatively. "Thank you for the flowers, Blaine. Savvy's not feeling well, so it'll be a few days before I can go out, but I would like to see you again."

Surprise and something else flickered in his eyes. She had a feeling he would be looking for more than just some mild flirting the next time she saw him. She mentally shrugged. She'd deal with that when she had to.

"I guess I'd better go."

"We'll talk soon. Okay?"

Nodding, he turned away and gave Quinn an awkward smile as he passed him.

Quinn barely glanced his way, his blue eyes glittering dangerously. She'd seen him this furious only once before. Her entire body tensed up. Was he upset about Blaine?

As he stopped in front of her, his voice was quiet but held a seething fury. "Why didn't you tell me someone almost ran you down last night?"

More than aware of Blaine sitting in his car, staring at them, Samantha backed up and motioned for him to come inside. The instant the door was closed, she said, "Midnight's gossipers at it again?"

"No, your brother-in-law told me. He's concerned and so am I."

Surprised that the usually closemouthed Zach would reveal that, she said, "When did you talk to Zach?"

"He called to thank me for my help earlier. He said since he was taking a few days off, he thought it'd be a good idea if I knew about the incident so I could keep an eye on you."

She frowned. "I don't need anyone keeping an eye on me. I can take care of myself."

"Apparently not, since you were almost killed last night."

With a huff of exasperation, Samantha turned away. "I'm going to the kitchen for a vase. If you want to stand here and act like a jerk, feel free, but I don't intend to stay around and watch."

Quinn clenched his jaw till his teeth hurt. Behaving like an ass with Sam had apparently become an epidemic with him. Learning what had almost happened to her had brought out all of his protective tendencies. Unfortunately it had also turned him into a caveman. Instead of talking with her about the incident like an adult, all he'd been able to focus on was what could have happened and how it would have been his fault.

Only minutes after learning he had bought the Hartley property, a place he knew she loved, she had almost been run over . . . could have been killed. Their argument had likely distracted her. He shouldn't have let her leave like that. He'd known she was upset. It had been getting dark and she had been at least five miles from her home. The thought of anything happening to Sam twisted his insides.

The instant she returned, Quinn moved slowly toward her. More than anything, he wanted to touch and pet her, reassure himself she was truly okay. Since he figured he'd get a well-deserved put-down, if not more, he settled for what he hoped was a halfway decent smile and an apology. "I'm sorry, Sam. Can we start all over?"

"Gladly."

That had always been one of the things he'd liked most about this woman. Even when she was angry, she didn't hold a grudge.

"If I promise not to turn into a jerk again, will you tell me what happened?"

"I'll tell you on the way to pick up dinner. Faye's putting together a takeout order for us." She looked at the duffel bag he'd dropped at the door. "You want me to show you to your room first so you can drop that off?"

"It'll be fine there till we get back. How's your sister?"

"Resting."

Quinn nodded. "Best thing for her." As they walked out onto the porch, Quinn nodded at his Audi. "We can take my car."

She was silent until they were both in the car and then turned to him with a teasing grin. "You know if you walk into Faye's with me, you'll start up a whole new slew of rumors. Are you ready to be the talk of the town?"

She had been joking but his reply was as serious and honest as he could get. "More than I would have ever thought possible."

It wasn't until much later that Samantha and Quinn had the chance to talk. On the way to Faye's, he had gotten a call on his cellphone that had put him in a grim, silent mood. She hadn't been able to avoid listening, not that it had done her any good. The conversation had been one-sided, with Quinn giving short yes-and-no answers. After he'd ended the call, she had asked if everything was okay and had barely gotten a grim nod.

She had assumed he would remain that way the rest of the evening, but after they left Faye's with a boxload of food and dozens of good wishes for Savannah, the austere expression had been replaced with something else. In fact, he had looked almost jovial. For Quinn, who could make stoicism seem cheerful, that was something.

Dinner was surprisingly upbeat. Since Savvy couldn't leave her bed, Zach took dinner up to their room and they shared a cozy meal together. Samantha and Quinn sat in the kitchen, enjoying Faye's incredible chicken and dumplings, and talked about everything but serious things. A discussion of weather, football, and favorite holiday dishes was a welcome relief from the tension of the last couple of days.

When the subject of the Hartley place came up, she was thrilled that he asked her opinion on painting and decorating the interior. Closing her eyes, she pictured the house as she remembered it and gave him ideas for each room. When she opened her eyes again, she was surprised and touched that Quinn had jotted her ideas onto a napkin.

"The house will need a lot more than a coat of paint on the walls, though," she said.

"Yeah. In fact, when I talked to your brother-in-law earlier, I asked him for contractor recommendations. He suggested a company who specializes in renovations."

Samantha nodded. "He's a good person to ask. Before he became police chief, that's what he did."

Folding up the paper napkin of notes, Quinn tucked it into his shirt pocket. "So, the guy with the flowers . . . who was he?"

She was surprised it had taken him this long to ask. With anyone else, she would have been evasive, but there was no reason to be that way with Quinn. She trusted him to keep what she told him in the strictest of confidence.

"His name is Blaine Marshall and I'm investigating him."

"I heard that you and your sisters have opened a security agency. Is this one of your cases?"

"Yes, our only case, actually. We've barely scratched the surface of creating the agency. Bri and I went to Birmingham a few weeks ago and did some specialized weapons and tactical training. We'd just gotten back when we got this case."

"Can you talk about it?"

"There's not much to say. We're protecting a young woman who is being sought by a drug lord. She believes he'll send someone after her. Blaine is the only newcomer to Midnight in the last couple of weeks."

"And you suspect he might be the man who's after your client?"

"Possibly. He seems like a nice enough guy but I can tell he's keeping secrets. Whether they have anything to do with our client remains to be seen."

"We all have secrets."

"Some more than others."

"You said Marshall was the only newcomer to Midnight. Have you forgotten about me?"

"Absolutely not, but I trust you."

"Do you?"

"Yes." And then because they both needed to hear her say it, she added, "I'll never doubt you again, Quinn. I promise."

His gaze locked with hers for several long seconds, and then he breathed out a ragged breath. "You have any idea how much I want to kiss you right now?"

She wanted that, too, but that's where they'd gone wrong before. "Me too, but—"

"I know . . . I know." He stood and went to the coffeemaker. "Want more coffee?"

She shook her head. "It'll keep me awake and I didn't sleep all that well last night."

"Because of your accident? Or was it an accident? You think someone deliberately tried to run you down?"

"The more I think about it, the less convinced I am that someone wanted to hurt or kill me. Just makes no sense." She shrugged slightly. "It was probably just some kids who let a prank go too far."

"You piss anyone off lately?"

She grinned. "Just you."

"Yeah, but when you piss me off, I don't want to run you down with my car."

"What do you want to do?"

Heat returned to his eyes again. "If I tell you that, we'll be getting back into dangerous territory."

With just one look and those words, arousal flooded through her. From the moment they'd met, this incredible chemistry had been between them. Unfortunately it had also been their downfall. Instead of learning about each other, they'd learned what pleased each other physically. Important, yes, but not as important as sharing the information that revealed their true selves.

The decision to steer the conversation in another direction wasn't easy but was infinitely smarter and safer.

"Why do you never talk about your parents?"

Black brows furrowed in a grimace. "Hell, that was a hundred-eighty-degree turn of a pleasant conversation."

"I thought that was the purpose of us being together. Getting to know each other."

"You're right, it is. Still doesn't make it an enjoyable topic."

"I know they live in Virginia. Right?"

"As far as I know."

"You don't talk to them?"

"No. My mother called me out of the blue about nine months ago. First time I'd talked to her in years. Conversation was a stilted, one-sided mess. She asked about Charlene and I told her we'd divorced. She did the obligatory 'I told you so,' said my father was fine, and that was it."

"Your parents didn't like Charlene?"

"They never met her. But if they had, no, they wouldn't have liked her. My parents had certain ideas about who their sons should associate with—Charlene definitely wouldn't have been on their approved list. Besides, not many people liked Charlene, unless she was sleeping with them. Even then, I doubt that any of her lovers actually liked her."

"Tell me more about your parents. What are their names? Are they retired? What did they do for a living?"

The grim set to his mouth told her he didn't want to talk about them.

"Please, Quinn. I need more."

"Edward and Geneva Braddock. My father's family is in banking. My mother's job is to help my father succeed. They had little time for their children."

"Your family is Braddock Bank and Trust?"

"You've heard of them?"

"They have a couple of branches in Atlanta. You didn't know that?"

"No. Banking is their business, not mine."

"I'm so sorry about your brother. That must have been an excruciating time for your entire family."

He lifted a shoulder in a shrug. "Suicide is never pleasant but Dalton's life was over years before he took his life."

His answer was short and blunt, understandably so. Dead loved ones always left victims behind. And suicide could be the most hurtful.

As if remembering their promise to open up more, he went on. "My brother was barely a teenager when he was institutionalized. When he was seventeen, he apparently decided he'd had enough. I think my parents were relieved."

Horrified, she said, "Why? What did they do?"

"They held a memorial service and went on with their lives."

"You don't think they grieved?"

"With anyone else, I might say yes. But I knew them too well. When they were out of sight of the public, their concern was about their reputation and how to protect it. So, no. I don't think they grieved . . . at least not like normal people."

She shivered at their coldness. "No wonder you don't talk to them often. And they didn't come to your wedding?"

His mouth twisted with a grimace. "We eloped. Charlene's only family was an older brother she hadn't seen in years. And inviting my parents to our wedding would have been hypocritical. They probably wouldn't have come anyway."

"From what I know about Charlene, she seems so different from you. Why did you marry her?"

Another grimace. "Stupidity. Met her at a party. I'd been focused on my career, not having a social life. She latched onto me like I was some kind of rock star." His smile was a mixture of embarrassment and self-deprecation. "She was beautiful. And even though I was old enough to know better, I reacted with all the sophistication of a sex-starved, awestruck kid."

"Yet you stayed married to her for three years?"

"I'd never given up on anything in my life. Stupid thing is, I knew within a few months I'd made a mistake. She turned from a witty, exciting woman into a manipulative shrew.

"I was working eighteen-hour days; she was bored. I told her to get a job or a hobby. At first I was too busy to notice. Then one night I came home, she was in the bathroom. I made the mistake of surprising her in the shower. I saw her body . . . thought she'd been raped."

"Why?"

"She had bruises, welts, and bite marks all over her."

"She hadn't been raped?"

"No. She confessed that she had cheated on me. Swore it was just the one time. Said she liked the kind of pain the guy gave her." He shook his head. "I think the only reason she told me was because she hoped I'd give her the same kind of treatment."

It took a lot to shock her anymore but the thought of a woman or anyone wanting to be physically hurt for pleasure amazed her. Sure, she knew enough about BDSM to realize it got rough sometimes, but this sounded more extreme than that.

"What did you do?"

"I told her 'Hell no,' of course. The thought of doing something like that disgusted me. I already knew the marriage was over, but she begged for another chance. We talked about going to counseling but I knew I was going to leave. I went to see a friend of mine . . . my old college roommate. I knew he had a condo he'd been trying to sell. Thought I'd buy it."

Gut instinct told her what happened next. Still, she asked, "What happened?"

"The receptionist wasn't at her desk. I figured Nate wasn't there, either. I was about to walk out when I heard sounds coming from his office. I stuck my head inside. Nate and Charlene were on his couch together."

"What did you do?"

"I stood in the doorway and laughed at them." He gave a dry, cynical chuckle. "You'll never know how relieved I was."

Quinn was the most controlled person she knew, but anyone, no matter how controlled, would be furious at the scenario he'd just described. If she had known about this before, would it have prevented her thinking he had murdered Charlene?

"After I told her I was divorcing her, she confessed to all the other affairs she'd had. Apparently they started a few months after our marriage. I told her to get a hobby . . ." He shrugged. "She did."

"How on earth did you keep from knocking the hell

out of her?" The words were out of her mouth before she could stop them.

He looked at her then, the pain she had dealt him in his eyes. "I don't hurt women, Samantha."

"I wish you had told me about her earlier. I wouldn't have—" She stopped again. She was making this worse.

"I didn't know I needed to explain that I don't hurt or kill women for you to trust me."

"I screwed up, Quinn. I'm so sorry."

He stood and went to the sink to pour out his cold coffee.

Samantha watched him. There were so many things she wanted to say, ways she wanted to show him how sorry she was for not trusting him. Instead she stayed silent.

"It's getting late. I think I'll go on to bed." He headed out of the kitchen and then surprised her when he stopped at the door and said, "I said I don't hurt women. That last night . . . I hurt you, Sam. I was rough with you. I'm very sorry about that."

Before she could respond, he was gone.

Her chest ached. She had hurt him so very badly, and instead of holding it against her, he wanted to give them another chance. And even though it scared the hell out of her, she wanted that, too.

But where were they headed? Back to what they had been before, or had this opened a new door for them? He had admitted early on that he didn't want anything permanent, but the actions he'd taken—coming to Midnight, buying a house here. Didn't that mean he wanted more than what they'd had before? Something permanent?

She was going to do it—she had to give them another chance. She loved him . . . wanted a future with him. And his actions proved his feelings for her were strong. Staying-power strong? She would soon see.

CHAPTER NINETEEN

Quinn stood at the window of the guest bedroom. Darkness outside prevented him from seeing anything but the reflection of a grim-faced man. A man whose career was officially in the toilet. Of all the turns he had imagined his life taking, this hadn't been one of them. Since Charlene's murder, rumors had run rampant throughout the hospital. Everyone, even the people he'd worked with for years, had started looking at him differently. Ignoring them hadn't stopped the talk. The hospital board had claimed they were behind him, but they had caved to pressure. They hadn't said the words but he had no problems reading between the lines. They wanted him out.

The court of public opinion didn't give a damn about charges being dropped and witness testimony. Suspicion had been cast, and until Charlene's murderer was caught, he was still a suspect in their eyes.

In one of her last temper tantrums, Charlene had told him that she'd give anything if she could ruin him. Little had she known that that's exactly what she would do.

He had agreed to come back to Atlanta and discuss his future. As much as it galled him to give up what he'd worked over a decade for, he knew what his decision would be.

He hadn't mentioned anything to Sam yet. What was

the point until he had figured out where he went from here?

The knock on his door had him turning in an instant. Sam stuck her head inside the room. "Do you have everything you need?"

He told himself to honor their agreement—nothing physical. But with her only a few feet from him, looking so damned sweet and sexy, it took every bit of will-power to stay at the window and say, "Yeah, thanks."

"There're more blankets in the bottom drawer of the chest, if you get chilly."

"I'll be fine."

"If you get too warm, you can lift the window. It gets stuck sometimes, so you may have to tug on it a little."

Her anxious expression reminded him of their first night together. She'd been nervous and had needed reas-surance. He was known for his patience and never had he been more rewarded for it than that first night with her.

"And there should be plenty of towels in the bath-room, too."

Quinn fought a smile. She didn't want to leave either but they'd made the damn pact. "Sam, do you want to kiss me?"

When she blushed and then nodded, Quinn willed himself to stay put. "But we agreed to nothing physi-cal."

"I know . . . it's just . . ."

"How about I meet you halfway?"

He was surprised and pleased that instead of hesitat-ing or saying no, she was in the middle of the room al-most as soon as he got the words out. Quinn wasted no time, either. With a groan, he reached for her. He should be going slower, easier . . . less urgently. But he'd waited too long for this kiss.

Standing on her toes, Sam wrapped her arms tight

around his shoulders. Quinn plastered his body against hers and moved his mouth gently, thoroughly, over her sweet, luscious lips. He tasted passion and surrender. Though he was hot, hard, and aching, he made no move to take it further than the kiss. Hell yeah, he was hurting. Everything within him told him to pull her down onto the bed behind him and thrust hard and deep into the sweet heat that waited for him. But he couldn't. This was too important, she was too important.

They broke away from each other, gently, reluctantly. Quinn saw what he wanted to see in her eyes. Desire, need, and sexy, sweet submission. He'd seen that look many times in the past. And in the past, he had fulfilled everything she'd asked for. Tonight was different. He wanted more than her acquiescence.

"Go now, before we change our minds."

Her sigh one of resignation and regret, she backed away from him. "Good night."

"Sleep tight."

"You too."

As she opened the door, he said, "Anytime you want to end our pact, I'm game."

With a smile full of promise and something more, she blew him a kiss. "I'll keep that in mind."

The door closed on his abrupt bark of laughter. How the hell had he gone all these months without that smile?

Samantha sat in the sunroom, sipping coffee and enjoying freshly baked blueberry muffins brought over by Logan Wright. Brody was with Lauren. Logan had said he wanted to give his report to Samantha in person, but she strongly suspected he needed to get some distance from their client. Didn't take a psychic to see that Lauren and her experiences had deeply affected the stern, reserved Logan.

After waking from the best sleep she'd had in months, she had come to the kitchen for coffee and found a note on the counter from Quinn.

Went for a run. Wish I were running with you. Q

That had made her smile. She and Quinn had only run together a few times, but she'd loved it. Even though she was in good shape, when compared to Quinn's strength and stamina, she was definitely at a disadvantage. That hadn't mattered, though. He'd never pushed her to do more than she wanted.

Savvy was still asleep and Zach was doing paperwork in the study. Samantha had been prepared to enjoy a lone cup of coffee and had been seriously arguing with herself that the chocolate cake on the counter would make a halfway decent breakfast. Seconds later Logan had shown up with a basket of muffins, resolving the argument.

"The good news is," Logan was saying, "we've got everything recorded—all of Lauren's recounting of Cruz's twisted, fucked-up deeds. Bad news is, we've got nothing to back it up."

Logan wasn't one to sugarcoat anything. When she and her sisters had made the decision to form their own agency, they had relied heavily on the advice and support from both Logan and Brody.

Samantha had always thought the men made an interesting partnership. Both had served with Zach in the army and had moved south after they left the service. Their security agency was thriving in Mobile. She wondered if the differences in their personalities helped with their success. Brody had a tendency toward optimism. Not that one would ever call him lighthearted, but when compared with Logan and his brooding demeanor, Brody might be considered positively jolly.

"Is Lauren getting stir-crazy in the safe house?"

An interesting light brightened Logan's forest green eyes. "She's turned into a domestic diva. I swear I've packed on five pounds since I got here."

Considering the man's six-foot-five frame and rock-solid muscles, five pounds wouldn't show. It was nice to see a lighter side of Logan, though. She'd often wondered if his experiences in the war were what had made him so dark or if he had been like that before.

"Is it going to be a problem for you staying with her full-time?"

"No. Zach needs Brody's help. We've got everything covered back at our office, so until this thing's over or you guys don't need us anymore, we're here for the duration."

"And that's the biggie. We don't know how long this thing is going to last."

"Have you heard from Bri?"

Samantha shook her head. With Bri going undercover, she had known she wouldn't, but that didn't lessen the worry. Especially since Savvy had asked about her a couple of times already.

"Your sister's a smart girl. She won't do anything stupid."

"I know she won't, but combined with Savvy's health problems, I'm feeling just a little anxious." Samantha shrugged. "Our only option is to maintain status quo until we hear from Bri. If the police can get what they need to arrest him, Lauren's testimony should be phenomenally helpful."

"And you're still keeping an ear to the ground on newcomers?"

She grimaced. Compared with what Bri was doing, it seemed insignificant, but she knew it wasn't. As long as Lauren stayed hidden, anyone who came to Midnight would have to show themselves to search for her. And

Midnight's gossipers would be all over it. Who knew that the people who had irritated her for years as nosy busybodies might end up saving a life and much more?

"Yes, I'm going to Faye's at least once a day and I'm getting my hair done at Tillie's tomorrow."

His mouth lifted in a slight smirk. "That's tough work."

"I'll trade you."

"No thanks." He tugged on a hank of shoulder-length ink-black hair. "I promised myself that once I left the army I'd never have to put up with the sound of an electric razor again. That's one promise I kept."

Which brought to mind what promises he hadn't kept. She knew not to ask.

"What about that Marshall character? Anything new on him?"

"Not yet. He came by yesterday and seemed awfully interested in getting inside the house." She shook her head. "Could be my own paranoia at work and he just wanted to see the inside of the mansion."

"Brody told me he followed the guy around a couple of times, just to see what he was up to. Said the man didn't do anything more than eat a couple of times at Faye's and go to the library."

"That's the problem with Blaine. He seems like a nice, decent guy but then he says something that gets me suspicious. Like the way he reacted to my questions about Florida." She shrugged. "And yet, his explanation might well be the truth."

A glint of humor hit Logan's eyes. "If he is just a mild-mannered accountant, he'd probably get a kick out of being considered a hit man for a drug lord."

Samantha laughed. "Maybe I can tell him someday."

Logan got to his feet. "I'll head back over to the safe house so Brody can get back to help Zach. I probably won't be back for a while. Call if anything changes."

Walking Logan to the door, she nodded. "Will do."

As Logan's truck traveled down the drive, she was pleased to see Quinn striding toward her. He gave a cursory glance at Logan and then moved his gaze to where she stood at the door.

She took in his appearance and could only imagine the heart palpitations that had occurred in town. Dressed in black running shorts and a black T-shirt, Quinn could make even the most committed woman stand up and take notice. Samantha knew she would never be immune. His long, muscular legs ate up the distance between them, and with each step, her heartbeat picked up speed. She had gone to bed thinking of that delicious goodnight kiss they'd shared and wishing she'd had the courage to ask for more.

He stopped at the steps to the porch. "Morning."

To keep herself from running down the steps and throwing herself into his arms, she gripped the door hard. "Did you run through downtown?"

He stepped up onto the porch. "Went to check on the house and then came back through downtown."

"That's at least twelve miles."

"Had a lot to think over."

He stopped inches in front of her. As he gazed down at her, what he wanted was reflected in his eyes. But she knew he also wanted her to make the first move.

Samantha leaned forward and softly kissed his unsmiling mouth. "Good morning."

"How are you feeling? Still sore?"

His words were the exact ones he'd asked her the day Charlene was killed. He had promised her an all-over body rub and never had the chance to fulfill that promise.

Knowing that if she mentioned that day, it would spoil this still fragile and new beginning, she said instead, "Not as bad as yesterday. Maybe we can run together tomorrow."

"Can't. I'm leaving tomorrow."

Her good spirits took a nosedive. "I thought you were staying a couple more days."

"I need to get back and take care of some business."

She told herself not to be surprised or disappointed. He now owned a house here in Midnight. He would be back. Hadn't he said he would be spending holidays here? Thanksgiving was a little more than two weeks away.

"Don't look like that, Sam." Surprising her, his fingers trailed down her face in a tender caress. "I have to do this."

"When will you be back?"

"As soon as I can."

She nodded and straightened her wobbly legs. Okay, that was good enough for her. "How about some breakfast?"

"Faye's?"

"Yes. I need to get my daily dose of Midnight news."

"Give me ten minutes to shower and change."

"I'll go check and see if Savvy needs anything."

As they went up the stairs together, she watched Quinn out of the corner of her eye. He had something on his mind. He didn't seem grim or sad . . . actually he appeared almost peaceful. She wanted to ask him but she resisted. Rebuilding their relationship meant trusting him. He would tell her in his own time.

CHAPTER TWENTY

The instant Quinn and Sam entered the diner, the busy, noisy restaurant went silent. This was how it had been every time he walked in. He and Sam headed to a booth close to the back. On their way, she received several cordial greetings while Quinn received nods and even a couple of glares.

As they settled into their booth, Quinn sent a halfway-amused, halfway-irritated glance around the restaurant. "I always seem to cause an explosion of silence when I walk in here."

"That's because you're a tall, dark, handsome stranger."

He grinned. "So if I were short, pale, and ugly, they'd accept me better?"

She laughed and shook her head. "No, but they might not be as interested. Midnight has a stringent screening process for newcomers. Once they've gotten the lowdown on everything about you, they'll either decide you're all right or . . ."

"Or what?"

She shrugged. "Or you'll be a visitor forever."

"No matter how long I stay?"

"Midnight residents are friendly but wary. Just don't piss them off and you'll fit in fine."

He tilted his head toward the tall, broad woman behind the counter.

"What's her story?"

"Now, Faye is someone they accepted without knowing her secrets. No one knows more than she's willing to share. This diner is the oldest restaurant in Midnight, but for as long as I can remember, it's been Faye's. And she's had the same expression on her face since I was a little girl."

Sam glanced warily over at the object of their discussion. "Even now, if she looks at me, I'll sit up straighter in my seat. She just commands that kind of attention and respect."

"She's a damn good cook."

"Don't expect that by giving her a compliment it will help you. She's not one to be swayed by kind words or a handsome face."

"What about you? Think I could persuade you?"

"Dr. Braddock," Sam leaned closer and said softly, "I think you know that you can persuade me to do just about anything you want."

It was probably a good thing that Faye chose that moment to come to their table to take their order. If not, he would have had to pull Sam toward him and capture her beautiful mouth with his.

"What'd you want?"

Sam immediately answered, "I'll have the special, eggs over easy. Oh . . . and a side order of pancakes."

Pleased that her appetite had apparently returned, Quinn closed his menu and looked up at the stern-faced Faye. "I'll have the same."

With a small grunt, she turned away. He couldn't tell if that was approval or disgust.

Sam answered that question, her green eyes glittering with amusement. "She likes you."

"She does? How do you know?"

"She usually glares at strangers." She laughed and

grabbed his hand. "See, you're on your way to being accepted already."

Unable to resist, he leaned forward and dropped a kiss on her smiling mouth. "I'd say being in your company helps."

"Possibly. I used to be popular round these parts."

"Were you born here in Midnight?"

She shook her head. "Mobile, actually. Mama told us that my dad took a hotel room close to the hospital when she was about eight months pregnant. She said they knew we'd come early and he didn't want to be so far from the hospital when that happened."

"Tell me about your parents."

A brief flash of grief crossed her face. "They were wonderful. Mama had the most beautiful smile you could imagine. My dad was sweet, funny, and incredibly handsome." She shook her head and added wistfully, "We had such fun together."

"I know you said it was murder-suicide, but that's changed, hasn't it?"

She grimaced. "Yeah, you probably heard about that your first day here." Her eyes took on a faraway look. "We were ten years old when it happened . . . away at summer camp. A first for us." A small smile teased her mouth. "I was so excited because Mama said we could swim every day and eat roasted hot dogs and s'mores to our hearts' content.

"The day after we left, my granddad showed up. I remember it was right after breakfast. I knew something bad must have happened. There was no other reason for him to be there. I can still see his pale, grief-stricken face. He put his arms around all three of us and said Mama and Daddy were dead. It wasn't until we got back home that we learned Mama had been brutally stabbed and that Daddy had hung himself. A note of confession and apology was supposedly found in his pocket."

"Hell," Quinn whispered.

"We didn't believe it at first. We kept looking at each other, trying to make sense of it all. There was never any indication that our dad would ever do such a thing. We'd never even seen him lose his temper. But that's what we were told and what we believed."

"How did you find out differently?"

"Savvy came back here last summer for a few weeks. She found some letters from my granddad to my grandmother. He wrote her every day, even though she'd been dead for years. In the letters, he said he didn't believe that's the way it happened but he couldn't get the police chief to investigate further. The chief apparently made some vague threats against us." She shrugged. "Granddad made a hard choice: pursue it and possibly put us in danger, or let it go. He let it go."

"And I bet it ate at him like acid."

"I'm sure it did, but he never let on. He was a wonderful man. I just wish he had told us when we got older. I think he was afraid the killers could still hurt us. And he was right."

"What do you mean?"

"Savvy was almost killed when she started investigating."

"But the killers were caught."

"Yes, the trial was a couple of months ago. They're both in prison. Thankfully."

"So it was a cover-up, making it look like your father killed your mother and then killed himself out of guilt."

"Yep. Pretty slick, huh?"

"And sick."

"Definitely sick. If Savvy had never found those letters, we would have kept on believing the lie."

"You must've hated your father for years."

"Hated and still loved him, too. That's a lot for a little girl to deal with." Her eyes went even sadder. "I know it's no excuse but that's why I doubted you at first. I never saw the evil in my father, believing him perfect and then . . ." She shrugged. "Here you were, so seemingly perfect . . ."

"And you were afraid you'd made the same mistake again."

"I know that's not fair, but I wasn't exactly thinking rationally."

"But instead of giving up on me, you proved my innocence."

Green eyes went wide with surprise. "How did you know?"

"Your friend Murphy. Why didn't you tell me, Sam?"

"I was going to but—"

"But instead, I got drunk and acted like an ass."

"Something like that."

"Can we start again, forget what happened?"

She gave him that sweet, sexy smile that instantly made him hard. "I'd like that."

"Breakfast." Reality, with the sour face of Faye, broke into Samantha's giddiness.

Letting go of Quinn's hands, Samantha grinned up at the woman, not one bit put out by her grim countenance.

"Thank you, Faye."

Breakfast platters slid in front of them and then Faye relented enough to say, "Eat up. You're too skinny."

Samantha swallowed a laugh. Coming from Faye, that statement was tantamount to an "I love you."

They both dug into their breakfast. Samantha couldn't remember enjoying a meal more. Amazing what the feeling of forgiveness and optimism could do for an appetite.

"Well, if it ain't one of the Wilde sisters."

Recognizing the obnoxious voice immediately, Samantha looked up at a chubby, bearded Clark Dayton, a vile, obnoxious creep of a man she'd gone to school with.

Nodding a greeting, she returned her attention to her plate, hoping he'd get the message that she didn't want to talk. Unfortunately Clark was as thick-skinned as he was disgusting.

"Heard you were back. Couldn't hack it as a big-city cop? I'm not surprised."

Instead of looking at Clark, she cut her eyes over to Quinn. Dark flames of blue fire gleamed in his eyes. She'd once watched Quinn at a gym, sparring with one of the trainers. There was no doubt in her mind that he could handle himself with anyone, especially an out-of-shape slug like Dayton. But what she absolutely loved was the fact that instead of getting all macho and defending her honor, he raised his brow in a questioning look. He wanted to know if she wanted to handle the creep herself or let him take care of the problem. She loved that he trusted her to know what to do.

Leaning back in her chair, Samantha looked up at the jerk who'd once terrorized her sister Savvy. "Since you're no longer working for Midnight's police department, I'd say I handled my big-city-cop job a hell of a lot better than you handled your small-town-deputy job."

His chest puffed up thicker. "I quit because I couldn't stand working for your jerk of a brother-in-law."

"Is that right? Want me to challenge you on that in front of everyone here? Because, believe me, I will."

With the appearance of a hairy, furious blowfish, Clark muttered something unintelligible and twisted away. He took two strides and then turned around again, a smirk back on his face. "Tell Zach that my sister, Lindsay, is living with us again. That money he gave her ran out. Reckon he'll give her some more?"

Samantha knew nothing about Zach giving Lindsay

Milan, Clark's sister, money. If he did, it was most likely to help her get away from her creep of a brother and father.

"Give Lindsay my condolences."

He opened his mouth, she was sure to issue another put-down, but was stopped by the tall, broad-shouldered Faye, who stood inches from his face and said in her harsh, no-nonsense voice, "You either sit down and behave or I'll kick your ass out of here. Your choice."

No one challenged Faye, especially not in her own place. His mouth pursed in a pout, like a little boy who'd been punished unfairly, Clark stomped off. Samantha had to give him credit, though. Instead of leaving the restaurant, he went to the back booth and sat down. But then again, Faye's delicious food overruled hurt feelings or embarrassment a thousand to one.

"Thanks, Faye."

Grunting an acknowledgment, Faye turned and headed back to her station behind the counter.

"That was interesting."

"Yeah, Clark has an unpleasant history with the Wilde sisters."

"Seems like Faye's got his number."

Samantha grinned and took a giant bite of her delectable pancakes. "Faye's got everybody's number."

"Can I ask you a question?"

His face had gone serious again. Samantha tensed and said, "Sure."

"I know you don't want to stay at the Hartley house and oversee repairs, but would you consider checking on it from time to time?"

"I still can't believe you bought the place. Did you remember it from what I told you?"

"That if there was one place in the world you could live forever, it was this beautiful old house on a small lake right outside your hometown. And the man who owned it would never sell it piecemeal." He nodded. "I remembered."

"Why, Quinn?"

He leaned forward and murmured in a soft, delicious growl, "You sure you want to have this discussion here?"

That was the voice that could get her thinking about hot, sweaty nights, silk sheets, and multiple orgasms. A shiver of arousal went through her. Quinn must have seen it, because his gaze focused on her mouth as if he were seconds from devouring her.

Leaning closer, she whispered his name in a way that left no doubt what she wanted.

Quinn's deep voice was low, intimate. "I'd really like to kiss you without an audience."

So immersed in the man across from her, she had paid little attention to the other restaurant customers. Tearing her gaze away from what she wanted most in the world, Samantha looked around the room. Of course, everyone was staring. She even saw a few leaning closer, trying to hear their hushed conversation. And they weren't being subtle about it, either.

Quinn caught her attention again, using that same growling tone. "We need to get out of here. Now." He went to his feet. "I'll pay the check."

The instant Quinn stood, an amazing thing happened. The entire restaurant turned their attention back to their own tables and meals. For the first time in her memory, they seemed satisfied with what they had learned. Samantha had no real clue what that was.

While Quinn paid for their food, Samantha spotted Inez Peebles sitting at the counter and made a beeline for her. Instead of doing her job and getting the lowdown on possible newcomers to Midnight, all of her focus had been on Quinn. Talking to the most knowledgeable busybody in town would remedy her need for information in seconds.

"Inez, how're you doing?"

Whirling around in the stool like a teenager, Inez grinned up at her. "Better than most, not as good as a few. What about you, Sammie?"

Inez was one of the few people outside her family who called her Sammie. As the oldest resident of Midnight, the elderly woman believed her seniority came with special privileges. And Samantha supposed it did.

"I'm doing just fine. I—"

"You ever figure out who tried to run you down the other night?"

Samantha resisted the urge to roll her eyes. No secrets in Midnight. Since everyone in town seemed to know everything before it happened, maybe she should be asking people their opinion on who it was.

As if she'd read her mind, Inez cut her eyes over to Clark Dayton, who was openly glaring at Samantha. "That one would do it, completely sober and for free, too. Just for the hell of it."

Now, there was a thought . . . she hadn't considered Clark. There was no love lost between him and the Wilde family. And Zach's firing him hadn't exactly improved relations. And that kind of cowardly act would be right up Clark's alley. Little to no risk to him, limited exposure, and if he didn't succeed in killing her, at the very least, he could scare the crap out of her.

"You're a wise woman, Inez."

"Course I am." Inez jerked her head over at Quinn, who was carrying on a one-sided conversation with Faye. "He fix what he broke yet?"

It would do no good to pretend she didn't know what the elderly woman was talking about. Nor would it help to ask her how she knew about Quinn. Sometimes she swore there were psychics in this town. Instead Samantha shrugged and answered vaguely, "He's trying."

A cackle erupted from Inez, bringing with it the ever-present odor of garlic. "Honey, it's my experience if a man tries to fix what he screwed up, you gotta give him points just for trying."

"I'll remember that." Samantha turned the attention to another issue. "So, what's going on around Midnight? Anything new?"

Eyes narrowed in suspicion, Inez leaned closer. "What're you looking for?"

"Nothing. Just making conversation."

The elderly woman snorted and guffawed at the same time. "Samantha Wilde, you can't lie worth a damn. But to answer your question, nothing new that I heard of. Just the same old stuff." Excitement brightened her face. "Should I be looking for something?"

Samantha almost laughed at the question, then abruptly swallowed her laughter. There was no one more knowledgeable about Midnight happenings than Inez Peebles. Why not enlist her help? "If you hear something interesting, like perhaps a stranger in town or someone asking odd questions, can you let me know first?"

Looking both intrigued and delighted, she whispered, "I'll not tell a soul but you."

Considering that sharing gossip was Inez's favorite thing in the whole world, Samantha felt humbled at her promise. "Thank you, Inez. You'll be a great help."

Blushing like a teenager, she patted Samantha's arm. "You can count on me, sugar."

Samantha walked away from the elderly woman with the strange feeling that she had just hired a new employee for the Wildefire Agency.

CHAPTER TWENTY-ONE

Samantha settled into the passenger seat of the car and waited for Quinn. She hadn't lasted very long, had she? Only one day had passed since they'd made the pact about nothing physical. So far they'd shared a deliciously steamy kiss, along with a few quick ones. The heated look he'd just given her in the diner said he wanted a whole lot more. So did she.

Major issues remained. There were still things they didn't know about each other. And their relationship—how would that work with her in Midnight and Quinn in Atlanta? But the issue that had torn them apart had been resolved. Now, more than anything, she wanted to rejoice in that with the man she loved.

Just as Quinn walked in front of the car, the door of the diner opened and Clark Dayton swaggered out. He said something to Quinn, and though she couldn't hear his words, she knew they weren't friendly. In an instant, Quinn had Clark pushed up against the diner's window and was in his face.

Quinn Braddock was all about control. Having him lose his cool meant one thing: he was more than pissed— he was furious. Clark Dayton had finally shot off his mouth to the wrong person.

She'd put her hand on the car door handle to get out when Quinn swung his head around and gave her a hard, telling look. The message was clear. With a small nod, Samantha settled back into her seat and quite happily waited for Quinn to handle the imbecile. She trusted him to know what to do.

Apparently satisfied she wouldn't interfere, Quinn turned around and devoted his full attention to the man plastered against the diner window. Whatever Quinn said made an impressive impact. Clark's face was crimson red, his eyes so wide they were almost bugged. No doubt about it, Quinn was scaring the crap out of the jerk.

It was over in seconds. Quinn took one step back, nodded at the dozen or so people who were unashamedly gawking at the confrontation, and then headed to the car.

When he got inside and shut the door, she glanced over at him and asked mildly, "Feel better?"

The twitch at his mouth told her he was fighting a grin. "Much."

"Good. Let's go before he shows his stupidity again and one of us has to slug him."

Starting the engine, he pulled out onto the road and then threw her a concerned look. "Did you want me to step in the first time? I got the impression you wanted to handle it on your own."

"No, I appreciated your self-control. As much as I'd like to slap the smirk off his face, I refuse to lower myself to his level."

"Sorry I don't have the same restraint."

She grinned. "Actually, I thought you showed incredible restraint. I expected blood. You want to tell me what he said?"

"No."

She didn't push it. Whatever it was, she knew it had been uncomplimentary and, from Quinn's reaction, most likely about her. Clark Dayton's opinion of her meant nothing.

They were at the Hartley place before she knew it. Though she guessed she needed to start referring to it as Quinn's place from now on. Yes, that definitely had a nicer ring.

Quinn parked in front of the house. She opened her car door but he was there before she put her foot on the ground, holding his hand out for her. "Let's go christen our new home in the right way."

Our new home. Her heart pounding at his words, she took his hand and then gasped when he pulled her from the car and into his arms.

A rush of emotion overwhelmed her, and Samantha sighed with delight as Quinn's mouth smothered hers in a soul-deep kiss she felt all the way to her toes. Oh, how she had missed these kisses.

Way too soon, his mouth lifted. "Let's get inside before we get arrested for indecent exposure."

Hand in hand, they walked to the house. The instant the door closed behind them, Samantha went back into his arms. Quinn cupped her butt in his hands and lifted her. "Wrap your legs around me."

Samantha lifted her legs and locked them together at the ankle behind his back. Kissing her as if he would never stop, Quinn carried her up the stairs. She knew they were probably heading to his bedroom, but her mind was on other things, like the hard length that ground into her in rhythm with his steps, causing a fire within her to burn out of control. While Quinn ate greedily at her mouth, Samantha lost herself to sensation after sensation as she climbed to the peak of pleasure.

The movements abruptly stopped and she was dropped onto a soft bed.

"No," she whimpered. She was on the edge . . . she didn't want to let go yet, not until she'd reach that insurmountable, exquisite moment of ecstasy.

"Shh, baby, I'll take care of you."

When he released her and stepped back, away from her, she knew he meant something different from what she'd thought. "Wait . . . what?"

Heat rippling through her, she watched beneath her lashes as he pulled her shoes off and then stripped her jeans and panties down her legs. Before she could fathom his intent, his mouth was on her, his tongue delving deep. As she arched upward, climax crashed into her like a meteor and then completely shattered around her. Her mewling scream of ecstasy echoed through the house as she soared into another dimension.

Long seconds later, she landed softly back to earth to find Quinn still loving her with his mouth and tongue. With each gentle, thorough lap, arousal became more urgent and fierce. But this time, she wanted them to ride that spectacular wave together.

"Quinn?"

Not lifting his head, his voice muffled, he said, "Yeah?"

Before she could answer, his tongue speared deep again, and instead of answering him, her body arched off the bed as she found herself back on the edge of orgasm. Gritting her teeth to hold back the pleasure, she spoke, quickly, urgently: "I want you inside me." And in case he didn't understand her need to have him with her, she said, "Now."

He stood, his gaze sweeping over her, deep blue eyes smoldering with intent. "I love it when you tell me what you want."

Thankfully he didn't make her ask again. As he stripped off his shirt, jeans, and shoes, Samantha lost her breath. How could she have forgotten? When dressed, Quinn was a striking man, causing men and women to follow him with their eyes. Without clothes, that beauty became something different. She had never gawked at a naked body before, but she could stare at his for hours. He was every woman's fantasy of powerful masculinity. Broad shoulders and arms, muscular without being bulky; hard, flat stomach; long, lean legs that revealed the hours he spent running.

How wonderful it felt to be with him again. To see the desire in his eyes, his beautiful body aroused and ready to give and receive pleasure.

He crawled onto the bed, but instead of giving her what she wanted immediately, his mouth moved up her body, kissing, licking, nibbling. First a kiss on both feet, then the inside of each calf and thigh, then one tender, lingering kiss on her mound. From there, his mouth traveled to her stomach, then midriff, and then stopped at her breasts.

Lifting his head, he stared down at them. "I missed these."

She laughed unexpectedly. Quinn had always been able to bring almost as many smiles to the bedroom as he had orgasms.

"They missed you, too."

"Then I guess I'd better make it up to them."

Her nipples, already aching for his touch, tightened even more in anticipation. Hot breath coated her skin and then his tongue bathed her entire breast. At the same time, one of his hands traveled down to her stomach and then she felt him between her legs. Opening for him, she gasped as a long, hard finger pressed deep just as his mouth clamped onto her nipple, sucking hard and deep. In seconds she was back on the precipice of a mind-blowing climax.

He released her nipple with a loud pop and pulled his finger from her. As much as she wanted him inside her, she couldn't stop a disappointed groan. Chuckling softly at her reaction, he moved over to her other breast and gave it the identical treatment. And as before, his mouth clamped hard onto her nipple and, at the same

time, he plunged deep. Only this time, it wasn't his finger. At the first hard thrust, Samantha screamed, shaking the rafters of the old house. Wrapping her legs tight
around his hips, she buried her face in Quinn's neck to
muffle her cries of intense pleasure as an orgasm once
again crashed over her.

His mouth clenched to control his need to let go, Quinn
pushed Sam away and pressed her shoulders gently onto
the pillow. "I want to hear your pleasure. Don't hide it
from me."

Green eyes, darkened with pleasure, gleaming with
love, gazed up at Quinn. A part of him wanted to deny
what he saw; another part reveled in the fact that this
amazing, beautiful woman could feel this way about
him. How the hell had he gotten so lucky?

Coherent thought vanished as she writhed beneath
him, allowing him to go even deeper. Hooking her long,
silky legs at her knees, Quinn lifted them, spreading her
wider, and then buried himself as deep as he could go.
Her inner muscles gripped him like a vise as he set up a
pistoning rhythm of thrust and retreat. His own impending climax zipped up his spine. Locking his eyes
with hers, he growled, "One more time, Sam."

With a keening cry, her entire body arched and she
gave him what he asked for, just as Quinn's release
flooded inside her. They held each other tight as both
their bodies went stiff and then collapsed into each
other, shuddering in recovery.

Pressing tender kisses against her elegant neck and
silky shoulder, Quinn realized that for the first time in
months, he knew true and total peace.

Not wanting to smother her with his big, sweaty body,
he rolled and collapsed beside her. Both of them were
panting like thoroughbreds after a race. He propped
himself up on his elbow to look down at her and felt his
heart flip over. Her face. Had he ever seen Sam more

serene or peaceful? She glowed like she had a brilliant light inside her.

"I think we can say that this house has been well and truly christened," he said.

She rolled over on her side, facing him. Her smile was both sweet and sexually confident. So different from the timid, almost frightened Sam when they'd first had sex. He loved seeing that confidence.

"I wonder if we've shocked it."

He shook his head. "The house is over a hundred years old. I'll bet she's seen her share of risqué bed antics."

She smiled dreamily. "I hope so. I love the history here. Babies have been born in this bedroom; thousands of meals have been cooked in that giant old kitchen. Families loving each other, husbands and wives growing old together. Just the way it's supposed to be."

"I guess having a crusty old bachelor living here will be quite a change for her."

Samantha dropped her head back onto her pillow. Quinn's words reignited a worry she hadn't let herself face. She had wanted to be with him, share herself with him. She loved him and that was only natural. But now those demons of doubt had returned. She had to know where she stood.

Feeling more exposed and vulnerable than she'd ever felt in her life, she whispered words she didn't want to say: "Where is this going, Quinn?"

"What do you mean?"

It took more courage than she thought possible to roll back over on her side and face him. "I mean, you're here in Midnight. You bought a house that you knew I loved . . . called it our new home." She swallowed around the lump of fear clogging her throat. "Have you changed your mind about a permanent relationship?"

He blew out a long sigh and shoved his fingers through his hair. Despair increased the throat lump to softball size. He didn't need to say the words. She had no trouble reading his thoughts.

"I don't understand, Sam. You were okay with that arrangement before."

She sat up. Lying beside him, having his warm body next to hers, tempting her, wasn't conducive to this kind of discussion. She swung her legs over to the side of the bed, with her back facing him. "And I've had a lot of time to think about things." She turned and looked at him over her shoulder. "I don't want an *arrangement*. I want permanency."

"You mean marriage?"

"Marriage, children, commitment to spend a life together." She shrugged. "Everything."

"Sam, I care about you . . . more than anyone I've ever known." He shook his head. "But after my divorce, I swore never again. If it helps, I want more than what we had before, too. A long-term relationship—that's more of a commitment than I ever thought I could agree to again. But marriage? That's out of the question."

She had known what his answer would be . . . had always known. She just hadn't wanted to face it.

Pulling in every bit of her reserves, she stood and faced him. "Then I can't do this."

Regret and something else darkened his eyes. "I don't want to lose you."

Already feeling too exposed, she picked up the first thing she saw—Quinn's shirt—and slipped it on. She looked around the beautiful old bedroom and wondered if anyone else's heart had been broken within these four walls.

"You really shouldn't have bought this house, Quinn. She deserves a family to live in her and love her."

"That's why I—"

"No. Stop." She backed away from him . . . away

from temptation. "I'm not going to live in it for you. It's your home, not mine."

"What does that mean?"

"It means this is goodbye."

Surprising her, he jumped from the bed and grabbed her shoulders. "Before this all happened, we were good together. We were happy. Don't deny that."

"I can't . . . I wouldn't. But having you put limitations on us before we even get started again won't work. Not like before."

"Why not?"

"Because I can't. From the first time you kissed me, I knew a temporary relationship wouldn't work. What you said . . . about nothing permanent . . . I kept hoping you'd change your mind."

"Why the hell do we have to put labels on things? We're good together. We could be good together for years."

"Dammit, I don't want term limits. I want a future. With you. A commitment that you're not going to walk away when things get tough. I want the knowledge that we can fight and disagree with the assurance that we're still one." She swallowed again and whispered, "I want it all, Quinn."

"I can't give you those promises."

"Then I guess this is it."

"It doesn't have to be."

"Yes it does." She gazed around again at the beautiful old room that had known intimacy, happiness, heartache, and love. The things that made up a family. "This house deserves to be home to a family who love each other and are committed to a life together."

She went to the window and lovingly caressed the wood that was in desperate need of a coat of paint. "It's going to take some work and elbow grease, but when it's finished, she'll be as beautiful as she once was."

Turning back to him, she stretched her trembling

mouth into what she hoped looked like a smile. "The people Zach recommended will do a good job for you. I doubt that you'll need anyone to oversee it."

Grim acceptance stamped on his face, he nodded. "You're welcome to come here anytime. I'll give you a key."

She ignored the offer. She doubted she would ever come back here again. Why return to the place where your heart was torn from your chest? Unless . . . "Will you sell it once the repairs are done?"

Quinn could only shake his head. Hell, he was making it up as he went along these days. Not having a plan for his future had him stumped. With his career going up in flames and Sam giving him an ultimatum he couldn't accept, he felt like the captain of a ship with no rudder or sails.

He answered honestly. "I don't know."

The smile she gave him was bright but didn't disguise the pain in her eyes. "Keep me in mind if you decide to sell."

The tightness in his chest almost constricted his breathing. Hadn't he always known she would want more? Of course he had. He just hadn't wanted to accept it. Sam was a small-town girl with old-fashioned values. He had expected her to give him this ultimatum at some point. He had just hoped it would be far into the future, when the thought of living without her wouldn't be so bleak. He refused to believe that day never would have come. Everything ended eventually, even the things you didn't want to end. That was just the way life worked.

Quinn gazed down at her beautiful face and felt the words tremble on his lips. How he wished he could give her what she wanted, what she deserved. He didn't want to lose her but neither could he promise something that could never be.

If he were a different kind of man, he would tell her what she wanted to hear. But those would be promises he couldn't keep. He'd hurt her already; he refused to be a total bastard.

One of the hardest things he'd ever had to do was turn his back on her and say, "I'll take you home."

"Then we got dressed and he brought me home."

Savvy's eyes were compassionate and sad as Samantha gave an entire account of her breakup with Quinn. When she finished, she held her breath, hoping her sister would come up with a solution. It was a silly hope. There was no solution other than giving up her dreams.

"I can't believe he would buy a house here if he didn't plan something permanent."

"I made the mistake of thinking that, too. Especially when he said he bought the house for us."

"So you think he meant for you guys to move in together?"

"Yeah, I do. He never said the words, but having him refer to it as our house . . ." She swallowed, unable to continue.

Samantha wasn't a prude or a hypocrite. She and Quinn had slept together and she wasn't ashamed of giving herself to the man she loved. However, living together in her hometown? She would be fodder for every self-righteous, gossiping resident. And old-fashioned or not, she didn't like the thought of living with a man who had no intention of marrying her. That just wasn't her.

"Did he say when he would be back?"

"No. I'm assuming he will come back at some point to check out the repairs."

"Maybe when he comes back, he'll have realized what a dodo-head he was."

"I don't think so, Savvy. He was too adamant." And

because being with Quinn was what she wanted most in the world, she doubted herself again and asked, "Do you think I was wrong?"

"No, I don't. When we were little girls, before Mama and Daddy died, you always played the bride."

Even heartbroken, she could smile at that memory. "You played the schoolteacher, I was the bride, and Bri was . . ."

Both grinning, they finished her sentence in unison: "Indiana Jones."

Savvy giggled. "That was a really hard class to teach. You always showed up in that old white nightgown Mama gave you. And every few minutes, you'd pop up from your desk and throw your plastic flower bouquet."

Samantha nodded, loving these memories of happiness before their world fell apart. "And remember, Bri had that nasty-looking hat she found at Goodwill when we were dropping off some donations?"

"Yeah. And she used our jump rope as her whip."

"Little did I know that getting to be that bride wasn't going to be as easy as it looked."

"I'm so sorry, Sammie. I really believed Quinn came back for you to make a commitment."

"I think he did. At least all the commitment Quinn can give." She shrugged. "Sometimes things just don't work out the way we hoped." The words were bland and trite but they were the best she could manage right now. That damn lump had apparently decided to make a permanent residence in her throat.

Wanting to get on to something else, pleasant or not, she said, "We had a little altercation with Clark Dayton at the diner."

In the middle of shifting on her pillow for a more comfortable spot, Savvy stopped to give her a grimace. "What did the asshole do?"

"Oh, you know, the usual insults and snide looks. Quinn, however, had more than a little run-in with him."

"What happened?"

"I don't know. I was in the car, so I didn't get to hear anything. Clark came out of the diner and said something that Quinn took exception to. Before I knew it, he'd shoved Clark against the window and had a few choice words for him."

"Oh, how I would have loved to have seen that."

Even though she'd never felt less like smiling in her life, she forced her mouth into a grin. "Everyone in the diner got a good view of it. I wouldn't be surprised if *Midnight Tales* doesn't run a story. Thirty seconds of excitement in Midnight."

"Someday Clark's going to say the wrong thing to the right person at the wrong time."

"We can only hope. By the way, he did say that Lindsay was back in town. Didn't Zach help her get a job in South Carolina?"

"He did but it apparently didn't work out. I hate to hear she's back. Living with those Dayton men has got to be hellacious. I just hope now that Zach is married, she'll leave him alone."

"Maybe I should introduce her to Blaine."

"You've decided he's in the clear as far as Cruz is concerned?"

"No. Not really. Even though his background checks out, it's easy enough to create a fake one these days. And that conversation we had about Florida. I don't know . . . it was kind of weird. Also, some of his questions regarding the agency make me think he's digging for information. But other than those things, he's given no indication that he's anything other than what he says. And he's been a complete gentleman on our dates."

"If we decide he's in the clear, do you think you'll continue to see him?"

"I don't think so. I told him I'd like to see him again because I'm hoping he'll reveal himself, one way or the other. But if he's not Cruz's man, then it's not fair to lead him on." She laughed, wincing at how raw it sounded. "Besides, going out with anyone after Quinn would be like settling for cold grits instead of filet mignon."

Even though she wasn't all that sure of Blaine, she felt guilty. Comparing Quinn to any other man was unfair. No one could measure up.

"So," Savvy said casually, "when were you going to tell me that Bri is working undercover in Cruz's camp?"

Samantha sat frozen, staring at her sister. Speechlessness for her was a rarity, but for the life of her, she couldn't think of anything to say. And though Savvy was smiling, Samantha saw the hurt.

Finally finding her voice, she hurriedly said, "Savvy, please don't be upset with me. I just didn't want you to worry."

"I know that, Sammie. But you have to understand, not knowing what's happening to the people I love the most in the world hurts much more than the truth."

Samantha let go of a ragged breath. Hell, she felt like she'd lived a thousand years today. Breaking up with Quinn and hurting her sister. "I'm so sorry."

Savvy waved her hand. "Apology accepted. Just remember, when we agreed to this venture, we said we were all in this together. Okay?"

"I promise I'll never keep things from you again. So who told you?"

"In a roundabout way, Bri told me herself."

"How's that?"

"Zach was in the shower and had left his cellphone on the nightstand. It chimed with a text message, so I picked it up. It was from Bri. She said you knew about her undercover job but wanted to make sure that Zach knew about it, too, so he could help you cover for her."

"Uh-oh."

"Yeah. Turns out he already knew about it." She grinned. "At least *you* didn't try giving me a lecture before you apologized. I got a three-minute 'You shouldn't read other people's text messages.'"

Laughing, Samantha hugged her sister. "I wish I could have seen your response."

A slight flush appeared on Savvy's cheeks. "He apologized in a most satisfactory way."

Samantha snorted as she got to her feet. "Typical guy. He screws up and gets a treat for it."

"I'd say we both got a treat."

"I'm going to take a shower. You need anything?"

"No." She held up her cellphone. "Zach's in the nursery, doing some painting. If I need anything, I've been instructed to call."

"You have a craving for anything for dinner?"

"Oh yes, I'm glad you asked." She held up a list she'd apparently been thinking about a lot. There were at least a dozen items scribbled on it.

Samantha took the list and winced at some of the unappetizing combinations of foods. "You want all of these?"

"No, maybe just a few today and then tomorrow and so on."

Samantha laughed as she opened the door. "I get the message."

"Sammie?"

She turned back to her sister. "Yeah?"

"Quinn Braddock will come to his senses one day. Don't give up on him."

She gave her sister the best smile she could muster and closed the door. Giving up on Quinn wasn't the problem. It was Quinn who had given up on them.

CHAPTER TWENTY-TWO

"So you're telling me a woman can get murdered in one of the best neighborhoods in this city and no one, not the police or a private investigator, can find one damn clue to lead to the murderer?"

"Sorry, Dr. Braddock, but that's about the size of it. I understand if you don't want to keep me on the case."

Private investigator Paul Haney had come highly recommended. Quinn had researched the man, too. The PI had successfully handled some high-profile cases in Atlanta. If anyone could find Charlene's killer, he had hoped this man could. But so far, Haney, like the Atlanta homicide detectives, had come up empty.

"What about the sketches of the men Charlene had been seeing?"

"We found all but one of the men. Apparently the unidentified man was someone new. The neighbors didn't recognize him as a regular visitor. The neighbor across the street identified him as the man who came to Charlene's house just minutes before you. I believe this man was her killer.

"Both the police and I showed the mystery man's sketch to everyone we could think of. No one recognized him."

Quinn couldn't fault anyone for that. He had seen the sketch himself. The man could have been one of thousands of men. There'd been nothing distinguishing about him. Had that been the killer's intent all along? Looking like no one in particular was a great way to not be identified.

Who and why? Hell, he might never know.

"Your ex-wife didn't have a lot of friends. She went to the gym four days a week, the grocery once a week, and a beauty shop over on Sinclair Avenue twice a month. None of those people had ever seen this man, either."

"And all the other men had alibis?"

"Yeah. I think two marriages broke up over this. Charlene didn't have a problem sleeping with married men."

There was a lot he could say about that, but he wouldn't. Charlene was dead. There was no point in discussing her lack of morals.

"What about the video of her memorial service? There were several men there."

"They were all accounted for, too. I'm sorry . . . I just don't know where else to turn."

Quinn didn't, either. He had come to Haney's office on the off chance there was something encouraging he could hold on to. Something he could take with him to the meeting at the hospital to show that the dark cloud of suspicion would soon be lifted from him. Even though he knew the PI would have called him if there had been a break in the case, he'd had to give it a shot.

Standing, he shook the other man's hand. "Don't stop trying to find her killer. My career may be shot here in Atlanta, but I'll be damned if I plan to stay a suspect the rest of my life."

"Will do. And I'm sorry to hear about your career. People are a fickle bunch. As soon as you're cleared, they'll come to you in droves and swear they believed you were innocent all along."

Maybe, but that didn't help the here and now.

"Call me if you discover anything new."

Haney nodded, but his grim expression said not to get his hopes up. Quinn closed the door behind him, thinking that hope was about the last thing he had these days.

His mind on a myriad of issues he had to deal with, he was in his car and headed toward downtown Atlanta before he even realized it. Good thing he could make this drive with his eyes closed. Samantha had once told him he noticed everything, that he had an eye for detail. Not today.

Sam. He still couldn't believe it was over. After all they'd gone through. All the distrust set aside and all the apologies made and accepted, he had believed they were heading in the right direction. Unfortunately her direction wasn't the same as his.

He was stupid for not seeing this coming. Even when they'd first started dating and he'd made that unromantic ultimatum that he wasn't looking for anything long term or permanent, he'd seen the doubt in her eyes. And why shouldn't she doubt him? Sam was a beautiful, intelligent woman. Any man would be incredibly fortunate to have her as his wife. That man couldn't be him.

He hadn't told her about his earlier plans, before Charlene's murder, of asking her to move in with him. What was the point? Would her answer have been different then? Would they have been living happily together, growing closer, if none of this shit had happened? Who the hell knew.

He had hurt her again. How he hated that. The drive back to her home had been painfully silent. After searching for and not finding anything remotely encouraging to fill the silence, he had kept his mouth shut. Anything he said would have just made it worse anyway. He couldn't give Sam what she wanted and she wouldn't accept what he could offer.

Quinn pulled into the hospital parking lot and parked in a designated spot for doctors. No doubt the last time he would park here. He had no illusions what would happen when he walked through those doors.

He was glad to see Bob Dixon standing outside the front door, waiting for him. Having his attorney with him was an added precaution. Hell, the way his life had been going lately, maybe he needed to travel around with one. Another benefit of Bob's presence was his support. A friendly face in a sea of doubting Thomases was a welcome relief.

Smiling grimly, he shook Bob's hand.

His friend looked equally grim. "You sure you want to do this?"

Bob had wanted him to fight it. Any other time, Quinn might have agreed, but he was tired of it all. The suspicious looks, the whispers. The conversations that stopped the minute he entered a room. He'd fought all of his life not to give a damn about other people's opinions. His parents had lived their lives with the opinion of others as their guiding compass. He had been determined that would never happen to him. But now when it came down to it, he had caved. Grim pragmaticism was his new reality.

Quinn opened the door. "Let's get this done."

MIDNIGHT, ALABAMA
TWO WEEKS LATER

She was being stalked. And they weren't being very discreet about it, either. Everywhere she went in Midnight, either Brody or Zach was there, too. It was getting damn irritating.

Pushing open the door to the police station, Samantha nodded at the thin, gray-haired woman sitting behind the desk. Hazel Adkins was the police department's dispatcher, receptionist, and secretary.

"Hey there, Samantha. How're you doing?"

"I'll be doing just fine as soon as I give my brother-in-law a piece of my mind."

"That's going to have to wait, hon. He's over at Tillie's Hair Today. Somebody threw a rock at the window last night."

Since Tillie's was her next stop, that worked out well. "Thanks, Hazel." Turning to the door, she took one step and ran straight into Brody James.

Glaring up at him, she snapped, "Stop following me."

He raised a questioning brow. "That's quite an ego you got there."

"Oh, don't even try to pretend with me. This town might be small, but there's no reason I should see either you or Zach every time I turn around. Now, tell me why."

One thing she had always appreciated about Brody, he wasn't one to beat around the bush. In that way, he reminded her of Quinn. *No, don't go there.*

And Brody didn't disappoint her. Shrugging, he said, "Ever since your so-called accident, we've been tailing you. Doesn't hurt to be extra careful."

She said quietly, "While I appreciate the concern, I'm a former cop. Since that happened, I go nowhere without my gun. And I'm trained in self-defense. I've even taken down men bigger than you. So please, give me some credit. Okay?"

"Bigger than me?" He grinned. "Didn't know there *was* such a thing."

Samantha had to laugh. Brody had such a good sense of humor. Why, oh why, couldn't she have fallen for him instead of a commitment-phobic control freak who confused her at every turn and made her toes curl at just the thought of him?

"I appreciate everyone's concern, really I do. But I'm not going to go on any long runs by myself or be caught in situations I can't handle. We've got more than enough issues on our plate here in Midnight. Babysitting me shouldn't be one of them."

"Heard and understood." Big shoulders lifted in a slight shrug. "Just following orders."

"Zach's?"

"No, your sister Savannah."

Samantha sighed. Of course Savvy would be worried. Her doctor had given her a clean bill of health, assuring her that she and the baby were fine. And Savvy, being Savvy, was just back to taking care of those she loved.

"I'll talk to her."

"I missed breakfast. Want to head over to Faye's with me? My treat."

Samantha recognized the invitation for what it was. Brody had asked her out twice since Quinn left. She had turned him down both times. This was another invitation, probably the last one he would make. And as much as she wanted to say yes in hopes that eventually she would stop hurting, she couldn't do that to him. Brody was a good man and deserved a woman who would be totally focused on him and not using him as a fill-in for another man.

"Can't. I'm heading over to Tillie's for a manicure. Gotta pick up my daily quota of gossip."

His smile one of regret and understanding, he nodded. "I'll see you later, then."

More than aware that Hazel had been eating up the conversation with both eyes and ears, she hurriedly said goodbye and walked out the door and straight into another man.

Irritated at her lack of attention, she forced her mouth to smile at Blaine Marshall. He'd had to go out of town a couple of weeks ago and had canceled their date. Samantha had been relieved. Now she wondered if she should give him the same kind of message she'd just given Brody. Dating this man made little sense anymore. Even if he was one of Cruz's men, he wasn't going to give up any information. There was no point in pursuing an avenue of investigation that was producing no results. Their best bet was to keep Lauren hidden until either the Miami police or Bri dug up enough information to bury Cruz.

"Samantha, I'm glad I ran into you. I just got back into town." He winked and added, "Miss me?"

Since telling him the truth would be cruel, she just maintained her smile and said, "Did you have a good trip?"

He grimaced. "Not really. Had some business to take care of back home. It's damn cold up there."

She laughed and tightened her sweater around herself. "I think it's damn cold here, too."

"You Southerners don't know what cold is. We had two feet of snow on the ground the whole time I was there."

What was it about the weather that made people brag as if they had something to do with it? Northerners bragged about their cold winters and made fun of Southerners who couldn't drive in the snow. Southerners were equally proud of their heat and humidity, often calling Northerners wimps and pansies. She mentally shrugged. Since the War Between the States was over, maybe this was their battle.

She shivered again. "This is as cold as I like to be."

"I'm sorry I had to cancel our date. Want to go out tomorrow night?"

"I don't think so, Blaine."

"What do you mean? Why not?"

"I'm not looking to get involved with anyone. It just wouldn't be fair to you."

He gave her his usual charming, self-deprecating grin. "We'll form our very own broken hearts' club."

Midnight's grapevine never failed to disappoint. Blaine might have been back only a day or two, but it was apparently enough time to hear that Quinn had left town. His smile invited shared understanding.

"I just think it would be best—"

"Look, it's dinner, not a relationship. I'm single, you're single." He held up his hands. "I'm looking for nothing more than friendship, I promise."

Samantha wavered. Maybe something uncomplicated was what she needed. A good meal, pleasant company, and absolutely no expectations. And if she could dig a little deeper, perhaps she could decide once and for all whether or not Blaine was connected to Cruz.

She smiled her appreciation. "When you put it like that, how can I resist?"

"Excellent. So tomorrow night's okay with you?"

Samantha shook her head. She had promised Aunt Gibby she'd come over to her house and help hang her new kitchen curtains. In exchange, Gibby was going to make one of her famous casseroles. As much as Samantha dreaded the meal, she enjoyed spending time with Gibby.

"I have plans. How about Monday night?"

Blaine's eyes searched her for several seconds, and she knew he was wondering if she had another date. She didn't want to alienate him, but her plans were not his business.

Thankfully he just nodded and said, "Monday it is. Six o'clock okay?"

"Sounds good."

Samantha walked away, neither dreading nor looking

forward to her evening with Blaine. She was beginning to think this would be her attitude and way of life, at least for the foreseeable future. A life with Quinn wasn't possible. Though she knew that, she had yet to come to terms with how to return to the Samantha she'd once been. Optimism seemed as far from her as the earth from the moon. At some point, she'd have to get there. But today wasn't that day.

Still, she entered Tillie's with the sunny smile everyone expected. Having carefully crafted a reputation that life and its disappointments didn't impact her the way they did most people, she wasn't about to give in and show just how badly the real Samantha was hurting.

After learning that Zach had already left, Samantha seated herself in the waiting room and picked up a magazine. Her ears open for anything odd or unusual that might alert her that one of Cruz's men might be snooping around, she almost missed that someone was speaking directly to her.

She raised her head from her magazine. "I'm sorry, what did you say?"

Justine Lewis, blowing her long, blood-red nails dry with short puffs of air, stopped mid-huff. "I said, I just saw that doctor friend of yours headed to the Hartley place. Reckon he's here to stay for good?"

The genial demeanor she was working so hard to keep up was abruptly shot to hell. Not caring what kind of impression she was making, Samantha threw down the magazine, shot to her feet, and went out the door.

CHAPTER TWENTY-THREE

Quinn shifted into park and sat for a few minutes, staring at his house. Was he stupid for coming back here? Seemed like lately all he could lay claim to was stupidity.

His attorney was handling the details, but bottom line, he no longer had a career or a life to go back to in Atlanta. At some point, he'd return to medicine, either emergency or private practice. He'd worked too hard and enjoyed it too much—and dammit, was too good at it—to turn away from it for long. But for right now, he was officially unemployed.

So no, coming back to Midnight made no real sense. He only knew a few people in town, and one in particular would not be happy that he had returned. The last thing he wanted to do was hurt Sam more. He would do his best to stay out of her way.

Quinn got out and grabbed his duffel bag from the trunk. He'd taken the back roads, going three miles out of his way to avoid downtown Midnight. It was useless to hope that he could live here long before everyone, including Sam, knew. But a couple of days of peace would be a reprieve from all the insanity over the last couple of weeks.

The thought had barely entered his mind when he heard the roar of an engine. Turning, he squinted against the late afternoon sun and tried to make out the identity of the driver. He told himself he didn't want it to be Sam. Too bad he didn't believe it.

An electric-green Ford Fusion sped toward the house. *Not Sam*. He took the disappointment and absorbed it. This was just the beginning.

Quinn stood and waited for the car to reach him. It stopped a couple of yards from him, and a young woman he had never seen before got out. In one hand was a casserole dish and the other held a bottle of wine.

As she came toward him, he observed the way she walked. Hell, except for the reddish-brown hair color, she looked way too much like Charlene. With a long-legged, swaying walk and a smile that reminded him of a barracuda, the woman exuded a hungry, sexual energy. A younger Quinn might have been intrigued, but he'd been there and done that and it definitely hadn't been worth the trip. Sam's beauty, intelligence, and lack of pretense outshone this woman a thousand to one.

"Hey there, sugar. Welcome to Midnight. I'm Lindsay Milan."

Quinn nodded a hello. Having had more than enough experience with this kind of woman, he knew not to show the least bit of encouragement.

Not deterred, Lindsay held out her offering. "I brought you a casserole for dinner and some wine to wash it down with. Hope you're hungry."

Her eyes traveled down his body, leaving him no doubt what she hoped he was hungry for.

"How did you know I was here?"

"I was walking by Tillie's and heard you'd come back. I didn't get to meet you when you bought the house. I'm real glad you came back so soon. How long you planning to stay this time?"

Her quickness surprised him. Lindsay apparently had

casseroles ready on the off chance someone new popped into town.

"That's nice of you but I'm afraid I can't invite you in." He searched for an excuse that sounded reasonable. "I just got here and haven't had a chance to check the place out." Seeing her shiver slightly, he added, "I'm not even sure I have heat."

She grinned. "Oh, but you've got something better."

Not really wanting to know, he asked anyway. "Really? What's that?"

"You've got fireplaces."

"Can't use them yet. They have to be cleaned out."

Holding up the bottle, she winked. "This'll warm you up."

"I'm not much of a wine drinker, but thanks."

Her red lips pursed in disappointment but still she persevered. "At least let me show you how to heat the casserole." She took a few steps toward the house. Quinn was about to call her back when he heard another car pull into the drive. Hell, was there a welcome sign posted somewhere he wasn't aware of?

At the sight of the silver BMW headed toward them, Quinn felt a lift to his spirits. Didn't matter that he had vowed to avoid Sam at all costs. She was the one who'd come to see him.

Lindsay shot him a frustrated look. "I thought y'all broke up."

Focused on the woman getting out of her car with mutinous determination on her beautiful face, he didn't acknowledge Lindsay's comment.

Sam stalked toward him and Quinn fought a smile. This was the Sam he admired and wanted like none other. She was furious and wasn't bothering to hide it.

"Why are you here?"

"Hello to you, too."

"I thought you—"

She broke off when Lindsay touched his arm with a caressing glide. "Quinn and I were just about to sit down to eat. Why don't you stop by another time?"

Quinn didn't know who was the most stunned, he or Sam. What the hell did this woman think she was doing?

"I wasn't aware that you and Quinn knew each other, Lindsay," Sam said.

"He's an easy man to get to know." She turned back to Quinn, her eyes wide with seeming innocence. "This casserole is getting cold, sugar. We'd better go in before it ruins."

Since he neither wanted to have dinner with this woman or have Sam believe there was anything going on between them, he shook his head. "Again, thanks but no thanks. I have unpacking to do." And because he wasn't a total prick, he said, "Thanks for your thoughtfulness."

Her smile frozen, she shoved the casserole at Quinn. "Here. Heat for twenty minutes at 350 degrees."

She nodded at Sam and stalked to her car. Quinn thought it interesting that her walk was so different from when she arrived.

Lindsay gunned the car, creating a cloud of dust as she sped away.

Waving away the dust, Sam said, "I didn't expect you back."

"I wanted to get in a few days of repairs before the holidays."

"You're doing the repairs yourself?"

"Some of them, yeah."

"What's going on, Quinn? With your work schedule, you barely used to have time to eat."

He shrugged. "I took some more time off."

"Why?"

"Come inside and let's talk."

He'd meant nothing more than it was getting dark and he was holding a damn casserole in his hands that he didn't want. When she took a step back, she seemed to think it was another kind of invitation.

"I need to get home."

"What are you afraid of, Sam?"

"I just . . ." Her eyes darted to the house and then came back to settle on him. "I just don't know why you came back, Quinn. There's nothing for you here."

"Maybe you're right, but I'm here. Now, are you coming in or not?"

She shook her head and started for her car.

Quinn watched her drive away, the ache in his gut not easing. It was clear she didn't want to be around him.

Shrugging, he headed to his new home. She was just one of many who felt that way these days.

Samantha threw her keys on the hall foyer table. She was torn between wanting to go for a long, body-aching run and just running to her bedroom and crying her eyes out. Why had he come back here? They had broken up. It couldn't be the house. It meant nothing to him.

At first she had thought he had somehow changed his mind. Silly, she knew. Quinn wasn't fickle like that. Once he made a decision, he stuck with it. But still she had hoped.

Seeing him with Lindsay had almost knocked her off her feet. Even though the woman's reputation in high school had been one few girls would want, Samantha had always felt sorry for her. Lindsay had lived with her brother and father, both of whom were known to be jerks. Her home life couldn't have been easy.

From what she knew about Lindsay's life since then, it hadn't gotten better. She'd been through two divorces and had acquired the reputation of being a desperate,

man-hungry woman who would sleep with anyone.
Having immersed herself with the gossips of Midnight,
Samantha had heard more than she wanted about many
people, including Lindsay.

"What's wrong?"

She turned to Savannah and tried for her best fake
smile. "Nothing."

"Sammie, stop it. We used to tell each other everything. Please don't let my pregnancy change that."

"I'm sorry. It's just hard to talk right now."

Her sister took her hand and led her to the kitchen.
"A good cup of hot sweet tea is what we both need."

Hot sweet tea had been their panacea when they were
kids. Granddad had insisted that the soothing drink
made everything just a little more bearable.

Samantha sat at the kitchen table and watched her
sister put the kettle on and prepare the cups. Even in her
misery, she saw something different about Savvy. There
was a serenity that hadn't been there hours before.

"What's going on? You look like a cat who's just been
given a canary farm."

Her sister threw a grin over her shoulder. "Is there
such a thing as a canary farm?"

"Don't change the subject."

Facing her, Savvy said, "Tit for tat?"

Meaning she'd have to spill her news before Savvy
would give up hers. Her sigh ragged, she said, "Quinn's
back."

Instead of looking disturbed, excitement flared in her
green eyes. "I knew he wouldn't be able to stay away
from you."

Samantha wished she could laugh, because it really
was kind of funny. She and her sister had apparently
reversed roles. Savvy had always been the pragmatic,
logical one, not prone to romanticism. And Samantha

had been the romantic in the family, believing in happy endings.

"He's not here for me. He's here to do some work on the house before the holidays."

As if she hadn't spoken, Savvy turned away to pour the hot water into the cups. Holding two steaming mugs in her hand, she carried them to the table and set one in front of Samantha. Then, with what sounded like the most contented of sighs, she sat down and said, "Let's invite him to Thanksgiving dinner."

"What? Have you lost your mind? I'm not going to ruin everyone's holiday by having the man I just broke up with at our dinner table."

Savvy opened her mouth, probably to argue, but before she could speak, Samantha weakened and said, "Do you think he'll spend it alone?"

"What do you think?"

"Lindsay Milan was at his house when I got there. Maybe she'll invite him."

Savvy grinned. "Quinn having Thanksgiving dinner with Clark Dayton and his father. You really see that happening?"

Of course she didn't. And the thought of Quinn spending Thanksgiving by himself was too painful to contemplate. No matter that he didn't want a permanent relationship, she still cared deeply about him.

"Maybe it wouldn't be too awkward. With the houseful we're expecting, I doubt that we would even have to speak to each other much."

"Excellent. Give him a call and invite him."

"Why can't you do that?"

"Well, for one thing, he hardly knows me. And secondly, I'm having a baby girl."

Samantha was concentrating so hard on her reluctance to call Quinn, she almost missed the last part of Savvy's comment.

Squealing her delight, she jumped to her feet and ran around the table to throw her arms around her sister. "What? You are? When did you find out? Does Zach know? What did he say? I thought you guys were going to wait to find out."

Savvy laughed as she returned the hug. "We went to the doctor this morning. When he asked if we wanted to know, Zach and I just looked at each other and said yes at the same time."

"Oh, Savvy, I'm thrilled for you guys. No one deserves this happiness more than you do."

Her face glowing and happy, she giggled. "Zach had to sit down when the doctor told us. I've never seen him so rattled."

"I can't wait until we can start decorating the nursery. This is going to be the most spoiled baby in the entire world."

"And the most loved." Savvy's smile dimmed slightly. "I tried calling Bri this morning. Had to leave a voice mail. Have you heard from her?"

"No. I tried calling and texting this morning, too. I'm sure everything's okay. You know how she is when she gets into a case. Tunnel vision on steroids."

"I know. I just worry that she's in over her head. The thought of Bri being exposed to that monster chills my blood. Lauren's account of her experiences with him make it obvious the man's a psycho."

"Bri's smart. She knows how to play the pretend game better than anyone. She'll be fine."

Savvy nodded and took a sip of her tea. Samantha went back to her seat and practically gulped her own tea down, needing the extra comfort. She hoped to hell she was right about Bri. If anything happened to their sister, neither she nor Savvy would get over it. They'd been one another's best friends since they took their first gasps of air. Their bond had no psychic connection. It was just part of who they were.

"Okay, so let's talk about Thanksgiving dinner. Who all is coming and who is going to cook if Bri can't make it home?"

Samantha got to her feet, glad to have something to concentrate on besides her heartache or her worry for Bri. "I'll make a list. If Bri can't get back in time, let's get the turkey and trimmings from Faye's and add our favorite side dishes to them."

"Sounds good to me. Don't tell Bri I said so, but Faye's chicken and dressing is almost as good as hers."

Grinning, Samantha put her finger to her mouth and traced a giant X. "My lips are sealed."

Quinn propped his long legs up on the railing of his front porch and took a long swallow of beer. Spending the day painting a bathroom and a couple of bedrooms might be a different kind of work than he was used to, but he felt damn good about his progress. Now as the late afternoon sun turned the sky into a crimson and orange blaze, reflecting a path of gold on the lake, he thought about where his life had led him.

He'd never been one to dwell on the past. Mostly, he figured, because he always had a plan and knew where he was headed. Having parents who were so self-involved hadn't been all bad. Even though his mother and father would never get a Parents of the Year award, he had to give them credit. Being ignored had helped him become self-sufficient and focused.

Edward and Geneva Braddock had been simplistic in their child rearing. The first few years, they had paid enough attention to their children so that they didn't get killed or starve to death. Once he and his little brother were old enough to do a few things for themselves, much of the attention had stopped. The responsibilities of parenting had been placed in the hands of nannies and babysitters.

Both heavy drinkers who denied alcoholism like the plague, the booze only made them more selfish. Not that they would ever acknowledge anything like that. If their kids did any wrong, it wasn't on them. Denial had been a daily activity in the Braddock household. Odd how their self-absorption had affected his little brother so differently. He and Dalton had been as different from each other as a scalpel was to a hammer. Quinn had loved him and tried to look out for him, but Dalton had issues long before they became too drastic to deny.

Having had the advantage of skipping a few grades in school because of his academic achievements, Quinn went away to college at sixteen. His career path had always been clear to him. He was part of a banking family, and whether he respected his parents or not, he was a Braddock. The family business was banking; Quinn's course was set.

Until his life took another unexpected turn.

One day he was walking by the army recruiting office, and instead of passing by like he had hundreds of times before, he went inside. An hour later, he had enlisted.

Six months later, he was in Iraq.

Looking back on it now, it amused Quinn how arrogant he'd been. Having always prided himself on his restraint and discipline, he saw the army as an opportunity to reinforce his strengths. Instead he had learned how unfocused and out of control he really was. Nothing forced control and focus like being in the midst of battle and trying to prevent a man from bleeding out, or having a gaping hole shot in your arm and still having to shoot your way out of a deadly ambush.

Four years later, he was back in civvies with a whole new focus. He applied to medical school with a plan to specialize in emergency medicine. And had never looked back. His CO, career army and damn proud of it, had told him more than once that things worked out the way they do for a reason. Quinn agreed with him.

Once he was stateside again, he'd made a point to go see his parents. After a tense fifteen-minute visit during which they'd mostly just stared at him, he'd left. On his way out of town, he'd stopped at the cemetery. The overlarge tombstone hadn't surprised him. His parents would want only the best to impress their friends. But he had been stunned at the engraving on the shiny limestone: *Dalton Braddock, beloved only son of Edward and Geneva Braddock*.

Seeing those words coalesced memories, thoughts, and feelings into an indisputable truth. Whatever his parents had felt about him, it for sure hadn't been love. He'd driven out of town and hadn't bothered them since.

When Sam had asked him about Dalton, he hadn't handled it well. She had every right to know. Hell, he should have told her way before that. Instead she'd learned the truth and had assumed the worst. Was it any wonder she had thought he was guilty?

He wondered if she had given thought to what he carried in his blood. Alcoholic parents and a psychopath for a brother. How in the hell could anyone want to have children with a man who had a freak show for a family?

He set his half-finished beer on the porch and stalked back into the house. Other than holding Sam in his arms, only one thing could calm and center him. In seconds he had stripped out of his jeans and pulled on running shorts, a T-shirt, and running shoes. Within five minutes, he was out the door and off for a body-punishing run.

Running from his demons or chasing them? Quinn could no longer tell.

CHAPTER TWENTY-FOUR

Samantha waved at the late afternoon crowd at Faye's Diner as she jogged by. Since Savvy was back on her feet and Inez was keeping her informed of any new arrivals to Midnight, she had stopped going to Faye's. Going there brought back too many memories of her last breakfast with Quinn. She'd walked out of the restaurant with such hope, and barely an hour later, all hope had been obliterated.

And now he was back. For two weeks she had been living in a numb kind of limbo, but now she could feel the zing in her blood again. That infuriated her. She didn't need a man in her life to make her feel alive and purposeful. Her sense of self was strong enough to function without Quinn. Problem was, she still wanted to be with him. She'd gotten almost no sleep last night, thinking about Quinn being so close by again.

Rounding a corner on Fifth Street, she made a right onto Magnolia Avenue. For as long as she could remember, she had ended her runs in the exact same spot. The middle of the town square, in front of the mimosa tree fountain. Slowing her pace, she crossed the street. Her focus on avoiding traffic, she was in front of the fountain and stopping before she realized someone else was there, too.

Quinn stood before the fountain staring at it as if it

had all the answers. She could tell him from experience that it didn't.

He didn't look at her as he said, "I can just see you coming here as a kid and making wishes. Did you do that?"

"Yes."

"Did they come true?"

"Some. Not as many as I'd hoped."

He turned then and Samantha's heart leaped to her throat. Those piercing blue eyes that could make her feel a million and one emotions at once were clouded, almost vulnerable. She ached to reach out to him and console him. "What's wrong, Quinn? Did something happen?"

A half smile twitched at his lips and then his mouth went straight and grim once more. "Just life, Sam."

"Why are you really here in Midnight?"

His broad shoulders shifted in a shrug. "Like I said, I'm here to work on the house."

Why had she expected anything different? Hell, when they'd been sleeping together, he had rarely told her what was on his mind. Now that they were broken up, did she think he'd suddenly become less reticent?

About to retreat and go on her way, she stopped abruptly when he said, "Want to go to Faye's for coffee?"

"You really think that's a good idea?"

"Probably not." Again that half smile appeared. "Come on, Sam, we're adult enough to have a cup of coffee together without anything happening, aren't we?"

Adult enough? Maybe. But putting herself through another experience like the last one? She was no masochist. Each time she said goodbye to this man, her heart fractured a little more.

Shaking her head, she backed up. "I don't think so, Quinn."

He surprised her when he didn't argue, just gave her a solemn nod and turned away.

Refusing to be so pitiful as to watch him until he disappeared from sight, Samantha went the other way. As she passed by Faye's again, she stopped abruptly. Going back home held no appeal. Savvy and Zach were in Mobile picking out baby items for the nursery. And Samantha wasn't due at Gibby's until seven. If she went home, she'd just worry about Bri or think about Quinn. At least here she would be around people and might pick up some valuable information.

Mentally shrugging, Sam went through the doors. Why did she feel she had to justify going for a cup of coffee?

After waving, nodding, and offering several hellos, Sam chose a booth close to the back. She felt out of sorts, and it wasn't just because of Quinn. She was restless and bored. Having had a profession that could take more hours of the day than was even possible to give, she now felt directionless.

Bri was diligently working Lauren's case. In between research on Cruz and all the paperwork involved in setting up their business, Savvy was planning for the baby. This left Samantha with way too much time on her hands. She either needed to drum up more business for their fledging security agency or go find another job.

Immersed in her moment of self-pity, she barely noticed that the diner door squeaked open again. What she did notice was the cessation of sound. She looked up and swallowed a gasp. Quinn had come in. He nodded to the room, at no one in particular, and headed toward her. Hadn't she just told him this wasn't a good idea? Why would he follow her? They couldn't be just friends . . . didn't he understand that? And if he thought they could go back to what they had before, he was wrong.

All the wind was taken from her sails when he chose

the booth behind her. She knew immediately when his big body slid into the bench seat. Dammit, he was inches away from her, so close she could practically feel his body heat through the thin material of the partition. If she leaned back, her hair would brush against his neck. And she could smell his heated skin, a mixture of clean male sweat and the musk aftershave he favored. She closed her eyes as a wave of longing rushed through her. She reminded herself the last time she'd inhaled those delicious scents, she'd gotten her heart broken.

A masculine voice asked, "So, how's the apple pie here?"

She kept her voice to a furious whisper. "What are you doing here, Quinn? I thought we agreed we couldn't do this."

"Do what, Sam? I just came in here for some coffee and pie. If I'm not mistaken, there's no law against that."

"Why couldn't you have gone to another restaurant or at least a different booth?"

"Because Faye's coffee is the best. And if you'll look around, the restaurant is full. There is no other place to sit."

She quickly scanned the room, noting that he was right. Not only that, every eye was on them. There was no way people didn't know they were talking to each other. Holding her menu up in front of her face, she said, "I still don't like that you came here."

"I was the one who asked you here for coffee. You had to know I would come in here. So, tell me, Sam, are you following me?"

She heard the humor in his voice. Any other time, she might have laughed at the ridiculousness of the situation. She didn't feel any laughter within her. "Fine. Just don't talk to me."

"You started the conversation, Sam. I was only being polite in answering you."

"You asked me about the pie."

"No, I asked Faye. She's standing only a few feet away from me."

She peeked over her shoulder and sure enough, Faye stood barely three feet away staring down at both of them. Samantha turned back around. "Fine. Whatever. Just do what you came here to do and leave me alone."

There was complete silence.

"Quinn?"

Still no answer. Unable to help herself, she turned around and almost bumped noses with him.

"Yes?"

"Why didn't you answer?"

"You told me not to talk to you."

With a huff, she turned back around. "Glad we got that straight."

She couldn't be sure, but it sounded as if he swallowed a laugh.

"I'm so happy you find this situation so amusing."

"I don't, Sam. In fact, I'm damn lonely. If you like, you can join me in my booth and we can talk like two adults instead of seventh graders with a secret crush."

The enticement was great. She had no doubt if she wanted to, she could join Quinn at his booth and they could have a wonderful conversation. And after they left here, she knew she could follow him to his house and they could make love. Quinn had made no bones about the fact that he was open to having her back in his bed. But she wanted more than just a bed partner. She wanted him in other places besides the bedroom. She wanted to be his companion, his friend and his lover. Forever.

"That's okay. I'm perfectly happy here."

"Suit yourself."

"What're you going to have?"

Samantha looked up into Faye's tired, lined face. "Coffee."

"No dessert? You're still too skinny."

"Why not get the apple pie, with ice cream?" This came from Quinn.

Ignoring him, Samantha said, "Coffee is just fine. Thanks."

Faye walked a couple of steps sideways to Quinn.

"What're you going to have?"

"Coffee, extra-large slice of apple pie, two scoops of ice cream . . . why don't you bring two spoons, just in case."

"You got it."

The humor in Faye's voice was unmistakable. Samantha turned around and gaped. She had never heard or seen Faye have any kind of humorous moment. Though her mouth was still set on grim, there was a twinkle in her wise brown eyes. Despite her irritation at Quinn, Samantha was suddenly glad he was here. If he could give a lift to Faye, who had always seemed unliftable, then the aggravation of his presence was worth it.

Deciding to ignore him as best she could, Samantha took out a notepad and pen from the little pack attached to her waist, having learned to never go anywhere without something to write on or with. Now to figure out how to get their name out so they could grow their business. She opened to the first page and sighed. She also needed to decide on the menu for Thanksgiving dinner. Which reminded her. She had yet to invite the aggravating man behind her.

"You still there?"

"Where else am I going?"

"Savvy wanted me to invite you to Thanksgiving dinner."

"And what about you? Did you want to invite me?"

"You can come if you want." She winced, well aware that she had sounded like a bratty teenager.

"What a lovely invitation. So heartfelt and sincere."

"Fine. Would you please come to Thanksgiving dinner? We'll have a massive amount of food and lots of people."

"So you can ignore me."

"Whether I like it or not, Quinn, you're not exactly ignorable."

"Thank you, Sam. That's probably one of the nicest things you've said to me in a while. And yes, I would love to come to Thanksgiving dinner with your family."

"Fine. Be there at two. We—"

"Hey there, Dr. Braddock. Did you enjoy the casserole?"

She stiffened, recognizing the sugary-sweet tone of Lindsay Milan. The woman had somehow slunk up to Quinn's booth without Samantha seeing her pass by.

"Hello, Mrs. Milan. That was a fine casserole."

Quinn didn't bother to tell the woman that it was still in the fridge. He hadn't even thought about eating it last night. What he wanted to do was ask her to leave so he could continue flirting with Sam. An outside observer might think they were sniping at each other, but this was the friendliest conversation he'd had with her in a while. He wanted to continue.

"I'm making Thanksgiving dinner for my family at my house. We'd love it if you could come."

Considering that one of those family members was Clark Dayton, Quinn seriously doubted that. The bastard had called Samantha a slut. Saying that about any woman wasn't something Quinn would allow. Having it said about Sam? Hell, the man was lucky he hadn't lost some teeth in the altercation.

"I appreciate the invitation, but I already have plans."

He watched Lindsay's eyes travel over to Sam, who was still sitting behind him. And though he couldn't see her, he knew her back was board stiff and she was listening to every word.

"Maybe we could go see a movie or something. The

holiday movies are starting. There're going to be some good ones."

"I'm going to be tied up with the repairs to my house. Thanks, though."

"What about dinner tomorrow night. I mean . . . you gotta eat."

She stared silently for several more seconds. The longer she stared, the more he felt sorry for her. Even as she stood there, trying to act seductive, the look in her eyes said she was expecting a rejection, like she was used to getting turned down. He'd never in his life accepted a date with a woman because he pitied her, but he heard himself saying, "Dinner tomorrow night sounds good."

Three things happened simultaneously. Lindsay smiled like she'd just won the lottery. Faye slammed his apple pie à la mode onto the table with a killing glare. And Sam got up and walked out of the restaurant.

Quinn cursed silently. Nodding his agreement to Lindsay's plans, he stood and threw down money for the dessert he no longer wanted. "I'll see you tomorrow."

"Aren't you going to eat your apple pie?"

"Can't. Just remembered I gotta be somewhere. You're welcome to it."

He didn't stick around to see if she took him up on his offer. As he walked through the restaurant, he felt the disapproving glares drilling a hole into his back. He knew he had made a tactical error. It was obvious just from the short time he'd spent here that Sam was a favorite of many in Midnight. She was a favorite of Quinn's, too. Unfortunately it wasn't enough for her.

Monday night, Samantha sat across from Blaine and worked hard to hang on to her smile. She didn't want to be here with him but neither did she want to be at home, moping about Quinn. At least dinner with Blaine meant she was doing something constructive.

"Do you not like your steak?"

"It's delicious." She swallowed the small bite she'd taken and added, "Guess I'm not as hungry as I thought."

"For a Podunk town, Midnight has some pretty good restaurants, but I thought coming to Mobile would be a treat for both of us."

She ignored the slight to the town she loved and said, "Are you not liking Midnight as much as you did?"

Blaine gazed over her shoulder, as if he were seeing something in the distance. "Things just haven't worked out the way I wanted them to." Before she could comment on that, he said, "How goes the security business? Have any jobs yet?"

"Not yet. It takes time to establish a business like that."

"Takes keeping secrets, too. Doesn't it?"

"What do you mean?"

He shrugged. "Just that every time I ask about your business, you've been evasive. I finally decided that it makes sense for you not to tell me. After all, if you're doing secretive stuff, you can't exactly broadcast it, can you?"

Her senses heightened, she tentatively opened a trapdoor and offered some bait. "You're very smart to pick up on that. We do have a case but it's not something I can talk about."

"That's what I figured. Is it dangerous?"

"It could be."

He stared hard at her for several seconds and then said, "You like danger?"

"I was a cop. I like to right wrongs."

"So do I."

"What do you mean?"

He gave a self-deprecating smile. "I was an accountant. I righted wrongs every day."

"Are you not looking for an accounting job in Midnight?"

"Not yet. I'm trying to decide if I'm going to stay. I haven't found what I was looking for yet."

"What are you looking for?"

"Peace. Healing."

"You think that's possible?"

Surprising her, Blaine took her hand from the wineglass she'd been fiddling with and held it to his mouth. "I think it's something we can work on together."

Whoa. Where had that come from? Just when she was thinking he might have some connection to Cruz, he threw her for another loop. He had claimed he wasn't looking for a relationship beyond friendship. And now this?

Samantha gently pulled at her hand but Blaine held it tight. Tugging more forcibly, she finally succeeded. "Blaine, no. I'm sorry but I just don't have those kinds of feelings for you."

"But you could. If you try, I know you could." He gave her another gentle smile. "Give us a chance."

She had found herself in many uncomfortable situations in her life, but this ranked near the top. The restaurant was small, so conversations weren't private. She'd seen more than a couple of people glance their way during this exchange.

In the past, she had been able to extricate herself from such situations with relative ease. The determined set to Blaine's mouth told her this wasn't going to be as simple.

"We could never be more than friends. That's never going to change."

"I could change your mind . . . I know I could." He

put his napkin down and pushed his chair back. "Come home with me and let me show you how good we could be together."

She had chosen to be short and curt hoping to cut this conversation off at the quick. Either she hadn't been as blunt as she had thought or Blaine was more stubborn than most.

"No, that's not going to happen. I don't want you in that way, Blaine." And because he still looked unconvinced, she added with brutal honesty, "I never will."

As if realizing he had attracted the attention of nearby tables, he gave a self-conscious glance around and then turned back to her. She braced herself for his anger but was relieved when he said, "I'm sorry. I didn't mean to push you." He nodded at her still-full plate. "Do you want to take that home?"

"No."

"Then I think we'll both be more comfortable if I drove you home now."

Glad to be going but sad that she had hurt his feelings, Samantha stood and walked with him out of the restaurant. The silence was stiff and awkward. She scrambled for something to break the ice and ease the tension.

When in doubt of what to say, a Southerner always turns to weather. "I heard that a winter storm is headed for the North. Think Indiana will get much?"

Thankfully Blaine went along with her lame attempt. "Yeah, I heard that, too. I checked online . . . looks like it's going to blanket half the country."

That conversation got them to the car, but once they were both seated and Blaine had pulled out of the parking lot, the tense silence returned. Samantha chose not to try again. She wished they had eaten at a restaurant in Midnight as opposed to one in Mobile. A forty-minute drive home could feel like hours in situations like this.

Glancing at his profile to see if he was feeling the same level of discomfort, she was stunned to see him smiling at her.

"Something amusing?"

"I was just thinking how I really know how to end an evening on a sour note."

"Blaine, I am—"

He held up a hand. "Please . . . don't apologize again. You did nothing wrong. I obviously misinterpreted things."

Since she had made a point of telling him she wasn't interested in anything but friendship when he had asked her out for this date, she wasn't sure how he had misinterpreted her. Reminding him was useless, so she didn't. Instead she said, "The restaurant was good. I've never been there before."

Apparently lame conversation starters weren't going to work, since he just nodded his head and was once more silent. Samantha let it go. She'd done her best to minimize his hurt, and she couldn't change her mind about her feelings. There was nothing more she could do.

When at last they turned onto Wildefire Lane, tension eased from her body. Just a few more seconds and she would be out of this awkward situation. She made a solemn vow to herself never to agree to go out with a man again unless she was romantically interested in him. Then she grimly acknowledged that since she would never be interested in anyone that way but Quinn, she would likely never date again. She mentally shrugged. So be it.

Blaine pulled in front of the Wilde house and parked. Hoping to get away without any more dramatics, she opened the car door.

"Samantha . . . wait."

She turned to him and said, "Really, I think it'll be best if we just leave it like this. Okay?"

"I'm really sorry it turned out this way. I hope we can still be friends."

Friends? Even if he wasn't one of Cruz's men, she didn't see a friendship happening between them. However, getting into another discussion was pointless.

"I've got to go, Blaine. Again, I'm sorry."

He nodded and allowed her to exit the car. She was relieved that he didn't try to escort her to the door. Her foot had just hit the first step of the porch when Blaine called out, "Samantha, wait."

Cursing softly, she turned to see him jogging toward her, holding a small wrapped box.

"I meant to give this to you earlier and then . . . well . . ." He shrugged.

Feeling even more uncomfortable, Samantha backed up, taking another step up to the porch. "Blaine, no."

"It's a simple token of friendship . . . nothing more."

"Friendship or not, I cannot accept it."

Instead of taking no for an answer, he grabbed her hand and placed the box in it. "Keep it. I can't return it."

Before she could say anything else, he turned on his heels and jogged back to his car. Weary and disgusted at how the night had gone, Samantha let herself into the house.

Even though it was only a little past nine, the house was silent. She trudged up to her room and undressed. Just as she was about to settle into bed with what she hoped was an uplifting romance, her eyes caught a glimpse of the beautifully wrapped box she'd dropped on her dresser.

Determined to return the box unopened to Blaine the

next time she saw him, she opened her book, ready to put the disastrous night behind her by immersing herself in a story in which it appeared that happily-ever-afters really did exist. She already knew that unless something drastic changed with Quinn, a happily-ever-after for her was definitely out of the question.

CHAPTER TWENTY-FIVE

The sun rose like a hot, bright beacon on Thanksgiving morning. The weather for the last few weeks had been decidedly chilly, but for some reason, Mother Nature chose to return warm weather as a Thanksgiving gift.

Samantha stood in the garden at the back of the Wilde house. This had been a favorite place of hers since she was a little kid. She'd often come here to breathe in the fragrance of nature and find the serenity she needed.

Today was such a day. Quinn would be coming for dinner. She'd been so busy with the preparations over the last couple of days, she hadn't had time to think about that. Now, with most of the preparations complete, she drew in the fresh, springlike air and searched for that centeredness she counted on to get her through tough times.

It wasn't like they were going to be alone. There would be almost a dozen people here with them. She doubted they would have the chance to say hello to each other, much less have any kind of conversation.

And what did she have to say to him anyway? *How was your date the other night?* Hearing him accept a date with Lindsay Milan had hurt. She couldn't deny that. But she knew it meant nothing. She'd heard the compassion in his voice when he had accepted her invitation.

No, that wasn't what bothered her. What had been on her mind for the past few days was a bigger problem. How was she going to stay in Midnight with Quinn owning a house here? Even if he came only a few times a year, what was going to happen when he arrived one day with his new lover? She wasn't naïve enough to believe he wouldn't find someone else. Quinn wasn't the type of guy to play around with a lot of different women. He would find another woman to share his bed and maybe his life. Just because he didn't want to marry again didn't mean he wouldn't have a long-term romantic relationship.

What would she do if she ran into them? She already knew she wouldn't handle it well. So what was she to do? Only go out when she knew he wasn't in town? Leave town when he arrived?

"Looks like everything's under control. Why so glum-looking?"

Gasping, Samantha jumped from her chair and threw her arms around Bri. "I was so afraid you weren't going to be able to come."

Bri returned her hug and then pulled away to give her rare, brilliant smile. "Miss my favorite holiday with my favorite people? Never."

Joyful tears threatened. She had been so worried about Bri these last few weeks. Being in the midst of monsters could be rough on the toughest people. The toughness in Bri was mostly a façade to cover the hurts life had thrown at her. Most people saw only what she wanted them to see. Samantha and Savvy saw their sister for who she really was, and they loved her just the way she was.

Drawing Bri down onto the bench with her, Samantha examined her sister's face. She looked a little tired but not overly so. There were no shadows lurking. No hint of sorrow. This was a good day.

"What's going on with Cruz? Have you made any progress?"

"The guy's a creep of the first order, but I've made some progress. I mostly just sit around, look clueless and beautiful, and try to stay out of his way. I'm finding that's one of the best ways to learn a lot. He tends to forget the women in the room."

"Yeah, Lauren mentioned that."

"Enough talking about that louse for today. Tell me about Savvy. She's really okay?"

"She's perfect. The doctor said both she and the baby are healthy as horses."

"What a relief." She grinned and added, "She texted me that it's a girl. That's wonderful. We need another feminista in this house."

"I agree. Though I think Zach is feeling a little overwhelmed. He and Savvy were arguing the other night on what age it's okay for her to start dating. His suggestion was not until after she gets her second doctoral degree."

"I can't wait to meet her." Her eyes went serious. "Now, tell me what's going on with you. When I came out here, you were looking like someone ate your last cookie."

"Quinn's back."

"I didn't know he'd left."

"That's because you didn't need any additional things to think about." Samantha shrugged. "He left a couple of weeks ago."

"And?"

Without going into too much detail, Samantha told her about how Quinn had taken her to his new home and made love to her like she was as important to him as breathing and then admitted he still wanted nothing permanent.

"So why is he back?"

"That's exactly what I asked him. He just said he was

taking some time to get a few repairs done on the house before the holidays."

"He came back because of you, Sammie."

"No . . . maybe." Samantha shook her head. "I don't know. I guess it doesn't matter, since he won't change his mind and neither will I. Seeing him here is killing me. What if he brings a girlfriend back with him someday? I couldn't handle that."

"So this town's not big enough for the both of you?"

"Yeah, something like that, I guess."

"I still don't think you're seeing the big picture. You're the only reason he has to come back to Midnight."

"He has a house here now."

"Yes. A house he bought for the two of you."

"There is no two of us any longer."

"Of course there is. You're just too stubborn to admit it. You still love him, and from all accounts, he's crazy about you."

Samantha fought back a smile. This coming from the Queen of Denial. Ian had been in love with Bri forever. And if Bri allowed herself to stop and think about it, she'd admit she felt the same way. But her sister was right about one thing. She did love Quinn and knew her feelings would never change.

"And a man doesn't dole out hundreds of thousands of dollars for a house on a whim. He was looking for something permanent with you."

"But that's not the kind of permanency I want. I can't live with him, Bri. Even as modern as I tell myself I am, that just isn't me. Especially in my hometown."

"Then don't live with him, for gosh sakes, if that's the only thing holding you back."

It wasn't the only thing but it was a big factor. "But what if he never wants to make it more permanent? I want more, Bri. Marriage, kids, the whole shebang. He's told me he doesn't want that."

"Then I guess the question is, is your need for those things more than your need for Quinn?"

The truth shot through her like a precisely targeted arrow, penetrating her most cherished beliefs. Did she want those things more than she wanted to be with Quinn?

"I'll let you ponder that while I go freshen up. I spotted the dressing and turkey you got from Faye's on the counter. From the looks of everything, you guys have everything under control. I'll make a cake, a couple of pies, and maybe another casserole or two. Dinner still at two o'clock?"

Samantha absentmindedly nodded. Thanksgiving dinner now a thousand miles from her thoughts, she barely noticed that Bri dropped a kiss on top of her head and walked back into the house.

She had some decisions to make. And she needed to make sure she could live with her choices. Quinn had made it clear he wouldn't change his mind. So that left them exactly where?

Lindsay Milan glared down at the pitiful excuse for a turkey. She'd waited too late to shop for a good one and had gone by old man Henson's grocery on the way home last night. There'd only been this scrawny-looking thing left. Hell, what did she care? The only people to eat it would be her daddy and brother. They barely looked at the food before they shoveled it into their mouths.

The unfairness of it all hit her hard. Both men went out deer hunting this morning. They'd woken her just before dawn for one reason only—to tell her what time they'd be back for dinner. They didn't give a damn that she'd be spending the entire day in the kitchen. All she was to them was a cook and housekeeper. And she didn't even get paid for it.

She shouldn't have come back to Midnight but it was the only home she knew. A few months ago, she'd left town with two thousand dollars in her purse and the promise of a job in Charleston. Zach Tanner, the police chief, had provided her with both. That hadn't exactly been what she'd wanted from Zach, but when he encouraged her to make something of herself, she had believed she could. But the job had been boring and the money had run out sooner than she had expected. When she got fired for pilfering a few lousy bucks from the kitty, she'd left town. She knew she was lucky her boss hadn't filed charges against her. She'd never been so sloppy before.

Maybe she had secretly wanted to come back home. Her daddy and Clark were the only family she had left. Had she thought they would have missed her and might treat her better? Of course, she hadn't just fallen off the turnip truck. She'd figured they'd want her to be their housekeeper again, but when she'd demanded they pay her, she didn't know who had laughed the hardest, her daddy or brother. Both of them were assholes, and if she weren't so scared of them, she'd put something in their Thanksgiving dinner that'd give them the runs till springtime. But damned if she wanted any more bruises.

She had a funny feeling deep in her gut that things were about to change. Her ship was about to come in. She just knew it. For so long, Zach Tanner was the only decent-looking man in Midnight, but the other day she'd met someone who had literally blown her socks off. Okay, not exactly her socks. More like her panties.

She'd never had a man take control of her like that. In fact, it was a wonder she had been able to walk the next day. They'd only had one date so far and she had been a little disappointed when he had taken her out of town to eat. She had wanted all the tongue wagglers in Midnight to get an up-close-and-personal view of her with him.

In the end, it hadn't really mattered. After taking her to a nice restaurant in Foley, he'd stopped halfway home and pulled over to the side of the road. She'd been a little unsettled. After all, she didn't know that much about him.

When she had asked him why they were stopping, he'd just smiled and said, "So I won't have to share you with all those busybodies in Midnight." And then he had kissed her, taking control of her mouth and then her body. Just the memory of all the delicious things he'd done to her caused her to go wet with desire.

The car wasn't her favorite place to get her rocks off, but he had made it worth her while. She'd come home that night worn out and deliciously sore. The morning after, she'd woken to find several bite marks on her breasts, stomach, and the inside of her thighs. When and how they'd happened she had no clue. Considering she'd had two husbands who'd beat up on her, plus a daddy and brother who thought nothing of backhanding her on occasion, having a man bruise her like that shouldn't be so sexy. But it was. And she wanted him to do it to her again, as soon as possible.

She dumped a can of pumpkin pie mix into a pie shell, slapped it smooth with a spatula, and shoved it into the oven, beside the turkey. She'd never been much of a cook. After her mama left, she'd been put in charge of all the household chores. Cooking had been forced on her and she'd had no real interest in learning how to do it right. Daddy and Clark hadn't cared. As long as it was edible and they could fill their gullets, they were satisfied.

Her ex-husbands hadn't been much better when she'd

been married to them. They hadn't expected much out of her and she'd been glad to give them what they expected. They'd both kicked her out of the house for screwing around, not because she was a bad cook. There was some kind of irony in there somewhere.

She jerked at the sound of the doorbell. Hell, she wasn't about to answer it. She looked like something the hounds had dragged home—no makeup and wearing a ratty old housecoat she'd had since she was a teenager. Whoever it was would go away. They didn't get pleasant visitors at their house anyway. Just salespeople and bill collectors.

She was in the middle of mixing up a green bean casserole when she felt a presence behind her. Frowning, she turned and dropped the spoon she was holding.

"What are you doing here? How'd you get in?"

The charming smile was missing today. His eyes were serious and intense and the smile he gave her was cold and slightly creepy. "I thought we could spend Thanksgiving together."

Despite her unease, she couldn't help but be flattered. A man as good-looking as him probably had lots of places he could spend Thanksgiving. She glanced around at her messy kitchen. "I'm afraid it's not going to be ready for several hours. Daddy and Clark are out hunting and I just now put the turkey in the oven."

"That's okay." He pulled the shirt from his pants and began to unbutton it. "That'll give us time to get to know each other better."

Instantly aroused at his masterful attitude, Lindsay unzipped the ancient housecoat and dropped it to the floor. Her naked body was a hell of a lot better to look at than that old thing anyway.

He held out his hand. "Let's go to your bedroom."

Her dreams were more important than dinner. As he led her to her bedroom, she gave little thought to how he knew where it was or how he'd been able to get inside the house. He had worked magic on her body, so maybe he knew things that couldn't be explained.

All questions could wait. She had more important things on her mind. Just like she'd hoped, her ship had finally come in.

CHAPTER TWENTY-SIX

His hand wrapped around the most expensive bottle of wine he could find at Midnight's one and only liquor store, Quinn rang the doorbell of the Wilde mansion. Other than the alcohol, he felt like a teenager going on his first date. This was Sam's family. The people who meant more to her than anyone. It was stupid, he knew, since he and Sam weren't even together anymore, but he wanted them to like him. He wasn't holding out much hope.

The door flew open and a small, cheerful-looking elderly woman with silver-gray hair and lively brown eyes assessed him. He withstood her scrutiny, figuring she was trying to decide if he would be allowed in. Finally she nodded and said, "Yes, I can certainly see why." She stepped back and said, "Come on in, young man."

Having no idea what her first comment had been about, Quinn stepped inside the giant foyer of the mansion. Sam had described her aunt so well, he immediately knew the older woman's identity. "You must be Sam's aunt Gibby."

Lively, shrewd eyes continued to examine him as she answered, "Lorna Jean Wilcox. Most people call me Gibby."

Not sure if that included him, Quinn held out his hand and said, "I'm happy to meet you. I'm Quinn Braddock."

She took his hand, but instead of shaking it, she held it between her two hands and examined it. "You have beautiful hands for a man. Healing hands."

Quinn was beginning to wonder if Sam's aunt had a touch of dementia when he heard a soft snort to his left. Turning, he saw a young woman with short, white-blond hair and Sam's features. This was apparently Sabrina.

"Don't mind Aunt Gibby. She's just trying to figure you out."

The elderly woman finally let go of his hand. "I was reading one of those magazines over at Tillie's when I was getting my hair done the other day. It said you could read a person's character by examining their hands."

Before Quinn could ask if she had learned anything, Sabrina said, "What my aunt means is she's trying to figure out if you're just a jerk or you have another reason for breaking the heart of one of the most beautiful and gentle-hearted people in the world."

"I guess I deserved that."

"No you didn't."

Sam came to stand beside her sister. "Quinn is a guest. I didn't invite him here for you guys to interrogate him or treat him badly."

"We weren't doing anything other than trying to get to know him," Sabrina said. "Were we, Aunt Gibby?"

"Oh, heavens no." Her eyes sparkling, the elderly woman smiled up at Quinn. "In fact, I think I got the answer I was looking for. And you're right, Samantha. He is quite beautiful."

He heard Sabrina snort but his eyes were only for Sam, who was blushing at her aunt's comment as she came toward him. Quinn stopped breathing. Had she ever been lovelier? Wearing a body-hugging sweater dress in gray and dark red, she looked elegant, feminine, and so damn sexy. If her aunt and sister hadn't been watching, he would have pulled her to him and followed the curve of her mouth with his tongue. Whether she would have let him was another matter.

Meeting her halfway, he took her hand and held it to his mouth. Though her full lips were tilted up in a smile, her eyes remained solemn, their brightness dimmed.

"You okay?"

She nodded. "I'm fine. I'm glad you could come." She peeked around him. "And I apologize for my sister and aunt. They sometimes let their overprotectiveness get the better of them."

Still bothered by her too-serious demeanor, he glanced over his shoulder and nodded at both women. Neither of them looked particularly repentant. "You're fortunate to have a family who loves you like that."

"You're right, I am."

She pulled her hand from his and turned away. "Come on into the family room. We have appetizers and wine. Everyone is here."

"Not everyone."

Samantha turned back to her aunt. Still reeling with the thousand emotions Quinn always created in her, she barely wondered about Gibby's comment as she said, "Who else is coming?"

"A nice young man I met at the grocery store the other day. He's new to Midnight and was buying a turkey TV dinner for Thanksgiving. Well, you know I couldn't let that happen."

She stiffened with dread. Even though the identity of their coming guest was obvious, she asked, "What's his name?"

"Blaine Marshall. He said he was a friend of yours, Samantha. I'm surprised you didn't ask him yourself."

She hadn't asked him for obvious reasons. "I wish you had told me, Aunt Gibby."

Her shoulders drooping slightly, Gibby said, "I'm sorry. I didn't realize it would be a problem."

Immediately she felt guilty. Gibby had done nothing wrong. "No, I'm sorry, Aunt Gibby. You have every right to invite anyone you want. And we have more than enough food." Turning to Quinn, she said, "Could I talk to you for a minute?"

Questions in his eyes, he nodded. "Sure."

Instead of heading to the family room, where everyone was gathered, she led him into the study. Letting Quinn in on what was going on would hopefully quell any possible outburst.

Once inside the room, she closed the door and turned back to him. "I just wanted to remind you that Blaine's the man I told you about . . . the one I was investigating for our case."

"You are so damn beautiful."

She'd been so intent on defusing the situation, she hadn't noticed that Quinn had other things on his mind. Even as she told herself not to leap to conclusions, her heart pounded against her chest. A little breathless, she said, "Thank you. You look nice, too." And he did, in gray slacks and a dark tan sports coat that covered a white open-necked shirt. Understated and classic.

"I've been doing some thinking." The words burst from her before she could stop them. She'd thought of nothing else since her conversation with Bri earlier. Did she have the courage to go through with this, and could she live with the consequences? The answer always came back to one thing—she wanted Quinn in her life, any way she could get him.

"Thinking about what?"

"Us." Standing on the precipice of what to her was a major leap of faith, she said, "I don't want us to be over."

Relief, hope, and wariness were all reflected in his eyes. "Neither do I."

He started toward her but she held up her hand. "No, wait. We need to talk."

"Okay, but first . . ." Taking the hand she held up, he pulled her into his arms and covered her mouth with his.

Groaning in surrender, Samantha sank into his hard body. After all the lectures and recriminations she'd given herself over the last few days, it all came down to this. What she felt for this man defied her arguments. She didn't want to give up on her hopes of the family she'd always dreamed of, but hanging on to those fantasies was small comfort if she had to give up the man she loved. She didn't want a family with anyone else. She didn't want to be with anyone else. Quinn and only Quinn.

As her fingers weaved through his thick hair, she rubbed against his body, creating an intense, hot friction of need. When Quinn's big hands grabbed her hips, she thought he was going to stop her; instead he pressed her deeper into his erection. Her gasp one of excitement and arousal, Samantha held his shoulders as she rode the wave of arousal and then climbed the peak to something more.

Only seconds from climax, she swallowed a moan of denial when Quinn pulled his mouth from hers and growled, "I want more than this."

"I do, too."

"Can we go somewhere?"

Reality crashed, destroying the deliciously achy need thrumming through her bloodstream. There were a dozen or so hungry people in the family room waiting for dinner, probably wondering why it hadn't been served. Dropping her arms, she pushed away and strode to the door. "I've got to get back to the kitchen. Savvy and Bri are going to kill me."

"Sam."

She leaned her head against the door. How could a

voice make her insides turn to liquid flame? "I need to go, Quinn."

"Promise me we'll finish this later. That it's not just a moment of weakness for both of us."

Turning, she faced him with the truth. "I can live without you, Quinn, but I don't want to. I've been miserable without you."

She braced herself. Baring her soul wasn't easy for a girl who liked to keep it light and fluffy. But Quinn, as usual, knew what to say.

"That makes two of us."

The heavy weight of aloneness lifted and she smiled her brightest. "Let's get dinner behind us."

"Deal."

She stepped out the door but his words caught her. "Happy Thanksgiving"

"You too, Quinn." She closed the door and leaned against it. So what if she didn't have all she wanted. For now she had Quinn. That was more than enough. And if it wasn't forever? She refused to go there.

Quinn settled back into his chair and took everything in. Every Thanksgiving food imaginable had been loaded onto the long cherry dining table. Elegant china, silverware, and crystal were a fitting complement to the feast waiting for the hungry guests seated around the giant table. Sam and her sisters had outdone themselves.

Laughter, gentle ribbing, and varying conversations created a comfortable but festive environment. How different this was from the Thanksgiving dinners of his childhood. The meal had been catered from one of the finest restaurants, servants had stood at solemn attention, and conversation had been either stilted or nonexistent. The atmosphere had been as loving and warm as a morgue.

"Dr. Braddock, would you like some of my corn casserole?"

He turned to Sam's aunt and took the dish from her. "Thank you, Miss Wilcox. But there's no need to call me Dr. Braddock. Call me Quinn."

She beamed. "And you can call me Gibby."

Feeling like he'd made a slight inroad to Sam's family's approval, Quinn spooned out a large helping of the casserole. Under Gibby's watchful eye, he took a giant bite and had instant regret. Tasting like something between an old sock and burnt rubber, the casserole was enough to stop him from ever eating corn again.

"Do you like it? It's an old family recipe with a few additional secret ingredients. I make a big batch every year and freeze them for special occasions."

Grateful he hadn't made a face, he swallowed the lump of torture and smiled at the sweet old lady who apparently had no taste buds. "Best corn pudding I've ever had."

As if he'd just given her a thousand dollars instead of a lie, her eyes lit up. "Let me get you some more."

Before he could stop her, she had heaped another tablespoon onto his plate. She was in the middle of adding another when Sam said, "Aunt Gibby, don't let Quinn eat all of your casserole. Send it down here."

Shooting her a grateful glance, he was surprised to see a knowing amusement in her eyes. And then he remembered a comment she had once made about her beloved aunt and her penchant for very bad casseroles. He heartily agreed with her description.

After a long swallow of iced tea to wash away the bad taste in his mouth, Quinn dug into the rest of his meal. His conversation with Sam had left him with an appetite . . . something he hadn't had in weeks. If he hadn't misunderstood the look in her eyes and her words, what he wanted most in the world was about to come true.

"Where did you say you were from?"

Quinn looked up from his plate, thinking the question was for him. Instead he realized that Savannah had asked the question of the man sitting three chairs down. Blaine Marshall was the guy that Sam said she had been investigating for their case.

"Indiana. The northern part, close to Merrillville."

"I spent some time in Indiana when I was growing up. Nice place to live," Brody James said. "You get back there much?"

He'd been eyeing Marshall, but when the question was asked, Quinn turned his attention to James. The man had been introduced as one of Zach's closest friends, but the expression on his face was anything but friendly.

"I don't have family there anymore but I have a couple of friends I go back and visit from time to time." He glanced over at Sam and smiled. "My home is in Midnight now."

Oh hell, now he knew why Sam was unsettled when her aunt mentioned she had invited Marshall.

"And we're delighted to add a new resident to Midnight," Savannah said.

Savannah was most likely the peacemaker of the family. Sabrina, on the other hand, seemed to be focused solely on Quinn. The statement she'd made earlier had stung but he couldn't deny the truth. Sam was beautiful and gentlehearted and he had hurt her numerous times. But with their conversation earlier, he hoped like hell they could put all of that behind them.

"Quinn," Sabrina said, "Sammie's not told us a lot about you and your family. Where did you grow up?"

"Northern Virginia."

"Your family still live there?"

Quinn nodded. "My mother and father."

"What about brothers or sisters?"

"I had a brother. . . . He died."

"Oh, how sad," Savannah said. "Was he younger or older than you?"

"Younger by two years."

"That's just awful," Gibby said. "Did you read in the paper where . . ."

Quinn stopped listening. He had just shared more with the Wilde family than he had ever told anyone other than Sam herself. For some reason, it wasn't painful . . . not like he had feared.

Sam caught his eye and mouthed the words "Hurry up."

Breath caught in his throat and his heart flipped over. He had to find a way to make this work. He couldn't lose her again.

Hurriedly swallowing the last of her pecan pie, Samantha stood and started gathering empty plates. She needed to get Quinn out of here soon. He had that closed-down expression on his face that he got when things went beyond his comfort zone. That look had occurred often at the few parties they had attended in Atlanta. Quinn was such a private person. She wished so much that she had realized sooner that his need for privacy coincided with a deep hurt in his past.

"Here, Sammie, let me help you."

Blaine tried to take the plates from her. Having him here for dinner hadn't been as awkward as she'd feared. He had been polite and friendly but not overly so. However, she didn't want him to misunderstand again where she stood. And his calling her Sammie was downright irritating.

"That's okay, Blaine." She pulled the plates from his grasp. "Go visit with everyone else. My sisters and I have this down to a science."

"Nonsense. A beautiful woman shouldn't have to work on a holiday."

She laughed. "If women didn't work on holidays, there sure would be a lot of hungry people."

Backing away from him, she caught Brody's eye and he gave her a slight nod.

"Blaine, you up for a game of poker?"

Whether it was his need to feel like one of the guys or because Brody put a hand on his shoulder to steer him toward the family room, Samantha didn't know. Whatever the reason, she shot a grateful look at her friend, who winked back at her.

As she watched the two men walk away, she chewed her lip in indecision. She needed to return the gift Blaine had given her the other night. The longer she had it in her possession, the more it would look as if she had accepted it. Problem was, if she tried to do that now, it would most likely cause a scene, spoiling everyone's Thanksgiving. Making a mental note to take care of that deed tomorrow, she turned toward the kitchen and bumped into Zach.

"Here, let me take those."

She eyed him suspiciously. Though Zach was always helpful in the kitchen, he seemed a little too eager today. "What's going on?"

His expression one of exaggerated innocence, Zach shrugged. "It's Thanksgiving." He leaned closer and whispered, "Besides, Savannah told me if I didn't help you sneak away with Quinn, she wouldn't let me have dessert."

Since she had watched him devour almost half of a pumpkin pie less than ten minutes ago, Samantha had a feeling "dessert" meant something else.

"How does Savvy know I want to sneak away with Quinn?"

"I think she and Bri had a talk."

Samantha cut her eyes over at Bri, who was chatting with one of Gibby's best friends, Hester Shook. As if she knew she was the subject of conversation, her sister lifted her head and grinned. "Go for it, Sammie."

Shooting her a brilliant smile of thanks, she turned back to Zach and handed him the empty plates. "Thanks, Zach, I owe you."

"I figure you'll pay back plenty in babysitting."

"With pleasure."

Heading to the other side of the room, where Quinn seemed to be in a deep discussion with Aunt Gibby, Samantha was filled with both exhilaration and anticipation. She couldn't wait any longer.

"Aunt Gibby, did you get enough to eat?"

"Oh heavens, honey, I won't need to eat for another week." She patted Samantha's cheek. "You're looking rosy and happy today. It's good to see you like that again."

She then turned to the man responsible for Samantha's rosy cheeks. "Young man, I hope you know how lucky you are."

"Yes, ma'am, I most certainly do."

"Excellent. Now you two run on. I'm going to settle back with another cup of coffee and catch up with Sabrina."

Grateful that her aunt realized how much she wanted to be with Quinn, Samantha leaned down and kissed the wrinkled, weathered cheek. "Happy Thanksgiving, Aunt Gibby."

"You too, honey." She winked. "Now y'all go and have fun."

Swallowing a startled laugh, she grabbed Quinn's hand. Making a brief stop in the hallway for her jacket and purse hanging from the coatrack, she pulled him toward the kitchen.

"Wait. I thought we were leaving," he said.

"We are, through the back door. I want to get away without anyone stopping us."

Samantha burst through the kitchen door and then stopped abruptly. Savvy and Zach were in the midst of a kiss. She winced and was about to back out again when Savvy pulled slightly out of Zach's arms and peeked around his broad shoulder. "Go, you two, before anyone sees you. We've got this covered."

Blowing her a kiss, she ran to the door with Quinn striding behind her. "Thanks, sis."

The instant they were on the patio, Quinn pulled her into his arms and held her tight. She melted against him and savored being this close to him again. Her voice was muffled against his chest. "We'd better leave before we get caught."

"Stay the night with me?"

She leaned back so she could look up at him. "Can I borrow your toothbrush?"

He grinned and dropped a kiss on her nose. "You bet."

"Then let's go."

Taking her hand, he pulled her around to the front of the house, toward his car. Samantha settled into the passenger seat and breathed in a quiet, steady breath. She had made her decision and nothing would change her mind.

As they drove away, she caught a glimpse of Blaine's glum, wistful face at the window of the family room. Knowing she had nothing to feel guilty about didn't take away the sadness. Hopefully he would soon find someone to mend his broken heart. As for her, she had everything she needed.

CHAPTER TWENTY-SEVEN

Quinn turned in to his driveway. Though every particle of his body wanted to rush Sam into the house and into his bed, he refused to give in to temptation. This was a new beginning for them. She had said she wanted to be more to him than a bed partner. That meant sharing more than just their bodies. And Sam meant a hell of a lot more to him than just a warm body to lose himself in for an hour or so. If he had to deny himself to show her that, then he'd damn well do it.

He glanced over at her. She'd been quiet on the drive over. He hoped to hell she wasn't having second thoughts. "Ever sat on the pier and watched the sunset?"

"I thought the sunset was in the west. The lake faces the east." She frowned as if she wasn't quite sure.

"Yeah, but the sun still turns the water a brilliant gold before it sets." He took her hand and pressed a kiss to it. "Want to watch?"

"I'd like that."

They got out of the car and walked toward the pier. Halfway there he stopped. "You're not exactly dressed for this, are you?"

She looked down at her dress and four-inch heels and grimaced. "I should have taken the time to change." Raising her head, naked longing blazing in her eyes, she said, "I couldn't wait any longer."

No way could Quinn prevent himself from kissing her. Lowering his head, he touched her lips with his, moving softly, slowly, tasting, teasing. When she leaned in for a deeper connection, he gave her what she wanted and what he was dying for. Sealing his mouth to hers, his tongue plunged deep, tangling with hers. Her finger-nails dug into his shoulders as she leaned more into him, needing, like he did, more contact. A growl began deep in his chest. He cupped her beautiful ass in his hands and brought her flush up against him. Still wasn't enough. Anchoring his feet to keep his legs steady, he lifted her and fit himself into the soft, giving V of her mound. The instant he did, she pressed into him and began a slow, sensuous ride.

The growl that had been building let loose. Sliding his hands beneath her dress, he cupped her almost naked ass and squeezed gently. What had begun as a soft, gentle taste test had turned into an erotic, mind-blowing experi-ence. As his mouth continued devouring her sweetness, he pressed himself as deeply into her as their clothes would allow. He knew exactly the moment she was coming. Her body went stiff, and even through clothing, he could feel her sex pulse and throb against him. He held her tight, loving the mewling sounds she made as she reached the top and then plunged into her release.

When her body went slack, it took every bit of will-power to let her slide down his body until her feet were firmly on the ground. Loosening his arms, he pulled away enough to look down at her flushed, beautiful face. Despite his throbbing erection straining for re-lease, Quinn knew he wouldn't take it further than this.

His chest tightened at the look in her eyes. Soft, dewy, and full of love. Giving pleasure without taking his own wasn't something he had a lot of experience with. He had always made sure his partner was satisfied, but had also ensured he got his, too. But with Sam, seeing her gratification and knowing he had given her what she needed . . . Quinn mentally shrugged. It was enough.

Her face softly glowing, she whispered, "Let's go inside."

Shaking his head, he backed away. "It's almost sunset." He scooped her into his arms, laughing at her small squeal of surprise.

"What are you doing?"

"Carrying you so you won't stumble on the ground."

Moving swiftly, he covered the distance in a matter of seconds. An old bench that needed refinishing and painting was the only place to sit. Quinn lowered himself to the bench but kept her on his lap. "You'll snag your dress if you sit on the wood." And then he said softly, "Just wait . . . and watch."

Samantha's heart was so full it was almost to the bursting point. Never had Quinn been so tender and gentle. And never had he given her such delicious pleasure without taking it further.

She pressed a soft kiss to his neck, inhaling the delicious all-male scent of him. Then, because she could tell it meant something to him to share this with her, she turned her head and waited. What followed was a gentle flush of crimson on the water. Samantha gasped in delight as slowly, surely, the sun sank lower behind them, turning the entire lake a yellow gold.

"In the mornings, seconds after sunrise, the lake turns an even lighter shade." He lifted several strands of her hair. "Almost this color."

"I'd like to see that, too."

"We'll make a point of it."

Darkness washed slowly over the entire area, leaving them in a soft, dusky light.

Quinn stood. "We'd better get inside before it gets too dark."

Wrapping her arms around his neck, she laid her head

on his chest and whispered, "Thank you for sharing that with me."

He tightened his arms around her and headed toward the house. Anticipation sang through her bloodstream. This was only the beginning of many nights to come. Quinn's actions today showed her how much he cared for her. Whatever the future held for them, Samantha knew she would never regret the decision she had made today. She was where she belonged.

"Want some more wine?"

Sam shook her head. "You know me—a 'one glass is plenty' drinker."

Quinn refilled his glass and then pulled her back into his arms. They'd done nothing more since they'd come inside the house but sit in front of the fire he'd built and talk softly about everything and nothing. Strange how even the nothing parts had been interesting.

"How is your security business doing?"

Huffing out a breath, she said, "Still only the one case so far. And Bri's doing most of the work on it. Logan, Brody's partner, is staying with our client, protecting her. My only part has been to investigate Blaine Marshall and listen to the gossip for news of visitors or newcomers."

"Marshall seems to be very interested in you, too."

"That's my fault. I shouldn't have gone out with him again. He said friendship was all he was looking for, but things got pretty uncomfortable on our last date. I'll definitely not be seeing him again socially."

"You decided whether or not he's got anything to do with your case?"

"I still don't know. He's said some things that made me suspicious. But then, the other night, he acted like a lonely guy looking for a girlfriend." Sam lifted her shoulders in a shrug. "Either way, I'm not going out with him again. If he is associated with Cruz, he's not going to get any information from me, and if he's not, then it's unfair to lead him on."

"You ever figure out who tried to run you down?"

"No. I think it was probably someone trying to scare the hell out of a jogger—and that person just happened to be me. I haven't felt the slightest danger since then. To be on the safe side, though, I take my gun everywhere now."

"You didn't before?"

Her silky head rolled side to side on his shoulder in a lazy no. "Never thought I'd need it in my hometown. Which is crazy since there are evil people in this town, just like any other."

Quinn gave her a one-armed hug. "Nice to know you can protect me."

She snickered. "Yeah . . . right."

They went silent, peaceful again. Quinn stared into the fire, fighting the need to take her to bed. He'd vowed to treat her as something more than a bed partner, but with every passing minute, the need to lose himself inside her was growing stronger.

"Quinn?"

"Yeah?"

Instead of answering, she pulled from his arms and then went to the floor on her knees, facing him. Her hands parted his legs and then she scooted up, placing herself between them.

Quinn had stopped breathing, hoping and waiting to see what she would do. Her next move did not disappoint. Soft, slender hands slid up his thighs and then met in the middle, on top of his growing erection.

"Sam?" he whispered.

Samantha looked at the beautiful man above, his deep blue eyes glittering with need and hot desire. No one would ever accuse her of being sexually assertive. With Quinn she had timidly explored that side of her sexual nature, but so many times he had overwhelmed her with his needs and his ability to pleasure her, so that she'd never really gone beyond her comfort zone. She had once joked to herself that if anyone looked up "sexually assertive" in a thesaurus, her picture would be beside the antonym.

Her lack of confidence in the bedroom had plagued her for years. Quinn had given her the confidence to go further, and tonight she wanted to go as far as she could. A million miles past her comfort zone. Whatever he wanted, she wanted to give to him. His pleasure was all she sought.

Her fingers clumsily unzipped his pants. Not a good beginning if she wanted to behave like the vixen she wanted to be with him. Her heart plunged to her stomach when his hands stopped her.

She lifted her eyes to his. "What's wrong?"

He held her gaze for several long seconds. Samantha couldn't breathe, couldn't move. If he rejected her advances . . .

Finally, giving her that rare beautiful smile, he shook his head and said, "Not a damn thing."

She started breathing again when he removed his hands but then gasped when he took her face in them, bent forward, and kissed her softly on her lips. Before she could respond, he released her and leaned back against the couch once more.

Shivers of arousal blended with heat to create a throbbing need unlike anything she had ever felt. Samantha didn't know what turned her on more, Quinn looking at her with such burning need, his large, beautiful hands lying on the couch clenching and unclenching as if he were having trouble keeping them off her, or the massive erection now poking through the opened zipper. Whatever it was, she loved every single nuance of this moment of self-discovery.

Needing to see him, touch and taste him, she quickly unbuckled his belt, unbuttoned the single button at his waistband, and then opened his pants. The dark navy briefs barely contained him. She had seen Quinn's penis many times, both aroused and not. But now, with new eyes, she wanted to explore every long, hard inch of him. She moved the material of his underwear slightly and his erection sprang out, as if eager for attention.

Her first tongue swipe at the head caused an interesting reaction in Quinn's body. Breath caught in his throat and his entire body went stiff. Smiling her delight, she licked again, loving the salty, masculine taste of him. After several licks and swirls, she sat back a little and considered him. She didn't care what books and magazines said about the male appendage. He was beautiful.

"Sam . . . please . . ."

Quinn's groan made her realize that while she had been delightfully admiring him, he had been in torture, waiting for her to continue. Since his torture was definitely something she didn't want, she bent forward and, without any hesitation, took him inside her mouth. When he touched the back of her throat, she jerked back quickly, afraid she would gag. Then she tried it again, finding it easier each time. Setting up a steady rhythm, she soon lost herself in his taste, the texture of hot, smooth steel on her tongue and the responding hisses and groans above her.

So into her own delicious findings, she was startled out of her sensual world when Quinn gripped her shoulders and pushed her away.

"What's wrong?"

Instead of answering, he lifted her from the floor. The hard, glittering look on his face might have terrified her at one time, but she knew that expression. He was teetering on the edge of control. She wasn't surprised when he raised her dress, stripped her panties down, and growled, "Step out of them." When she complied, he picked her up and placed her in his lap, facing him, with her straddling his hips. She felt his fingers testing her readiness. Apparently satisfied with the moisture he found there, he pushed her down hard and thrust deep.

Swallowing a gasp at the fullness, Samantha grabbed his shoulders and closed her eyes. Quinn's hands were on her hips, pulling her up and then pushing her down. Pants and groans filled the room, and as if coordinated, their bodies stiffened as one. Samantha felt Quinn's release at the exact moment she fell over the edge into dark oblivion. Holding on tight, she allowed herself to soar, knowing that when she landed, Quinn would be there to catch her, just as she would be there for him.

CHAPTER TWENTY-EIGHT

"Is this how you remember it?"

Samantha snuggled into the blanket covering them as she leaned back against his chest and looked out over the lake. The frogs and crickets were quiet, most likely enjoying a long winter's nap. Millions of stars reflected on the water. With a gentle wind blowing, it looked as though fireflies were dancing across the lake.

"It's more peaceful than I remember, and still beautiful." She shook her head in wonder. "I still can't believe you remembered what I said about this place."

The hard arms that were wrapped around her tightened as he nuzzled his face into her neck. "There's not a moment that we spent together that I don't remember."

The quiet sincerity in his words brought an unexpected lump to her throat. "I feel the same way," she said softly.

"There's something I need to tell you."

"What's that?"

"I no longer have a job."

She twisted around to look up at him. "What are you talking about?"

"With Charlene's murderer never being caught, the suspicion and doubt that I could have done it is still there. The board thought it best that I step down."

"Oh, Quinn, that's so unfair. You shouldn't give in to those idiots."

"I could've fought it. Probably would have won, too. Bob, my attorney, certainly thought so. But I didn't want to be in a place where that kind of doubt exists. I went into medicine to save lives, not to scare people." He shrugged. "I thought I'd take a couple of months and work on the house. Then, when I'm ready, I'll either go back to a hospital or I might consider private practice."

"I'm so sorry this has happened."

He pulled her back into his arms. "On the upside, we can spend some time together. Maybe even Christmas, if you like."

"I like." Even though she tried to sound cheerful, she knew the huskiness of her voice revealed her true feelings. She wanted to cry and stomp her feet at the injustice of it. She also wanted to go to Atlanta and tell the bastards who didn't want Quinn in their hospital that they were imbeciles.

"I ever tell you the reason I went into medicine?"

Unwilling to break this fragile new beginning by reminding him that he had shared very little with her, Samantha just shook her head.

"I saved the life of the woman my brother tried to kill. She wasn't breathing and I gave her CPR. I was glad to be able to save her, but I never gave what I did much thought after that. I guess all the other shit covered up the fact that I'd done something worthwhile. My plan was to be in banking, like all the Braddocks before me. I went to college with that goal in mind, never even considering anything else."

"But you joined the army, didn't you?"

"Yeah, after college."

"Was that part of the plan, too?"

Quinn snorted. "As far from it as possible. But my parents did something so unbelievable and outrageous . . . I don't know. I think I went a little crazy. The last thing I wanted to do was be like them."

"What happened? What did they do?"

"The last semester of my senior year, my mother called to tell me that Dalton had committed suicide. It crushed me. I felt almost as bad as I did when I first realized he was sick. I'd tried repeatedly to see him but he refused all of my visits. I hadn't seen him in years but kept hoping one day he'd change his mind and agree to see me."

"How awful that must have been for you. But what did your parents do to make you so angry?"

"I didn't know about the suicide until after they'd already held his memorial service. I never got the chance to say goodbye. And actually, I think the only reason she even called me then was because she thought I might read about it in the newspaper."

The callousness of his parents disgusted her. How could they treat their own son that way? "Why wouldn't they want you at the service?"

"My parents blamed me for what happened."

"Blamed you for what?"

"Dalton's crime." He shrugged. "They've never accepted responsibility for anything in their lives. They had to blame someone."

"How could they blame you for your brother almost killing someone? You're the one who prevented him from committing murder."

"According to my parents, I should have called them, not the police. They would have figured out a way to cover it up. Because of me, Dalton's life was ruined and their reputation was in jeopardy."

"That's ridiculous."

"Yes, but that's my parents for you. Anyway, with Dalton's death, then the cold-blooded way they buried him and went on with their lives . . . I don't know, I just couldn't imagine having anything to do with them again. So instead of doing what they expected of me and following in the family business, I signed up for the army."

"Were they furious?"

"I have no idea. I sent them a letter from boot camp and told them. I didn't hear from them while I was in the service. When I got out, I went by to visit. Stayed only a few minutes." He shrugged. "Haven't seen them since."

"They missed out on knowing what a phenomenal man their son is."

His arms tightened around her and he pressed a kiss to the top of her head, thanking her.

"So did the army pay for your medical school?"

"No, the Braddock money paid for it. I received a trust fund when I was twenty-one. My career choice might not have been what my parents wanted, but they couldn't prevent the money from coming to me. My grandfather had set up the trust when I was baby. It was mine to do with what I wanted. And medical school seemed a whole lot more worthwhile than banking."

"What made you decide on emergency medicine?"

"My commanding officer, one of the toughest and smartest SOBs I've ever known, put the idea of emergency medicine in my head. I already knew I wanted to be a doctor, but he said the way I kept my head in the heat of battle wasn't something to take for granted. That struck a chord with me. I was already a combat medic. . . . Specializing in emergency medicine just made sense. So that's what I chose."

"Any hospital should call itself lucky to have you on staff."

Once again his arms tightened briefly around her. "You're good for my ego."

"Just stating the facts."

They were silent for several seconds and then he said, "There's something else I should have told you. I guess I never thought it would come up, but I wanted to make sure you understood where I stand."

She tensed. Even as much as she wanted Quinn to share with her, it seemed when he did, it was always disturbing news. She hoped someday they got to share the silly and mundane like other couples. "What is it?"

"I know you don't understand my dislike of marriage, but something I don't think you've given thought to is the very real possibility that if I fathered children, they might inherit the same kind of sickness that my brother had or maybe even my parents' alcoholism. The thought of that happening is enough to swear me off the idea of children forever."

There was an instant sadness but she refused to dwell on it. Yes, she had wanted Quinn's children, but she had already accepted that he couldn't give more than he already had. There was no use arguing that the chances of a child inheriting those sicknesses were rare. Quinn would have given this a lot of thought before coming to that decision. Her assurance would not change his mind.

"Thank you for telling me. This will be good enough, Quinn. We're good together."

"Yes, we are." His teeth gently scraped the lobe of her ear. "Ready to go back inside and be good again?"

"Absolutely." She stood and Quinn wrapped the blanket tighter around her. Just as she turned to go inside, car lights illuminated the house. It had to be close to one in the morning or later. Who would be coming by this late? Had something happened to Savvy or Bri?

"Why don't you go get some clothes on. I'll see who it is."

The solemnity of his voice told her he was concerned as well. She rushed back inside and hurriedly ran to the bedroom where she'd left her clothes. She had just started to unbutton Quinn's shirt that she'd been wearing when she heard a man shouting curses. Not bothering to dress, she grabbed her Glock from her purse and dashed out the door. The instant she was on the porch, she knew something terrible had happened. Clark Dayton stood on the first step, holding a shotgun pointed straight at Quinn.

Samantha stood beside Quinn. "What the hell are you doing, Clark?"

"I'm here to kill the son of a bitch who killed my baby sister."

Her heart dropped. "Lindsay's dead?"

"Found her in bed, stabbed." He jerked the shotgun toward Quinn. "This bastard's responsible."

Sick with dread, she glanced briefly over at Quinn. Instead of focusing on Clark and the shotgun pointed at his head, his eyes were on her. He was waiting for her to doubt him. She didn't.

Trying to convey her faith in him with just a look and a small nod was tough, but she did her best. Any more than that would have riled Clark even more. The last thing she wanted to do was piss off a man who would shoot Quinn without blinking an eye.

Samantha turned her gaze back to Clark. "What makes you think Quinn had anything to do with this?"

" 'Cause I heard the talk. He killed his ex-wife in Atlanta. Now he's come here and done the same thing to Lindsay."

"He was cleared of those charges. Besides, he's been here with me all night."

She was about to move forward when Quinn stepped in front of her. "Call Zach. I'll stay here."

"You're damn right you'll stay there, asshole. I'm a gnat's ass away from blowing your fucking brains out."

Quinn pushed aside the sick feeling of déjà vu and focused on one thing—getting Sam out of harm's way. He knew she had her gun behind her, but if Dayton fired his shotgun at her, she'd be dead in an instant.

Once she was clear and he'd talked some sense into the man, he'd let himself think about this new horror. Two murders directly tied to him? No way in hell was this a coincidence.

"I'm not leaving you out here with this maniac, Quinn."

He turned his head slightly so he could see her better. Still dressed in his shirt, her golden hair tousled, lips slightly swollen from his hard kisses, Sam had never looked more wonderful to him. Or more out of his reach.

"Go. Now."

He barked the order at her, but though she flinched at his harsh tone, she continued to stand there with a mutinous expression.

To get her attention, he snapped, "Look at me."

Moving her gaze slightly, she said, "What?"

"We're at a standoff here. I don't know about you, but I'd like to get this cleared up. Since Dayton isn't going to stop pointing that gun in my face, the only recourse is for you to call Zach."

"Fine." Holding the gun so Dayton could see, she said, "Clark, I swear with everything that's in me, if you so much as harm a hair on Quinn's head, I will fill you with so much lead they'll have to lift you with a bulldozer to bury you."

If he didn't have a twelve-gauge shotgun pointed directly at his head, and weren't facing the possibility of being charged with another murder, Quinn would've been laughing his head off. Sam's threat would've made Charles Bronson or Clint Eastwood proud.

When she finally disappeared inside, he turned his attention back to Dayton and said quietly, "I didn't kill your sister, Clark. I'm sorry she's dead. She didn't deserve that."

"As if I'm going to believe you. Being accused of two murders in less than a year? That ain't no coincidence."

"You're right, it's not. I don't know who is doing this or why it's happening."

"Then until I know one hundred percent you're innocent, you're my number one suspect."

"I—" Quinn broke off when he heard sirens and spotted the lights of two police cars. He didn't know how the hell Zach had gotten here so fast and didn't really care. Feeling a slight easing, he kept his mouth shut and decided to let the police chief handle the man.

The patrol cars pulled in behind Clark's vehicle. Zach got out of one and a deputy got out of the other. As the two men strode toward the porch, Zach called out, "What's going on here?"

Not taking his gaze off of Quinn, Dayton snarled, "Lindsay's dead. This asshole is the most likely suspect."

"Put the gun down, Dayton. I'm sorry to hear about Lindsay, but you're not a deputy any longer. We'll investigate to determine who the murderer is. Now hand the gun to Deputy Odom."

"I ain't doing no such thing." For the first time, Quinn saw real sorrow in the man's expression. "Lindsay was stabbed repeatedly. She looked like she was raped, too. Until you prove different, this asshole is my number one suspect."

"He may be your suspect, but until I investigate, everyone is a suspect. Now. Put. The. Gun. Down."

The instant Clark lowered the rifle, Zach grabbed it and tossed it to the deputy, who emptied the chamber.

"Okay, let's talk," Zach said. "What happened?"

"Daddy and I went hunting. Lindsay was going to cook Thanksgiving dinner and have it ready for us when we got home." He shrugged and glanced down at his feet, looking slightly guilty. "We got sidetracked. I didn't get home until around midnight or so. I figured Lindsay would've put dinner in the fridge, but when I went to the kitchen, the food was still sitting out on the counter. The turkey was in the oven but it'd been turned off. I called out for her but nobody came. Her robe was in the middle of the kitchen floor. I went to her bedroom."

He swallowed hard. "There's blood everywhere. She was lying on the bed, naked. The bastard had a good time with her."

"Then we need to get over there and check this out." He looked at his deputy. "Stay here with these two. I'll grab Brody and head over to Clark's house." He turned back to Dayton. "Where's your daddy?"

"He's at Mamie Dillinger's. Daddy hooked up with her at the bar and went home with her. He doesn't know."

"We'll call and let him know." Turning to Quinn, he said, "Where's Samantha?"

"I'm right here."

Quinn turned to see that Sam had changed back into the dress she'd worn for Thanksgiving dinner. Hell, had that only been a few hours ago? He felt like he'd lived a lifetime since then.

Zach's eyes roamed her from head to foot. "You okay, Sammie?"

"I'm fine, Zach. And Quinn's been with me all night. There's no way in hell he had anything to do with this."

Instead of agreeing with her, Zach just said, "We'll get to the bottom of it."

"I'd like to go over to the house with you," Sam said. Zach shook his head. "Having you over there will only complicate the matter."

His sweeping gaze taking in Dayton, Sam, and Quinn, the deputy nodded his head toward the door. "Why don't we all go inside and have a seat?"

Quinn turned to do just that and was surprised and humbled when Sam reached for his hand. No doubt she wanted to show her support and belief in him. He couldn't let her. He turned away without a backward glance and went inside the house.

The fury he'd been holding back rushed through him. How fucking stupid they'd all been. Two murders linked to him a coincidence? Not bloody likely. Charlene's murder had apparently been an attempt to frame him. It had almost worked. And now Lindsay.

Whoever this was, he was out for revenge, wanting to hurt Quinn in the worst possible way. And the worst possible way to hurt him was to harm Sam. As long as she was associated with him, she had a giant target on her forehead. No matter how much it clawed at his insides to do so, his relationship with her was over. At least until this was settled. And if the murderer was never caught or she wouldn't forgive him? He mentally shrugged. Better a lonely life without Sam than the gut-deep agony of being responsible for something happening to her.

Samantha sat on the sofa, across from Quinn. Clark was at the other end of the room, in a corner. He was behaving better than she expected. Other than the occasional glares at Quinn and her, he was acting remarkably mature. Shock was most likely settling in. Finding the body of a dead person was a traumatic experience. That the murder victim was a relative would be much harder to deal with. Despite her antipathy for the man, she felt sorry for him.

Quinn wouldn't talk to her, would barely look at her. Did he think she believed he had something to do with Lindsay's murder? She hadn't given any indication that she had anything other than total faith in him. So why was he acting so cool? An hour ago, he'd held her gently in his arms and shared more with her than he ever had before. She had finally felt as if she was making a dent in that impenetrable, stoic mask he wore.

Now she was cold and worried . . . and so unbelievably scared. Someone was trying to set Quinn up. That was the only explanation she could come up with. But who?

Even though she hadn't seen the crime scene, the way Clark had described it sounded almost identical to the murder of Quinn's ex-wife. Charlene hadn't been raped but that may have been from lack of opportunity. But even if the killer had been trying to frame Quinn, how would he have known that Charlene had called her ex-husband to her house?

She needed to call Murphy and get his thoughts. She hadn't talked to him in months. Last time she had, he'd indicated they were no closer to finding Charlene's murderer than before. He'd definitely want to know about this new one. New evidence and old evidence could be combined to hopefully give them a profile of the killer.

Wanting to break the tense silence, Samantha looked over at Deputy Bart Odom, who was standing guard at the door. "How did you guys get here so fast?"

Bart's eyes briefly flickered over to Samantha. "We were half a mile away at the Greens' house. Malcom and his son-in-law got into a fight about the football game. His wife, Louise, called us to come break it up. We were just leaving their house when your call came in."

Samantha nodded numbly. Alabamians took their football seriously, sometimes too much so. Just like in most of America, watching college football on Thanksgiving was a tradition in Midnight. And almost every year here, a family fistfight broke out when things didn't go a certain way.

The radio attached to Deputy Odom's shoulder squawked out Zach's voice: "Bart, you there?"

"Yeah, Chief."

"Bring Dayton and Braddock to the station."

"Be there in a few minutes."

Bart Odom opened the door. "Okay, let's go."

Samantha grabbed her purse and stood. "Quinn and I will follow you."

"No way in hell are you driving in," Clark said.

"No problem," Quinn said calmly. "I'll ride with Deputy Odom."

He finally looked at her then and a deep ache developed in her stomach. He had gone to that place he went when it became too much. She had hoped never to see that look on his face again.

"Sam, take my car. Dayton can follow behind us."

"That'll work," Clark said.

Unable to let Quinn go without words of encouragement, she grabbed his wrist. "Everything's going to be okay."

Instead of answering, he pulled away from her. "Go home, Samantha. I don't need you. I'll pick up my car as soon as I'm released."

She dug deep and ignored the cutting words. "What's wrong?"

His response was a humorless laugh. "Sorry I can't kiss and make it better for you. I'm a little busy."

Her entire body stiffening at his cruel words, she backed away and watched silently as he walked out the door.

Clark's glare barely penetrated her hurt. "You always did have lousy taste in men. You should've stayed home and married one of the local boys. You might've not thought they were good enough for you, but at least they wouldn't have murdered you or anyone else." He stomped out the door.

Samantha stayed frozen for several seconds and then grabbed her purse and Quinn's keys. Whatever the reason for Quinn's cruelty, she wasn't about to let him be held accountable for a crime she knew he most definitely didn't commit. Whoever had done this was out there, waiting to see what would happen. If it was the last thing she did, she was going to find the bastard. And then she would deal with Quinn.

CHAPTER
TWENTY-NINE

"So how is it that you knew Lindsay?"

Quinn had to hand it to the Midnight Police Department. They were a helluva lot more accommodating than the Atlanta cops. He'd been given coffee and a comfortable chair in Zach's office. He knew there were interview rooms because they'd passed by them on the way. He didn't fool himself. This special treatment was all due to Sam. Any other suspect would have been grilled in an interview room with half a dozen people watching.

"I didn't know her well. When I came back to Midnight last week, she showed up a few minutes after I arrived with a casserole and a bottle of wine. I thanked her and she left." In case he needed further proof, he added, "Samantha was there and heard everything."

"Clark said you dated her."

Never had he regretted a date more. "It wasn't really a date. She came into Faye's the other day when I was there. She asked me out." He shrugged and added, "I felt sorry for her, so I said yes."

Nodding as if he understood, he said, "Anyone around then . . . to hear you?"

"Sam was there then, too."

Zach's expression went from understanding to furious in a second. "You were with Samantha when you accepted a date with another woman?"

Put like that, it sounded damn insensitive, and he supposed it was. "We weren't together. Sam was sitting behind me, but she heard me accept."

Zach's glower didn't lighten up. Quinn could understand why. His explanation hadn't exactly made him look any better.

There was no real excuse he could give for accepting the date while the woman he loved sat close by. *Loved?* Hell, where had that come from? Not loved. Cared about. He cared deeply for Sam. That was it. Not love. Hell, his brain must be fried.

Quinn continued, "We went out the next night. I took her to Esmeralda's Garden over on the bypass. We ate and left. I brought her home around eight-thirty."

"That's a damn short date."

"It wasn't a date. I bought her dinner." Quinn shook his head. "Hell, I know I was an asshole for saying yes. Sam's the only woman I want to be with."

"Have you seen Lindsay since that night?"

"No. She wasn't happy that I brought her home so soon. She tried to invite me in. I said no and left. That's the last time I saw her." Quinn leaned forward in his chair. "I know this looks bad."

"Two murders and an attempted murder. And you were associated with all three. Yeah, it looks real bad."

"Attempted murder? Who?"

"Did you forget that Samantha was almost run over a few weeks back?"

And he hadn't believed he could feel any colder. Sam had dismissed that as someone trying to scare her, but now, after this . . . *Shit!*

He surged to his feet. He needed to make sure Sam was safe. She had driven home by herself.

Zach nodded at the chair Quinn had vacated. "Sit down."

"Not until I check on Sam. I need to make sure she made it home safely."

"She did. I talked to Savannah a few minutes ago. Samantha's fine. Now sit down."

Quinn dropped back into his chair. "You didn't buy her theory that someone was just trying to scare her?"

"I think she was trying to convince herself. When nothing else happened, I eventually let myself believe it, too. Now, after this . . ." Zach shook his head. "There's no doubt in my mind that someone tried to kill her."

"And it happened right after I came back here."

"So either you did it or someone's trying to frame you."

Yes, but who and why? A former patient he'd pissed off? A relative of someone he'd treated? He had practiced medicine long enough to have lost a few patients. Was this revenge or payback?

Hell, why hadn't he given this any consideration before? Why hadn't the police?

His expression grim, Zach speared him with a cold look. "So the question is, Dr. Braddock, who hates you so much they'd kill three women to hurt you?"

Samantha leaned back against the headboard, her arms wrapped around an oversized bed pillow for comfort and support. "He didn't do it."

"Zach'll get to the bottom of it, Sammie."

She and her sisters were gathered in her bedroom— a common practice when one of them had a problem. From childhood, they'd banded together to talk things out and either provide moral support or solve issues. This would be no different but the stakes were higher than ever. Quinn's life was in danger.

"I know he will, Savvy, but we can all work on it together. I know Zach has procedures to follow, but he's got to give me access to the crime scene. He wouldn't let me go before, but I need to see it. I can compare it to Charlene's murder. See the similarities and differences." She paused. "And you can research Quinn in Atlanta. Find any complaints made against him. As soon as I can, I'll talk with him. See if he's got any idea who might have a motive to hurt him."

Bri went to her feet and pulled her cellphone from her jeans pocket. "I'll call my Miami contact and let them know I'm out as far as Cruz is concerned."

"No, Bri," Samantha said. "As much as I'd love for you to get as far away from that monster as possible, you've made too much progress to back out now. It would take too long to get someone else inside. It's a Wildefire case, too. Savvy and I will work this one. Logan will guard Lauren. And if Brody agrees, he can help us with Quinn's case."

"I agree," Savvy said. "I don't want you close to Cruz any more than Sammie does, but you're in now. You need to work that angle till it's done."

"Okay, fine. But if you guys need me, I can be here in hours."

Smiling her gratitude at both of them, Samantha said, "I hope Zach lets Quinn leave soon. He would hardly even talk to me before he went to the police station."

"That's the way of men, Sammie. Especially the strong, silent type."

Savvy was right, she knew. And the description fit Quinn perfectly. She just hoped to hell she could get him to talk. If they were going to find out who was doing this, his cooperation was vital.

"Did Zach tell you anything about the crime scene?"

"Not much. I think he's too afraid it'll upset me." Savvy rolled her eyes. "Silly man forgets that I used to prosecute these kinds of crimes."

"What did he tell you?"

"Just that the door had been jimmied, so we know the killer broke in. Said it looked like Lindsay was in the middle of making Thanksgiving dinner. There were dishes halfway prepared. The turkey was half done, but it looked like the oven was turned off in the middle of cooking."

The break-in was different from Charlene's murder but that wasn't necessarily significant. Samantha tightened her arms around her pillow and tried to put herself in the mind of the killer. "Think he killed Lindsay, then went back to the kitchen and turned off the stove to prevent a fire?"

"That makes sense," Bri said. "He does the deed but doesn't want to call attention to the murder. If he'd let the turkey burn, smoke alarms would have gone off. Fire department might have been contacted."

"Anything else, Savvy?"

"Not much. From what I could get from Zach, it was a gruesome scene. He said he wouldn't know until the coroner can confirm, but it looked like she might have been raped, too. And he counted thirteen stab wounds."

"Thirteen . . . just like Charlene."

"Think that's his signature?" Bri asked.

"Who the hell knows?"

"Did Charlene have bite marks?" Savvy asked.

"No. Just the stab wounds." And then the significance of her sister's statement hit her. "Are you saying Lindsay had bite marks on her?"

"Yes. Zach said some were fresh and others looked like they were a couple of days old."

Did this have anything to do with Charlene's penchant for rough sex? Even though Charlene had no fresh bite marks on her, she remembered the coroner's report mentioning some older marks that were of unknown origin. Could they have been healing bite marks?

"Quinn told me Charlene liked rough sex. That's how he found out she was cheating on him. He saw bite marks on her and thought she'd been raped. The coroner's report mentioned some markings on Charlene that looked like they were healing. I wonder if those marks would match up with Lindsay's?"

Samantha rolled off the bed and stood. Her need to see the crime scene and Lindsay's body was now even more imperative. "I need to get over there ASAP."

Savvy held up her cellphone. "I'll call Zach. If he goes there with you, there should be no reason you can't see it. If this was the same man who killed Charlene, having a person who saw the scene in Atlanta is essential."

While Savvy made the call, Samantha went to the closet to dig out her camera. She would send photos to Murphy and let him compare them to Charlene's murder scene. This had to be the same person, didn't it?

A sick thought occurring to her, she turned back to her sisters. "Have you guys considered that Clark could be the murderer and just staged this to look like Charlene's murder, hoping to pin it on Quinn?"

Her finger poised to press a key on her cellphone, Savvy looked up with a grimace. "There were rumors that both Clark and his daddy were abusive to Lindsay. That's one of the reasons Zach helped her get out of town and got her a job."

"Too bad she didn't stay gone," Bri said.

"So could Clark Dayton be that sick and disgusting?"

"Actually, he probably could, I just don't know that he's bright enough to stage the scene to make it look like someone else did the deed."

Samantha nodded. "He seemed genuinely upset that Lindsay was dead."

Her phone to her ear, Savvy said, "Let's see what Zach says."

"Ask him if he's through talking with Quinn."

Anxious to get something—anything—going, Samantha paced back and forth the length of her bedroom and listened to the monosyllabic, one-sided conversation Savvy was having with Zach.

Finally the call ended but the expression on her sister's face wasn't encouraging.

"What's wrong?"

"Zach will be here in a few minutes and take you over to the crime scene. Clark and his daddy are staying at the motel over on the bypass, so it'll just be you two looking."

That was good news but there was something more . . . something her sister didn't want to tell her.

"And what else?"

"Zach said that one of his deputies took Quinn home."

"But why didn't he bring him here? I've got his car."

"He didn't want to come here. He asked Zach to have his car brought to his house."

She tried not to be hurt. Quinn had to be exhausted. Of course he would want to go home, maybe shower and catch some sleep. Her own eyes felt as if they had ten pounds of sand in each one, and she hadn't been questioned by the police for endless hours. It was just past four o'clock in the morning. Once he had some sleep, they would talk.

"No problem. I'll leave the keys here." Samantha knew she wasn't fooling either sister but thankfully they didn't comment.

She took the camera and her purse and headed out the door. "I'll go wait for Zach downstairs."

Apparently unable to let her go without offering some kind of comfort, Savvy said, "I'm sure Quinn is exhausted, Sammie."

Nodding, Samantha walked out of the room before she did something she would regret, like diving into her sisters' arms and bellowing out her hurt feelings. She had more important problems to deal with. The man

she loved was once again being accused of murder. She
had failed Quinn before. There was no way in hell she
would fail him again.

Quinn sat on the sleeping porch where only a few hours
ago he and Sam had been wrapped around each other.
All that peace had been decimated. Someone was once
again fucking with his life. And another woman was
dead, apparently because of him.

Who the hell had he pissed off so much that he
thought murder was a proper revenge? A former patient
or colleague? Someone he'd known in medical school
or the army? Hell, someone he'd known in college?
Throughout his life, he hadn't exactly been known as
Mr. Charming. There could be hundreds of people who
didn't care for him. Being liked had never been one of
his top priorities.

Until he'd met Sam. Quinn rubbed his grit-filled eyes.
God, what was he going to do about her? Just when
every obstacle that had stood in their path seemed to be
gone, now this monumental FUBAR stood in their way.

When Zach had told him he was free to go, the words
had trembled on his mouth to be taken to Sam. The
need to hold her in his arms had almost been enough to
weaken his resolve. But he hadn't. Being anywhere near
her right now was out of the question. Two women were
dead because of him. If anything happened to her,
Quinn knew without a doubt he wouldn't survive.

The slam of a car door was his first clue that he had
a visitor. Hell, he needed to get some sleep. He hadn't
heard the car or even seen the lights. He stood and
headed back inside the house to the front door. If he
were a betting man, he would have placed money that it
was Sam.

Quinn would have lost the bet. He opened the door to

a woman with Sam's features but with short, white-blond hair and a fierce, determined look in her eyes. Her sister Sabrina.

"You're a prick."

Despite himself, he felt a smile twitch at his mouth. "Greetings in Midnight aren't what they used to be."

"I thought you finally realized how lucky you are."

Since he didn't feel too damn lucky right now, Quinn waited, figuring she wouldn't leave until she'd had her say.

"But now you're acting as if she means nothing to you. I never figured you for a fuck-her-and-forget-her kind of person."

"Have you ever considered that I'm staying away from her for her own good?"

"How's that?"

"Whoever is doing this wants to hurt me. And the number one way to hurt me is to hurt Sam."

Sabrina gave him a hard stare as if trying to delve deep into his brain to see if he was lying. Finally she gave a derisive snort. "If you think Sammie's just going to sit back and not get involved, then you don't know my sister."

"What do you mean?"

"I mean whether you've hired us or not, you're now a client of Wildefire Security Agency. Sammie's over at the crime scene right now, taking pictures that she can compare with your ex-wife's murder. We're going to work the case until we find the killer."

Hell, he really wasn't with it. Of course that's what Sam would do. Even though he'd hurt her, she wasn't going to let this go.

"How do you know I didn't do it?"

"Because Sammie believes in you. And I believe in Sammie."

She couldn't have pierced his conscience any better if she had shot a bullet into it.

"And what if I don't want the Wildefire Agency's help?"

"Tough shit."

"Then I guess I'd better cooperate."

"Your cooperation would be helpful but isn't necessary for us to do our job."

"I admire your confidence."

Her shrug said she didn't really give a damn what he thought. She confirmed it with "You fix it with Sammie or I'll bring a friend over next time I come."

"Someone to beat me up?"

"No, my favorite little Smith and Wesson. She's convinced plenty of people to my way of thinking."

Quinn had to laugh. Sabrina's tough talk reminded him of the threat Sam had made to Dayton earlier. He wondered if they'd watched a lot of Bronson and Eastwood movies when they were growing up.

"I'll keep that in mind."

Apparently satisfied she'd done what she intended, Sabrina nodded and turned away. Quinn watched as she walked down the steps and marched to her car. She opened the door and then stopped for one final parting shot. "You're damn lucky to have my sister's love. I hope someday you deserve it."

CHAPTER THIRTY

Samantha snapped another shot of Lindsay Milan's bloodied body, trying like hell to ignore the death glaze in her eyes and the fact that she had known the woman. Investigating murders had once been her job, and though she had on occasion gotten queasy, none of them had been acquaintances of hers.

Lindsay hadn't had an easy life; her death had been even tougher.

"What do you think?" Zach asked.

"She put up a hard fight. The cuts on her hands are slices, not stabs. Defensive wounds." Samantha drew closer, snapping shots of her extremities. "Think he restrained her?"

"Don't think so. No ligature marks on her wrists or ankles. The bruises on her wrists look like finger bruises to me . . . like on her neck."

"What about the bite marks? You think that was consensual?"

Zach shook his head. "Hard to say, but if he didn't restrain her, then my guess is she was okay with it. At least at first. Especially since she's got several that are a couple of days old."

"Breasts, stomach, and inside of her thighs. Anywhere else?"

"Yeah, we turned her over. She's got one on her back,

below her right shoulder blade, and a couple on her buttocks."

"So this guy gives them the rough sex they like and then kills them. Any evidence of semen?"

"No." He sighed and added, "I didn't mention this to Savannah, but if you'll notice the smell . . ."

He waited until she took a deep breath. Her eyes widened with knowledge of just how thorough the killer had been.

"Yeah . . . he used bleach to clean her up, inside and out. We found a turkey baster in the kitchen, filled with bleach."

Samantha's stomach lurched. Holy hell, that was cold. "Hope she was dead before that happened."

"Me too," Zach agreed grimly.

"Any idea on time of death?"

"We're approximating between noon and 6:00 P.M. Hopefully the coroner can pinpoint it closer."

Samantha sighed, beyond exhausted. She'd been through every room in the house and had taken at least two hundred photos.

"Come on and I'll take you home," Zach said. "The coroner is waiting for my call to come pick up the body."

Too tired to argue, she walked outside with Zach and took in a deep breath of fresh air. No matter how many murder scenes she saw, she would never get used to them. This one might not have been the most graphic or gruesome, but it had definitely been the most disturbing.

She glanced over at Zach, who seemed to be taking his own deep breaths. "We haven't talked about Quinn. Aren't you going to ask me if I think he did it?"

"Do you?"

"No, I'm sure he didn't."

"You weren't too sure once before."

"And that was a mistake. Someone is trying to make it look that way."

"Then if you're right, we need to figure out who it is before he kills again."

"Any ideas on how you're going to do that?"

Quinn's voice behind her had her whirling around. "What are you doing here?"

Instead of looking at her, his gaze was focused on Zach.

"Dammit, Braddock," Zach snapped, "you shouldn't be here."

"I'm not staying."

"Then why are you here?"

"For Sam."

Hearing Quinn's words in that deliciously growly tone he got on occasion sent a jolt of warm electricity through her bloodstream. When he held out his hand, she couldn't have stopped herself from joining her hand with his if she had wanted to . . . which she didn't.

She felt Zach's questioning look and gave him a smile. "I'll be home later. Tell Savvy not to worry."

Zach nodded and got into his car. The minute he drove away, Quinn pulled Samantha to his car.

"Where are we going?"

"Home . . . to bed."

She grinned at him. "Pretty sure of yourself, aren't you?"

Laughter rumbled in Quinn's chest. A few hours ago, he hadn't believed he'd ever laugh again. But now, here with Sam, he had the insane feeling that everything would work out. He had no good reason to think that. The last few months his life had been closing in on the edge of hell. And now that hell had come even closer. But being with Sam blurred all of that.

They were almost home before she asked the question he had been anticipating. "What made you change your mind?"

"What do you mean?"

"Don't." The one word held a mountain of emotion.

Quinn pulled into the drive. "Let's get inside, then we'll talk."

They got out at the same time. Meeting her in front of the car, he took her hand and pulled her up the steps, unlocked the door, and then pulled her inside. The instant the door closed behind them, she went into his arms.

The depth of his feelings for this woman was unlike anything he'd ever felt before. He had thought they were strong when they were in Atlanta, before Charlene's murder. Those were mild compared to what he was experiencing now.

"I'm so sorry this is happening to you, Quinn. But we'll figure it out."

She humbled him with her quick forgiveness. Without his asking for it . . . even with no explanation of why he'd been such a prick to her before.

"You know I don't deserve you."

She pulled away, apparently surprised at his confession. "Why would you say that?"

"Because I'm a dickhead."

Green eyes lighting up with teasing laughter, she cupped him in her hand. "If you'll remember our interlude from earlier, you'll know that I'm particularly fond of that part of your anatomy."

Laughing at her wicked sense of humor, he said, "Why don't we take a shower and then we'll talk."

"Separate or together?"

"I've heard Midnight's water supply is low."

"Then I guess we'd better shower together to conserve."

As they walked up the stairs together, Quinn wondered if it was possible to have these feelings last. He had little to no experience with couples staying together for more than a couple of years. He immediately discounted his own parents' marriage. From his perspective, love had nothing to do with why they had stayed together for almost forty years.

Quinn opened the door to the bathroom and waited for Sam's reaction. He wasn't disappointed.

"Oh, Quinn, when was this done?"

"A week or so ago."

Letting go of his hand, she walked around the oversized bathroom, touching the gleaming fixtures. "It's gorgeous."

"I found some photos in a magazine and asked the contractor to copy it."

"Where did you get the claw-footed tub?"

He shrugged. "Found it online."

Her glowing smile of approval made the hours he'd spent perusing magazines and online sites worth it. "I'll look forward to a good, long soak in it soon," she said.

He turned the shower on and began to unbutton his shirt. Sam's soft hands stopped him and she slowly unbuttoned the shirt for him.

Steam from the shower filled the entire room. Everything felt as if it was in slow motion. Quinn slipped Sam's shirt over her head, leaned down, and licked the moisture gathering at her neck. Hands caressed slick, moist skin, lips kissed, and tongues glided over each other as they lost themselves in a silent declaration of devotion. He had made love to Sam many times, but none had ever seemed more important or poignant. She had given him everything—her trust, faith, and loyalty. He wanted to show her how much he cared for her, appreciated her . . . cherished her.

When at last they were nude, Quinn nudged her into the shower, and with all the tenderness he knew how to give, he gently washed her body, lingering over soft mounds and delicious curves. And then, when neither of them could stand it anymore, he pressed her back against the wall of the shower, fitted his erection into her hot, welcoming sex, and thrust deep.

With a soft cry of surrender, Sam wrapped herself around him. Buried deep within her heat, Quinn stilled. Everything within him told him to piston back and forth, to take the explosive pleasure Sam's sweet body offered. But he waited and watched.

Glittering green eyes, dark with passion and love, gazed up at him. "What's wrong?"

"Not a damn thing."

"What are you waiting for?"

"You."

"What do you . . ." She broke off, gasping as he shifted, stroking hard . . . pressing deep.

"Come for me, Sam."

Their gazes locked, he watched her eyes widen, felt the pulse of her coming climax as if tiny aftershocks were developing into a massive reaction. And then it happened. With a soft, sexy cry, she came. And at that moment, Quinn gave himself permission to let go, pounding again and again until pleasure drove everything from his mind. Only in this woman's arms had he ever found this kind of peace.

Burrowed against his chest, so relaxed she could barely move, she whispered, "Hard to believe I could feel so wonderful after all that's happened."

"I'm sorry for how I acted before."

One of the many things she loved about this man was his ability to apologize. She had known some men who would barely make a token apology and assume all was forgiven. And granted, Quinn had hurt her on several occasions, but he was man enough to admit his mistakes.

"You were pushing me away from you. Why?" she asked.

"I would think that would be obvious. Some twisted freak is killing women I'm associated with. You think I want to put you at risk?"

Even though that thought had crossed her mind, his rejection had stung. "So what made you change your mind?"

He hesitated and she knew he was considering not telling her. Shifting in his arms, she looked up at him. "Quinn?"

"Your sister came to see me."

Breath whooshed from her. She didn't need to ask which one. "What did Bri say?"

"Hmm, besides the insults? She reminded me that whether I want you involved or not, you were going to be."

A little let down, she said, "And that's it?"

"Should there be another reason?"

Shrugging, she turned her head away. "I guess not."

Quinn made a sudden abrupt move and Samantha found herself on her back looking up at him. Though they had closed the blinds to shut out the daylight and the room was dim, she had no problem seeing the fierce gleam in his eyes.

His voice gravel rough, he said fiercely, "Do you want me to say that staying away from you for more than a minute is painful for me? That the thought of not having you in my life tears at my soul? That just seeing your face creates a peace inside me I've never felt before? That having you in my arms is like coming home?"

Tears filled her eyes. Quinn had stripped himself bare, exposed his deepest thoughts and feelings—ones she had never expected. Whether he used the words or not, he had just told her he loved her. That was all she had ever wanted to hear from him.

Cupping his face in her hands, she brought him down to her mouth and whispered softly, "I love you, Quinn Braddock. With all of my body, heart, soul, and strength, I love you."

She heard a groan, wasn't sure if it came from her or him and didn't care. His mouth moved tenderly, softly over hers, and Samantha pushed aside everything but the glory of the moment as she gave her heart and her body to the love of her life.

CHAPTER THIRTY-ONE

Quinn crumpled the newspaper in his hands and threw it into the fireplace, where flames greedily consumed the salacious lies. In the days since Lindsay Milan's murder, *Midnight Tales* had printed outlandish innuendos mixed with facts to make the story sound as scandalous as possible. They hadn't let the grim reality that a woman had been brutally murdered get in their way of what they apparently believed to be an exciting event for Midnight.

"Guess you don't think a lot of our local newspaper."

He turned to see Savannah standing at the doorway of the Wilde house's living room with a tray of drinks. Taking the tray from her, he set it on the oversized oval coffee table behind him. " 'Newspaper' isn't a name I would call that rag. Where the hell did they come up with that crap?"

She dropped into a chair close to the fire. "It's mostly just a gossip page now. I think it started going downhill right after our parents were killed, and never recovered."

"Who never recovered?"

Quinn turned to see Sam standing at the door. Though she looked incredible in her red sweater and tan skirt, he saw the shadows under her eyes and the tension at her mouth.

"Our illustrious newspaper is at it again."

"Two scandalous stories in one year. First our parents' murderers are finally caught and now this. The Wildes are keeping them in business."

Quinn noticed Sam's inclusion of him in the Wilde family wasn't lost on Savannah. What surprised him was her nod of agreement. It'd been years since he had been a part of a family, and even then, it had only felt like happenstance and not because he belonged.

The clomp of heavy-footed men alerted him that the meeting was about to begin. Zach came into the room, gave a soft kiss to his wife, a smile to Sam, and then a grim nod to him. Sam and Savannah might have accepted him into the family, but it was evident Zach wasn't quite as willing to bring him into the fold just yet. Which was understandable considering the man was the chief of police and was investigating a murder Quinn was directly tied to.

Brody James came in after Zach, winked at both Sam and Savannah, then gave him the same kind of look as his friend had. Another person not one hundred percent on board with his innocence.

Zach poured himself a cup of coffee and then looked around the room, meeting everyone's gaze. "Since the Wildefire Agency is working this case, too, I figured it'd be a good idea to pool resources and see if we can come up with some likely suspects."

The police chief's eyes zeroed in on Quinn. "And I sure as hell wouldn't normally include a possible suspect in the investigation. But since Samantha is going to include you anyway, I don't have much choice. Your innocence hasn't been proven yet, so don't assume you're here because you're no longer a suspect."

Quinn jerked his head in acknowledgment.

Zach pulled a notepad from his pocket. "Here's what we know. Lindsay had thirteen stab wounds. Cause of death was asphyxiation caused by choking. The stab wounds were in nonvital parts of her body, so it would have taken her some time to bleed out. It's hard to say if she was raped or just engaged in rough sex prior to her death. Either way, there was no semen."

"So he used protection?" Savannah asked.

Quinn noticed Zach briefly shifted his eyes to Sam before answering. "Hard to say. He used bleach to wipe away any evidence."

Quinn frowned, not liking where the scenario was taking them. "So he's angry enough to stab a woman thirteen times but is calm enough to clean up the evidence after it's over."

Zach shook his head, his expression even grimmer. "I don't think he was in a rage."

"What do you mean, Zach?" Sam said. "That kind of overkill usually indicates anger."

"Not this time . . . at least not according to the coroner. He said the stab wounds weren't thrust with a lot of force. It was almost as if the killer slid the knife in as slowly as possible."

He glanced over at Quinn. "Atlanta PD sent me a copy of your ex-wife's case. Her murder was both brutal and angry. The killer intended to cause her as much pain as possible. The stabs were so hard, a couple of them went all the way through her body."

Shaking his head, Quinn said, "Are you saying the killer wanted it to hurt less for Lindsay than Charlene? The force of his stabs wouldn't have made any difference to their pain. It would have been excruciating either way."

"No, that's not what I'm saying." Zach blew out a sigh. "Maybe he enjoyed this kill less or more than the other one."

"Or it was all staged."

"What do you mean, Sammie?" Savannah asked.

Sam stood and began to pace. "The thirteen stab wounds in Lindsay have always bothered me. Someone in a murderous frenzy isn't counting how many times he inserts the knife into his victim. With Charlene, the number of stab wounds didn't stand out because we just assumed he stopped at thirteen because he wanted to stop."

A cold chill of dread, not unlike moments he'd felt on the battlefield, went through Quinn. "So what you're saying is, he was aware of how many times he stabbed Charlene and wanted to make sure he gave Lindsay the exact same number."

"Exactly."

"So you think the number thirteen is significant," Savannah said.

"Yes . . . maybe . . . possibly." Sam blew out a harsh breath. "Hell, I don't know."

"The number thirteen has a lot of different meanings. I'll do some research. Maybe there's some correlation we're just not seeing."

A soft hand touched Quinn's arm in a comforting caress. He looked up into Sam's worried face. Her sister Sabrina had said that Sam was beautiful inside and out. There was no doubt of that in his mind.

"What about the weapon?" he asked.

"Kitchen knife," Zach answered.

"You said the door was jimmied," Quinn said. "Wouldn't that imply that she didn't know her attacker?"

"Not necessarily," Savannah said. She looked at her husband. "Zach, didn't you say there was an old housecoat in the middle of the kitchen floor?"

At his nod, Savannah went on, "If the doorbell rang and she was wearing the housecoat, she probably wouldn't have answered. From what I remember about Lindsay, she was very careful of her appearance. She wouldn't have wanted anyone to see her in an old robe."

Giving Quinn one last caress, Samantha turned away and continued pacing. Sitting down calmly was beyond her at the moment. "I agree. Lindsay was very vain about her appearance." She winced as she said the words. At one time, there had been no one more vain than she was. And like Lindsay, she wouldn't have been caught dead in an old housecoat.

"So he breaks in and she, what . . . just goes along with it?" Brody said.

"If she knew him, she might've thought it was romantic," Savvy said.

Samantha huffed out a disgusted breath. "I'm the romantic in the family and that would've scared the crap out of me."

"Me too," Savvy said, "but we know that Lindsay had some issues. She saw men as either conquests or rescuers."

"Okay, let's go with the theory that he broke in and she possibly knew him," Quinn said. "He takes her to the bedroom, they have sex, and then he brings out the knife he stole from the kitchen?"

Zach nodded. "That's the going theory. Coroner said she was killed between noon and four."

That news confirmed what she feared. "He's watching Quinn, isn't he?"

"Yeah," Zach said. "I would think so. To frame him, he's going to want a window of time where Quinn's whereabouts can't be verified."

"I arrived here at this house right at two o'clock. Before that, I was at my house, alone."

"You saw no one until you came here?" Brody asked.

"No. I was in the back of the house, working on some bookshelves for the study. My car was in the drive, so anyone could have driven up and seen it."

"What about it, Braddock?" Zach said. "You come

up with any names of people angry at you enough to kill?"

Quinn shook his head. The blank look in his eyes tore at Samantha's heart. He was retreating behind that wall again and she couldn't let him. Zach didn't know Quinn the way she did. He might look at Quinn's cool control as deceit. She knew different. When it became too much, that was his fallback mode.

His voice devoid of any emotion, Quinn said, "I'm sure there are hundreds of people I've pissed off in my life but none to the degree that they'd kill someone for it. A few might've wanted to kill me but . . ." He shrugged. "Not sure why he wouldn't just come after me instead."

"Because he wants to torture you," Samantha said. "Killing you might be his endgame, but until then, he's enjoying making you sweat."

She made her statement deliberately blunt, hoping to see that fire back in his eyes. And for a moment, there was a flare of life. Then like a blast of arctic ice, the coldness returned.

"Then he's going to be disappointed. I don't sweat."

Biting her lip, she glanced nervously at Zach, sure that he would question the cool arrogance in Quinn's statement. Instead she saw approval and understanding. They were both former military. Maybe Zach understood Quinn's control.

"What about at the hospital?" Savvy asked. "Could someone have blamed you for a loved one's death?"

Quinn shrugged. "Possibly. But I've not lost any patients this year in a way that was remotely questionable."

"I talked with the head of the emergency department," Zach said. "She concurred with your assessment. Said there had been no threats of lawsuit or any indication of a bereaved family member wanting vengeance."

Feeling desperate, Samantha pulled up a footstool and

sat in front of Quinn so she could see his face. "Then someone from your past? Maybe in medical school or when you were in the army?"

Quinn shook his head. "I've racked my brain, Sam. And as I said, I'm sure I've pissed more than a few people off, but none come to mind."

Samantha surged to her feet again. "Then we need to look at this from a different angle. This person came to Midnight . . . might still be here."

Brody, who had been uncharacteristically quiet, said abruptly, "A man would be hard-pressed to come into this town without someone seeing him. Especially in the middle of the day."

Savvy said. "But remember, the Daytons' house is on the outskirts of town, down an old dirt road. It would be very easy to sneak in and out without being seen."

"Yeah, but how would this person know I went out with Lindsay or even knew her?"

"Maybe they didn't," Samantha said. "Maybe he killed her at random, knowing you would be a suspect because of Charlene. He could've stopped on the outskirts of town, done the deed, and left."

"That's damn chancy," Zach said.

Samantha knew she was grasping at straws, but so far straws were all they had.

"There is one new person in Midnight," Brody said. "Any reason we're not considering him a suspect?"

"You mean Blaine Marshall?" Savannah asked.

Brody nodded. "There's something off with him."

Poor Blaine. Little did he know he'd been considered a hit man for Cruz and now a murder suspect.

"I checked him out . . . dug as deep as I could," Savvy said. "From what I can tell, the man is who he says is."

"I've followed him around a little. Those comments he

made to Samantha about Florida bothered me." Brody shrugged and added, "I might not like the guy, but I have to admit, I've seen nothing that would indicate he's not what he says he is."

"Doesn't mean he's not connected to Braddock in some way," Zach said.

Samantha threw a glance over at Quinn. "You've seen him several times. Does he look familiar to you?"

Quinn shook his head. "Not at all."

"I agree, though," Savvy said. "I watched him at dinner the other day. He's charming but . . ."

"Exactly," Samantha said. "Finish that sentence. There's just something there but I can't place my finger on what that is. Which reminds me, I have to return something to him. Why don't I meet him for lunch? I'll wear a wire like I did before and ask some direct questions." Before anyone could protest, she looked over at her sister. "And Savvy, see if you can tie Blaine to St. Catherine's Hospital or to Atlanta. Also, check to see if he has any military ties."

Quinn's disapproval of her plan was obvious, but thankfully all he said was, "What are you returning?"

Samantha grimaced. "He gave me a gift the other night when we went out. I was going to return it the next time I saw him but didn't want to do it on Thanksgiving."

"I don't like the idea of you being around him if he's got anything to do with this," Quinn said.

"I've been out with the guy several times. We've been alone. And the other night, we drove all the way to Mobile. He was a perfect gentleman."

"That was before we were considering him a murder suspect," Zach said.

"True, but we thought he was a hit man, so what's the difference?" At the sea of unconvinced faces, Samantha added, "How about I meet him at Faye's? Nothing gets said or done there without witnesses. I'll be perfectly safe."

No one looked thrilled with her solution but it made sense to her. Whether Blaine Marshall had anything to do with Lindsay's and Charlene's deaths, was Cruz's man or simply a lonely guy, she needed to return his gift.

"Okay, everyone," Zach said. "Let's end this meeting with the acknowledgment that we still have no real clue who we're looking for and why."

The announcement deflated Samantha's optimism. Zach was right. They had no solid ideas or theories.

"The coroner has released Lindsay's body. Her funeral is set for tomorrow at one o'clock. Brody, Bart, and I will be there. I've asked Savannah not to go and she's agreed."

By the expression on Savvy's face, it hadn't been an easy agreement. Still, it was best. Not that anyone was expecting trouble, but Clark Dayton was volatile by nature and this had been his sister. No matter that neither he nor his father had been terribly kind to the woman in life, rumor was they were taking the loss hard.

"I think that's best, Savvy. Heaven knows what Clark might do. I heard he's been on a drinking binge since this happened."

Her sister sighed and shot her husband a quick smile. "I know. I just feel like I should pay my respects."

"I'll represent the family," Samantha said. And before Quinn could make the same suggestion that Zach had made to Savvy, she said, "It'll look very strange if someone from the Wilde family isn't there."

"Braddock, it'll be best if you're not there, either," Zach said.

Though his jaw clenched, Quinn nodded curtly, agreeing.

Glad that was settled, she stood and held out her

hand to Quinn. "Let's go." She wanted to get him alone as soon as possible. She had a feeling the discussion of Lindsay's funeral was getting to him. Having taken an oath to save lives, the idea that someone had killed two women because of him couldn't be easy.

Zach sat on the arm of Savvy's chair, put his arm around her shoulders, and looked at Quinn. "Since Savannah won't be at the funeral and I have to be, I'd be grateful if you would stay with her until I can get back home to her."

The tension she could feel in Quinn's arm loosened slightly. "I'd be honored."

Throwing her sister and brother-in-law brilliant smiles, Samantha walked out of the room by Quinn's side. Zach's request had most likely been prompted by Savvy but he wouldn't have asked if he didn't have total belief in Quinn's innocence. And the look on Quinn's face had been priceless. He would soon learn that being part of the Wilde family meant total faith and loyalty. And whether Quinn wanted to acknowledge it or not, he *was* a member of their family.

CHAPTER THIRTY-TWO

Rain slashed against the windshield, hindering her vision. Samantha squinted in between the swipes of the wiper blades for a clearer view of the road in front of her.

What an awful day for a funeral. Yesterday the weather had been sunny and warm; tomorrow's forecast was also supposed to be filled with sunshine. Burying Lindsay on a day like today seemed like a final insult to the poor woman.

"I do hope they put tents up at the gravesite. Funerals are depressing enough without getting soaked, too."

Samantha glanced over at Gibby. Her aunt had insisted on attending. Even though she had a cold and was probably running a fever, she refused to miss the event. Samantha hadn't even thought to discourage her. The entire town of Midnight, with the exception of only a few, would be there.

That was the way in Midnight. Weddings, christenings, baptisms, and funerals were attended by as many of the townspeople as possible. Citizens worshipped and celebrated together; it only made sense that they mourned together, too.

After the funeral, the inevitable consumption of a massive amount of food would commence. Tears followed by nourishment had been the tradition for as long as she could remember. Since the Daytons' house was still a crime scene, Faye had offered to host the mourners at her diner.

"Do you reckon Zach'll be able to find out who killed poor Lindsay?"

"I'm sure he will, Aunt Gibby. It just takes time."

"And to think someone is doing this to hurt Quinn. I swan, I don't know what the world is coming to."

"Who told you that?"

"Why, it's all over town, honey."

Of course it was. Had she thought Midnight's gossipers would let her down this time?

"So people don't think Quinn had anything to do with Lindsay's death?"

"I'm sure there are some who have their doubts." She jutted out her chin. "I, for one, *don't*."

Unexpected tears sprang to her eyes. That was Gibby— always loyal, always loving.

"Thank you, Aunt Gibby. That means a lot."

"He's a tough nut to hatch but I think if anyone can crack him, it's you."

Grinning at one of her aunt's wacky sayings, Samantha slowed and then turned in to the parking lot of the First Methodist Church. The parking lot was already packed and Samantha silently sighed. She was going to have to park across the street in the overflow lot.

"I'll let you out under the porch so you won't get wet. Can you save me a seat?"

"Be glad to, honey."

Samantha pulled underneath the protective overhang. "I'll see you in a few minutes."

The passenger-side door opened and Blaine Marshall's handsome face appeared as he stooped down. "Hi there, Miss Gibby. Want me to escort you inside?"

"Why, thank you, dear boy. I'd appreciate that." Gibby

smiled at Samantha. "Be careful crossing the road, honey. It'll be slick."

Blaine took Gibby's arm and gently pulled her from the car. Despite her misgivings about him, it was a kind, gentlemanly act. "Thank you, Blaine. I'll see you both in a few minutes."

He nodded and closed the door. Samantha pulled out into the parking lot again and then crossed the street to the overflow. Since the rain continued to pour like some-one had opened up the floodgates of heaven, no one loitered about.

Grabbing her umbrella from the back, she opened her car door and then gasped when it was wrenched from her hand and Clark Dayton's bushy face appeared inches from hers. His sorry appearance confirmed what the gossips had described—he'd been on a major drinking binge. Bloodshot eyes glared, and when he opened his mouth, the distinctive smell of hard liquor was undeniable.

"Tell your boyfriend we're coming for him," he snarled. "Once we're through with him, he won't have anything left to rape a woman with, much less have the sense God gave a goose."

"He had nothing to do with Lindsay's death, Clark. If you weren't so drunk and could think rationally, you'd be able to see that."

"All I see is a man who's gotten away with one murder already. He ain't about to get away with another one."

Disgusted and furious at his threats, Samantha used the pointed end of her umbrella to jab him in the chest. "You come anywhere near him and Zach'll have your ass in jail before you can take another breath."

"Zach won't be with him all the time. We'll strike when he least expects us."

"And we'll know who to arrest and prosecute, too."

Clark grinned, showing yellowing, crooked teeth. "Hard to prosecute without finding a body."

"Did you just make a death threat?"

"Oh, hell no, sugar. I just gave a friendly warning."

Disgusted, she jabbed the umbrella again, this time deep into his soft gut. He grunted and backed away. In one smooth move, Samantha exited the car and pulled her gun from her purse. Holding it steady, she issued her own warning: "You come anywhere near him and I promise, you'll regret it."

His grin dimming slightly, he kept a wary eye on the gun as he backed away.

"Samantha, everything okay?"

Hearing Brody's voice behind her, she said, "Clark just made a death threat against Quinn."

"Is that right?" Brody's laid-back voice held a sharp edge.

Swallowing hard, Clark shook his head. "I didn't do no such thing. Your word against mine, Samantha."

"Then I'm sure you'll want to make sure that Quinn stays healthy so you won't be accused of anything."

"Sure thing." He glanced toward the church. "I gotta go."

Samantha kept the gun on him until she saw him cross the road. Then, breathing out a long sigh, she dropped it back into her purse.

"We're going to look like we took a swim if we don't get out of here," Brody said.

She grimaced and opened her umbrella. Though the rain had lightened to a mist, they were both getting soaked.

Brody took the umbrella from her grasp and held it above them as they headed to the church. She was surprised that he hadn't made any mention of what just happened. They were to the edge of the church, about to go into the foyer, when he broke his silence.

"You really believe in his innocence, Samantha? Enough to stake your life on it?"

Speaking with complete assurance, she said, "I am one hundred percent sure. Quinn had nothing to do with Lindsay's or his ex-wife's death."

He nodded as if his doubts were completely gone and confirmed it by saying, "Then that's good enough for me."

"Would you like to know anything about Sammie?"

Quinn turned from looking out into the soggy backyard and the rain-drenched sky. "What do you mean?"

"Oh, I wouldn't give any secrets away or anything. It's just when I fell in love with Zach, I wanted to know all the little things that can take forever to learn. Like what kind of cereal he liked or what his favorite cartoon was when he was growing up."

Savannah's face was innocent, devoid of any hidden agenda. Her assumption that he was in love with Sam was natural. Telling her that he wasn't in love with her sister would have been both boorish and possibly wrong. He couldn't define his feelings for Sam. They were just there, powerful and passionate.

"I already know her favorite breakfast is Cheerios and Froot Loops mixed together."

Savannah grinned. "She stole that recipe from me."

Chuckling, he seated himself across the kitchen table from her and said, "What was her favorite cartoon?"

"She had two, *Teenage Mutant Ninja Turtles* and *G.I. Joe.*"

"Doesn't surprise me. She likes to pretend she's tough."

"She's tougher than she looks but a whole lot more vulnerable than she lets on."

Quinn's chest tightened at Savannah's protective tone.

The love the Wilde sisters had for one another was what he'd always thought family should be about.

"I know she is, Savannah," he said gently.

The atmosphere had gone from lighthearted to serious in seconds. Savannah's eyes, so much like Sam's, seared him with questions she wasn't going to ask. He wished he could reassure her that he would never hurt her sister again. It wasn't his intention but they still had a gargantuan mountain to climb. Being crazy about her didn't negate the fear that he was shitty husband material.

Since he couldn't make those assurances, he returned to asking about her favorite things, hoping to lighten the mood again. Thankfully Savannah cooperated and he managed to learn that Sam had been a cheerleader, homecoming queen, class president, and the lead in two class plays, one of them a musical. None of which surprised him. Samantha Camille Wilde was a beautiful, multilayered woman with many talents. He just hoped like hell he could figure out a way they could be together without breaking her heart or her spirit.

Savannah was in the middle of telling the story of how the eight-year-old triplets went an entire week at school pretending to be each other when his cellphone rang. Chuckling, Quinn answered the phone but barely got a hello out before Sam was saying urgently, "I just had a run-in with Clark Dayton. He threatened you."

Quinn wasn't surprised. Dayton didn't seem the type to let the law get in the way of what he wanted to do.

"No worries, we're safe here."

He looked up, surprised that Savannah was no longer in the kitchen.

"Savannah?" Striding out of the kitchen, he was just in time to see her about to open the front door. Dropping the phone, he took off running, making it in time to scare the hell out of both Savannah and the delivery-man standing at the door.

"Quinn, what on earth is wrong?" Savannah asked.

"Sorry, when I couldn't find you, I got worried."

"I saw the van drive up. Thought I'd catch him before he rang the doorbell."

"Everything okay?" the deliveryman asked. Dressed in a brown suit, holding a medium-sized box, he looked worriedly at the hand Quinn had wrapped around Savannah's arm.

Releasing her slowly, Quinn held out his hand for the package. "Everything's fine." He grinned and winked conspiratorially. "Christmas present for the wife. I wanted to make sure she didn't open it."

Savannah giggled and said, "Oh, honey, that's so sweet."

Grinning at both of them, the man said, "I have to hide the presents from my wife, too." He nodded, wished them a good day, and returned to his truck.

Quinn closed the door. "I'm sorry if I startled you."

"You did, but it was my fault for not telling you where I was going." She grinned. "If you were Zach, you'd be yelling a blue streak about now."

"And if you were Sam, I'd probably be yelling, too." Quinn closed his eyes. "Damn . . . Sam." Turning around, he grabbed his phone from the floor, relieved that it wasn't broken.

Holding the phone to his ear, he said, "Samantha, you there?"

"What the hell happened? I've been yelling for the past five minutes."

"Sorry, delivery truck came by in the middle of you telling me about Dayton. Savannah was about to open the door."

The shaky sigh she blew into the phone told him he had scared her, so he wasn't surprised when she said, "I'm almost home now. When I couldn't get you to answer, I jumped in my car."

"Sorry about that. Do you need to go back?"

"No, I'll call Brody and ask him to bring Gibby to the house. Until this thing is over, I want to keep an eye on her, too."

"Okay, see you soon."

Quinn pocketed his phone and turned back to Savannah. "You think your husband would let me leave town?"

"Why would you want to do that?"

"Because I'm endangering everyone with my presence."

Shaking her head, she started back to the kitchen. "No matter where you go, this sick freak knows who you care about. We Wildes fight together."

Arguing that he wasn't a Wilde would do no good. This was the second time she had included him in the family. And like before, his chest tightened at her words. Having this kind of support, something he never got from his own family, did something to his heart.

Quinn followed Savannah back to the kitchen and watched as she took a pair of scissors from a drawer and began to open the package. She stopped abruptly, gently set the box on the table, and stepped back.

"What's wrong?"

"I just noticed that it's addressed to you."

"What?"

Glancing down, he saw his name and this address. Why the hell would anyone be sending anything to him here?

"Hand me those scissors."

When she complied, he said, "Now open the back door for me."

Quinn carefully lifted the package and walked out the door, past Savannah's wide, frightened eyes. Dammit, if he had any idea that he'd be putting Sam and her family or anyone in danger by coming here, he would have stayed as far away as possible.

"Maybe we should call a bomb expert or something," Savannah said.

Even though he'd never felt less like smiling, he threw her a grin. "Used to do these in my sleep in Iraq." He nodded at the door. "Go inside, then out the front door. Stand in the yard, away from the house."

As soon as the door closed, Quinn began cutting. He'd detected no smell of chemicals and the package itself weighed less than a pound. Still, he wasn't about to put Savannah's life at risk just because he didn't think it was an explosive. He'd make damn sure it was safe before he let her anywhere near it.

The package opened easily. Just as he was about to peer into the opening, an angry Sam snapped from behind him, "Dammit, Quinn Braddock. What do you think you're doing?"

"I'm opening a package," he said mildly.

"But what if it—"

"It's not." Holding a plastic-wrapped object with the tips of his fingers, he instantly identified it. "It's a knife . . . looks like a butcher's knife."

"What?" She came to stand beside him. "Was there a note?"

He lifted the package again, unsurprised to see a piece of paper float out, message side up. Quinn had seen profane, obscene, and disgusting things in his life, but the printed words on the paper twisted his stomach unlike anything ever had before.

I'd be honored if you'd use this to gut your girlfriend, Samantha Wilde.

. . . A fan of your work

CHAPTER THIRTY-THREE

"I need to get the hell away from you and your family."

"You're not leaving, Quinn."

"I'm endangering all of you by being here."

Samantha sat on the sofa in Quinn's house. This had been the day from hell and it wasn't getting any better. First the altercation with Clark Dayton and then her scare when she'd called Quinn and had heard him shout her sister's name. Then, when she got home, she'd been told he was opening a suspicious package in the backyard. Samantha had felt like she was slogging in quicksand as she ran around to the back, praying she could prevent Quinn from opening an explosive.

The knife and its accompanying note hadn't been an explosive, but they'd had a monumental impact on them all the same. Brody had taken Savannah and Gibby to Mobile to stay at his house, with one of his employees guarding them. She and Quinn had round-the-clock police protection from Midnight's two deputies, and Zach was out searching for Clark Dayton and his father, Carl—both of whom had disappeared immediately after the funeral.

And now Quinn was talking about leaving. If she had any extra energy, she'd release an ear-piercing scream of frustration.

"Look at me, Sam."

Raising her head, she was surprised to find him sitting on the coffee table right in front of her.

"I don't want to go but I don't want anything to happen to you or your family, either."

Her eyes roamed over his tired, worried face. Even though exhaustion had etched lines around his eyes and mouth, he was still the most handsome man in the world to her. And so very dear.

"We're all safe now and we'll stay that way," Samantha said. "Once Zach finds the Daytons, we can go back to finding this killer."

He took her hand, pressed a kiss to her palm, and surprised her by asking, "What do you want for Christmas?"

Loving him even more for his calm, steady courage, she drew in a long breath and shared one of her fantasies with him. "I want to wake up in your arms on Christmas morning, in this house. After a delicious breakfast, we'll sit in front of our giant, beautifully decorated tree and unwrap presents. Then we'll get dressed and go over to the Wilde house for a Christmas feast and open more presents. In the early evening, we'll return home and drink hot chocolate in front of the fireplace."

"You left out one important thing," he said softly.

She shivered at the gravelly, sexy voice. "What's that?"

"You forgot to mention when I do this." Leaning forward, he captured her mouth with his, roaming gently and thoroughly.

Before she could deepen the kiss, he pulled away and whispered, "And this." His fingers deftly unbuttoned her blouse. Already anticipating his mouth on them, her nipples went instantly erect.

Unclasping the front closure of her bra, he pulled both her blouse and bra away till they draped on her shoulders. His eyes devoured what he had uncovered and Samantha felt exposed, sexy, and beautiful.

A long, masculine finger traced her erect nipple, making it tighten even more. "Have I ever mentioned that you have the most beautiful breasts in the world?"

"No," she whispered.

"Very remiss of me. Let me clear up any doubt. Your breasts are beautiful, sweet . . . infinitely suckable."

Mesmerized and totally aroused, Samantha sat enrapt as he seduced her with his words and voice.

"Now, where were we? Oh yes, what you left out of your perfect Christmas Day. You forgot the part when I do this." His hands went beneath her knees and pulled her to the edge of the couch, then he spread her legs with his.

Samantha held her breath, the anticipation of his next touch almost more than she could bear.

Large, competent hands glided up her thighs, heading in the direction she desperately wanted him to go. Heat and moisture pooled at her core; she was throbbing, wanting, needing. Almost to the edge of her panties, he stopped and said, "Sam?"

"Yes?"

"Breathe. I don't want you passing out before the good part."

As far as she was concerned, the good part was every single moment she spent with this amazing man. However, she did need to breathe. Slowly releasing her breath, she was rewarded when one of those long fingers eased beneath the lace of her panties and delved gently, tenderly into her crease.

Moaning, she whispered, "Quinn . . . please."

"Oh, I will, sweetheart. I promise. I—"

She was so immersed in the sensual seduction, the cheerful Christmas jingle barely penetrated her consciousness. It was when Quinn stopped and pulled away from her that she realized her cellphone, only inches from her, was ringing. She had set the song as her ringtone, hoping it would cheer her. The sound of it was most definitely not cheering her now.

Giving her a grin, he kissed the tip of her nose and growled a promise: "Later."

Samantha watched longingly as he headed to the kitchen. Blowing out a frustrated breath, she grabbed the phone and answered, "This had better be good."

"Sammie, it's Savvy."

Any other time, she knew her sister would have laughed at her greeting, correctly guessing that she had interrupted something steamy. The seriousness of her tone alerted her something wasn't right.

"What's wrong?"

"Something fishy came back on Blaine Marshall."

Wedging the phone between her ear and shoulder, she quickly closed her bra and buttoned her shirt. "What'd you find out?"

"I was looking for a connection between Blaine and Quinn."

"And?"

"I didn't exactly find that but I did discover that he went to Atlanta a few weeks ago."

"Really? He told me he went to Indiana, to take care of some business. Said there was two feet of snow the whole time he was there."

"I can't find any evidence that he went to Indiana. He flew from Mobile to Atlanta the day after Quinn left. He was there for two weeks and came back the same day Quinn did."

"That can't be a coincidence. Any idea what he did when he was in Atlanta?"

"I know that he stayed at the Marriott downtown, but other than that, no, I don't know what he did. I'll keep digging."

"I still need to set up a meeting with him to return that gift."

"Maybe you should wait on that. Finding this information has kind of freaked me out."

"It is weird but not exactly a smoking gun. There could be all sorts of reasons he went to Atlanta. When I see him, I'll—" Her breath caught in her throat as she was plunged into darkness.

"Sammie, you there?"

Her heart slamming against her chest, she whispered into the phone, "The lights just went out."

"Where's Quinn?"

"In the kitchen."

"What about the deputies?"

Blindly she reached for her Glock that had been beside her cellphone. Its reassuring weight in her hand, she walked toward the window and opened the blinds. Thankfully the night was bright enough to see that the patrol car was still in front of the house, but she couldn't see anyone inside it.

"Savvy, call Zach."

"Sammie, please be careful."

"I'll be fine. Just call Zach." Closing the phone, she called out, "Quinn?"

No answer.

With dread and a stark fear, she moved toward where she believed the kitchen was. It was so damn dark. Halfway there, the lights flickered and then blazed back on. Breathing out a relieved sigh, Samantha dashed to the kitchen and then came to an abrupt stop. Quinn lay facedown on the floor, unmoving. Clark Dayton, Carl Dayton, and two men she didn't know stood over him.

"What the hell are you doing?" Samantha yelled.

"We're taking justice into our own hands," Clark snarled. "Gonna teach this murdering son of a bitch a lesson he won't ever forget."

She tried not to stare at Quinn. Was he breathing? *Oh God, please let him be okay.* Bringing her gun up, she held it steadily on Clark, who seemed to be the ring-leader. "You're an idiot, Clark. If you would just think rationally for a minute, you'd realize that Quinn had nothing to do with Lindsay's death."

"You only believe him because you're screwing him."

"I believe him because I know he's innocent."

Clark smirked. "I always knew you were the stupidest of the Wilde girls." He reached down toward Quinn.

"Touch him and I swear I will blow a hole in your gut."

He glanced hesitantly around at his father and friends as if looking for encouragement. When he moved his gaze back to her, his eyes appeared to see beyond her, to something over her head. The obnoxious smirk became a full-fledged grin.

And that's when she felt a presence behind her. She managed only a half turn before she felt a sharp pinch on the side of her neck. She tried to complete her turn but stumbled unsteadily back. Her legs wobbled and the faces of the four men blurred into one giant blob. Samantha knew she was about to pass out. If she did, what would happen to Quinn?

Fury helped burn some of the grogginess away. *The bastards.* She didn't care if she killed them all. Barely able to keep her grip on her gun, she raised it slightly higher to make sure she didn't shoot Quinn and fired.

She heard a shriek and a curse, then something slammed into her head and she felt herself falling forward. She flung her hands outward to catch her fall but they were useless as she fell on top of Quinn.

Breathing in his beautiful masculine scent, Samantha felt tears fill her eyes. Her mind registered shouting, angry voices. And then she fell into a soft, deep darkness.

"What if he really didn't do it?" a harsh male voice whispered.

"Yeah," another male voice said, "that Samantha Wilde seemed pretty sure about that."

"Stop it, you two. You said you were on board with this. Remember, my sister is dead because of this bastard."

Pushing past the throbbing ache in his head, Quinn lay still and tried to get his bearings. He knew he was in a vehicle, probably an SUV. His hands were tied behind his back and he appeared to have some sort of cloth bag over his head. The people who'd abducted him, Dayton and his buddies, were arguing about whether they should have abducted him—a little too late in his estimation.

Where was Sam? Had they hurt her? Even though he couldn't see, he knew she wasn't in the vehicle. Rage boiled within him. If they had touched one hair on her head, they were going to die. He wasn't a violent man. After leaving the service, he'd deliberately avoided war movies and rarely talked about his time in the service. Hell, he didn't even own a gun. But if they harmed Sam, he wouldn't hesitate to tear them limb from limb.

"What do you think that man is going to do with Samantha?"

Quinn stopped breathing. A man had Sam? Who? From the sound of it, he was someone they didn't know.

"I don't know," Clark answered. This time there was worry in Dayton's voice. "He seemed like a nice fellow. And he said they'd dated."

"Then why'd he drug her?"

"Hell, I don't know. I got enough problems without worrying about somebody else's. I just—" Dayton broke off and then said, "Wait, there it is."

The vehicle jerked to a stop. Quinn clenched his jaw to prevent a groan as his head rammed into something hard.

He heard shuffling as the door clicked open and Dayton and his friends got out of the vehicle. Quinn stayed still and prepared to strike. Sam was in trouble. The only way to get back to her was to go through these idiots. He had to work as quickly as possible.

The back of the SUV squeaked open. Quinn waited . . . waited . . . Someone grabbed his ankle. With a violent kick, he shoved his foot forward and connected with a soft cushioned body part—maybe a stomach. He heard a grunt and a curse.

"He's awake!" Dayton shouted. "Watch his legs."

"No shit, asshole," Quinn snarled. "Think you're man enough to take me on without tying me up?"

"You're going to get the beating of your life tonight, you bastard," Dayton said.

Quinn stayed silent. Telling them once again that he hadn't killed Lindsay would do no good. They were out for retribution. Why let a little thing like his possible innocence stand in the way?

Having learned a lesson, they were more careful when they reached for him again. A man grabbed one of his feet; another man grabbed the other one. With a massive yank, they pulled him from the back of the vehicle and threw him down on the ground, where he landed faceup. Quinn barely felt the impact. Adrenaline was surging through his system like a geyser, washing away everything but his one purpose. The quicker he dealt with these sons of bitches, the sooner he could get to Sam.

With his hands tied behind him, he was limited in his ability to fight, but he was far from helpless. Hell, how many times had he trained for this exact scenario? Just because he hadn't practiced it in years didn't mean he didn't remember exactly what to do.

Still, he gave goading them one more try. Having his hands free would make this go much faster. "You guys really are macho, beating up a tied-up man. Why don't you untie me and let's see who's got the biggest balls?"

Hard hands grabbed his arms, jerked him to his feet.

"Shut up," Dayton said, "or I'll forget about the ass-whooping and go straight for the kill."

Maybe he couldn't get them to untie his hands, but it'd help a hell of a lot to be able to see. "At least let me see who's going to whoop my ass."

"I don't—"

"Take the bag off, Clark." The voice was that of an older male, one Quinn hadn't heard before.

"Daddy, you okay? I didn't think you were going to wake up."

"It'll take more than the peashooter that Wilde girl had to put me down."

Sam had apparently been able to get off a shot. Even though he was up to his neck in assholes, Quinn smiled. That was his tough, beautiful Sam.

Abruptly the bag was yanked off his head. Swaying slightly, Quinn faced his opponents. They were a scraggly-looking bunch. Three of them, including Clark Dayton, were medium height and slightly thick in the middle. Handling them with his hands tied behind his back was no big deal. The fourth man was the one he needed to worry about. The guy was about Quinn's height of six two but outweighed him by about fifty pounds. This was the one he needed to take down first.

Clark and another of the smaller men rushed him at the same time. Quinn gave them no time to touch him. He threw out a kick, slamming one man in the nose, then whirled and kicked again. His foot connected with Clark's mouth. Blood spurted like a busted water pipe and both men held their hands over their faces. Unfortunately they were still standing.

The big guy came next. This was the one he wanted. Wasting no time on finesse, Quinn went straight for the groin shot and kicked as if he were making a one-hundred-yard field goal attempt. A squeal of anguish echoed through the trees, and the man toppled like a giant oak.

Clark and his bloodied friend came at him again. One managed to slam a giant fist into the side of his head. Temporarily stunned, he barely felt Clark's fist punch him directly in the face. Quinn saw the blood but paid little attention. Kicking out once again, he slammed one foot into Clark's face and then followed it up with another kick to his stomach. And before the other man could come at him again, Quinn whirled once more and kicked the man in the groin with only a little less force than he'd used on the big guy. Another squeal and then the man went down.

Spewing curses, Clark jumped on top of Quinn, taking him to the ground, and started pummeling in earnest. Quinn absorbed every blow as he maneuvered his body to the exact position he needed. While Clark concentrated on brutality, Quinn used his distraction against him. Straddling Clark's head, Quinn twisted and rolled. Suddenly the man realized that not only had his ability to punch been impeded, he was now at the mercy of hard, muscular thighs. With one quick jerk, Quinn could break the bastard's neck like a twig.

Quinn looked up into the astonished face of the older man, apparently Carl Dayton, Clark's father. "You've got one second to untie me or your son's neck will be shattered."

Clark gurgled something and Quinn's legs tightened around him.

The father pointed a shotgun at Quinn's head. "Or I could just shoot your sorry ass to hell. You'd be dead in seconds."

"True, but I'm taking your son with me. The reflex of my body will cause my legs to tighten. Clark will die instantly." Quinn doubted his own words but the elder Dayton didn't know that.

Carl glared down at them, indecision in his eyes. His son's face was beet red and he kept his body stone-still. Apparently Clark had enough smarts and survival instinct to believe that Quinn could easily snap his neck.

"Shit," Carl growled, and then withdrew a knife from his pants.

Quinn watched him warily as he walked behind him. Then finally the rope around his wrists loosened. The instant he was free, Quinn leaped to his feet and grabbed the shotgun from Carl Dayton's hands.

"Hell, boy, where'd you learn to fight like that?"

"Army." Gesturing with the shotgun, he pointed at the three men on the ground. "Tie them up and together."

As Carl headed toward them, Quinn asked, "You got a cellphone?"

"In the truck."

Quinn waited until Carl began tying the men up and then he walked backward to the SUV. Peering inside, he spotted the cellphone in a pocket of the door. One hand holding the shotgun steady on the men, he grabbed the phone with the other and pressed in the numbers for Zach.

"Chief Tanner," Zach answered tersely.

"It's Braddock. Somebody's got Sam."

"Yeah, I know. Both my deputies were found tied up and unconscious. We figured they got both of you."

"No, the Daytons and a couple of his friends knocked me out and took me. I didn't see who got Sam but I think it's Marshall."

"Shit," Zach said softly. "Where are you?"

"Hold on." Quinn walked a few feet to where Carl Dayton was busy tying up his son and the other men. "Where are we?"

"About three miles west of Midnight." He nodded at the little shack in the distance. "That's my hunting lodge."

Speaking to Zach again, he said, "Dayton's hunting place. Three miles from town."

"Where are the men who took you?"

"They're being tied up by Carl Dayton as we speak."

"Impressive," Zach said. "Can you get back to town?"

"Yes, I'll be there in less than five minutes."

"Okay, we're at the Wilde house. Looks like someone broke in . . . the security alarm went off but nothing seems to be missing."

"I'll see you in a few."

Closing the phone, he looked at Carl Dayton again as the man finished his task. "You got any more rope?"

"In the back of the truck."

Quinn located the rope, then said, "Put your hands behind your back."

"Dammit, you can't leave us like this. We'll freeze to death."

"You'll be together . . . you can keep each other warm. I'll send someone back for you."

Cursing under his breath, Dayton reluctantly put his hands behind his back. Quinn made quick work of tying the man up. Then he pulled him toward the other men, all of whom were now awake.

Pushing Carl into the heap of men, he said, "For the record, one last time: I did not kill your daughter, Mr. Dayton. I'm very sorry for what happened to her and I intend to find out who did it."

Quinn ran to the SUV, jumped in, started it, and headed back to Midnight, the lump of sorry-assed men he'd left behind completely forgotten. Now his one and only focus was finding Sam. He refused to consider that the same thing that had happened to Charlene and Lindsay could be happening to Sam right now. He couldn't lose her. He would move heaven and earth to find her, and when he did, he was never letting her go.

CHAPTER THIRTY-FOUR

The first thing she noticed was the sound of someone moaning. Where was it coming from? She held her breath to hear better and it stopped. When she began breathing once more, the moaning started again. A part of her brain acknowledged the sounds were coming from her, but she couldn't fathom why, or why she should care.

Darkness surrounded her and she was cold to the bone. Not the normal kind of cold, but the clammy kind that came from being outside too long. Where was she and what had happened?

She put her mind to work, forcing sanity through the cloudy haze. Like a rocket blast, Quinn's image came to her. He had been lying on the kitchen floor, unconscious. Was he dead? No, she couldn't let herself think that. He couldn't be dead. Besides, Clark and Carl Dayton knew they couldn't get away with murder. They might be willing to spend time in jail for beating someone up, but murder was a whole new ball game. They were more the type to fight and leave the person broken and bruised. Not easy to let herself think of Quinn being beaten, but it was a hell of a lot better scenario than thinking him dead.

What had they said? They were going to teach him a lesson. And then what happened? Why couldn't she remember? She blinked, wishing for some kind of light to give her surroundings substance. If she could get her bearings, maybe her brain would work better.

She strained for a memory. She had been looking down at Quinn and . . . someone had come up behind her. Then she had felt a sting at her neck and everything became one big blur. She had fallen on top of Quinn and remembered nothing else after that.

"Samantha," a singsong familiar male voice said. "Wake up, Sammie, and talk to me. I'm lonely."

The voice belonged to Blaine Marshall but never had it sounded so childlike or creepily sadistic. If she continued to lie here and pretend she was unconscious, could she perhaps take him off guard?

"I heard your breathing change . . . I know you're awake." Hard hands shook her shoulders. "Come on, baby. Wake up and let's play. We're about to get to the good part."

Pointless to pretend unconsciousness. Maybe she could get him to talk and she could find out why the hell he had done this. As odd as it seemed, she would like to believe he was one of Cruz's men and had kidnapped her to get information about Lauren. Given a choice between a hit man and a sadistic murderer, she'd take the hit man any day. She might be able to reason with a gun for hire. Negotiating with a conscienceless lunatic would be nearly impossible.

Her gut told her the truth. Even though it was hard to believe that the seemingly mild-mannered Blaine Marshall could have done these terrible deeds, she didn't see any purpose in pretending otherwise. He had cold-bloodedly murdered Charlene Braddock and Lindsay Milan. And she didn't doubt for an instant that he intended to murder her, too. That didn't mean she would let him, though. She had resourcefulness and training the other two women hadn't had. She'd been in tough spots before . . . she would get out of this one.

She moaned uncontrollably when his hard hands shook her again. "Come on, wake up or I'm going to have to hurt you much sooner than I'd planned."

"Where are we?"

"At last the sleeping beauty awakens. We're in the woods, far away from Midnight, far away from your precious Quinn."

"Why are you doing this, Blaine? What did I do to you for you to treat me like this?"

"Sit up and let's chat. We've got some time."

She allowed herself to be pulled into a sitting position. She tried once more to get her bearings, but it was still dark as pitch. Her arms were bound at the wrists and then tied to the inside of her ankles. She felt like an animal about to be branded.

"Why is it so dark?"

"Is it? I hadn't noticed, but then again, I've been in the dark for years. You might say darkness and I are old acquaintances."

"Could you turn on a light so I could see you?"

"Sure, I don't see why not."

Seconds later she heard the scratch of a striking match and then watched as its small flame lit a lantern. A soft glow surrounded them now. Samantha gazed around. As he had said, they were in the woods, but not just any woods. This was swampland, where creatures lived that few people ever got to see. And few people wanted to see.

"We're in the swamp."

"I prefer 'woods' but I guess 'swamp' will do, too. I found this little place a few weeks ago when I was scouting for the place of execution."

Oh God, she didn't want to ask, but she did anyway. "Execution?"

He gave a giant belly laugh. "Oh, you thought execution as in death? Well, I suppose that, too, but that's not the execution I was talking about. The execution of my plan."

"What plan?"

"Where the truth will be revealed and Quinn will finally understand that actions have consequences."

"What did Quinn do to you? Why do you hate him so much?"

"Not so fast, my dear. This is a moment I've been waiting years for. I'm not about to spoil the surprise for everyone."

"How do you know he'll even come? Dayton and his friends were going to beat him up."

He shrugged. "He'll get away from them. I do hope they don't hurt him too badly."

"How did you get Dayton to go along with your plan?"

"Are you kidding? There's nothing easier than riling up a good old boy who's had too much to drink. He and his buddies were at the bar. I became a sympathetic ear and then an instigator."

"How will Quinn know to come here?"

"Very easy. I made sure to bring your cellphone. I turned it off until we were ready. Besides, Quinn's a good tracker. Did he not tell you about his army experience?"

He grinned at her as if he already knew the answer to that question. "He's not one to brag. Let's just say that if he doesn't find us, he's not the Quinn Braddock I know."

"How do you know him?"

"Nuh-uh. You're not going to get me to spill before it's time."

He came around to stand in front of her. In the dim light of the lantern, she could see his face. And once again, that charming smile he always seemed to be wearing was in place. Samantha shivered. The smile was the same, but now that she knew it was the smile of a killer, she thought it looked way past creepy.

"Could I have a blanket or something?"

"I'll heat you up. Don't worry."

She didn't like the sound of that. He hadn't raped Charlene but he'd had sex with and possibly raped Lindsay. Is that what he had planned for her? Rape, then murder? No, she would kill him before she let him touch her like that.

"Why did you kill Charlene and Lindsay?"

"There you go, trying to get me to tell you before it's time."

"But your plan was to frame Quinn . . . right?"

"I guess there's no harm in admitting that. Yes, I had hoped it would work with killing Charlene. But it was a hasty and ill-conceived plan. Way too many witnesses around. When she told me he was coming over, I thought, What the hell, I'll give it a try and if it doesn't work, I'll have another chance." He smiled and added, "As you might have guessed, I'm a very patient man."

"So you knew Charlene?"

"Oh yes. Intimately. She was so easy to get close to. Never seen a hornier woman in my life. I knew screwing her would eventually pay off. Too bad it didn't pay off enough to get Quinn put in jail."

"You arrived in Midnight before Quinn. How did you know he would come here?"

"I didn't . . . not really. But you obviously meant something to him. After you left town, he didn't do a damn thing but work. I followed him for days, waiting for him to find another woman so I could make her acquaintance. Instead, all he did was go to that frigging hospital, run those damn marathons of his, or go to the gym. So I decided to come here and establish myself. I was going to give him a couple more weeks, and if he hadn't shown up, I was going to take you and use you as an enticement."

"I'm assuming you're the one who tried to run me over?"

Another wicked smile lit up his face. "Gotta say, you can move fast for a girl. Not that I wanted to kill you. If I had, you'd be worm food by now. But that would've been too easy. Couple of weeks in ICU might've been fun, though. I could've played the concerned friend. Brought you chocolates, flowers, crossword puzzles. I play that role quite well."

"But why kill Lindsay?"

"I admit, that was a bit self-serving. She was so hot for a good time. And the lack of witnesses this time gave me more cover." If possible, his grin became even eviler as he added, "And more time."

"You're a sick, sadistic bastard."

The hard slap to her face wasn't a complete surprise. She had known insulting him might set him off. Didn't lessen the pain, though.

Blinking back tears from her watering eyes, she said, "You know you won't get away with this, don't you? Quinn won't come alone."

"Oh, don't you worry, I have everything planned."

He stood and pulled something from his back pocket. "I anticipate Quinn will be here within the hour or so, which means we'd better get down to it."

First she heard a click and then she saw the gleam of the knife in the light as it came toward her. She leaned back as far away as possible.

"Don't flinch or move or I'll cut you and that's not my intent. Yet."

"Blaine, I—"

"And don't talk, either. This takes careful concentration."

Within seconds she realized what that careful concentration was for as he sliced at her clothes. Her heart thudded like a manic drum against her chest, and the convulsive shivering of her body had more to do with horror than cold. When at last he stepped away, her clothes lay in shreds all around her. She was now completely nude.

She told herself to face him, mock and deride him. That she had to be strong, show no weakness. That he would not get the best of her. Despite the knowledge of what she should do, fear swamped her. She rolled over to her side, away from the man standing above her with eyes glittering with a killing lust. Paralyzed by a dreadful terror, her mind went numb and blank. Blaine's mocking laugh brought her back to reality.

"You were a hell of a lot easier to subdue than I thought you would be. Damn, this is going to be fun."

Numbness evaporated and fury returned full force. Rolling back over so she could see him, she snarled, "You're a piece of shit . . . a pathetic excuse for a man."

"You're going to regret saying that."

His words were meant to be a threat, but the way his triumphant smile wavered, she knew her insults had made an impact. It gave her encouragement that this was the path to take.

Samantha laughed, making the sound as loud and mocking as she could, hoping he didn't notice the hysterical edge. "Regret telling you the truth? How about this—the only reason I even went out with you was because I was investigating a case for our agency and you were a possible suspect. I was never attracted to you. What sane woman would be?"

He grabbed the rope that held her ankles and hands together and jerked her until she was on her knees. Terror threatened to return. Samantha concentrated on the ache in her ankles, hands, and knees. Pain helped her to refocus.

Throwing her head back, she glared up at the maniac. "Truth hurts, doesn't it, asshole?"

His smile was now completely gone and in its place was an expression not unlike that of a wounded child.

"You only dated me because of an investigation? You don't think I'm good-looking and charming?"

"I think you're boring, pretentious, and incredibly ordinary-looking."

He dropped to his knees in front of her, and they faced each other—she with her false bravado she prayed he didn't see through and he with his crazed eyes and hurt feelings. The stare-down lasted several seconds.

Just when she thought he would get up and walk away, the knife reappeared . . . cold steel touched her cheek. "Want to see what a boring, pretentious, ordinary-looking man can do to your pretty face in a matter of seconds?"

Biting the inside of her mouth till she tasted blood, Samantha glared up at the psychopath. Refused to flinch.

Cheerful Christmas music, totally incongruent with the atmosphere, floated toward them.

Blaine surged to his feet. "Saved by the jingle bell." His good humor seemingly restored, he grinned down at her. "I wonder who could be calling."

Quinn held the phone so everyone in the car could hear. Sam's phone had been switched on, giving Zach the opportunity to trace it. The bastard wanted to be found. And he probably wanted to talk, if only to taunt.

"Hello, Dr. Braddock. Fancy hearing from you."

"Is Samantha all right?"

"But of course she is. What's the point in having dead bait?"

"Can I talk to her . . . to make sure?"

"I guess I should be insulted you don't believe me, but since we don't know each other all that well, I'll forgive the slight."

Quinn waited. He had plenty of questions to ask, but until he heard Sam's voice, he could do nothing else.

"Quinn," Sam said. "I'm all right."

She sounded shaky and weak but—*Thank you, God*—alive. Something else he heard was the thread of steel in her voice.

"Are you hurt?"

"No. Are you okay?"

Quinn closed his eyes. "I'm fine, sweetheart. Stay strong for me. I promise I'll—"

Blaine's voice cut him off. "Enough sweet stuff. Now let's talk turkey."

"What do you want?" Quinn asked.

"You. Alone."

"Where?"

"You're tracking me, so you know where. If I see anyone, hear the slightest sound that someone other than you is close by, Samantha's neck will be sliced and she'll be dead before she hits the ground."

"If I come, will you let her go?"

The line went dead.

Quinn continued to hold the phone, his only connection with Sam.

"What do you think?" Zach asked.

"I think he's telling the truth. He'll kill her unless I go in alone."

"You do this alone, both of you are dead."

"And if I don't, he'll kill Sam. I'll get her out."

"How?"

Quinn looked in the rearview mirror. Three trucks followed them. What he had learned in the last hour about Midnight's residents had reinforced his faith in mankind a hundredfold. He had arrived at the Wilde mansion and found cars and trucks parked up and down the long drive. At least a hundred residents, probably more, had stood in the front yard. They'd heard about Sam's kidnapping and all wanted to help.

Now at least a dozen men filled the vehicles following

them. Five times that many had wanted to come. Zach had agreed to allow the ones he knew were crack shots.

They had discussed the plan but Zach wasn't totally on board. Quinn could understand that—the victim was his sister-in-law. Also, as police chief, he was putting his job on the line by letting civilians assist in a rescue. If any of them were hurt, it was on him.

"I'll do it just like we discussed. Stop a quarter mile before we get there. I drive the rest of the way alone. These people are hunters. They know how to move without making a sound. I'll distract the bastard, draw him away from Sam. The instant she's safe, I'll take him down. If I'm not able to, someone else gets the honor."

Zach threw him a sharp look. "The plan is for everyone to survive."

"Agreed. But if there's only one, it damn well better be Samantha."

With a grim nod, Zach turned his eyes back to the road.

They should arrive at their stopping place in about fifteen minutes. From what they could discern from the GPS signal on Sam's phone, Marshall had taken her to the middle of nowhere. A map indicated swampland. Since Marshall had no doubt been planning this from the moment he entered Midnight, Quinn knew the man would be prepared.

The knowledge of what Sam might be going through pounded like an out-of-control jackhammer, trying to penetrate the wall he'd built around himself. For as long as he could remember, that barrier had shielded him from feeling too deeply. When it was in full force, it had rarely been breached. Now, as if it were made of sawdust, he could feel the wall crumbling around him. Quinn fought against its destruction for all he was worth. Sam's life depended upon him being able to shut out all distractions, including his feelings for her. Nothing mattered but getting her out safely.

Regret that he had come to Midnight was like bitter bile. And even after Lindsay had been killed, he had continued to see Sam. Why the hell hadn't he stayed away from her? He had used the excuse that she would be working the case anyway, and he had believed he could protect her. Never had he hated his arrogance more.

The ringing of Zach's cellphone pulled Quinn from his misery.

Without looking at the readout, the police chief answered with "Savannah . . . babe, we still haven't gotten there yet."

He listened for several seconds and then said, "Hold on." Handing the phone to Quinn, he said, "She's got something she needs to tell you."

Expecting curses and tears, he was surprised to hear a husky-voiced Savannah say, "Quinn, she's going to be fine. Remember, she's tougher than she looks."

"Thank you, Savannah. I'm just sorry that—"

"But that's not why I called. I've dug deeper into Blaine Marshall." Her voice went hard as she added, "I've used avenues the bastard probably doesn't even know exist."

When she paused, he knew she wasn't doing it for dramatic effect. There was something she dreaded telling him. Since he still had no clue why Blaine Marshall, a complete stranger, hated him enough to kill, he figured whatever she had to tell him would be a surprise. "And?"

Savannah pulled in a deep breath and Quinn found himself bracing for the news. No matter how much he prepared himself, he never would have been ready for the words "Quinn, your brother isn't dead."

CHAPTER THIRTY-FIVE

Samantha lay on her side, shivering beneath a plastic tarp he had thrown over her. It provided absolutely no warmth but at least it kept the dampness to a minimum. Also, having her body exposed to the bastard was something she could no longer stomach.

He had wanted to rape her and failed. Now, even though she knew it wasn't going to happen, she couldn't prevent the shudders of fear and revulsion. The minute he had ended his call from Quinn, he had sliced the rope, freeing her. She hadn't been able to move. After having been bound for so long, her arms and legs had been pierced with thousands of tiny pinpricks of sensation.

Curled up with pain, she had seen his hand reach for his zipper and had known what was about to happen. He wanted her submissive and compliant . . . to lie there like a victim. Damned if she would give him the satisfaction. She had opened her mouth and surprised even herself as she spewed as many insults and curses as she could think of, calling him every disgusting name she'd ever heard and a few she had made up.

Her words had saved her from rape. They hadn't saved her from his wrath. The knife slid into her before she realized it. One moment she had been curled up on the ground, screaming at him, and the next, agonizing pain bloomed in her back.

As long as she didn't move and breathed in shallow breaths, there was little to no pain now. She knew she was bleeding. How much, she couldn't tell. Her only hope was to minimize movement to prevent more blood loss.

"Get up, bitch. Quinn'll be here soon. I want you dressed for the occasion."

She actually did try to move but couldn't make herself do it.

Blaine had no problems forcing her. Pulling the tarp off her body, he grabbed her arm and jerked her to her feet.

Agony speared through her back and her knees buckled.

He caught her before she could drop back to the ground. "Stand up," he snapped. "I've been planning this a long time. You're not going to ruin it for me now."

She managed to lock her knees in place and gaze around. Blaine had turned on his car's headlights. Their brightness, along with the light from the lantern he'd lit earlier, enabled her to get her first good look at their location. It was basically a wide, semi-dry spot in the middle of a swamp. Giant trees towered over them, their gnarled limbs stretched eerily outward. A ghostly mist rose from the ground, spiraling toward the Spanish moss that hung from the trees like dark, misshapen ghouls. The area was creepily atmospheric—a fitting place for the monster before her.

If there was one blessing, it was that the weather was too cool for the creatures who usually inhabited this area to come out and investigate. Although an alligator intent on chowing down on Blaine would be a welcome sight.

"Come over here and sit." He pulled her toward a folding chair he'd set up in front of his car.

She eased down into the chair, glad to get off her wobbling legs.

Blaine walked around behind her; Samantha tensed. He had stabbed her in the back once, would he do that again? She jerked slightly when something cold touched her neck.

"Be still," he snapped.

"What are you doing?"

"I'm giving you the gift you refused before. I had to break into your house and go through every fucking bedroom to find it. Ungrateful bitch, you never even bothered to unwrap it."

Samantha glanced down and wasn't surprised to see the necklace Quinn had described to her. The Braddock necklace—the one he had gone over to get from Charlene.

"So after you killed Charlene, you took her necklace?"

"Yeah. She was wearing it, most likely thinking Quinn would find that enticing. She was a two-bit whore wearing jewelry fit for a queen."

Samantha leaned sideways against the back of the chair, careful of her wound. She had to figure out a way to disarm him. Quinn would be walking into a trap. There was no way Blaine didn't plan to kill him.

"Here, put this on."

He held some kind of cloth in his hands. She didn't care what it was—anything was better than being stark naked.

She reached for it and gasped when he pulled it out of her reach. "Stand up."

Bracing herself on the chair, she stood swaying and felt something soft go over her head. Suddenly she was covered to her knees in a dress.

Somehow, just with that bit of clothing, strength and purpose returned. She had been behaving like a whipped animal, not a former homicide detective, a security specialist, or a Wilde.

Lifting her chin, she glared at the bastard in front of her. A smirk had replaced the charming smile. The cheerful gleam in his eyes was gone, replaced by a sick malice. He looked like the sadistic psychopath who had killed at least two women.

Whether it was the clothing or just sheer stubbornness on her part, she didn't know, but she was feeling stronger. The wound in her back throbbed but had apparently stopped bleeding again. She didn't feel as woozy as she had before.

"So what's the plan?" she asked.

"You just sit still and look pretty."

The longer she waited to act, the more likely it was that Quinn would face him without cover. At least if she were gone, he wouldn't have the distraction of her presence.

He walked behind her again and she felt a tug on her hair. It took several seconds for her to realize that he was brushing her hair. Of all the things he had done, for some crazy reason, this particular act roiled her stomach. She had expected his violent behavior but not this deed of almost tenderness. Her stomach revolted and she bent forward to gag. In mid-gag, her eyes spotted what looked like her salvation. Bending lower, she surreptitiously picked up the fist-sized rock. A brutal tug on her hair jerked her back up.

"Sit up or I'll tie you to the chair."

Since that would greatly hinder her escape, Samantha complied and once again suffered his hands brushing and smoothing her hair. She waited for several more seconds, trying to regulate her rapid breathing. If he suspected anything, he would tie her up and she might never get this chance again.

"I love your hair." He buried his face against the back

of her neck and breathed in deeply. "It smells good, too."

Swallowing bile, she waited until he pulled away. Then, surging to her feet, she whirled and slammed the rock into the side of his head. He went down, but she wasted no time checking to see what kind of damage she'd done. As if her feet had wings, she took off like a wild animal, undeterred by the darkness or the lack of shoes to protect her feet. Better to die of exposure than let the bastard get the chance to kill her or Quinn.

Without light, Samantha had to rely on other senses besides sight. Mist floated all around, saturating the thin dress she wore. Being barefooted was probably her biggest worry. If she injured her feet, getting away would be even more difficult.

Running noiselessly was almost impossible. The ground was soggy but covered with broken twigs and leaves. Every step she took sounded like a blast of dynamite to her ears. Her breath wheezed through her lungs and the wound in her back throbbed. The warmth streaming down her back told her she was bleeding again. Since there was nothing she could do about it, she forced herself to focus on one thing only—getting as far away from the lunatic as she could.

She ran with her arms stretched out to avoid slamming into a tree, and barely grimaced as a blob of something slippery smacked her in the face. Moss most likely. Her fingers touched a broad tree and she took a moment to lean against it to catch her breath and listen. Nothing but the sound of her own breathing, the distant hoot of an owl, and wind whistling through the trees.

Had she knocked him out cold? Maybe even killed him? If so, the nightmare was over. If not, she would—

An inhuman scream sounded in the distance. He had apparently just woken and realized what had happened.

She could rest no longer. Drawing in a shaky breath for courage and strength, she took off again.

"*Samantha! Where aaaare yooouuuuu?*"

His voice echoed eerily through the trees. It was impossible to tell how far away he was. *Keep running . . . keep running . . . keep running* became a mantra in her mind, matching the rhythm of her thudding heartbeat.

A flood of light in the distance gave her the first sight of where she was. Headlights . . . from a car. Quinn was here. She had to get to him, stop him before he faced the maniac alone.

Renewed optimism gave her a burst of energy. Quinn was here and everything was going to be okay. Samantha took a giant leap toward light and safety. Cruel, brutal hands grabbed her arms and jerked her backward. She screamed and something soft but noxious covered her mouth and nose. Trying not to breathe, she fought with all her strength; kicking backward, she connected with his shin and heard a slight grunt.

Her mind whirled and her muffled cry of defeat was drowned out by the sound of triumphant laughter that followed her into darkness.

Quinn pulled to a stop a few yards from the GPS location of Sam's phone. He was armed and ready, a Glock 22 in his pocket, a Kel-Tec P-32 in an ankle holster, and a Ka-Bar knife hidden in the lining of his fleece jacket. He was also armed with knowledge and information.

An hour ago, he had been stupidly ignorant. Now vile, dirty family secrets had been revealed. He had called his parents and learned more about the filth he'd come from than he'd ever wanted to know. The rage, pain, and disgust would have to wait. Compartmentalizing had saved his ass in the army. And now it would save Sam. He had no choice in the matter. He cared about nothing else but getting her to safety. If that entailed killing his brother to do it, so be it. If that also included losing his own life, then that's the way it would have to be. Nothing mattered but saving the woman he loved.

And yes, he did love Sam. His stupid, idiotic need to control every aspect of his life, including his heart, had kept him from admitting the truth. But there was no doubt in his mind that he loved this beautiful, gentle-hearted, and courageous woman. He just prayed that he got the chance to prove it to her and make it up to her.

Quinn opened the driver's-side door and stepped out. In the distance, he saw two dim lights and assumed they were from a car. He heard no voices or sounds other than the normal noises of a quiet, eerie night in a swamp. Not hearing anything gave him hope. Dalton would correctly assume that he was armed. And he would probably realize that there were a couple of people behind Quinn who would step up and help. There was no way he would know that he was surrounded by at least a dozen of the best hunters in Midnight. They knew how to be silent and how to wait for the right time to take the shot. And their mission was clear—save Sam.

Zach, both of his deputies, and his friend Brody James were among the crowd, along with many others Quinn didn't know. One of their own had been taken, and if there was one thing the citizens of Midnight didn't take kindly to, it was that.

The lights went dark and a voice called out, "Stop right there."

Quinn jerked to a stop. He couldn't see anyone but it sounded as if Dalton was about fifteen feet in front of him.

"Using your left hand, take the gun out of your right pocket."

Quinn had known he'd have to lose that one. Slowly,

carefully, he complied and dropped the Glock on the ground.

"Come closer."

Taking slow, measured steps, Quinn moved forward. Clouds that had obscured the moon moved away, giving him some semblance of light. As he got closer, dark shapes began to materialize. Two people, one sitting, one standing. He released a quiet, relieved sigh. The one sitting was smaller, slighter—Sam. Just the knowledge that she was within touching distance gave him a certain kind of peace.

"That's far enough."

Again Quinn stopped and waited for further instructions.

"Long time no see . . . brother," Dalton sneered.

"Hello, Dalton."

"You knew?" His voice had the disappointed sound of a petulant child who had been deprived of a favorite dessert.

There was little need to lie about this. "Yes, but not until a few minutes ago."

"Ah . . . I'll bet you talked to our dear mother. How is the old hag?"

"Worried . . . about you."

"But of course she is. I'm her only son."

The image of Dalton's headstone came to his mind, and like before, something clicked. Holy hell, had his entire life been a lie?

Apparently taking Quinn's silence as shock, Dalton laughed. That sound was familiar and Quinn wished he had heard him laugh before tonight. If he had, he would have recognized the distinctive sound.

"You didn't know, did you?"

Already suspecting, Quinn gave Dalton the opportunity to spring the truth on him.

"You're adopted. You're the son of some knocked-up

teenager Mommy Dearest hired one summer. She didn't think she could get pregnant, so she purchased a kid. But then I surprised her. She found out she was pregnant with me when you were about a year old. Too bad she didn't get rid of you then. Life would have been much simpler."

"How do you know all this?"

"She was trying to convince me how much she loved me." His voice was confident, smug. "All the things I had to give up, all the indignities I had to suffer, because of you. She wanted me to know I was her only son. Blood of her blood."

"What is it you want, Dalton?"

"That should be pretty obvious, don't you think? You took my life away from me. You had to pay. Because of you, I had to change everything. My face, my career. You took it all and left me nothing."

Knowing it was useless, Quinn said anyway, "You tried to kill a woman."

"Nobody had to know about that." His tone turned sly. "Did you get the message? Thirteen stabs—thirteen years?"

If he'd had any idea Dalton was alive, yeah, he would've gotten the message. Dalton was thirteen years old when he was put away.

When Quinn didn't answer, Dalton went on. "I admit it was a bit self-serving, but a guy's gotta have a little fun."

Refusing to contribute to his smugness, Quinn went on to something that he couldn't get his head wrapped around. "Why wait so long to come after me? You had to know where I was."

"The fucking medications they forced down my throat. They kept me from thinking clearly. Every single day I had to take the things. I was like a zombie. Went to work, came home. I had no life.

"Then one day I was driving down the road, minding my own business, and some bitch cut me off in traffic. And that delicious anger returned. Damn, it felt good. I followed her home and took care of her. I'd forgotten that incredible feeling of power. I left town the next day and knew exactly where I needed to go and what I needed to do. It took me a while to set it all up. But finally, my mind was clear and I was thinking straight again. And I knew it was time for you to see the consequences of your actions."

"Why not just come after me? Why did you have to kill Charlene and Lindsay?"

"Because you needed to suffer. If I'd just killed you, then it would have been over. And because they were so damn fun."

"I have suffered."

Dalton gave a loud snort of disgust. "Not nearly enough."

"You've taken what was most important to me—my reputation and my career."

"Really?" Dalton paused and suddenly a lantern flickered on.

Quinn knew if he survived this night, the image before him would haunt his nightmares for years to come. Sam sat slumped in the chair. Her eyes were closed, indicating she was either unconscious or dead. He detected no life. The light was too dim for him to see if she was breathing. The only thing that gave him hope was that she had tape over her mouth. Why would Dalton need to gag her if she was dead?

"I think killing this little lady might hurt you the most of all."

Quinn shook his head and forced his mouth into an amused smile. "Now, why would you think that?"

"You bought a house here to be close to her. I saw you kissing her. And remember, I was there at the Thanksgiving dinner. You were looking at her like there was no one else in the room."

His shoulders were so stiff with tension, he barely managed a slight shrug. "That's called lust, dear brother. Surely you know all about that. She's a sweet piece of meat, nothing more."

"Then why'd you buy a house here?"

That was harder to explain but he did his best. "Because I like to fuck in private. If I hadn't bought a place, the gossips would be watching my every move. I got a place that's far enough away from town so I can do to her what I damn well please."

"I don't believe you."

"Then wake Samantha up and ask her. She'll tell you what I told her."

"How do you know she's not already dead?"

Quinn stopped breathing and his heart screamed a denial. Then sanity returned. Dalton wanted to torture him. If he intended to kill Sam, then he would want to do it in front of Quinn.

"I saw her breathing," he lied.

Sam's head jerked back—Dalton must've pulled her hair. Though her eyes were closed, he did finally detect signs of life. He saw the rapid movement of her chest, indicating she was alive and was most likely awake. Had she heard him deny his feelings? He couldn't let that matter now. Once this was over, he would do anything and everything he could to make up for all of this, including the lies he'd had to tell his brother.

"Wake up, Sammie, and say goodbye to your lover."

Her eyes flickered and then finally opened. She stared at him and he wondered if she was in a daze. Brody had found an empty hypodermic needle on the floor of the kitchen, and Quinn figured that was how she was taken.

Dalton leaned down and whispered loudly in her ear,

"My brother here is telling me tales about your relationship."

"We have no relationship. We sleep together . . . that's all."

Her voice was cold and hard, devoid of emotion. Quinn hoped like hell she was lying and wasn't saying the words because she believed them.

"No, that can't be true. You're just saying that."

Quinn held a hand up. "Scout's honor. She's no different from any of the other women I've slept with. Hell, you really think after being married to that slut Charlene, I'd want to tie myself down to any woman ever again?"

"It's true," Sam whispered. "That's what he told me."

Dalton shook his head. "No, I don't believe it." He jerked Sam up and kicked the chair to the side. Holding her as a shield in front of him, he snarled, "Then if you don't care about her, you won't mind if I do this."

Quinn shouted, "No!" and dove for the knife in Dalton's hand. An instant before he reached him, he knew he was too late. The knife sank deep into Sam's stomach.

Fury and fear coalesced into a driving need to destroy. Using every bit of force he could muster, Quinn slammed his fist into his brother's face. The crunching sound of breaking bone and cartilage barely penetrated his consciousness.

Quinn caught Sam in his arms and placed her gently on the ground. His hand firmly over her wound, he said sharply, urgently, "Sam, can you hear me? Wake up. Look at me."

Her eyes blinked slightly and she mumbled something. Quinn leaned closer.

A gleeful laugh came from several feet away. Quinn glanced up briefly. Dalton, his entire face a bloody mess, stood swaying as if he could barely stand. And he was smiling.

Quinn returned his attention to Samantha. "Sam, you're going to be fine. I—"

The sound of a rifle shot registered. Quinn jerked his head up in time to see Dalton waver unsteadily right above him, the knife clutched in his hand, ready to strike. Then, as if in slow motion, he crumpled slowly to the ground.

Quinn turned away, grabbed the lantern, and pulled it closer to check Sam's wound. The cheap cloth of the dress ripped as he pulled at it. She had a deep gash on the right side of her abdomen, just below her rib cage. Until he could get her to a hospital for a CT scan, he wouldn't know for sure if her liver or bowel—or both—had been punctured.

Forcing his mind to ignore that this woman was his life was almost impossible. The only thing keeping him from going berserk was the knowledge that if he failed, Sam died. That stark truth focused him like nothing else could.

He tore off his jacket and then his shirt. Folding the shirt, he again pressed firmly over the wound to slow the bleeding and then covered her with his jacket. Her skin was ice cold and clammy. Hypothermia was almost as much a concern as her wound.

Zach materialized beside him. "How is she?"

"I won't know till I can get her to a hospital."

"Here." Zach handed him a blanket. "Stretcher's coming. Someone's bringing your medical kit, too."

Quinn covered her with the blanket and then pressed his fingers against her neck to feel her pulse. Rapid, a little thready. Her respiration was slightly elevated. As soon as he had his blood pressure kit, he'd be able to determine more.

"Quinn?" Sam whispered softly.

"Shh. I'm here, baby. You're going to be fine."

"You're a terrible liar."

"I'm not lying. You will be fine. I promise." And then because he could no longer hold back the words, he leaned over her and said softly, "I love you, Sam."

She seemed to stop breathing for a second and then she whispered, "Like I said . . . a terrible liar."

Her eyes closed. Checking her pulse again, Quinn's breath rushed out in relief. She had passed out, nothing more.

He heard several loud footsteps behind him and looked over his shoulder. Two men were holding a canvas stretcher much like the army used to carry their wounded. As he helped them lift Sam onto the gurney, he glanced over to where his brother lay.

"He's dead," Zach said.

Nodding, Quinn turned away. He'd deal with that later. Now he had only one thing on his mind. Keeping Sam alive.

CHAPTER THIRTY-SIX

She was floating. Pain existed but was distant. Voices surrounded her, some familiar, some not. Dimly, she knew she had been injured. How and why she didn't know and somehow she thought maybe that was best.

She'd heard Quinn's voice, hoarse and strained. And Savvy's, too, though it sounded thick, like she'd been crying. And once she thought she'd heard Aunt Gibby's quivering voice.

Her eyes felt like they'd been sewn shut. She told them to open and they refused. As awareness came, her vague thoughts coalesced into a solid reality. Crap, there was the pain. Though everything seemed to ache, there were two distinct throbs, one in her back and the other in her stomach.

Once again she told her eyes to open. And dammit, they refused. Opening her mouth to verbally issue a command, all she heard was this strange moan.

"Sammie? Oh my gosh, Sammie, you're waking up. You're going to be fine." A hand squeezed hers and for the first time she realized someone had been holding her hand all along. Savvy?

"Quinn's right outside, talking to the doctor. I'll be right back."

Quinn? Was he okay? She wasn't quite sure why she thought something might have hurt him, but for some reason, her heart thudded and dread washed over her. But Savvy had said he was right outside, which meant he was fine.

She heard the sound of the door opening and the thud of footsteps. Even with closed eyes, she knew Quinn had entered the room. When a large, warm hand gripped hers, she wanted to smile her relief that he was okay, but couldn't gather the energy.

"Sam?" The voice was definitely his but again it sounded hoarse. Maybe he had a cold. Was that why she had been worried?

"Sam, open your eyes and look at me."

She wanted to see him . . . she really did. Straining with effort, her eyelids flickered and she saw a minuscule glimpse of light.

"That's it, sweetheart."

Encouraged, she continued to fight against the incredible weakness that seemed to have taken over her entire body. A couple more flickers and finally she got them open enough to see Quinn's unshaven face and bloodshot eyes. He looked as though he'd been to hell and back more than once.

Then an amazing transformation took place as a smile of pure joy lit his face. Never had he looked more dear or handsome to her.

"What's wrong?" she asked. Was that tiny little voice really hers?

"You're in the hospital. You were injured but you're going to be fine."

Hurt? How? She frowned. What had happened? Car wreck? Her muddled mind scrambled for knowledge and facts.

"Sammie, it's okay that you can't remember. It'll come back to you soon."

Turning her head slightly, she realized that Savvy was on the other side of the bed. She looked exhausted, too.

Her eyes were puffy and her mouth trembled as if she were trying to keep from crying. "Savvy, you're okay?"

"I'm fine . . . Little Bit, too." Her wobbling mouth tilted into a smile. "We've just been so worried about you."

"Bri . . . here?"

"Yes . . ." Savvy looked over her shoulder and then turned back to say, "She just stepped out for a few minutes."

"What happened?"

"All that can be discussed later," Quinn said.

Her eyes returned to the man who held her hand. "Sleepy."

"I know you are. Go back to sleep. When you wake up, you'll feel much better. I promise."

As if she'd been waiting for permission, Samantha closed her eyes again. Quinn's stubble brushed her forehead as he kissed her gently. And despite not knowing the reason for her injuries, she fell into a deep sleep, oddly content.

Quinn allowed himself one last look at Sam before he went out the door. She was going to be fine. He had known that hours ago but it wasn't until she opened her eyes that he gave himself permission to feel the slightest amount of relief. He had come so close to losing her.

It hadn't been until they were in the car, headed back to Midnight, that he'd realized she had a wound in her back. Less deep than the one in her abdomen, but her blood loss had been greater than he had feared.

They'd made it back to Midnight in record time. A medical helicopter had been waiting and had transported them to Mobile in a matter of minutes. Zach had made the call immediately after Sam had been stabbed. His quick thinking had saved her life.

The stab to her stomach had missed her liver by less than an inch. His entire body jolted every time he thought about how close she had been to dying.

Now that he knew Sam would be all right, he had some massive cleanup to do. Atlanta PD had been notified and wanted to talk with him. Dalton had admitted to Charlene's murder but it was the necklace around Sam's neck that would prove his guilt. Once the questions were dealt with in Atlanta, he would face his parents . . . no, correction, he would face Edward and Geneva. They weren't his parents, and of all the shit that had happened in the last twenty-four hours, that was one piece of good news. And Dalton wasn't his brother. Knowing he didn't have the taint of their blood inside him was incredibly freeing.

Quinn turned to Savannah, who had dropped into a chair in the hallway. "You'll call me if anything happens?"

She nodded. "Absolutely. I hope you can get things in order quickly, though. She's going to want to talk to you as soon as she's conscious again."

"I'll do my best. When she wakes, call me on my cellphone."

"Your brother's body won't be ready for release for a couple more days," Zach said as he ambled down the hallway toward them.

Quinn knew he owed this man everything. Because of the police chief's professionalism, Samantha was alive. And Zach's willingness to allow the townspeople to participate had been crucial. One of them had shot Dalton, saving both his and Sam's lives.

He held out his hand to shake Zach's. "Thank you for all you did."

Zach nodded and returned the handshake. He then sat down beside his wife and pulled her toward him. "You feeling okay, babe?"

Savannah nodded. "I'm fine." Her smile reminding him of Sam's, she added, "Now that I know Sammie's going to be okay, I feel like a ton of bricks has been lifted off of me."

Zach kissed the top of Savannah's head. "As soon as Bri comes back, I want you to go home and get some rest."

Worry returned to Savannah's eyes. "Something's going on with her but she won't talk to me."

"She will," Zach said.

"You know what it is?"

"Not much but a little. Give her some leeway. Okay?"

She blew out a shaky breath and nodded. "Okay."

Quinn glanced down at his watch. He needed to get going, but holy hell, he didn't want to leave. "I should get to Atlanta by mid-morning. Once I'm through there, I'll probably head up to Virginia for a quick stop before coming back here. I'll try to get back as soon as possible."

Zach nodded. "I talked with Detective Murphy. Told him I'd fax my report to them. Hopefully this will wrap up any doubts about who killed your ex-wife. When you get back, we'll need to discuss the Daytons and their friends. I'm not inclined to give them much of a break."

"Neither am I," Quinn said grimly. "Without their help, Dalton wouldn't have been able to get to Sam."

Quinn glanced back at Sam's hospital room door. He was so tempted to go back in, just for another glimpse. But the sooner he left, hopefully the sooner he could return for good.

Turning back to Savannah, he said, "Tell Sam I'll call her."

"I will. Have a safe trip."

Walking out of the hospital was one of the most difficult things he'd ever done. He didn't want to leave but he had no choice. He just hoped to hell Sam understood.

SEVEN DAYS LATER

"Have you talked to Quinn today?" Savvy asked.

Samantha rose slowly from the chair beside her bedroom window. Staring out of it for endless hours was pointless, but since she'd been home that's all she seemed to be able to do.

"No. He usually calls by this time." She couldn't hide the disappointment. Even though their conversations were often stilted and one-sided, she looked forward to them. His daily phone calls were the only contact she'd had with him since that first night in the hospital.

"Do you know when he's coming back?"

Her gaze turned toward the window again. "He hasn't said."

"I still don't understand why you're mad at him, Sammie. I'm sure he's doing everything he can to get back as soon as possible."

"I'm not mad, I'm just . . ." She was what? Listless? Tired? Lonely? Yes to all of those. She had no energy, no drive. Never had she felt so apathetic. She'd gotten out of the hospital two days ago, and so far all she wanted to do was sit around and mope. Not that she wanted to run a marathon, but a little energy would be nice.

"Once he gets back, you'll be able to sort out what's wrong."

Would she? What was there to sort out? Nothing had changed. She and Quinn had gone through a life-altering experience, but from what she could tell, it hadn't altered their lives one bit. He was still the same, and other than a couple of scars, so was she.

Savvy's sigh was so loud it echoed through the room.

"I wish at least one of my sisters would tell me what's wrong. For the first time ever, I feel like a stranger to both of you."

"Oh, Savvy, I'm sorry." She shook her head. "I guess I'm just kind of sad that after everything that's happened, Quinn and I are back to where we started."

"Why do you say that?"

"Because when we talk on the phone, it's all business-like. 'How are you feeling? Any unusual soreness? Weakness?' I feel as though he's my doctor, not my lover. Like that's our only connection."

"I'm sure he has a lot on his mind."

Guilt sliced at Samantha. Truer words were never said. Quinn's life had been upended. His parents weren't his parents; his brother, who he'd thought was dead, wasn't really his brother. And two women were dead. Not to mention the fact that she had almost died, too.

"I know I'm not being fair. I guess if I had seen him after I started recovering, I'd feel better. And I know he had issues to handle, so I'm not blaming him. I just wish things could be different."

"Have you changed your mind about being with him?"

"No. If there's one thing I did learn, it's that you have to appreciate every moment. I love Quinn and that's just going to have to be enough."

"But he told you he loved you, Sammie. You remembered everything, including that."

"He thought I was dying. And he's not said anything like that since."

"Well, maybe he wants to say it to you in person."

"Or maybe, since he thought I was dying and . . ." She couldn't finish the sentence. She was too scared to even hope. If she kept telling herself that nothing had changed, at least she wouldn't be disappointed.

"Don't lose hope, Sammie. If you had seen him when

they brought you to the hospital, you wouldn't doubt his feelings."

Quinn did have deep feelings for her, she knew that much. But did they have staying power? The kind that would see them through rough patches? Was the love he professed the type to build a future on, or was it the kind that weakened when times got tough and fizzled out eventually? She knew her feelings were strong enough to weather any storm . . . but were Quinn's?

Needing to focus on something other than her potential heartache, she said, "So you've still not been able to get anything out of Bri?"

"No. She just made that one announcement that Cruz was dead and Lauren was no longer in danger."

"What do you think happened?"

"I have no idea. I've read the news reports. They just claim Cruz was found washed up on the beach with a bullet hole in his head. No suspects so far, but the man had plenty of enemies."

Samantha hated to ask the question, but it needed to be said. "Do you think she killed him?"

A soft snort came from the doorway. "I can be reckless on occasion, but I'm not insane."

Samantha and Savvy turned at the same time. Bri stood at the bedroom door. Wearing a pair of gray fleece sweatpants and a FSU T-shirt, she looked about sixteen years old. The defiant, stubborn look on her face was an expression both sisters knew well. She was on shutdown.

"You've been so secretive, that was the only scenario I could come up with on why you won't tell us what's going on. I thought we agreed to share everything," Samantha said.

"Don't try to guilt me into telling you something that I can't. It's better that both you and Savvy stay out of this."

"Stay out of what?" Savvy asked. "We don't even know what we're staying out of."

Bri chewed her bottom lip worriedly for several seconds, then shook her head again. "No, it's safer this way."

"Safer for whom?"

"For all of us. You guys are just going to have to trust me on this."

"Trusting you isn't the issue, Bri," Samantha said. "You know we trust you with our lives."

"Then let it go. Believe me, it's better this way."

"Better for whom?"

"For all of us." She bit her lip and added, "Most especially for me."

"Did you tell Zach?" Savvy asked.

"No. He asked me what was wrong. I told him what I've told you guys."

"Which is nothing," Savvy said. "You know there isn't anything you could tell us that would shock us or we would reveal to anyone."

"I know that, Savvy. I just—"

Dreading to know the answer, Samantha asked anyway. "You're in danger, aren't you?"

"I don't know. Maybe." She shook her head. "Probably not, but it's safer if we just pretend we never even knew about Armando Cruz. Lauren is perfectly safe. No one's going to come looking for her."

"And is someone going to come looking for you?" Samantha asked.

Chin up, green eyes lit with that rebellious streak that was so Bri, she shook her head emphatically.

Samantha met Savvy's eyes and saw resignation and acceptance. When Bri went into one of her silent moods, there was no going further with her.

"If you change your mind, you know we're always here. Right?" Samantha said.

"Thanks, you two. You know I love you lots."

Though Bri's smile was brilliant, the solemnity of her eyes said there was something major bothering her. But until she agreed to share, there was nothing else Sam or Savvy could do.

"Now that we've got that settled." Savvy cut her eyes over to Bri. "Or not. I've got something I need to talk to both of you about."

Apparently deciding she wasn't going to have to bolt to avoid being questioned, Bri finally came farther into the room. And because she couldn't stay irritated with either sister for more than a couple of minutes, Samantha motioned her over to sit in the oversized chair with her.

With another brilliant smile, this one reaching her eyes, Bri settled into the chair. Leaning her head against Bri's shoulder, Samantha turned to Savvy and said, "What's up?"

"Brody and Logan mentioned something to me a couple of days ago. I told them I'd talk to you guys about it because unless we're all on board with it, it's a no-go."

"What is it?"

"They want to know if we want to partner with them on the security agency. It would stay the Wildfire Security Agency, but we would be equal partners."

"We do work really well together," Bri said.

"And they have more business than they can handle," Samantha added.

Savvy grinned. "Whereas we've had one case so far."

"Would they keep their office in Mobile?"

"Yes, though if we agree to the partnership, we'll run the main business here at the Wilde house. Both Brody and Logan would move to Midnight but would go to Mobile a couple of times a week to meet with clients, if necessary."

For the first time in days, Samantha felt a spark of

excitement. Still, that excitement was tempered with practicality. "One of our biggest problems is lack of exposure. If they come here, isn't that going to compound the problem?"

Savvy grinned and Samantha realized her sister had probably figured all of this out beforehand. One of the things she admired most about Savvy was her planning skills.

"We're going to get plenty of exposure. I've talked to a Web designer. She's sending me several mock-ups we can choose from. And Brody and Logan both have a load of contacts, which is where most of their business has been coming from."

"And?" Bri asked.

"I got a call this morning from a pharmaceutical company in Atlanta. They're interested in retaining us for a fraud investigation."

"Why us?" Samantha asked. "There're a dozen or more security agencies in Atlanta, all with more experience."

"It's on the hush-hush. They didn't want to use anyone close by. And someone you used to work with, Sammie, told them about us."

"Who's that?"

"Captain Mintz."

That brought a smile to her face. She was glad there were no hard feelings that she had so abruptly left the force.

"So what do you guys think?" Savvy asked. "If we start getting more jobs, we're going to need more people to work them."

"I'm in," Bri said. "I like working with both men."

Samantha nodded. "I do, too. And I don't know what we would have done without them the last few months."

"Then it's settled. How about we set up a meeting January 2 to discuss moving forward?"

"Why wait so long?" Samantha asked.

"For one thing, you're still recovering. And another thing, Logan is gone for a few days."

"Visiting family for the holidays?"

Both of her sisters shook their heads but it was Bri who said, "My fault. I told Lauren she was no longer in danger. Within the hour, she was gone. Didn't say goodbye to anyone. Left a note, along with ten thousand dollars in cash."

"What did the note say?"

" 'Thanks for your help.' "

"And Logan has gone after her?"

"Yeah." Bri grimaced. "To put it mildly, he was pissed. He came by to tell us and then tore out of the drive like a bat out of hell."

Logan's attraction to Lauren had been apparent to anyone who was around him for more than five minutes. Had she left because of that or something else?

"Okay, I'll give Brody a call and let him know we're in. Hopefully Logan will be back by then." Savvy stopped at the door and turned back to leave some parting news. "By the way, we've settled on a name—Camille Sage. What do you think?"

Tears sprang to Samantha's eyes. As she had so many times before, Savvy was showing her love for her sisters. Camille was Samantha's middle name and Sage was Bri's. "That's perfect, thank you," Samantha said.

Bri nodded her agreement. "I love it, too."

"Good. Couldn't resist using two of my favorite people's names."

The instant Savvy disappeared, Bri got to her feet. "I'm in the mood for some major cooking."

Bri cooked massive amounts of food when she had something on her mind.

"Are you sure you can't tell us—tell me—what's going on?" Samantha asked.

"I can't, Sammie. Believe me, I would if I could."
Stopping at the door, she turned and said, "Jambalaya
sound good to you?"

Refusing to let it go without one more push, she said,
"If there's anything I can do, will you let me know?"

Bri grinned. "After the way you handled that bastard
Blaine Marshall, you bet. You'll be the first person I
call."

The worry increased as Samantha watched her sister
leave the room. Not for a moment did she believe her.
What in the world had Bri gotten herself mixed up in?

CHAPTER THIRTY-SEVEN

Quinn pulled in front of the Wilde mansion. He'd been back for two days, and as far as he knew, only two people in town, Zach and Brody, knew he was back. Somehow the gossips of Midnight hadn't detected his presence. Of course, it helped that he had arrived before dawn the day before yesterday and hadn't stepped foot off his property since.

It had almost killed him to walk away from Sam. Every day he was gone felt like he'd lost something of himself. And with each phone call, she seemed to be drifting further and further away from him. Most of the time, she gave monosyllabic answers to his questions. Getting her to tell him what was wrong had been impossible. She'd said she understood why he had to leave, but dammit, something was off.

So he'd come back two days ago and had been working night and day since. Grand gestures weren't his forte and there wasn't a woman in the world that would call him the least bit romantic. But for Sam, he would try.

He got out of his car and marched up the steps. He almost felt like he was starting all over again, the way he did when he'd first come to Midnight to apologize. Her reception had been cold then. Would he meet with the same resistance?

He rang the doorbell and wasn't surprised when it

was opened immediately by a brilliantly smiling Savannah. He'd figured Zach would probably tell his wife what he and Brody had been helping him with.

"Thank goodness you finally came."

"What's wrong? Is Sam okay?"

"Oh, she's fine physically. And I have a feeling she'll soon be fine in every other way, too."

"I hope so."

"Why don't you go on up? Her bedroom is on the second floor, the fourth room on the left."

His heart rate increasing in anticipation, Quinn raced up the stairs. He stopped at Sam's bedroom door, took a breath, and knocked.

"Come in."

Opening the door, he stood for a moment and just drank in the sight of her. The panicked feeling he'd been having slowly melted away. Everything was going to be all right.

She was sitting by the window, looking outside. She wore faded jeans, the kind that made her slender, beautiful legs look impossibly long; the deep red of her sweater made him think she was trying to get into the holiday spirit. He hoped to help her with that.

Apparently thinking it was one of her sisters who'd entered, she said, "I think we need to get started on rebuilding the guesthouse. That way I can live there and Bri—"

"But you already have a house here."

She gasped and turned. "What are you doing here? When did you get back?"

Since it was easier, he answered the second question first. "Day before yesterday, around three in the morning."

"But why didn't you tell me you were back?"

"I wanted to surprise you."

Instead of the brilliant smile he'd hoped for, she gave

him one of her solemn, too-serious looks. Something was definitely wrong and it wasn't just his absence the last few days.

He walked slowly toward her. "What's wrong? Aren't you glad to see me?"

"Of course I am. Did you get everything taken care of in Atlanta?"

"Yeah. Charlene's murder case is officially closed. You don't have to do more than the statement you gave Zach. That, with the necklace, sealed the deal."

"I'm glad. And your parents—did you see them?"

"Yes, I saw them."

Quinn waited for the anger to reappear and was surprised when he felt nothing. The people who had claimed to be his parents were no longer a part of his life. And there was a possibility that Geneva Braddock could be in serious trouble. She swore she had no idea what her son was capable of. That was up to the judicial system. As far as Quinn was concerned, she no longer existed.

"Turns out Geneva's been sending money to Dalton for years. Even paid for extensive plastic surgery."

"Why plastic surgery?"

Quinn shrugged. "Everyone believed he was dead. He had a new face, a new identity, so she could pretend he was a new person, too. Most of his surgery took place in Florida."

"That's why he had such an extreme reaction when I asked him about spending time in Florida."

"That'd be my guess."

Quinn still couldn't get his head wrapped around the fact that Geneva had hidden from the world that her sick freak of a son was roaming the countryside. Since he had a new identity and a new face, no one could tie him back to the Braddocks of Virginia.

"Dalton was released into his parents' care when he was seventeen. To avoid the stigma of having a mentally unbalanced son, they claimed he committed suicide. So much better to be the grieving parents of a deceased child than the parents of a live psychopath."

The memorial, the giant tombstone, the fabricated grief—all had been lies perpetrated by two people who were so fucking selfish and self-absorbed that a taint on their reputation was worse than the knowledge that they'd freed a lunatic.

"Geneva swore that the doctors had him well in line. Dalton had an apartment, a job . . . just like a regular person. She said she believed he was perfectly sane. That the medications he was on prevented the violent temper tantrums and destructive behavior. About ten months ago, he went off the grid. Didn't keep his doctor's appointments and no one knew of his location." Bitterness entered his voice as he added, "She didn't know what to do, so she did nothing."

Sam gasped. "That's why she called you out of the blue nine months ago."

"Yeah. She knew Dalton might come looking for me."

And he had. Problem was, he hadn't sought Quinn out to reconnect with his older brother. The bastard had only wanted one thing—payback.

"Still don't know why they never bothered to tell me I was adopted." He shrugged and added, "Maybe they knew how happy and relieved that would've made me."

"You'd think someone in your town would have figured it out and told you." She gave him a quick smile, briefly looking like the old Sam. "If you had lived in Midnight, there'd be no way you wouldn't have known."

"I've missed you."

"Have you?"

He sat on the window seat, facing her. "Tell me what's wrong, sweetheart."

"Nothing." She turned and looked out the window again.

Quinn blew out a sigh. Maybe she would talk once he got her home. "Are you ready to go?"

"Go where?"

"To our house."

"I'm not sure that's a good idea. Shouldn't we—"

She broke off and swallowed a shriek when he stood and gently scooped her into his arms. "What are you doing?"

"I'm taking you home."

"You can't just come in and take me like this."

Loving the sparks he saw spitting from her eyes, he grinned and kept walking. "Oh yeah? Who's going to stop me?"

Not waiting for a reply, Quinn strode from the room and then down the stairway. A smiling Savannah stood at the front door.

"Savvy, don't you dare open that door for him. He can't just come in here and—"

Laughing, Savannah opened the door. "I'll see you tomorrow, Sammie."

"Traitor."

"Hey, what are sisters for?"

Feeling more confident by the minute, Quinn went down the steps and stopped at his car. He leaned forward and, with less finesse than he would have liked, opened the car door. Mindful of her still-healing injuries, he carefully placed Sam in the passenger seat and buckled her seat belt. Then, before she could unfasten the seat belt and open the door, he ran around the front of the car and jumped into the driver's side.

Thankfully she didn't seem inclined to want out, but neither did she look all that happy to be going with him. He hoped that would soon change.

It was dusk. As long as he didn't run into any unforeseen delays, the timing should be perfect. Then he would let his hard work speak for itself.

As they drove through town, she maintained her silence. Was she contemplating how to get away from him for good? After the hell she'd been through because of him, could he blame her?

At last Quinn pulled in front of their house. It was now pitch-dark. The stage was set . . . now for the main event. The instant he had the thought, it happened.

Sam gasped and grabbed his arm. "Oh my gosh, Quinn. It's beautiful."

He took in his handiwork. Thousands of Christmas lights outlined the entire house. Even to his jaded eyes, it looked like a Christmas card.

"I remember you told me how you would love to see it decorated for Christmas. Is it what you expected?"

Her voice filled with a hushed awe, she said, "Even more so."

"Wait . . . there's more."

He jumped out of the car and went around to open her door. Before she could step out, he picked her up again.

"I can walk."

"I know. I just don't want to let you go yet."

"Oh, Quinn, I—" Burying her face against his neck, she burst into tears.

Of all the responses he expected from her, this wasn't one of them.

"Sam? What's wrong?"

Unable to articulate what she couldn't even explain to herself, Samantha kept her face hidden and just shook her head. What a blubbering fool she was. He had done something so incredibly sweet and unexpected. And instead of thanking him, she'd fallen apart.

She felt a kiss to the top of her head and then he whispered, "It's going to be okay, sweetheart. I promise."

Refusing to keep her face buried like a wimp, she turned her gaze back to the house. It was even more beautiful than before. Every line of the house was lit up like in a picture book. It was so beautiful, it looked almost unreal . . . like a fairy-tale house.

"That's the sweetest thing anyone's ever done for me."

"Let's go inside and see the rest."

She knew she should protest again and tell him she could walk, but she didn't want to. All she wanted to do was hang on to his neck and never let him go.

Quinn took long strides toward the house, and the closer they got, the more she was in awe of his handiwork. "Did you do all of this yourself?"

"No. Your brother-in-law and Brody helped, too."

He shifted her slightly as they approached the steps. "I can walk from here."

"Not on your life. Do you know how long I've been dying to carry you into the house, just like this?"

She looked up at him then . . . really looked. There was tenderness, affection, and something more in his eyes. And then she realized it was true, everything *was* going to be okay.

Caressing his jaw, she whispered, "Let's go inside."

The rare smile curved his mouth and then he ran up the steps as if she weighed nothing at all. He opened the door, stepped into the foyer, and then stopped. Fragrances she only associated with Christmas surrounded her as she took in all that he had done. Garlands laced with holly berries were draped along the railing of the staircase, and everywhere she looked, there was evidence of the Christmas season. Framed pictures of Santa hung on the walls. Mistletoe hung from every entryway. A rug with Santa's jolly face covered half the foyer.

"I may have gone a little overboard." He swallowed hard and she heard the uncertainty in his voice as he continued, "I've never decorated for Christmas before. Growing up, all we had was a wreath on the door and a tree decorated by some designer. It this too much?"

Samantha swallowed a huge lump in her throat. Quinn must have bought out an entire Christmas store. And he'd done it all for her. He'd asked if it was too much. It was. But it was also absolutely perfect.

She looked closer and noticed something else. Christmas decorations weren't the only things he had done. The walls had been painted a light bird's-egg blue—just like the suggestion she'd given him weeks ago—and the molding at the ceiling and doors was a stark, marshmallow white. And plantation blinds covered the windows . . . just as she had suggested. Everywhere she looked was evidence that not only had he listened to her every word, he had implemented all of them.

"Quinn . . . I don't know what to say. It's beyond beautiful . . . it's absolutely perfect."

As if he'd been anxiously awaiting her verdict, he now released a long, slow breath. "The workmen have been working like crazy to get everything done."

She peeked up at him. "Everything?"

He grinned. "Let me show you one more thing and then you can explore to your heart's content."

Still holding her, he carried her across the foyer and down the hallway to the back of the house, to the family room and its gigantic fireplace. This was the room she had told him would be the perfect place for a family to gather Christmas morning and open presents.

After pushing the door open, he stood still and let her absorb the room. A giant tree, at least twelve feet tall, stood in the corner. Decorated with old-fashioned ornaments and a thousand twinkle lights, it looked like a Hallmark Christmas card. And in here, just like the foyer, he'd covered the room with a variety of decorations.

"I haven't had time to go shopping yet, so it's still kind of bare beneath the tree."

His features blurred as tears glazed her eyes. "Thank you, Quinn. It's everything I've ever wanted."

He stared down at her for several seconds. She wanted him to kiss her in this perfect room, at this perfect moment. Instead he just continued to gaze down at her, a frown furrowing his brow.

"What's wrong?"

"Sorry. Guess my lack of sleep is catching up with me." He dropped her feet to the floor. "Why don't you explore while I start a fire?"

When his arms dropped away from her, she instantly felt cold and alone again, much the way she had felt since she woke up in the hospital. Shaking off the ridiculous sensation of sadness, she began her tour as he had suggested.

Quinn felt like an idiot. Sam's feelings of melancholy were normal. Instead of giving her what she needed, he had stupidly behaved like the lovesick hero in a sappy movie.

Wishing he was agile enough to reach up and kick his own ass, he set his mind on getting a fire going and providing Sam with the comfortable, safe environment she needed. When he heard her walking around upstairs, he headed for the kitchen, where he hurriedly filled two cups with milk and cocoa mix and stuck them in the microwave.

The microwave dinged that their hot chocolate was ready. He topped the steaming drinks off with a swirl of whipped cream and set them on a tray with a plateful of cookies he'd purchased at Ava's Bakery.

He carried the tray to the family room and set it on the table. Knowing she'd find her way back to him, he settled onto the sofa and waited.

Barely a minute later, she appeared at the door. Face

glowing, eyes gleaming. God, how he loved her. "Come sit by the fire and have some hot chocolate."

"The entire house looks wonderful, Quinn. I can't believe all the things you've accomplished."

He handed her a mug. "You might say I was motivated."

"I'll say." She took a sip. "This is really good and just what I needed."

He returned his mug to the tray and draped his arm over her shoulder to pull her closer. Dropping a kiss to the top of her head, he settled back and waited. They hadn't talked about what had happened. Things needed to be said and aired out. He'd prompt her if he had to, but for now, he wanted her to feel comfortable and safe.

She sank into his body and nestled her head on his shoulder. Other than the crackling and popping of the blazing fire and the slight wind whipping up outside, there was silence. Minutes passed and Quinn told himself not to push her, not to question her or bring it up. It was her story to share.

Finally she issued a shaky, deep sigh. "I've never been so scared in all my life."

Quinn's answer was an encouraging tightening of his arm around her shoulders and pressing another kiss to her head.

"When I woke up, all I could remember was the sight of you lying on the kitchen floor. I didn't know if you were unconscious or dead."

"Takes tougher men than the Daytons to do that."

"How did you escape them?"

"They took me out in the woods to teach me a lesson. I don't think they counted on me being able to fight, especially with my hands tied behind my back. Once again the army came through for me. I doubt any of them had ever gone up against anyone trained in hand-to-hand combat." He paused for a second and then added, "Besides, I had more incentive to get loose than they could ever have anticipated. I had to find you."

"What's going to happen to Clark and Carl Dayton and the other two guys?"

"That's up to the DA's office. As far as I'm concerned, they can rot in jail."

She was silent for several more seconds and then breathed out another shaky sigh. "Dalton was a sadistic son of a bitch."

"Yes, he was."

"He . . . he didn't rape me."

Quinn closed his eyes. The doctors had assured him of that in the hospital, but the shaky way she said it confirmed his fears. The bastard might not have raped her but he'd traumatized her body and her spirit.

"He was going to . . . I saw it in his eyes. He cut my clothes off and then untied me. I couldn't move because my circulation had been cut off too long, but I screamed and shouted as many insults as I could. I took the chance he had performance problems unless he had a completely submissive victim."

"And it worked." Quinn winced at the sound of his strained, hoarse voice. He was no cool, calm professional listening to a trauma victim, but a man who would give his life for this event to never have happened.

"Yes, but unfortunately since he couldn't perform with an appendage . . ."

"That was when he stabbed you in the back."

"Yes. Then he walked away from me. I think he might have realized he would kill me if he stayed. And he wasn't ready for me to die yet."

Quinn knew he was weak but he couldn't let her go further until he said the words: "Sam, I am so very sorry. If I hadn't come to Midnight, none of this would have happened."

She was silent for several long seconds. Hell, had he

totally messed things up? Would she clam up and be unable to finish?

Finally, as if letting go of something monumental, she breathed out a long, ragged sigh and her entire body relaxed. "I know this might sound crazy but I'm glad it was me and not someone else. If you hadn't come to Midnight, he would have continued and most likely killed another woman. One who might not have fought back and survived. As much as I hated the experience, it's good that it happened to me."

Oh hell, he was going to lose it. Breathing in her hair, holding her delicate body close to his, Quinn shut his eyes tight to battle the moisture. He hadn't cried since he was a baby, but hearing her words reinforced his belief that Sam was truly one of the strongest, most beautiful individuals he'd ever met.

"You were so strong and brave. I'm humbled by your courage."

She shifted her head and grinned up at him. "I am pretty damn awesome, aren't I?"

He kissed her then, unable to stop himself. When her hands cupped his face, he deepened the kiss but only slightly. He didn't intend to turn this into a make-out session. Reluctantly he pulled away.

"That's the first time I've been able to talk about it. Thank you, Quinn."

"Thank you for being so strong, Sam."

Her head on his shoulder, she whispered softly, "Hey, I'm a Wilde. It's who we are."

CHRISTMAS MORNING

Samantha snuggled deeper into the covers as strong arms held her against a hard, warm body. She smiled sleepily. There was nothing like waking up in the arms of the man she loved.

Her eyes popped open wide. Quinn was in bed with her? When had that happened? She'd gone to bed last night, just as she had for the past couple of weeks, aching for him but still unable to articulate that need. He had given her time to heal, without any pressure for anything else.

"Don't panic, Sam."

She wanted to laugh. There were a lot of things on her mind right now, but panic was definitely not one of them.

"Remember when I asked you what you wanted for Christmas?"

Yes, she remembered that night all too well. Minutes after she had described her perfect Christmas morning, they'd both been unconscious and then abducted.

"Don't think about what happened after that. Just think about what you said you wanted."

Relaxing into his arms, she said softly, "To wake up in this house, with you beside me."

"And?"

"Open presents and have a delicious breakfast."

"And?"

"Go over to the Wilde house for a Christmas feast and open more presents. And come back here, sit in front of the fire, and drink hot chocolate." She grimaced. "Sounds pretty tame, doesn't it?"

His deep voice growled in her ear. "Sounds like heaven to me. And it's exactly what you're going to get today." He paused a heartbeat and then said, "Remember what I said?"

She went breathless and weak instantly. "Oh yes, I definitely remember that."

He rolled her over on her back and looked down at her. Concern mixed with desire seemed an odd combination, but she appreciated both. Quinn had treated her so tenderly these last couple of weeks. No pressure for anything more than a kiss good night before they went to separate beds.

And she had needed those days to come to terms with all that had happened. Going through that horrific event might have damaged her psyche for a while, but it had also shown her something about herself she had never before acknowledged. Despite her accomplishments, there had been lingering doubt within her that she wasn't as strong as she needed to be—certainly not as strong as Savvy or Bri. And now she knew she was. Not invincible and far from perfect, but she had faced down a monster and survived. The thread of steel she'd witnessed in her sisters was inside her, too.

She had told Quinn she was glad it had been her and not someone else. And while that was true, she knew it might take a while to completely overcome the terror of that night. Each day had been an improvement over the day before. Being able to talk with Quinn about it, having his steady presence beside her, had helped tremendously.

"Sam?"

She gazed up at the man she loved more than life. He was everything she had ever hoped for and dreamed about. People who didn't believe in strong, romantic heroes had never met Quinn Braddock. Sexiness and sensitivity were a rare combination.

Even now he was giving her a choice. If she wasn't ready, he wouldn't press her for more. Samantha loved him all the more for his gentleness, but she needed him, ached for him.

Brushing a strand of hair off his forehead, she whispered, "I love you, Quinn," and tugged him down to offer her mouth.

His groan sounded both tortured and thankful as he closed his mouth over hers and delved deep. In seconds, tenderness gave way to passion. Samantha's nightgown disappeared, landing on the floor. Quinn's sweatpants followed. At last they were both deliciously, wonderfully nude.

Each lingering caress was met with a gasp of delight; rasping sighs followed every delicious kiss. Quinn's mouth moved over her entire body, lingering with extra tenderness over the scars on her stomach and back. Samantha arched and purred like a cat, loving the exquisite gentleness laced with a fierce passion.

When at last he came over her and slid inside, Samantha wrapped her legs around his lean hips, arched her body, and gave herself up to the man who had given her so much—her very own romance hero.

Quinn clenched his jaw to maintain his control. He wanted to make this last as long as possible and be as perfect as she was to him. He'd been thinking about this for days. The perfect time, perfect place. But now, as he surged deep within her once more, the words broke free. Breathing them against her lips, he asked, "Want me?"

"Yes," she moaned.

He withdrew and then went deep again. "Love me?"

On a breathy sigh, she answered, "Yes."

Pulling completely out, he waited as Sam's eyes opened and then focused. "Marry me?"

She gasped softly. "Are you sure? Because you don't have—"

"Sweetheart, I've never been more sure of anything in my life. I love you, Sam. I want to spend my life with you, have babies with you. I want it all."

Delight brightened her eyes as she tightened her arms and legs around him. "Then yes, yes . . ."

He thrust deep within her just as she gasped out one last "Yes."

Happy that she'd given him the answer he wanted,

Quinn settled into a gentle, easy rhythm, wanting to build her arousal back slowly, carefully. And then when she was ready, they could fall over the edge together.

Sooner than he had expected, she was right there with him again, arching her body toward his, grasping his hips and taking him as deeply as she could.

Climax shot through him like thunderous, silk lightning. The convulsions of her inner muscles tightened around him as she found her own release. And Quinn gave himself, body, heart, and soul, to the woman who had given him her all. In her arms, he found peace and the knowledge that even in an imperfect world, one could find a perfect love. And that's exactly what Sam was to him—perfection.

ACKNOWLEDGMENTS

This book would not have been possible without the love and support of the following:

Jim, for a million and one things, including comic relief and chocolate gifts.

My mom, sisters, and aunts, who show me each day that girls raised in the South are something special.

My precious fur creatures, who shower me with unconditional love.

Anne, Crystal, Jackie, and Kara, for their help and wonderful words of encouragement.

Dr. Jennifer Grant, MD, who answered with extreme patience, kindness, and thoroughness my questions on medical careers, stab wounds, blood spatter, resuscitations, and a variety of other issues that I barely knew how to ask. Any mistakes are my own.

My editor, Junessa Viloria, for her insight. And to many people at Ballantine, including Beth Pearson, Deb Dwyer, Craig White, and Scott Biel.

Turn the page for an excerpt from the first book
in the Wildefire series

MIDNIGHT SECRETS

BY ELLA GRACE

Published by Ballantine Books

CHAPTER
SEVEN

"Has the jury reached a verdict?" Judge Henry House-man asked the group of twelve men and women to his left.

The jury foreman, her expression carefully blank to give no indication of the result, answered solemnly, "We have, your honor."

As the court clerk took the jury's decision from the foreman's hand and handed it to the judge, Assistant District Attorney Savannah Wilde stood behind the prosecutor's table, still and stiff. Though she had been through this process dozens of times, that moment of not knowing always twisted every muscle in her body into intricate knots of tension. She always found herself asking the same questions. Had she proven the case? Had she done everything she could to bring justice to the victim? Was this scumbag going to be set free like too many others had been?

His craggy face characteristically expressionless, Judge Houseman silently read the verdict. The anxiety through-out the room was like a living, palpable entity as the tension increased to a fever pitch. The entire audience held a collective breath, waiting.

The judge nodded at the foreman, who then read, "We the jury find the defendant Donny Lee Grimes guilty of murder in the first degree."

Breaths were expelled, some with anger, most with relief. Savannah fought the urge to shout, "Hallelujah!" Exhausted she might be, but the long days and nights she had worked this case had paid off. The murdering son of a bitch was going away, hopefully for a lifetime.

As the judge finished his instructions and set the date for sentencing, she glanced over at her boss, District Attorney Reid Garrison. Though his expression remained impassive, triumph gleamed in his eyes and the tension lines around his mouth had eased. They had needed this win. Not only because Donny Lee Grimes was a murdering creep who'd taken the life of a young father and husband, but because their record lately had been dismal. Watching murderers and rapists walk out the door due to technicalities or the prosecutors' inability to prove their case was not only gut-wrenching but reflected badly on the entire office. The mayor had chewed out Reid so many times lately, Savannah was surprised he still had an ass.

And the ass chewing he got from his superiors he gladly turned around and gave to his own people. Savannah had been on the receiving end much more than she cared to remember.

But all of that could be set aside today. This was a good day for justice. Donny Lee's connections hadn't saved him. The X-Kings, the gang he'd once been a prominent member of, had apparently cut him loose. Only a few veiled threats had been made against her— prompting an increase in her security—but nothing she hadn't been through before. Whatever influence Donny Lee once had with them was obviously gone.

The instant the judge stood and stepped down from behind the bench, Savannah allowed her tense muscles to finally relax. Exhausted, she dropped into the chair behind her and released a giant relieved whoosh of air. One more scumbag off the streets. One more victim's family had been given a slight amount of peace.

She ignored the weakness in her knees and the shakiness of her limbs. Having lived with the feeling for the last few weeks, she knew full well what it meant. She was on her final reserves. This was her last case for two weeks. Fourteen days of doing nothing more taxing than ordering takeout and turning pages of novels. She was about to take the first lengthy but very well deserved vacation of her career.

The sound of a ruckus caught her attention. Her head jerked up, too late. A large male body flew across the table toward her. A glimpse of Donny Lee's pockmarked face, red with fury, was all she saw before his two-hundred-pound body slammed into hers. Breath left her with stunning suddenness and Savannah crashed to the floor.

From a distance, she heard curses, screams, and shouts roar through the room. The disgusting man on top of her grunted almost unintelligible words of warning in her ear. Though dazed, Savannah wasn't too incapacitated to lift her knee and jam it directly into Donny Lee's groin.

Howls and curses almost split her eardrum. Donny Lee was lifted off her and Savannah could at last breathe. She sat up and leaned against the railing behind her, shaking her head to clear it.

The worried and furious face of her boss appeared above her. "You okay?"

"I'm fine," she answered, holding out her hand for him to help her up.

Eyeing her carefully, he pulled her to her feet. The lines

around his mouth and eyes had deepened. "We'll charge the bastard with assault."

Savannah breathed shakily as she flexed all moveable body parts, assuring herself that nothing was broken. The ache in her shoulders and back told her that she was going to be moving slowly and carefully for the next couple of days. Those fourteen days of doing absolutely nothing were going to be even more welcome.

As Donny Lee was hauled out of the room, shouting obscenities and threats to the room at large, Savannah kept a careful eye on him. He'd gotten away once; she wasn't betting on him not being able to do it again. She'd be ready this time. When the door closed behind him, she allowed herself to slump against the railing for support.

"You sure you don't need to go to the doctor?" Reid asked.

Savannah shook her head. "I'm fine. Just going to be sore for a few days."

"That bastard say something to you?"

"Nothing new. That it wasn't over . . . that they were coming for me." The silence after her statement had her gazing up at her boss. "What's wrong?"

"Maybe you need to extend your vacation till after sentencing."

A trill of fear swept through her. Not work for two months? She would go crazy. "I had to work my ass off just to take these two weeks. There's no way I can afford more—there are too many cases for the ADAs already."

"We'll make do. I'd rather have you alive and able to come back to work."

"Reid, seriously. Donny Lee was blowing smoke. Besides, I have police protection, I'll be fine."

He shook his head. "That police protection will be going away in a day or so." The stern, determined look that all his ADAs hated crossed his face. "I could order you."

A huff of exasperation caused the pain in her back to increase. Dammit, she wished she'd kneed Donny Lee even harder.

Reid continued his argument. "Just because we believe the X-Kings cut Donny Lee loose doesn't mean he doesn't have some old friends who wouldn't mind coming after you as a favor. As of now, you're off—two months minimum."

"I can't—"

Reid added, "Of course, I can't pay you full salary."

Though money wasn't scarce for her and he knew it, that wasn't the issue. "I'll hire a bodyguard. There's no reason for—"

He snorted. "Hell, Savannah, you'd think I was sending you to jail. Get out of town; get some sun. Go visit your sisters or take a long cruise. You've been working nonstop for more than three years without a break. You've got more vacation time built up than I do."

That was an exaggeration but he was right. Other than the one-weekend-a-month visit with her sisters, she hadn't taken any time off in years. And she wouldn't have taken these two weeks she had planned if it wasn't for the fact that she was just so damn tired.

But two months? An image of the Wilde mansion, empty and lonely, popped into her head. With two months to spare, no matter how much she dreaded the event, she had no excuses.

Her grandfather had passed away over two years ago. Other than the quick trip back to Midnight for his funeral, she hadn't allowed herself to think about what needed to be done. And neither had her sisters. Without her grandfather's larger-than-life presence, going back home had been too painful to face. As much as she hated the thought of returning to a place that held so many bad memories, it was going to have to be done at some point.

Her sisters wouldn't be able to spare the time. Samantha was a homicide detective in Atlanta and Sabrina was a private investigator in Tallahassee. Their caseloads were too heavy to take that much time off. Would she ever have a better opportunity to pack up their belongings and put the house on the market?

"You're not going to argue anymore?" Reid's voice indicated he was a bit disappointed.

Laughing, she shook her head. "Nope. I think you're right. I'll head back to the office and brief everyone. Then I'm off . . ." She swallowed hard. "For two months." A twinge of panic shot through her as she said those words. Work was her life, her panacea. Could she function that long without it?

Of course she could. She was going to be busy, just a different kind of busy.

Reid pulled his cellphone from his pocket, punched a key, and then held it to his ear. "I'll make sure you've got security until you leave."

Savannah nodded. Once she was out of town, they could all breathe a little easier. By the time she came back, Donny Lee would be in prison and any threats should be worthless. And she would be rested and relaxed. She would also have accomplished an important task that should have been handled two years ago.

Gathering her case file and notes, she shoved them into her briefcase. This definitely wasn't her idea of a vacation. Not only would she be dealing with the volatile emotions of saying goodbye to her grandfather one last time, she would again become immersed in the memories of her parents' deaths. Murder-suicide sounded so clinical and cold, but when it happened to the ones you loved most in the world, there was nothing clinical about it. Even eighteen years later, her stomach still twisted in grief as she remembered those dark days.

Her mind veered away from the other issue she had diligently forced herself not to think about since she had heard the news. Midnight had a new chief of police. No doubt she would be running into him. Seeing Zach Tanner after all these years wasn't something she even wanted to contemplate. What do you say to your first love? The first and only man who'd ever broken your heart? The one man you'd given your total trust to only to have it thrown back in your face? And the only man who, at the mere thought of him, could still cause shivers of arousal to strum through your body?

The best thing she could do was stay out of his way. She and Zach had nothing to say to each other. That ship had sailed a long time ago. And all of the hurt and sorrow from that time was just another dark moment in her life that she had put behind her.

As she made her way slowly out of the courtroom, a painful and humiliating thought flitted through her mind. Just because she remembered everything, down to the smallest detail of their short romance, didn't mean that Zach did. All the promises he'd made, including the last, most important one, had been lies. So what made her think he remembered her at all?

MIDNIGHT, ALABAMA

Police Chief Zach Tanner wasn't having a good day. It'd started too damn early. Getting a call in the middle of the night that Mr. Dickens's cattle were roaming free wasn't exactly murder and mayhem, but it was something he'd had to handle. By the time they'd been rounded up and Mr. Dickens had once again promised to get his fence repaired, it was long past dawn. Going home and

grabbing a couple of hours' sleep hadn't been feasible
Now, five cups of coffee later, he was looking at the graf
fitied wall of Henson's Grocery, one of the oldest store
in Midnight. Other than the misspellings, Zach couldn'
help but think that it actually looked better this way
Old man Henson had put off painting for years, bu
thanks to some idiots with nothing better to do, it looke
like the old store was finally going to get a face-lift.

"What're you aiming to do about it, Chief?"

The sarcastic tone of his last word bounced off Zach
with no impact. He and old man Henson had a past
and no matter how many years went by, neither of then
would ever forget it. Which was just damn fine with
Zach. Torturing the old bastard with his presence was
in its own way, a reward in itself.

Still, as chief of police, it was his duty to serve and
protect even holier-than-thou useless pricks like Hen
son. Problem was, with only three deputies in a town o
fourteen hundred people, Zach had learned early tha
certain issues couldn't get as much attention as he would
have liked. But this type of vandalism would continue
until either the culprits were caught or they found some
thing else to occupy their time.

"I'll put one of my deputies on it, but be warned, there'
not a lot of evidence here. Might want to reconsider thos
security cameras we talked about."

Brown tobacco juice splattered, landing barely thre
inches from Zach's boot. Henson wiped his tobacco
filled mouth with his sleeve and snarled, "Chief Mosb
would've made this his number one priority."

That was because Mosby hadn't been above taking
few under-the-table bribes to help him choose his priori
ties. Henson had made it more than clear that he ex
pected to be able to continue that service. At first Zach
had laughed in his face, amazed at the asshole's audac
ity. That'd pissed the old man off but good. Then, when

Zach had turned him down with the not-so-subtle warning that bribing an officer of the law was illegal, the man had been furious. Since then, Henson's hostility had become even more blatant.

Letting the man rile him wasn't worth Zach's time or energy. "I'll have Deputy Odom come by in a few minutes." With that, Zach turned away, ignoring Henson's mutterings.

He and Henson had never been on good terms. He hadn't known for a long time why that was and could have lived quite happily without ever knowing. Zach had just assumed that poor people pissed the man off. Of course, it hadn't helped that a teenaged Zach had been caught twice stealing food. The fact that it'd been from the dumpster in the back of the grocery store hadn't mattered to Henson. Until the trash collectors came by, that "gal-derned garbage in those dumpsters was rightfully his and nobody had a right to touch it."

He slid into his police cruiser, cranked the engine, and headed back to his office. The pile of paperwork on his desk wasn't something he was looking forward to, but it had to be done. When he'd agreed to become police chief, he'd made a commitment to do the best job he could.

Coming back to Midnight was only supposed to be a temporary thing for Zach. After two tours in Iraq and one in Afghanistan, he'd left the army with no real clear idea of what he wanted other than peace and solitude. He'd taken the time to finish up his degree and then had returned home with one specific goal in mind: sell the old house for what he could get out of it and then leave all the memories behind.

His mother had signed the house over to him when she and Leonard moved from Midnight. With Josh gone from home, too, and no one looking out for the upkeep, he had figured it would be in bad shape and he had been right. But something remarkable happened. In the midst of scraping, painting, and refurbishing the small, ramshackle house where he'd grown up, Zach had somehow found what he was looking for—a home.

Staying in Midnight made absolutely no sense other than the feeling that this was where he belonged. He had been treated like garbage by many of the good citizens of Midnight, so maybe it was his own twisted sense of humor that made him stay. Or maybe it was self-punishment for the sins he had committed. Most likely it was to piss certain people off. Whatever the reason, Zach was here to stay.

Finding a job hadn't been as big of a problem as he'd anticipated. Once his house was done to his satisfaction, he'd had a half dozen people approach him about doing work on their homes. Within a matter of months, he had a small business going with three employees and more job requests than he could accept. Though many folks still remembered the poor skinny kid that was always in trouble, Zach had no real problems until Henson's grocery store had been broken into. And who had Chief Mosby come to question? None other than Zach Tanner, former juvenile delinquent and still number one on Henson's shit list.

Zach had been torn between slamming his fist into Harlan Mosby's face and busting out laughing. He'd done neither . . . just quietly cooperated. Two days later, the punks had been caught.

There'd been no apology from Mosby or Henson; Zach hadn't expected one. However, Mosby's attitude had made him wonder just how soon he'd be called in to answer questions on another crime. It'd taken exactly a week. When Mosby had no idea of a suspect, Zach became his go-to guy. Though he was usually slow to rile, a fed-up and pissed-off Zach wasn't something most people wanted to tangle with. Ones who did lived to regret it. A very public confrontation had taken place in the middle of city hall. The results had been mixed. Many people had enjoyed watching a snarling Zach give Mosby his comeuppance. A few wanted to run Zach out of town. But Zach had gotten his desired result—the chief off his back.

Six months later, Mosby was calling it quits because of poor health and Midnight was in the market for a new police chief. The only person to step up for the job was Deputy Clark Dayton, a man who appeared poised to follow in Mosby's crooked footsteps. Time hadn't improved Dayton. He was still the same jerk he'd been in high school. At the urging of a few newfound friends, Zach had agreed to interview for the position. Much to everyone's surprise, including his own, he'd gotten the job.

Odd how he felt so at home in a place that held so many bad memories.

As if it had a mind of its own, the patrol car turned onto Wildefire Lane—something it did at least twice a day. Early on, he had told himself it was because he was the police chief and therefore it was his duty to keep an eye on vacant properties that might invite vandalism and theft. Empty homes were prime targets for all sorts of crimes. But he had long stopped trying to convince himself of something he knew wasn't true, especially since this had become a ritual long before he became police chief. No, he drove by the grand mansion for one reason only. Midnight held bad memories except for two magical months. And the woman who owned the house on Wildefire Lane had been the reason for that magic.

Ten years had passed since he'd seen her; held her in his arms, tasted her lips, heard her laughter, basked in her smile. She had gone on to fulfill her dreams. He had told her she would and he was glad to know that he'd been right. They'd been two kids who'd found what they needed at the time. Then life had interrupted in all its realistic and dirty glory.

As he came to the long drive leading to the mansion, Zach stopped the car. Even though it had stood empty since Daniel Wilde passed on, the residence was kept in perfect condition. Caretakers came weekly to mow the lawn, and a cleaning service dusted the furniture twice a week. He'd heard that fresh flowers were added to vases twice a week, too. With this place being the location of one of the most famous murder-suicides in Alabama in the twentieth century, gossip was rife about every aspect of the mansion. Some had even whispered that the ghost of Maggie Wilde still roamed the halls, calling out for her daughters. A few had claimed seeing a blond woman in white standing on the second-floor portico. Southerners did love a good ghost story.

The mansion was the traditional plantation-style home. Giant white columns, three on each side of the long, narrow porch, were so large and sturdy-looking, they appeared to be holding up the entire structure. White rocking chairs gave off the appearance of restful indolence, and blood-red roses creeping up the trellises splashed vivid color against the stark white background of the brick. Moss-draped giant elms and oaks hovered protectively over magnolia, mimosa, and weeping willow trees. In late spring and early summer, the scent of the flowering trees, along with the thick fragrance from the wild honeysuckle in the woods behind the mansion, was almost overwhelming in its sweetness.

A few people still came by on their way to Gulf Shores or Biloxi to take pictures and gawk at one of the most famous mansions in Mobile County. When Zach looked at the massive picturesque structure, he saw something else. In his mind's eye, he envisioned wavy, honey-gold hair that covered slender, delicate shoulders, eyes the color of new spring grass, and a smile like the first hint of summer after a bitter cold winter. And beneath that beauty, a genuinely sweet and kind spirit. Falling for Savannah had been so damn easy. Even ten years later, not a day went by that he didn't think about her. And not a day went by that he didn't curse himself for what he'd done to her.

The radio sputtered and the dispatcher, Hazel Adkins, croaked in her smoker's voice, "Chief, you coming back to the office anytime soon?"

Zach shook off his memories and grabbed the radio mic. "Headed that way right now. What's up?"

"Got a call from Reid Garrison, district attorney up in Nashville, Tennessee. Said he needed to talk to you real soon. Sounded kind of urgent-like."

Zach's heart stuttered. Savannah worked in the DA's office in Nashville. Did this have anything to do with her? He mentally shook his head. No. There was no reason the DA would even know about his past relationship with one of his prosecutors. This was probably about a case. Maybe some criminal was headed their way.

"Give me the number and I'll call him back right now."

While Hazel rattled off the number, in a small part of Zach's mind, temptation warred with his good sense. Should he ask about Savannah? As he pounded the number into his cellphone, he knew temptation would win out. Besides, finding out how she was doing was normal. They'd grown up in the same town. In fact, it'd be damn strange if he didn't mention her. Right?

Five minutes later, Zach ended the call and dropped the phone on the seat beside him. There'd been no need to ask about Savannah. The call had been all about her. Not only was she coming home, the DA wanted him to be aware of some threats that'd been made against her.

Zach checked the rearview mirror and then stepped on the gas pedal, his mind whirring with myriad thoughts.

He'd known that by coming back here to live, he'd see her again. The mansion was prime real estate and even in this economy would bring a pretty penny. He'd figured that she and her sisters would return someday and put the place on the market. Now that the day had finally arrived, Zach zeroed in on two major thoughts: It had almost killed him to let her go the first time. How the hell was he going to watch her come back to Midnight for only a short time and not try to convince her to stay forever?

And just how much did she hate him for breaking her heart?